Vows of Vengeance

ALANA DAIL

For the good girl with rage in her bones.

May your crown never slip,
And your enemies remember your name.

Long live the Black Serpents.

Playlist

Devil in a Dress – Teddy Swims
Wicked Game – Lusaint
Parachute – Camylio
Little Girl Gone – Chinchilla
Control – Halsey
House On Fire- Mimi Webb
Love Is a Bitch – Two Feet
You should see me in a crown – Billie Eilish
Take Me to Church – Hozier
Madness – Ruelle
The Way I Do – Bishop Briggs
Bury a friend – Billie Eilish
Lose Control – Meduza, Becky Hill, Goodboys
No Witness – LP
Glory And Gore – Lorde
Horns – Byrce Fox
Just Pretend – Bad Omens
Stiletto Gospel – Hellena Banner
You've Created a Monster – Bohnes
Against Me – Scout Speer, Austin Giorgio

Author's Note

Vows of Vengeance is a dark romance filled with morally gray characters, high emotional stakes, and graphic content. It is not intended for all readers.

This story contains themes and scenes that may be triggering, including but not limited to:

·Physical and psychological torture

·Stalking and obsession (romanticized within the fictional relationship)

·Violence, bloodshed, and murder

·Parental abuse (emotional and psychological)

·Abduction and captivity

·Panic attacks and PTSD

·Attempted sexual assault

·Discussions of revenge, trauma, and mental instability

·Intense power dynamics and emotional manipulation

Please know that this is a work of fiction, and while some characters romanticize their trauma and the darkness within them, your reality is different and deserves care, support, and gentleness. If any of these themes feel too heavy or unsafe for you right now, that's okay. Your well-being is far more important than finishing a book.

Your mental health matters.

Take breaks. Take care of yourself. And when you're ready, come back. The story isn't going anywhere.

With love and fire, Alana Dail

Chapter One

WRENLEY

THE SHARP CLICK of my heels echoes against the polished wood floors, each step a steady rhythm, a metronome for my unraveling nerves. The gallery stretches around me in pristine white perfection, the walls adorned with pieces I've spent years bleeding into. Every brushstroke, each layer of color, and even the flaws stand as silent judges in the arena I created for myself.

My name is everywhere. Banners, fliers, delicate programs tucked neatly into the hands of strangers.

Wrenley Ashford - Shadows of Silk

It looks surreal in bold, black lettering. My name, my work, my past laid bare for the world to see. My chest tightens every time my eyes catch onto the title, a constriction that won't ease no matter how often I tell myself I deserve this.

"You've got to breathe, Wren," a familiar voice teases, warm and laced with amusement. A hand lands gently on my shoulder, grounding me. "I swear, you're more nervous than a cat in a room full of rocking chairs."

I turn, meeting Margot's knowing smirk. She looks effortlessly put together, as always. A sleek black dress hugs her curves in a way that balances sophistication and rebellion—a skill she's perfected. Her dark eyes sparkle, bolder by the sharp red lipstick she wears like armor. She lifts a champagne flute, one she's undoubtedly pilfered from the reception area, and takes a leisurely sip.

"I'm fine," I lie, crossing my arms.

Margot raises an eyebrow. "Uh-huh. Sure. That's why you've been pacing like a lunatic for ten minutes." She steps closer, lowering her voice like we're conspiring. "Look, I get it. Big night. Big deal. But you're *Wrenley Ashford.* You survived those terrifying critiques in art school, moved halfway across the country, and built a career *on your own.* Honestly, these people are lucky just to be breathing the same air as you."

Her words should settle something in me, but they don't. The knots in my stomach remain tangled, pulling tight.

"It's not just the show," I admit, my gaze flickering toward the main room. The air crackles with energy as the hum of voices swell around me. "It's being... here. So close to everything I left behind."

My fingers drift absently to the thin scar beneath my right collarbone, tracing its familiar ridges. A reminder. A history written in flesh. Margot's expression softens, her sharp edges rounding into something gentler. She nudges me lightly with her shoulder. "Hey. You're not that scared kid anymore. And you're not alone. I'm here. If anyone gives you trouble, I'll trip them in my heels. Promise."

A laugh slips past my lips—small, fleeting, but real. Margot always knows how to pull me back when I start spiraling.

Before I can respond, a clipped voice interrupts. "Miss Ashford, we're ready to begin."

I flinch at the sudden intrusion and turn to find a gallery assistant standing nearby, clipboard in hand, her professional smile perfectly in place. She looks flawless, polished, like she belongs in a space like this. Next to her—and even next to Margot —I feel the familiar prickle of being a fraud.

Pushing the feeling down, I nod. "Thank you. I'll be right out."

The assistant hesitates, her gaze flickering past me, drawn to *it*. The centerpiece.

The one piece that's stirred more whispers than any other in this collection. I don't have to turn to know what she's looking at.

The Red Thread.

It breathes behind me, a ghost pressing against my spine. A woman ensnared in a delicate web of silk-like strands; a single red thread wrapped taut around her throat. It was cathartic when I started, by the time I finished, it felt like I had spilled myself across the canvas, every raw nerve, every hidden truth woven into its fabric.

The assistant doesn't say anything, but she doesn't have to. I nod once, a silent acknowledgment that I see what she sees. Margot squeezes my arm before falling into step beside me as I cross into the main gallery. The applause hits first.

It isn't overwhelming, but it slams into my chest like a physical force. A room full of strangers, patrons, collectors, critics, people analyzing, discussing, *judging*. My work glows beneath carefully curated lighting, shadows stretching across the walls, crimson hues breathing life into each brushstroke.

It should be exhilarating. Instead, something feels... off.

A weight lingers in the air, pressing against me like an unseen force. It's subtle, just beyond my reach, but it coils in my gut, sharpening my senses. It's not the crowd or the anxiety I've been wrestling with all day. It's *something else.*

Someone else.

I scan the room, searching. Dozens of faces, some familiar, most not. The gallery's more important donors nod at me politely from across the room. Critics whisper behind champagne glasses. None of them set off the alarm in my head, but the feeling doesn't fade.

"Wren? You good?" Margot's voice is grounding, cutting through the haze.

I blink and force a smile. "Yeah. Just... a lot to take in."

"Damn right, it is." She grins. "This is your night. Soak it up. And if anyone says something dumb, I'll handle them."

Her confidence pulls a laugh from me, shaky but genuine. I let her guide me through the crowd, exchanging handshakes, polite smiles, hollow pleasantries. But the feeling *lingers.* That presence. A shadow brushing against the edges of my awareness, again.

"Wrenley Ashford."

Turning, I find the gallery curator standing before me, tall, sharp in a suit that fits like it was made for him. There's something deliberate about his movement, his posture. He doesn't belong among the idle chatter and lighthearted admiration. He's here with a purpose.

"The Red Thread has been purchased." His words are clipped, precise. "By an anonymous buyer. Full payment has been made in advance of delivery."

I blink, letting the words sink in slowly.

"Already? But the show just started."

He gives a curt nod. "This client prefers privacy. And immediacy."

Before I can process it further, my stomach drops for an entirely different reason. Across the room, two figures step through the entrance. I don't have to see their faces to know who they are.

My mother. My father.

They haven't spotted me yet, but their presence is unmistakable. My father, severe and austere, his expression carved from granite. My mother poised and sterile, her elegance glacial and sharp.

Every muscle in my body locks. *Breathe. Move. Do something.* But I just stand there, gripping my clutch like a lifeline.

"Wren," Margot's voice is sharp, low. She's seen them too.

"I know," I whisper.

And just like that, the past I've been running from for years walks straight into my present, uninvited and impossible to ignore.

Chapter Two

WRENLEY

THE MURMUR of the crowd fades as I step onto the stage, swallowed by the quiet weight of a hundred eyes on me. The spotlight sears against my skin, leaving me feeling raw and exposed, like I'm laid bare for everyone to see. My grip on the microphone is tight—maybe too tight—but I need something solid to hold onto. Behind me, my paintings loom, bleeding crimson and shadow, whispering stories I can't take or get back.

In the front row, Margot catches my gaze. She gives me a slow, confident nod, her thumb barely lifting in encouragement. I exhale, centering myself.

"Thank you all for being here tonight," I begin. My voice is even, though my pulse still hammers in my throat. "This exhibit, *'Shadows of Silk,'* is deeply personal. It's a dark reflection of the moments that define me—the vulnerable, the strong, and the ones that force us to fight for who we are in a world that tries to decide for us."

A hush settles over the crowd, thick with expectation. I shift my gaze to *The Red Thread.*

"I owe a lot of this to someone who isn't here tonight. Someone who—" I pause, wetting my lips. The words are harder to push out than I expected. "—always reminds me that art isn't about perfection. It's about truth."

The audience listens. Motionless. Some nod, others simply watch. I don't elaborate. I don't name him. He has never been one for public acknowledgement.

A polite smile seals off the speech, and I step down from the stage, eager to disappear into the sea of bodies. But I don't get far.

"Wrenley."

That familiar voice that floods, smooth, cold, precise. The ice queen herself. I barely have time to brace myself before I see them up close.

My mother stands poised under the glow of the gallery lights, an ivory-and-gold Chanel suit draped over her like armor. A champagne flute dangles from her fingers, though she doesn't drink. My father is beside her, his presence formidable even in silence. He doesn't need words to exert control; his posture does it for him.

"Mother. Father." I keep my voice neutral and clipped. They don't offer pleasantries. They never have.

"Your speech was... heartfelt," my mother says, the smallest note of disdain curling around the word. "Though I must admit, I'm surprised you credited Benjamin so openly. I would have thought your instructors from school would deserve that recognition."

My jaw tightens. "He believed in me when no one else did. I wanted to thank him."

My father's scrutiny snaps to *The Red Thread*, his lips pressing into a thin line.

"Your work is... striking," he says, the deliberate pause giving everything away.

"Striking," my mother echoes with a quiet laugh. "I would call it gauche. So dark. So dramatic." She tilts her head, examining the piece with feigned curiosity. "Honestly, Wrenley, must you always create something so dark and sulky, bordering on obscene? You're better than this."

Her words land sharper than I expect, slicing through me with the same precision as one of her perfectly manicured nails.

Obscene. You're better than this. As if my art, my expression, somehow stains the pristine image she's spent years curating. As if who I am, what I feel, what I have survived, should be neatly folded away like one of her expensive silk scarves, never to be touched, never to be seen.

She doesn't see the truth in my work. She doesn't want to. The thought latches onto something deep inside me, dragging me back to that night.

The rain had been cold that night. That's the first thing I remember. Cold, soaking through my coat, chilling my skin.

Then—hands. Rough, unwelcome. The glint of a knife is too close. The pressure of it against my collarbone, sharp enough to draw blood. I remember struggling. The scrape of pavement against my knees when I fell. The weight of him, the stench of gin and sweat, the way my breath came in ragged, panicked gasps.

Just as a voice. Deep, firm. Cutting through the night like a blade of its own. Gin and sweat replaced with cedar, smooth whiskey, and rain itself.

The weight was gone. The attacker vanished into the darkness.

The rest of the memory is a haze, frayed at the edges. A figure, a coat draped over my shoulders, the echo of a voice I can't quite remember.

By the time the police arrived, he was gone. Like he had never been there at all.

As I snap back to the present, the bright gallery lights feel too harsh, too artificial. My mother's gaze is still locked onto mine, her expression sharp with disapproval. The air between us is thick with unspoken criticism.

She exhales, shaking her head, fingers tightening around the stem of her glass. "I just don't understand you, Wrenley." She says her voice is low but laced with frustration. "Why must you create something, bordering on erotic?" Her lips press together in a thin line as she sweeps her eyes over *The Red Thread,* like it personally offends her. "This is not how we raised you." She says, pointing a polished nail at my paintings.

The words hit harder than I expected, burrowing under my skin, setting every nerve on edge. *This is not how we raised you.*

Like I've failed some unwritten rule, like my art, my truth, is something that needs to be fixed, tamed, made more... palatable. Like I was supposed to follow the path they set, stay silent, and be the perfect little porcelain doll trapped in a glass case.

"You didn't raise me at all." I snap, sharper than I meant to be. "Not in any way that mattered."

Her expression barely flickers, but I know the barb lands. My father tenses beside her, his jaw constricting a silent warning *not* to make a scene. But it's too late, there's already a fracture in the pristine, calculated image they uphold.

"I am *so* tired of this little rebellion of yours," she mutters, her voice like gleaming steel. "You act as if you're some tragic victim when in reality, you've been given every advantage. And this..." She gestures toward the painting again. "This obsession with pain and desire—it's indecent. People are talking, Wrenley."

"Let them talk," I say, straightening my spine. "Because at least I have something to say."

My mother lets out a sharp breath, her frustration barely contained. "You may think this act of yours is liberating, but all you're doing is making yourself a spectacle."

I shake my head, a humorless laugh escaping my lips. "The only ones who see it that way are you two."

She doesn't answer. Instead, she takes a slow sip of champagne, her glare remaining cool and unreadable. When she sets the glass down, she simply says, "Brunch. Tomorrow. Ten sharp." It's not a request.

And then, just like that, she turns on her heel, my father following without another word, leaving me standing there, my fists clenched at my side.

Margot appears at my elbow, eyes narrowed. "What the hell was *that*?"

I release a slow breath, trying to shake off the conversation, but the weight of it lingers. "*That*," I murmur, "was my mother reminding me *exactly* where I stand."

Chapter Three

MAXIMILIAN

THE GALLERY HUMS with the kind of forced elegance that only wealth can buy—a carefully curated world of polished smiles, empty pleasantries, and overpriced champagne. These people move throughout life like marionettes, dancing their perfect steps, oblivious to the strings pulling them.

But I'm no puppet.

I move through them like smoke, unseen but undeniable, slipping past their laughter and their whispered judgments, my attention fixed on the only thing that matters tonight.

Her. Or rather, her work.

The Red Thread commands the far wall like a wound torn open for all to see. The crimson streak, jagged and raw, cuts through muted tones, daring anyone to look away. It is not beautiful—not in the way art is expected to be. It is violent. Unapologetic. It is a piece of *her*, and now, it will be mine.

"I'll take it," I say, barely looking at the gallery attendant hovering beside me. She hesitates for only a second before forcing a polite smile.

"Would you like me to inquire with the artist about—"

"No." My voice leaves no room for negotiation. "Just tell me the price."

She nods quickly, retreating to manage the details, but I am no longer listening. My gaze traces the crimson streak on the canvas, drawn to the energy hidden in every brush stroke. This is not just a painting. It is a map—one I intend to follow.

She is baring her soul, whether she realizes it or not. I suddenly recognize something in it. Something *broken*. Something like me. Something I *want*.

The first time I see her, it is through Benjamin Ashford.

We meet at his usual haunt—a private lounge tucked away behind a high-end restaurant, the kind of place that requires more than just money to enter. Benjamin has been useful to me. Cautious. Strategic. A man who knew how to navigate both the light and the dark without dirtying his hands.

Tonight, he's different. Distracted. His usual sharpness dulled by something lingering at the edges of his mind. And then, she walks in.

Wrenley Evelyn Ashford.

She doesn't even glance my way. She moves toward her uncle, a quiet force wrapped in a crimson dress, her red hair cascading down her back like ink spilled across silk. There is something almost other-worldly about her—an intensity in the way she carries herself. A wariness in the way she scans the room before she reaches him.

She is a puzzle I didn't know I needed to solve.

Benjamin's gaze softens when he sees her. A rare sight. "You shouldn't be here," he says, his tone lacking any real bite.

She rolls her eyes. "Relax, Uncle Ben. I was at an event downtown, and I just wanted to stop and see you before meeting friends for dinner."

"You should have called for a driver."

"I can take care of myself," she says, lifting her chin. She knows she is not a victim.

He sighs, shaking his head. "I know. That's what worries me."

For a moment, I almost see it, his weakness. Not in the way of business or power, but something far more dangerous. Sentiment.

It's clear he adores her. Protects her. Keeps her at a careful distance from men like me. That's when I know. She isn't just an Ashford. She is his greatest liability.

And now, she is mine. I will have her.

❧

Wrenley moves through the crowd, her presence impossible to ignore. Even surrounded by the elite, she stands apart, scarlet against a sea of polished gold and ivory. She wears her tension like a second skin, shoulders tight, gaze flicking between faces as if expecting something. Or *someone.*

She doesn't know she's being watched. Not by me. Not yet.

Her parents approach, their presence as cold and calculated as ever. I've dealt with them before—know the iron behind their carefully controlled exteriors. They are predators, circling their prey with measured words and quiet expressions.

I can't hear their conversation, but I don't need to. Her mother's sharp disapproval is written in the slight curl of her lips, the slow, deliberate sip of champagne that follows. Her father's silence is just as cutting, a presence heavy enough to press against her like a weight she can't shake.

I watch as Wrenley holds her ground, her chin lifting again slightly in defiance. But I also see the cracks. The way her fingers strangle the stem of her glass. The way her breath hitches—just slightly—before she speaks.

They think they can control her. Just as Benjamin tried to protect her. But control is an illusion. And protection? Protection *fails.* I would know.

Her parents' retreat is as deliberate as their approach. She stays behind, exhaling sharply, her mask slipping for just a fleeting moment.

She looks my way. Her gaze sweeps across the room, brow furrowing ever so slightly, as if she can *feel* something. Some presence lingering just out of reach.

I smirk, leaning against the wall. She doesn't see me. Not yet. I glance back at *The Red Thread.*

She doesn't know it yet, but the game has already begun. And when she learns the truth—about her uncle, about *me,* about why I'm here, the rules will change. For now, I'll wait.

Patience, after all, is a hunter's greatest weapon. But mine is running thin.

Chapter Four

WRENLEY

THE NIGHT IS thick with the scent of rain, the city streets slick with its aftermath as I step out of the gallery. It's close to one in the morning, the entire night had been exhausting—too many hollow compliments, too many lingering stares, too many people mistaking my art for an invitation to dissect me. I exhale sharply, my fingers tightening around the clutch in my hands as I make way to my car.

I hadn't expected Uncle Benjamin to be there tonight. He rarely attended public events, never cared for the spectacle or the suffocating social games the Ashfords played so well. But he had always been supportive of me, in ways that mattered. He never said it outright—he wasn't the type for flowery praise—but I saw it in the way he made sure I had everything I needed, the way he checked in after every show, the way he looked at my paintings like they were something more than just color on canvas.

He has always been proud of me. Beyond proud. Even when the rest of the family dismissed my art as nothing more than a frivolous hobby, he never did. That has always been enough.

That thought lingers in my mind as I pull my phone from my bag, expecting a message from him now, maybe a sarcastic quip about the Ashford name being whispered in hushed tones about *The Red Thread.*

But instead, I see it.

> Unknown Number: Benjamin Ashford is dead.

I stop walking. The words are wrong. They don't fit.
Dead? No. That's—no.
I saw him yesterday morning. *Yesterday.* He was fine. Healthy. The same calculated, meticulous man I have always known.

My heart pounds against my ribs as I stand frozen in the dim glow of the streetlights. The message just sits there, black text against white, like an omen carved in stone.

A joke. It has to be a joke. My fingers shake as I type out a response.

> Me: Is this some kind of sick joke?

The reply comes almost instantly, the screen flashing again before I can even take another breath.

> Unknown Number: It's not a joke. And he didn't just die. He was murdered. Be careful who you trust.

A sharp, cold wave crashes through me. *Murdered*?
No. This is impossible. I swallow hard, my eyes darting up from my phone, scanning the street, the parked cars, the quiet hum of distant traffic. Suddenly, the night feels too still, the shadows too deep.

I need to breathe and think. I reach into my purse, feeling the cold steel of the gun I've carried since I was attacked, and it settles the nerves a little.

Forcing myself to move, I cross the pavement with hurried steps, unlocking my car and slipping inside. As soon as I shut the door, I engage the locks, my fingers gripping the steering wheel as I try to process what I've just read.

Murdered.

I shake my head. I go over the conversation we had. He had made a wry comment about how the family would hate my latest work, how he was almost looking forward to their reaction. There was nothing that hinted at danger.

I press my lips together, my stomach twisting painfully. Whoever this person was, they had to be lying. Or knowing my family, someone knows something I don't.

Me: Who is this? How do you know this?

My message sends. The screen stays dark. I wait. And wait. Nothing. A cold prickle of unease crawls up my spine. Whoever sent this knows I needed to hear it.

However, they also understood when to vanish.

By midmorning, the sky is still thick with gray, the city drowning in a colorless haze. The storm may have passed, but something uglier has settled in its place.

Margot sits silently beside me, still in her pajamas with big sunglasses on like it's too bright outside, gripping a coffee cup in her hands. Clearly, too hungover to care about the fact that my mother will have something to say about us being late and under-dressed.

We step out of the car and onto the manicured path that leads to my parents' estate. The Ashford legacy, trimmed within an inch of its life and polished to hide the rot underneath.

"They could've told you over the phone," Margot mutters, her slippers shuffling beside mine. "Or, I don't know, called you when it happened."

I say nothing. My grip on the strap of my bag tightens. The double doors open before we reach them, timed, as always, by the meticulous staff. My mother is already waiting in the grand foyer, lips pursed, and spine rigid.

"Well," she says, dragging her gaze over our pajamas, "you're late."

"I didn't realize grief came with a schedule," I reply coolly.

Margot lets out a low hum in agreement behind me.

My father appears from the sitting room just off the hall, his expression unreadable. "Wrenley," he says. "Margot. Come in."

I step inside, the familiar scent of lavender polish and old money curling around my lungs like a noose. Nothing ever changes in this house. Not the rugs, not the furniture—and certainly not the temperature of the people who raised me.

"I heard about Uncle Benjamin," I say, voice steady. "Eventually."

My mother raises a brow. "We sent word."

I tilt my head. "Did you?"

She doesn't answer. My father clears his throat. "It's unfortunate he always did feed into your daydreams. But Benjamin's health has been questionable for some time."

A lie. His health was fine. He jogged five miles every morning and ate like a damn monk. But I'm not here to reveal what I know. Not yet.

"So you just...didn't think to call me?" I ask, tone deceptively calm. "To let me find out through someone else?"

My father stiffens. "You were going to find out today regardless. That's why we asked you to come."

"To inform me that the only person in this family who gave a damn about me is dead?" I laugh out humorlessly.

"Wrenley," my mother snaps. "This isn't the time—"

"No?" I shoot back, a bitter smile tugging at my lips. "When exactly is the right time to find out my uncle is gone? Or were you planning to wait until the funeral?"

"There will be service," my father says, tone clipped. "Saturday. Private. Close friends and family."

"And I'm what exactly?" I ask. "Peripheral blood?"

He doesn't answer. Neither does she.

For a moment, silence swells between the four of us. The kind of silence that speaks volumes. The kind that confirms everything I've always suspected: Benjamin was the last thread tethering me to this family. And now he's gone.

Margot shifts beside me, like she's ready to swing if I give the word. I take a step back, slipping my sunglasses down over my eyes.

"Thanks for the update," I say. "We'll see you at the funeral."

And without waiting for a reply, we turn and walk out the door.

Margot follows, muttering under her breath. "They're lucky I'm hungover. Would've punched your mom straight in the jaw."

I don't laugh. I don't speak. But as the car doors shut and we pull away from the house, I know one thing for certain. This isn't over. Not by a long shot.

Chapter Five

MAXIMILIAN

SHE STANDS APART from the mourners, a lone figure beneath a sprawling ancient oak, where shadows stretch long and restless. Wrenley Ashford does not weep. She does not bow her head in reverence like the others or seek the comfort of whispered condolences. Instead, she remains still, watching, waiting, as though she is not entirely part of the grief surrounding her.

She is an exquisite contradiction.

The black silk of her dress clings to her frame, stark against the pale marble of her skin. A single gloved hand rests on the tree trunk beside her, fingers tapping lightly, betraying the storm beneath her composed exterior. Defiant, distant, yet fragile in a way she likely doesn't even realize.

I watch her from a distance, concealed in the throng of solemn faces and empty platitudes. She has no idea who I am—not yet—but I have known her far longer than she would ever suspect.

Benjamin spoke of her often, always with an edge of wistfulness he rarely allowed himself. *She was meant for more than this family's weight,* he had said once, a glass of brandy in his hand, his gaze fixed on the fire. *And yet, she will never outrun it.*

He was right. And since then, she has been mine to understand.

I move toward her, slow and deliberate, my steps muffled by the soft earth. She notices me before I speak, her pointed glare locking onto mine. Her eyes, hazel, like the last breath of autumn before winter claims it. Beautiful. Fleeting. A dangerous flicker with wariness. She doesn't step back.

I admire that.

"Miss Ashford," I say, inclining my head slightly. My voice is measured, laced with just enough familiarity to unnerve her.

Her lips press into a thin line. "You seem out of place."

I left the corner of my mouth tilt upward in something that isn't quite a smile. "Your uncle and I had... dealings."

Her brows lift, skepticism flashing across her face. "Dealings, huh?"

"Of a personal nature," I clarify, offering nothing more.

Her silence is thoughtful, assessing. Then, "I didn't see you at the service."

I let my eyes sweep over the mourners in the distance, their sorrow perfunctory, practiced. "I don't grieve in the same way your family does."

Her fingers curl slightly, nails pressing into the fine leather of her gloves, the slight tension revealing their shape—elegant, almond-shaped, and meticulously kept. The polish is a deep, inky-black, glossy against the matte fabric, a subtle rebellion against the otherwise somber tones of mourning. Even in this small detail, there is something deliberate about her, something carefully constructed yet undeniably raw beneath the surface.

She tilts her head, studying me. "And how *do* you grieve, Mr...
"

"Maximilian," I supply smoothly. I do not offer a last name. Not yet. "Your uncle spoke of you often. Always with pride, but there was... a sadness too."

That gets to her. A flash of something behind those guarded eyes.

"He never told me about you," she says, but it is not quite an accusation. More of a test.

I step closer, just enough to let my presence settle around her, to let her feel the weight of it. The air between us shifts, carrying her scent to me—something light, laced with lavender, and something richer, darker—curls into my lungs, and my restraint tightens like a leash.

"You seldom came home," I murmur, my voice low, prudent. "And now it's too late."

Her jaw clenches. "How would you know I didn't come home? What do you know about regret, watching from the shadows, waiting for... what exactly?"

A sharp little thing, this one.

She turns to leave, but my hand finds her wrist, gentle yet immovable. I feel the moment her pulse jumps beneath my thumb, the betrayal of her body at odds with the resistance in her posture.

"You think you're running, Wrenley," I assert, voice just above a whisper. "But you've been walking straight into the lion's den."

Her breath shudders, barely perceptible. For a moment, she doesn't move. She slowly pulls her arm free. She doesn't flee. She doesn't demand an answer.

She simply meets my eyes with the same quiet defiance before turning away, disappearing into the sea of black-clad figures.

But I do not watch her go. Because I already know she'll come looking for me.

Chapter Six

WRENLEY

THE DREAM COMES as it always does. Unrelenting. Smothering.

I am twenty again, the air thick with the acrid stench of spilled alcohol and sweat. The alley is cold, damp, and pressing in around me like a living thing. My dress is torn at the strap, the silk slipping uselessly down my shoulder as I thrash against the grip of the man pinning me to the brick wall. His breath reeks of gin and something rotten, his laughter curling around me like smoke.

"You're prettier when you stop fighting." He slurs, his fingers digging into my waist enough to bruise. I fight harder.

He slams me back, my skull knocking against the bricks, and for a moment, the world wavers. Fear and pain crackle through me, hot and dizzying. I try to scream, but his hand clamps over my mouth, muffling the sound before it can reach the street.

No one is coming.

*My heartbeat pounds in my ears, loud enough to drown out the city around me. His free hand fumbles with the hem of my dress, yanking it upward, and I know—**I know**— that I am seconds away from something irreversible. Something that will carve itself into me in ways I will never be able to scrub clean.*

Then I see the glint of metal.

A knife.

Small, but sharp, its serrated edge catching the dim light of the alleyway as he pulls it from his pocket. My breath shatters in my chest. The game has changed. He isn't just a man looking for power, for control. He is something worse.

I buck against him, twisting, clawing at his wrist as he presses the blade against my collarbone.

"Keep struggling," he breathes, pressing in closer, the top of the knife biting into my skin. "See what happens."

Pain sears through me as the blade slices just deep enough to break flesh. Warmth blooms, slow and sticky, down my skin. The wound isn't fatal. It isn't meant to be. It's a warning. A promise.

And I know then—I am going to die here. I try to scream, but his hand stays locked over my mouth.

And then— A new voice.

"Let her go."

The words cut through the rain, sharp, authoritative. For the first time, my attacker tenses. His grip on me loosens, but not by much. His head jerks up. Scanning the darkness.

Another figure steps forward from the mouth of the alley.

Tall. Broad-shouldered. The storm swallows most of his features, leaving only fragments behind—the sharpness of his jaw, the wet strands of dark hair clinging to his forehead. His coat is heavy, soaked through from the rain, but he moves without fear.

He doesn't ask again. He moves. Fast.

The weight of my attacker is torn away, replaced by a sickening crack of impact, a body slamming hard against the opposite wall. I collapse to my knees, gasping for air, vision blurring as I scramble to pull my dress back into place.

A figure stands over my attacker, not just a man but a force, dark and merciless. His fist collides with the other man's face repeatedly, until the laughter turns to garbled choking. I hear the wet crunch of bone breaking, a gurgled sob of pain, and still, the stranger does not stop.

He only speaks when the man on the ground stops moving.

"You are no victim. Get up," he commands.

I do, trembling, my legs barely holding me upright. His voice is smooth, edged with something dangerous, but it doesn't frighten me. Not like the other man. Not like what almost happened.

I look up at him, just a glimpse, just for a second. The alley is dark, but the amber glow from a streetlamp catches the sharp angles of his face. He's younger but not like me. Mid-twenties, maybe. Strong. Cold. His knuckles drip red, his breathing steady despite the violence he's just unleashed.

I open my mouth to say something—to thank him, to ask him his name, to ask why—but he's already backing away, disappearing into the shadows before the moment can become anything more.

My eyes snap open, the echoes of the nightmare still clinging to me.

My breath shatters in my chest as I jolt upright, fingers tangled in the sheets. The hotel room is silent, save for the sound of my ragged breathing. My skin is damp with sweat, my heart hammering so violently I half expect it to tear through my ribs.

It was just a dream. Just a memory. But this time, something is different.

This time, I see his face *clearly.*

Not just the sharp lines of his jaw, or the way his eyes burned with something too controlled to be rage. *This time, I recognize him.*

The man from the alley—the man who saved me that night— is the same man who stood before me at my uncle's funeral.

A few more tattoos, and more tired, but unmistakable.

Maximilian.

The hotel room is quiet, wrapped in a thick silence that suffocates after a nightmare. My pulse stutters, breath unsteady, as I try to shake the memory of that knife against my skin. The wound has faded, but the memory remains.

I glance at the clock on the nightstand. **3:12 AM.**

Too early to be awake. Too late to convince myself I can fall back asleep.

With a quiet sigh, I shove the blankets off and slip out of bed, my bare feet hitting the cool floor. The city hums faintly beyond the window, but up here—on the twelfth floor— it feels like I'm floating somewhere between reality and the past.

Climbing over the bed, I reach for my laptop on the desk, flipping it open and watching as the screen illuminates the dark room. The glow feels harsh, making my eyes ache, but I don't look away. Not yet.

I hesitate for a moment, fingers hovering over the keyboard.

"What the hell do I even search for?"

I don't know his last name. I don't know who he was to my uncle, or why he was even at the funeral in the first place. But I know his face. I know his voice. And I know what he's capable of.

I start simple: **Maximilian. Dark hair. Tall. Connected to the Ashford family.**

Nothing useful. Of course.

I try again, adding **Northwyck** to the search, my fingers tapping impatiently against the desk as I scroll through irrelevant results. A novelist. A painter. A tech entrepreneur. None of them is him.

I stare at the screen, frustration simmering beneath my skin. "Think, Wrenley."

My uncle had clearly known him. And not in passing, *really* knew him. He spoke about me to him.

So, I shift my approach.

Benjamin Ashford: business connections.

This brings something new.

Dozens of articles pop up, detailing my uncle's wealth, his investments, and the network of people he surrounded himself with. I skim through the names, scrolling faster—until one stops me cold.

Maximilian Jude Blackwood.

I click the first article with his name. It's from a high-profile financial publication, detailing his rise in the business world. A once-underground fighter, turned entrepreneur, investment mogul, and self-made billionaire.

My stomach tightens as I scroll further, clicking link after link, reading between the carefully curated lines. His influence stretches farther than I realized. He's not just wealthy. He's dangerous in a way that doesn't require weapons. A kingmaker in the shadows.

My fingers tremble slightly as I click on another article.

Maximilian Jude Blackwood: The Most Powerful Man You've Never Heard Of.

The article is filled with speculation, whispers of the under-the-table dealings, businesses that exist in the gray spaces between legal and *something else entirely*. There's nothing that would hold up in court, but the implication is enough.

My throat tightens.

Who the hell are you?

I stare at the image embedded in the article. He looks the same as he did at the funeral—tall, impossibly composed, a presence that demands attention without needing to say a word. There are no photos of him with family, no wife or girlfriend, no kids.

My skin prickles. I need to stop that train of thought right now.

I should feel afraid. I should feel *something*. But all I feel is a strange, undeniable pull—like I've been circling something dangerous without realizing how close I already am.

And now, I know his name.

Maximilian Jude Blackwood.

And for better or worse, he knows mine.

Chapter Seven

MAXIMILIAN

THE SCENT of coffee and city rain lingers in the air as I stand by the window, looking out over the skyline. The morning light barely cuts through the thick clouds. Fitting. The Ashford family is in mourning, and the world itself seems to grieve in kind.

A knock at my door pulls me from my thoughts. I don't need to ask who it is. Only one person would show up unannounced and still expect me to let him in.

I open the door to find Elias Cade standing there, coffee cup in one hand, his phone in the other, looking entirely too pleased with himself.

"Morning, boss." Stepping inside without waiting for an invitation. He exhales dramatically as he settles into the chair across from me. "Guess what?"

I arch a brow; he knows I hate it when he calls me that. I say nothing, just stand there waiting.

He grins. "Your little obsession? She's looking for you."

That gets my attention. I turn from the window, watching as he sips his coffee like he has all the time in the world.

"She searched for me?"

Elias nods, flipping his phone around to show a screen filled with security alerts. "Multiple pings. Someone's been poking around for a *Maximilian Jude Blackwood*. Now, considering you're about as easy to find as a ghost, I'm guessing she's pretty damn determined." He leans back, smirking. "What have you *done* to this girl?"

I can't help but grin as I walk to the coffee pot and pour myself another cup. Sitting in the chair across from him, I smirk. "She's hunting, then."

"Oh, absolutely." Elias tilts his head. "And let's be real—you love it."

I take a slow sip, letting the silence settle. He's right, of course. Something is intoxicating about the idea of Wrenley looking for me, searching for answers she won't find.

Elias sighs, rubbing a hand over his face. "I hate to be the one to bring reality into your little game of cat and mouse, but do I need to remind you what we're actually doing here?"

I don't respond, so he continues, "She's smart. Too smart. And I don't know if you noticed, but the Ashford family tends to come with a whole lot of baggage. And murder plots."

I chuckle, shaking my head. "I need to see her again."

There is a methodical pause before Elias responds. "Of course you do. Why not? Nothing screams *healthy choices* like stalking a woman with serious trust issues and an entire family of sociopaths."

"I have somewhere to be, so I want you to sit in the lobby of her hotel later this morning. Follow her when she leaves."

Elias sighs in that exaggerated way that is like nails on a chalkboard to me. "Oh, sure. Let me just clear my whole schedule to babysit your fixation. You do remember the part where we're trying to dismantle an empire, right? The Ashfords don't just hoard wealth; they own people. Money laundering, offshore accounts, political manipulation, illegal arms deals—they don't just want power, they want control over every damn thing they touch.

I clench my jaw. I know exactly what the Ashford family is. What they've done.

"I know what I'm doing, Elias."

"DO YOU?! 'Cause this smells a lot like thinking with your dick, rather than that big brain of yours."

I exhale slowly, letting the silence stretch just long enough for him to shift uncomfortably.

"Follow her."

Elias stays silent, but he is about to resign to whatever madness I'm about to drag him into, again. He throws up his hands. "Fine. Whatever. But when this all goes to hell, I'm saying I told you so. *Twice.*"

I don't bother responding; I already know what I'm doing.

9:03 AM Elias

The coffee in my hand is absolute shit, but I drink it anyway. I lean against the marble column in the hotel lobby, my posture relaxed, eyes scanning the room with the kind of practiced ease that makes me blend in. The lobby is busy enough to provide cover but not so crowded that I'll lose her in the shuffle.

There she is.

Wrenley steps out of the elevator, moving with purpose. Black coat, gloves, sunglasses that hide her eyes, but not the sharpness of her attention. She's looking for something, no, *someone.*

I just wait until she passes me before peeling away from the column and following at a comfortable pace.

The city hums around us, people lost in their morning routines, heads down, earbuds in, coffee cups clutched tight. Wrenley doesn't rush, but she moves like someone who knows exactly where she's going.

And then, almost imperceptibly, she shifts. The kind of shift that says *she knows.*

I almost smile. Clever girl.

She doesn't stop, doesn't look over her shoulder, but she

adjusts—changes her gait slightly, varies her pace. Checking for a tail. I slow, matching her adjustments with my own.

A block later, she veers left, slipping down a side street lined with boutique storefronts and cafes. I follow, hands in my pockets, eyes on everything but her.

Then she ducks into a bookstore. Smart.

She wants to disappear. I wait a beat before stepping inside, pretending to browse. I keep her in my periphery, watch as she weaves through the shelves, her movements precise, controlled.

She's gone.

I don't stop moving, don't hesitate. I stride toward the back, past the rows of books, and push open the rear exit. And immediately, a gun is in my face. My own weapon is already drawn, pointed right back at her. We stare at each other, the air between us razor-sharp.

"Cute," I drawl, tilting my head. "You wanna talk, or are we just gonna kill each other and call it a day?"

Her grip doesn't waver.

I sigh, "I'm going to pull my phone out and make a call, don't shoot me yet." I mumble.

"Boss? You might wanna come down here before I have a bigger mess to clean up."

Chapter Eight

WRENLEY

THE COLD BARREL of a gun pointed at my head was not the way I planned to start my morning.

"Who the hell are you?" I demand, keeping my own weapon trained on the man in front of me. He's tall, broad-shouldered, built like someone who knows exactly how to throw a punch and make it count. Dark blonde hair, sharp eyes—annoying eyes, the kind that look like they see everything and enjoy the show.

"Elias Cade," he answers easily, like we're just exchanging pleasantries instead of holding each other at gunpoint. He tilts his head, studying me. "And you are?'

"You were following me, you already know who I am," I snap. "The better question is who the hell is the *boss* you just called?"

Elias smirks, the kind of lazy, cocky smirk that makes me want to pistol-whip him just on principle.

"Someone with better manners than you."

"Doubtful."

He lifts his gun a little higher. Not a lot, just enough to remind me it's there. "That attitude is why you're in this position, princess."

I scoff. "Oh, so this is my fault now?"

"Well, I don't recall *my* morning plans involving an alleyway standoff, but here we are." He nods toward my gun. "You want to put that away, or are we just gonna keep threatening each other like some kind of kinky foreplay?"

I glare. "I'd rather set myself on fire."

Elias grins. Really grins. "Knew I liked you."

"Yeah, well, the feeling is *not* mutual."

"You sure about that? You strike me as the type who likes a little danger."

"I like my danger in manageable doses, not idiot-sized ones."

"Ouch." Elias places a hand over his chest mockingly. "That one actually hurt."

"Good."

He chuckles, like this is the most fun he's had all week. "Damn. No wonder he's so interested in you."

I tense. "He?"

Elias just smirks. "Oh, you'll see."

Before I can fire back, the low growl of an approaching vehicle makes us both turn.

A black SUV, sleek and expensive, glides to a stop at the mouth of the alley. Tinted windows, blacked-out rims, the kind of car that belongs to someone with either too much money or too much power. The engine purrs like a well-fed predator, an understated threat. The driver's door swings open, and out steps *him*, gun in hand, pointed slightly at me.

Maximilian Jude Blackwood.

My breath catches despite myself.

He moves with an ease that is almost unnatural, every step controlled, deliberate, and dangerous. Dressed in all black, his tailored coat fits him too well, emphasizing the quiet strength beneath it. His dark hair is slightly tousled, but it's his amber eyes that catch me off guard. They're piercing and unreadable, holding something dark and knowing beneath the surface.

He looks like temptation wrapped in inevitability. *Damn him.* His lips tilt in something that's not quite a smile.

"Miss Ashford," he greets smoothly, his voice like a slow pull of whiskey over ice. "I'd say it's a pleasure to see you again, but I'm not sure you'd believe me."

I tighten my grip on the gun and level it at him. "What the fuck is going on? Why the hell are you having me followed?"

Elias makes a low sound—something between a laugh and a sigh—as he presses his gun just a little closer to me. "See, this is why I don't make promises, boss. She's clearly a bad influence."

I don't look away from Maximilian, but I can feel the smug amusement radiating from Elias like an actual heat source.

Maximilian, however, remains calm. *Too Calm.*

"Lower your weapon, Wrenley," he says, polite but firm. "I'll explain everything, but pointing a gun at me isn't going to get you the answers you want."

I hesitate. Every instinct in me screams not to trust him. But something about him, about the way he looks at me, about the way he doesn't seem remotely concerned about the gun in my hand, *makes me curious.*

Slowly, I exhale and slide the gun back into my coat.

Max inclines his head in approval. "Much better. Now, if you'd be so kind—" he gestures to the SUV "—get in."

I blink. *He's joking. He has to be joking.*

"You want me to just... get in your car?" I ask, incredulous.

"Correct."

"With you."

"Yes."

"And your *goon* who just had a gun in my face."

Elias grins. "I promise not to pull my gun out again unless you do. Scout's honor."

I narrow my eyes at him. "You were never a damned Boy Scout."

"True. But I was a *very* enthusiastic delinquent."

Max exhales, clearly done with our banter. "We're wasting time. I want to explain my... relationship with your uncle, and this is neither the time nor the place for that discussion."

I cross my arms. "And if I say no?"

Max steps closer, just enough that I catch the faintest trace of his scent—something dark and rich, like cedar and leather, mixed with a hint of something warmer... whiskey. His eyes hold mine, steady, unreadable. "Then I suppose we continue this conversation in a much less comfortable setting. Either way, Wrenley, you *will* hear me out."

I stare at him, weighing my options. The smart choice would be to walk away. But curiosity is a dangerous thing.

And right now, I think I'd rather risk death than walk away from the answer he's holding hostage.

I don't move toward the SUV just yet.

Instead, I keep my arms crossed and pop out a hip, glancing between the two of them, my gaze settling on Elias first. "So, what exactly is your job title? Professional stalker? Full-time asshole?"

Elias grins like I just paid him a compliment, "Freelance menace, actually. The pay's decent, and the health benefits are *fantastic.*"

I roll my eyes and turn to Maximilian. "And you? What's your title? Mysterious billionaire with control issues? Or just a thug with an expensive wardrobe?"

Max doesn't react the way most men would. He doesn't bristle or get defensive. He simply watches me with that unreadable intensity, like he's already figured out exactly how I'll respond before I even do it.

"That depends," he says smoothly. "Would you prefer an answer that puts you at ease, or the truth?"

The way he says it makes my pulse flicker with something I don't have time to analyze. I force myself to stay unimpressed. "Oh, I'm sure your version of the truth is *very* comforting.

Elias snorts. "Princess, if you're looking for comfort, you're barking up the wrong morally gray tree."

I glare at him. "You really can't help yourself, can you?'

"Not even a little."

Max lets out a sigh, the kind that says he's running out of patience. "Wrenley. Get in the car."

I huff a humorless laugh. "Yeah, because that's a *great* idea. Get into a car with two armed men I barely know, both of whom have already held me at gunpoint."

Elias gestures at me. "*Technically*, that was just a precautionary measure. *You* were the one pointing a gun first."

"Because you were following me!"

He tilts his head. "And? I followed you very professionally. You should be flattered."

"Oh, thrilled."

Max exhales sharply. "Enough. Wrenley, I understand your hesitation, but I assure you, if I wanted to harm you, I wouldn't have gone through the trouble of sending Elias to keep an eye on you."

"*To keep an eye on me?*" I repeat, skeptical. "That's what you're calling it."

Elias smirks. "Would you prefer 'casual surveillance'? Or maybe 'deeply concerned shadowing'?"

I glare. "I'd prefer if you both got hit by a bus, but clearly, I'm not getting what I want today."

Elias lets out a low chuckle. "I like her, boss. She's feisty. Can we keep her?"

Max ignores him entirely, his gaze locked onto me. "You want answers, Wrenley. I'm offering them."

I narrow my eyes. "At what cost?"

His expression doesn't change, but something in the air shifts. His voice drops just enough to send a shiver down my spine.

"The cost is *your choice* to step into this world or walk away from it."

I glance at Elias, who just shrugs like this is all some casual Tuesday morning inconvenience. "I mean, you *could* walk away," he muses. "But then again, curiosity *does* tend to get the best of people. And by people, I mean you."

I shoot him a look. "You don't know me."

Elias grins big. "Sure, I do. I know you're stubborn as hell, too smart for your own good, and *definitely* about to get into this car."

Damn him. He's right. I glance at the SUV again. I don't trust them. I don't trust any of this. But I need to know.

I sigh and point a warning finger at Elias before moving toward the vehicle. "If you even *think* about pulling your gun on me again, I will shoot you somewhere that doesn't kill you but makes you wish it did."

Elias grins wider if that is even possible. "Now *that's* the kind of energy I respect."

Max steps aside, gesturing for me to get in. I hesitate one last time before slipping into the SUV, telling myself this isn't the worst decision I've ever made.

Even though deep down, I know that's probably a lie.

Chapter Nine

MAXIMILIAN

THE CAR RIDE is thick with tension, the kind that settles into your bones and refuses to leave. Wrenley sits stiffly in the seat next to me, her hands curled into fists in her lap, eyes locked on the window. She doesn't speak. Doesn't ask where we're going. But I can feel the storm raging inside her, the questions piling up behind her lips.

Elias hums to himself as he drives, drumming his fingers against the wheel in a way that grates on my nerves. He's enjoying this far too much. I know he wants to say something, something to piss her off, something to get a reaction, but for once, he manages to keep his mouth shut.

When we finally pull up to one of the safe houses, Wrenley's eyes jerk to the house, studying it. It's sleek, modern, and deliberately unremarkable. A place meant to disappear into the background.

She doesn't move at first. Just stares at the house like she's weighing her options, as if she could make a run for it and somehow slip through my fingers. Not a chance. I open my door, stepping out into the crisp morning air. Elias stretches in the driver's seat, letting out an exaggerated sigh.

"Home sweet home," he mutters.

Wrenley finally moves, sliding out of the car with careful

precision, her eyes still scanning the area. Calculating. I can practically see the wheels turning in her head, mapping out every exit, every possible escape route.

I let her have the moment. Let her think she has control.

Elias smirks. "You planning on running, princess? Or do you just like the view?"

She shoots him a glare. "You talk *way* too much."

He grins. "I get that a lot."

I don't have time for their back-and-forth, so I motion toward the house. "Inside."

Wrenley hesitates but eventually follows. As soon as we step inside, her sharp gaze sweeps over the interior. The space is minimalistic, intentionally void of personality. No clutter, no personal touches. Just clean lines and neutral colors.

Her lips curve into something that isn't quite a smile. "You know, for someone with money, I expected something a little more... *lived in.*"

I close the door behind us. "I'm a man of simple means."

She snorts. "Right. I've seen enough crime shows to know a safe house when I see one."

Elais laughs from the kitchen doorway. "She's good, boss. Real good."

I shoot him a pointed look, and he holds up his hands in mock surrender before disappearing into the other room. Wrenley turns back to me, arms crossed, weight shifted to one hip. She's wary, but not afraid. Not yet.

I motion toward the couch. "Sit."

"I am not a dog."

I close the distance to her and say it again, "Sit." I can clearly see the effect I am having on her. She hesitates, then lowers herself onto the leather, keeping her posture defensive. I take the chair across from her, resting my forearms on my knees, watching her closely.

"I need to know how much you know about your family's business."

She exhales a short, humorless laugh. "Is that what this is about? Because if you're looking for insider information, you're going to be disappointed."

I keep my expression neutral. "Enlighten me."

She leans back, arms still crossed. "I left home when I was seventeen, right after I graduated from high school. I wanted no part in my family's business."

"*No part?*" I press.

She scoffs. "What part of *no part* isn't clear? I know what Ashford International does on the surface—the real estate, the investments, the ridiculous wealth—being in charge of an empire was not what I wanted, and my art pissed them off, so that's a bonus. That's why I left."

Ashford International. A name that carries weight, power built on control. I already knew she was distanced from the family, but hearing it from her lips solidifies the reality of it.

She shrugs, brushing an invisible speck of lint off her sleeve. "I put myself through art school working at a gallery because I didn't want their money. I didn't like what it did to them." A shadow crosses her face. "Benjamin was the only one who believed I could do it."

There it is again. That softness when she speaks about her uncle. The one decent Ashford.

"Your parents didn't help you at all?"

"Oh, they tried." Her lips twist into something bitter. "They gave me a trust fund when I turned twenty. But it's just been sitting there. Untouched. I don't want their money, Blackwood. It comes with too many strings."

I let silence settle between us, studying her carefully. She really doesn't know what her family is involved in. That complicates things.

After a long pause, I shift the conversation. "What about the night you were attacked?"

Wrenley tenses, her jaw tightening.

"Well, *you* were there," she says dryly. "Why don't *you* tell me?"

I don't respond right away. Instead, I hold her gaze, letting the weight of the memory settle between us. I exhale. "I was meeting with Benjamin that night. You came into the lodge, said hello. You didn't look at me."

She frowns slightly, as if trying to remember.

"I don't know what it was," I continue, my voice quieter now. "But the moment you walked out, I had this... *instinct*." I shake my head slightly. "So I followed you."

Wrenley stills.

"You didn't notice me at first. I kept my distance. And then I heard you scream."

A glimmer of something breaks through her mask, something raw, unprotected.

"I found you in that alley," I say, jaw clenching. "That bastard had you pinned. He had a knife." My eyes drift to her collarbone, where I know the scar is. "He'd already cut you."

Her throat bobs slightly as she swallows.

"I got there in time." My voice is steady, but there's an edge to it. I can still remember the look in that bastard's eyes when I got my hands on him. The way his screams echoed down that alleyway. But I don't tell her that.

She doesn't need to know how much I enjoyed spilling his blood that night. She clears her throat, shifting in her seat. "Why didn't you say something at the funeral?"

I tilt my head slightly. "Would you have believed me?"

She doesn't answer.

I take a slow breath, changing the subject. "You really don't know what your family is involved in?"

Her voice is quiet when she responds. "I *told you*. I left all of that behind."

I analyze her body language, breathing, her telling eyes, and wrestle internally with how much to tell her.

Benjamin wanted to dismantle Ashford International—to

strip the family of their power and break their greedy hold on this city. And now he's dead. And Wrenley? She's the only Ashford left who isn't corrupted by it. But if she learns just how deep this goes, there's no going back.

After a length of silence, I lean forward again, resting my elbows on my knees, my eyes locked onto Wrenley's. My voice is lower now, measured. "Benjamin and I had common interests, more than one, if you dig, if you learn the truth about what's really going on... things will never be the same." I pause, letting the weight of my words settle between us. "You have a decision to make, Wrenley."

She inhales sharply, her lips parting like she's about to speak, about to agree, but I hold up a hand, stopping her.

"Not now," I say, shaking my head. "Take some time. Think about it."

She presses her lips together in frustration. I stand, picking her phone up off the couch beside her, and I put my number in it. "Take my car back to your hotel. We'll retrieve it later." Then, without waiting for a response, I turn and walk out of the room.

Elias flops onto the couch beside her, stretching out like he owns the place. He holds up the keys and wiggles them between his fingers. "Well, look at you," he drawls. "Twenty-four hours in and you already have the boss giving you his car. You must be *very* special."

Wrenley snorts despite herself, a giggle slipping out before she can stop it. She quickly masks it, but Elias grins like he's just won something. "I *knew* you had a sense of humor," he says smugly, tossing the keys into her lap. "Try not to scratch it, princess. He may be generous, but he's still a bastard about his cars."

Chapter Ten

WRENLEY

I DON'T EVEN REMEMBER DRIVING BACK to the hotel or riding the elevator up to my room. I throw my phone and myself onto the bed and stare up at the ceiling.

What the fuck is going on?

Maximilian Blackwood's words won't leave me. *If you dig, things will never be the same.* What does that even mean? What was Benjamin doing with him? The room feels suffocating. I need answers, and there's only one person I can trust to help me find them.

I grab my phone and call Margot. She answers on the first ring.

"Are you up for a little late-night sleuthing in my uncle's mansion?"

There's a pause, then an excited gasp. "Breaking and entering? Wrenley, I thought you'd never ask."

Of course, she agrees. She's always up for an adventure, especially one that involves bending the rules. Less than ten minutes later, she's at my door, bouncing on her heels like she's had three espressos. She's still in the same leather pants and cropped sweater she wore to breakfast, her blonde hair twisted into a messy bun that somehow still looks effortlessly cool.

"You ready?" she asks, then eyes my outfit. "No. Absolutely not. You cannot sleuth dressed like a sad hotel guest."

I let out a sigh as I glance down at my sweatpants. "Fine, give me a second."

Margot lets herself in, immediately making herself at home by flopping onto my bed. She's staying at the same hotel, just a few floors below me, and I'd opted for separate rooms. I love her, but sharing a space with Margot means tripping over high heels, dodging discarded takeout containers, and pretending not to notice when she sneaks in a hookup at three in the morning.

Once I change into black jeans, boots, and a fitted jacket, I lead the way down to the parking garage. The dull thud of my boots echoes off the cold concrete walls. The air down here is thick with the scent of gasoline and faint traces of rain that must have drifted in earlier. Overhead lights flicker, casting long, distorted shadows along the ground.

I press the key fob in my pocket, and my matte black vintage Range Rover Classic flashes its headlights in response. Sleek, fast, powerful—exactly what I wanted when I bought it after selling my first painting. It's not just a car; it's a statement. A promise to myself that I didn't need my family's money to have something that was purely mine.

Behind me, Margot lets out a low whistle. "You know, I still think you should've gone with the drop-top Porsche. Champagne in the passenger seat. Instead, you're driving a retired bodyguard's dream car."

I unlock the door and slide in, the cool leather seat pressing against my skin. "I'd rather not spend the whole drive listening to you shriek about your hair tangling," I mutter as I start the engine. Margot rolls her eyes and climbs into the passenger seat, immediately propping her boots up on the dashboard. Without looking, I smack her leg. "Feet down, gremlin."

She sighs dramatically but obeys. "So, are we breaking and entering, or just politely letting ourselves in?" I shift into reverse, gripping the wheel a little tighter. "Benjamin always said I was welcome anytime I wanted," I say simply. "So, we'll call it visiting."

With that, I press the gas, the Range Rover rumbling to life as we pull out of the garage and into the night, the dark road stretching ahead like a question waiting to be answered.

The drive to Benjamin's estate is quiet, the hum of the engine the only sound between us for a while. The roads are winding, lined with towering trees that cast eerie shadows under the dim glow of the streetlights. The further we go, the less civilization there is, just the endless stretch of forest that surrounds the property. Benjamin always liked his privacy.

Margot drums her fingers against her thigh, watching the trees blur past. "So, are we expecting a security system, or did your uncle live recklessly?"

I smirk, "Oh, there's definitely security. But I know the codes."

"Handy." She tilts her head. "And you're sure no one's living there?"

I let out a slow breath. "No one that I know of. But... there might be a dog."

Margot turns to me, alarmed. "Excuse me? *A dog?*"

I shrug. "It's possible. Benjamin had a Cane Corso. Big, black, intimidating as hell."

Margot blinks. "And you're just telling me this *now*? What if it eats us?"

I fight a grin. "It won't eat us. Probably."

Margot groans, slumping back against the seat. "I swear, if I die via dog attack because of your family's secrets, I'm haunting you."

The iron gates of the estate come into view, looming over us like something out of a Gothic novel. I punch in the code at the keypad, and after a tense beat, the gates creak open. The house itself is just beyond a long, cobblestone driveway lined with old-fashioned lanterns. Even in the dark, the place is *imposing*, a sprawling stone manor with towering windows, ivy crawling up its side like nature itself was trying to reclaim it.

Margot lets out a low whistle. "This place is giving me major haunted vibes."

I smirk. "I know, it's perfect, isn't it?"

Pulling up near the entrance, I kill the engine. The air is thick with the scent of damp earth and pine. Everything is still, silent. Too silent.

We step out, and Margot huffs, rubbing her arms. "Okay, let's get in and get out before I start seeing ghosts."

I approach the heavy wooden door, reaching for the key Benjamin had once given me, when, from the side of the house, a deep, rumbling growl cuts through the night.

Margot stiffens. "No. Nope. Absolutely not."

A massive shape emerges from the shadows. A towering, muscular Cane Corso. His sleek black coat shimmers under the porch light, his dark eyes locked onto us with eerie intelligence. His growl is low, reverberating through the air as a warning.

Margot backs up so fast she nearly trips over her own feet. "That's not a dog. That's a horse."

I suppress a laugh and step forward slowly, keeping my voice firm. "Platz."

The dog immediately lowers into a sit, his head still held high, watching me carefully.

Margot's jaw drops. "Did you just—what did you say?"

I crouch slightly, extending my hand. "Braver Hund."

The dog's ears twitch, and after a moment, he cautiously steps forward, sniffing my palm before letting out a soft huff of recognition.

I glance at Margot. "His name's Hugo. And he's only terrifying if you don't know how to handle him."

Margot stares at me, then at the dog. "You speak German?"

I shrug. "Just enough to keep from getting mauled."

She throws her hand up. "Of course you do. And of course, your uncle had a killer guard dog trained in a foreign language."

Hugo gives another low, contented huff and leans his massive head into my touch. I scratch behind his ears, murmuring another soft command before looking at Margot.

"Are you coming, or are you staying out here to be haunted and eaten?"

Margot mutters something under her breath but stomps forward. "If I get drooled on, you owe me."

Smirking, I push the door open, stepping into the dimly lit house. Time to find out why Benjamin was working with Maximilian.

Chapter Eleven

WRENLEY

THE MANSION SMELLS THE SAME. A mix of aged leather, oak, and the faintest hint of cigar smoke lingers on the walls. It's unsettling how time hasn't touched it, as if Benjamin might step around the corner at any second, a brandy in his hand, ready to tease me about not visiting enough.

I push the thought down and press forward, leading Margot through the dimly lit hallways toward the study. If there's anything to find, it will be there.

Margot pauses in front of a large painting, tilting her head. "This is one of yours, isn't it?"

I glance over and feel a sharp pang in my chest; it's one of mine, the second piece I ever sold. Bold, textured brushstrokes with dark blues and crimsons layered together, chaotic but intentional.

"Yeah," I say softly. "Benjamin always told me he was going to buy one, but that he wouldn't be my first sale. Said I needed to stand on my own two feet." I let out a breath, shaking my head. Margot gives me a small smile before following me through the study doors.

Inside, the room is just as I remember, heavy bookshelves stretching to the ceiling, a massive oak desk at the center, and that ridiculous vintage globe bar cart in the corner. The walls are lined with dark green wallpaper and dim brass sconces that cast long shadows. The air is thick with him, his presence woven into every inch of the space.

I trail my fingers over the desk, but the second I reach for the keyboard, my stomach drops. The computer is gone.

"Of course," I mutter. "My father probably already took it."

Margot snorts. "That's not suspicious at all."

I move to the desk drawers, yanking them open, one by one, rifling through stacks of papers, old notes, and records. Nothing out of the ordinary. Just business documents, correspondence.

Margot wanders over to the bookshelves, running her hands along the spines. "I swear, rich people always have books they've never actually read." She pulls a thick, worn leather-bound volume from the shelf, and the moment she does, a crisp white envelope slips out, fluttering to the floor.

She bends, picking it up. Her eyes widen. "Uh, Wren... it has your name on it."

My pulse kicks up. I step over, taking the envelope from her. The handwriting is unmistakably Benjamin's.

My fingers tremble as I tear it open, unfolding the letter inside. The paper is smooth, the ink bold and deliberate.

Wrenley,

If you're reading this, then I am already gone. I won't waste time telling you to let this go; I know you won't. There are things I wanted to tell you, but time has a cruel way of stealing moments we thought we had. The truth is, your family has built its empire on more than what you were allowed to see. And I have spent years trying to undo what has been done.

I had hoped to tell you in person, to guide

you through the storm that is coming, but now...
now, you must decide if you want to see the whole
truth for yourself. There is one person you can
trust, stick to the shadow.

Find the false drawer in my bedroom. You'll
need what's inside. Be careful who you look to for
answers, renegade. The wrong question to the wrong
person could cost you everything
—Benjamin

My throat tightens. I read the words again, willing them not to mean what I think they do. But there it is. Laid out for me in his careful, steady hand.

"Wren?" Margot's voice is quieter now, the teasing edge gone. "What does it say?"

I fold the letter carefully, tucking it into my jacket. When I meet her gaze, my expression is grim. "It says we're not done here."

The old wooden staircase creaks under our weight as Margot and I ascend toward Benjamin's bedroom. The letter burning a hole in my pocket, my fingers itching to pull it out and read it again, just to be sure I didn't imagine it. The weight of its words presses down on my chest, making it harder to breathe.

Margot walks a step ahead of me, muttering under her breath. "I swear, if this is some secret treasure map leading to a bunch of IOUs and expired casino chips, I'm going to be so disappointed."

I roll my eyes, but don't get a chance to respond. Because as we pass a closed door at the top of the stairs, it bursts open.

Both of us shriek as a figure steps into the hallway, brandishing a bat like he's about to swing for the fences. Margot stumbles into me. "Holy shit, we're gonna die!"

Then I recognized the man in front of us, his wrinkled face caught somewhere between alarm and exasperation.

"Oh my God—Graham?"

The butler, who has been with this family since before I was born, lowers the bat, his blue eyes narrowing behind his glasses. "Miss Wrenley?" His crisp English accent is filled with disbelief.

I clutch my chest. "Are you trying to give me a heart attack?"

Graham straightens, smoothing his vest as if he is the one who were just startled. "I could ask you the same thing! What are you doing sneaking about? Your parents would be furious if they knew you were here."

Margot exhales loudly. "God, I think my soul just left my body."

I ignore her, stepping closer to Graham. "I just need to get something from Benjamin's room. We'll be gone in five minutes."

He studies me, his aged face pinched with worry. "Wrenley... you shouldn't be here."

"I know," I say, softer this time. "But I have to be."

After a long pause, he sighs, stepping aside. "Hurry."

I don't waste time. I pull Margot down the hall and push open the heavy wooden doors of Benjamin's bedroom. It's just as extravagant as I remember, all rich mahogany furniture and deep crimson bedding. A grand fireplace sits unlit against the far wall, and the entire space smells like him, leather, oak, and cigars.

Margot lets out a low whistle. "Damn, Even in death, he's still cooler than all of us."

I shake my head, heading straight for the dresser. "Start checking the drawers for false bottoms."

Margot grins. "You know, if we weren't looking for potentially incriminating evidence, this would almost be fun."

I roll my eyes, running my hands over the inside of the top drawer. Nothing. I move to the next, feeling along the seams. A minute passes, then two, then—"Bingo!"

I spin around just in time to see Margot pull an envelope from a hidden compartment in the bottom drawer. She hands it to me, and my heart hammers as I read the writing on my front. My name. Stapled to the outside is a small black card. I pull it off and flip it over. It's an address, nothing else. I meet Margot's gaze. "This is it."

She nods. "Then let's get the hell out of here."

When we reach the foyer, Graham is waiting with Hugo by his side, along with a suitcase. I slow to a stop. "What's going on?"

Graham exhales. "I'm leaving."

My brows pull together. "Leaving?"

He nods. "I don't feel safe in this house anymore. Not after Benjamin..." his voice trails off, and he shakes his head. "But I cannot take Hugo with me. He belongs to you now."

Margot blinks. "Uh—what?"

I glance at Hugo, who sits calmly beside Graham, watching me with his dark eyes. "I'm staying in a hotel. I can't possibly—"

"You think he'll be safer here?" Graham interrupts. "I don't trust your parents... to look after him. And he adores you, Miss Wrenley."

I hesitate, looking down at the massive Cane Corso. He lets out a soft huff, as if he already knows how this will end.

Margot smirks. "Yeah, Wren. You totally don't have a choice."

After a long pause, I sigh. "Fine. But you owe me for this."

Graham smiles. "I believe it's Benjamin who owes you."

By the time we get back to the hotel, I am exhausted.

But the moment we step into the lobby, the front desk clerk goes pale.

"Miss Ashford," he stammers, glancing between me and Hugo, who stand obediently at my side. "Dogs aren't allowed."

I pinch the bridge of my nose. Not tonight. I do not have the patience for this tonight.

I paste on my sweetest, most condescending smile, "Are you suggesting I leave this poor, defenseless creature outside all alone?"

The clerk blanches. "Well-no—no, but—"

"I'm so glad you understand," I say, stepping toward the elevator.

He sputters, grabbing the phone and calling for the manager. Within seconds, a middle-aged man in a suit appears, looking deeply unamused.

"Miss Ashford," he says with forced patience. "Hotel policy strictly prohibits large animals."

I sigh. "Look, I've had a very long day."

The phone rings. The clerk picks up, listens for a second, then wordlessly hands the receiver to the manager.

His expression shifts. "Yes, sir," he says stiffly. "I understand." A pause. "Yes, of course. It won't happen again."

When he hangs up, he clears his throat, looking far less smug. "You may keep your dog."

I lift a brow. "What changed?"

He forces a smile. "Have a lovely evening, Miss Ashford."

Margot waits until we're in the elevator before looking at me sideways. "Well, *that* was weird." I nod slowly. Yeah. It was.

Once inside my hotel room, I drop onto the bed, spreading the contents of the envelope in front of me: files, documents, names.

My stomach twists as I take in what I'm looking at. It's worse than I thought, much, *much* worse.

Chapter Twelve

MAXIMILIAN

IT'S BEEN three days since I left Wrenley at the safe house.

Three days of waiting. Three days of wondering if she was actually going to dig further or if she'd shove the documents aside and pretend she never saw them.

That first night, I wasn't sure which way she'd go—until I caught her on the hotel's security camera, waltzing into the lobby with that goddamn horse-sized dog.

I had to laugh. There she was, exhausted but determined, dragging that Cane Corso behind her while the front desk clerk looked like he was about to have a heart attack.

I didn't even hesitate; I picked up my phone, dialed the hotel manager directly, and told him in no uncertain terms that Miss Ashford gets to keep the dog. And anything else she damn well pleases.

Since then, I've been watching. Hacking into the hotel's security feed was easy for Elias. I've kept an eye on the footage, waiting for her to leave, to do something.

But Wrenley has barely left her room. The only times she's stepped outside have been to walk Hugo. A few times a day, short trips. No unnecessary outings. No suspicious behavior.

It makes me wonder... what the hell did she find at that

mansion? And why is she hiding away instead of running? Something about it doesn't sit right with me.

I grab my phone and call Elias.

"Took you long enough," he answers before I can say a word. "I was starting to think you finally took my advice and were letting this whole thing go."

"I need you to get over here," I say, ignoring him.

Elias sighs. "Oh, sure, because I don't have a life or anything."

I don't dignify that with a response, just hang up and wait.

Fifteen minutes later, Elias is slouching against my kitchen counter, nursing a glass of whiskey, smirking at me like he already knows what this is about.

"I gotta say," he muses, swirling the amber liquid, "this whole thing is a very, *very* bad idea."

"Elias—"

"No, no, hear me out." He interrupts, setting his glass down. "We have a plan. A solid, well-thought-out, *years-in-the-making* plan. You know what wasn't part of that plan?" He points at me. "You. Getting. Distracted. By. A. Woman."

I exhale slowly. "She isn't a distraction."

"She *is* a distraction," Elias argues. "And worse, she's an Ashford. The exact family we're trying to dismantle, in case you've suddenly forgotten."

I haven't forgotten. The Ashford's have their claws in everything. A dynasty of greed, corruption, and control. From luxury real estate to high-end art auctions to offshore investment firms—on paper, they're an empire of old money and prestige.

But underneath? Weapons trade. Drugs. Money laundering. Bribery. Assassinations. Every politician they can buy, they do. Every competitor who won't play by their rules mysteriously disappears. Every deal that benefits them screw over thousands.

And my father—

I grit my teeth. No. I won't go there. Not now.

"I know exactly what I'm doing," I tell Elias, my tone sharp.

He shakes his head. "Yeah? Then tell me, what's the play here,

Max? Because from where I'm standing, it looks like you're getting a little too wrapped up in the wrong Ashford."

Before I can answer, a loud knock echoes through the apartment.

Elias frowns. "Expecting someone?"

"No."

He sighs. "Great. If I get shot, I'm haunting your ass."

Elias swings the door open, mouth already forming some smart-ass remark, when—

"FUCK!"

He stumbles back, arms flailing as a massive black beast lunges forward, paws landing square on his shoulders.

Elias's scream is high-pitched—undeniably unmasculine—as he tries and fails to shake off the assault of slobbery kisses being enthusiastically delivered to his face.

"GET IT OFF, GET IT OFF!" Elias yells, voice muffled as Hugo's giant tongue drags across his cheek.

Wrenley stands in the doorway, amused but slightly panicked, trying to tug the dog back by his collar. "Hugo, down!" she orders, but the dog is not interested in listening to her right now.

I take one slow step forward.

"Sitz."

Hugo immediately drops onto all fours and sits his massive head tilting up at me expectantly. Wrenley's eyes widen as she stares between me and the dog.

"You've got to be fucking kidding me," Elias mutters, wiping his face with the sleeve of his jacket. "First, she shows up out of nowhere, and now the hell-hound listens to you?"

Wrenley blinks, still processing. "You..." She stops, shakes her head. "...You know German?"

I smirk. "Among other things."

She exhales sharply, still gripping Hugo's collar like she's expecting him to spring forward again at any second. Then, her attention shifts past Elias, taking in the penthouse behind me—

the clean lines, the open floor plan, the city spread out like a glittering kingdom beyond the windows.

Her expression shifts, momentarily thrown off balance.

"Huh."

I catch the brief flicker of uncertainty before she locks it all away again.

"*This* is your place?" She asks, though it's not really a question.

Elias, still grumbling about the attack, throws up his hands. "Okay, so are we just letting people and their war beasts into the apartment now, or... ?"

Wrenley shoots him a pointed look. "Did you want me to leave?"

Elias pauses. "I mean..." he glances at me. "Did you bring food?"

She rolls her eyes.

I just watch her, arms crossed over my chest. "You weren't sure who exactly would be here."

She shakes her head, exhaling. "Can't be too careful."

"And yet, here you are."

A beat of silence.

Then, Wrenley lifts the envelope, wiggles it slightly between her fingers. "Pour a drink, Blackwood," she says, stepping inside. "We have a lot to discuss."

I watch her, taking in the tight set of her shoulders, the sharp focus in her eyes. She wants answers. She has no idea what she's walking into. But she chose to come here. I take a slow sip of my drink, rolling the whiskey over my tongue as I debate.

How much does she really want to know? How much is she ready to hear? I set my glass down with a quiet clink and meet her gaze.

"Are you sure?" My voice is calm, but there's a weight behind the question. A warning.

Wrenley doesn't flinch. "Yes."

I hold her stare for a beat longer, searching for hesitation, for doubt. But there's none. She doesn't care. Good.

Pushing off the counter, I stride across the room to the bank of computers against the wall. With a few keystrokes, encrypted files unlock, revealing information she hasn't even begun to dig up yet, things that go deeper than what she pulled from Benjamin's house. Names, Numbers, deals, and accounts that shouldn't exist.

Behind me, Elias lets out a low whistle. Then, with zero hesitation, he throws an arm around Wrenley's Shoulder, pulling her into motion toward where I'm working. I grind my teeth, irritation curling hot in my chest. It shouldn't bother me—doesn't bother me.

But it does.

There is something about seeing Elias's arm draped so casually over her, the way she doesn't pull away, that makes my fingers tighten against the keyboard. Makes my jaw clench a little harder than it should. I say nothing. Because I don't give a damn. At least, that's what I tell myself.

"Welcome to the shitshow, sweetheart," Elias says, his voice dripping with amusement.

Wrenley lets out a laugh, soft at first, then louder, like she can't believe this is actually happening. Like she knows she should be terrified, but, for some reason, she's not.

And that...

That might just be the most dangerous thing about her.

The room is dimly lit by the glow of the computer screens, casting eerie shadows along the walls as I click through file after file, exposing layer upon layer of corruption, extortion, and bloody money.

Wrenley sits beside me, her eyes locked on the monitors, her brows drawn together in deep concentration. The more I show, the more that sharp, defiant edge in her gaze hardens.

"This..." she exhales, rubbing her fingers against her temple. "This is what my family has been doing?"

I nod. "For decades. They've built an empire on the backs of people who had no idea they were being used. Laundering money through shell companies, strong-arming politicians, bribing law enforcement, trafficking goods that should never make it past the border."

Her jaw tightens, her fingers clenching into fists in her lap. "And my uncle? How involved was he?"

I hesitate. She notices. She turns to me sharply. "Maximilian."

I don't answer right away. Instead, I shift the screen, pulling up another document, this one older, Benjamin's name is all over it, but so is his resistance.

"He wanted out," I say finally, keeping my voice even. "For years, he tried to pull away from the Ashford grip, but your father —" I shake my head. "He wasn't about to let one of his own walk away with family secrets."

Wrenley's throat bobs, her expression unreadable. She's processing.

Elias, sprawled across the couch with Hugo now curled against his legs, lets out a low, amused hum. "I gotta say, princess, your family is more fucked up than mine, *and that's saying something.*"

She glares at him. "Not helping."

He grins, stretching his arms behind his head. "Wasn't trying to."

I smirk slightly but keep my focus on her.

"How do you know all this?" she finally asks, tilting her head at me. "How did you get this information?"

I lean back slightly, weighing my words. I could tell her the truth, that I've spent years gathering every piece of dirt I could find, infiltrating their systems, following their trails, waiting for the perfect moment to pull the rug out from under them.

But I settle on something less revealing. "Benjamin trusted me," I say, watching her closely. "We had an agreement."

Her eyes narrow. "That's not an answer. What was the agreement?"

I just smirk. She exhales, clearly frustrated, but doesn't push —not yet.

Elias snorts from the couch, shifting to his side. "Damn, Blackwood, I think she might actually be better at interrogating you than you are at interrogating her."

"Shut up, Elias."

Elias just grins, stretching once more with zero concern for the gravity of the situation. For the next few hours, Wrenley asks more questions, some I answer, some I avoid. Elias occasionally chimes in, but eventually, he and Hugo both pass out.

It's nearing midnight when Wrenley presses her fingers against her temples, squeezing her eyes shut. "I need to lie down," she mutters. "I can't think anymore."

I push back from the desk, glancing toward the hallway. "Take my room."

She raises an eyebrow. "And where are you going to sleep?"

"I don't."

She studies me a moment before deciding not to push it. Instead, she rises, stretching her arms over her head before disappearing down the hall. I stay at the computer, fingers hovering over the keyboard, but I don't work. I don't look at the files.

I look at the hallway. I tell myself it's nothing. I don't care if she's in my room, in my space. She's just another part of the plan.

Elias stirs, not even opening his eyes, and mutters, "You're so completely fucked."

I scowl. "Go to sleep."

Elias smirks without looking at me. "She's still under your skin. You just don't wanna admit it."

I don't answer. Because I *don't* admit things. After a few beats of silence, I stand, pushing away from the desk. I don't think about where I'm going. But I already know.

When I reach my bedroom door, I pause for a second, fingers resting on the handle.

Then, without another thought, I push it open and step inside.

Chapter Thirteen

WRENLEY

I BRACE my hands against the cool marble countertop of the en-suite bathroom, staring at my reflection in the mirror.

The woman staring back at me should look exhausted, shattered by everything she's learned today. Instead, there's something else lingering in my eyes, something that has nothing to do with the Ashfords, my uncle's secrets, or the fact that my world is unraveling thread by thread.

No. It has everything to do with him. Maximilian Jude Blackwood.

The man who pulled me from the shadows the night I was attacked. The man who has haunted me ever since.

I've spent years wondering about the stranger who saved me. Until I saw him at the funeral, until I stood in his presence and realized that some part of me had always known.

And now that I do? I can't shake it. Something about him pulls at me, sets my nerves alight, makes my pulse thrash like I'm standing on the edge of something dangerous and irresistible all at once.

I grip the counter tightly, exhaling sharply. This is insane. "Wrenley, get a hold of yourself."

I should be thinking about the files, about my uncle's secrets, about the very real danger that could be creeping closer by the second. But instead, I'm standing here trying to get my heart to stop racing just because I'm sleeping in Maximilian's bed. Just because he's near.

I shake my head, trying to rid myself of the feeling, but it clings to me. When I finally push off the counter and step out of the bathroom, my breath catches in my throat. I hadn't noticed it when I first walked in. But now, hanging on the far wall, bathed in the faint glow of the city lights streaming through the windows, is my painting

The Red Thread.

The same piece that was sold anonymously at my exhibit. My stomach churns as I step closer, my gaze tracing the bold crimson streaks cutting across the canvas, the dark, silk-like strands swallowing the figure whole.

I painted this from a place of pain. Of defiance. It's not just a piece of art, it's a confession. A scar put on display. And it's here. In *his* bedroom.

"What the hell," I murmur under my breath.

"I had a feeling you'd notice that."

I spin, pulse spiking, and find Max standing in the doorway. He leans casually against the frame, hands in his pockets, his expression unreadable. The city lights cast a faint glow on the sharp lines of his face, making the shadows under his eyes look deeper, darker.

"*You* bought it?" My voice is breathless, still trying to catch up.

He tilts his head slightly. "Does that bother you?"

I glance back at the painting, at the way it stands out in a space that otherwise looks nothing like an artist's haven. It doesn't fit here, but at the same time, it's the only thing in this room that feels alive.

"No," I admit quietly. "But it makes me wonder?"

His gaze sharpens. "Wonder what?"

I swallow, my fingers brushing the hem of my shirt absentmindedly. Why me? Why my work? Why did you want it? Why does it make me want you even more?

I turn back to him, taking a slow breath. "Why?"

Max doesn't answer. He studies me instead, eyes roaming over my face, searching. Then he steps further inside.

"It shows me a confession of your soul, and I want it," he says, voice smooth, deep, indecipherable. "Are you alright? Do you need anything?"

His words hang between us, the silence stretching too long, too charged. I take another slow breath, steadying myself, trying to find the courage to say what's already forming in my mind. The truth is, I *do* need something. Not comfort. Not reassurance.

A distraction. From the weight of my uncle's death. From the files, I can't make sense of. From the family I don't recognize. From the way this man makes me feel like I'm burning from the inside out. I swallow, stepping closer, the air between us growing thinner, heavier with every step.

"I don't know how to explain this," I start my voice softer than I mean it to be.

Max doesn't move, but his entire body seems wired with tension. His sharp eyes are locked onto mine, waiting.

"There's something about you that is pulling me in." The words fall before I can stop them. "And right now, I need... I need to be distracted."

His brows furrow, not in disapproval, but in confusion, like he doesn't fully understand what I mean. I bridge the distance, reaching up, placing my palm against his chest. I feel his solidness, the warmth beneath the fabric of his shirt. His heartbeat is steady, controlled, so unlike mine.

His lips part slightly, but he doesn't pull away. Instead, he reaches up slowly, his fingers brushing against my cheek, a feather-light caress that makes my breath hitch. He studies me, his thumb skimming the edge of my jaw, as if he's waiting for me to change my mind.

But I don't. I tip my chin up, looking at him through my

lashes, and that's all it takes. Max closes the distance between us, his lips pressing against mine in a kiss that is soft, careful, searching. But as I press closer, my finger curling into the fabric of his shirt, something inside him shifts.

The kiss deepens, his hand sliding to the back of my neck, fingers tangling in my hair, tilting my head as he takes control. It's heat. It's fire. And for the first time in days, I stopped thinking.

Max pulls away, his breathing ragged, his forehead nearly touching mine. His hand still cups my face, his thumbs brushing against my skin as if he's memorizing the feel of me.

"I've been thinking about this," he murmurs, his voice rough, his lips barely ghosting over mine. "Since the first moment you walked into the lodge."

A shiver rolls down my spine. I believe him. I felt it then, the weight of his gaze, the pull between us, the way he watched me like he already knew how this would end.

Max lifts a hand, fingers threading into my hair, tilting my chin up to him. I let him, my pulse pounding in anticipation, my body already buzzing with the need for more.

Then his mouth moves to my neck, his lips dragging slowly across my skin. A soft nip, followed by a searing kiss. I let out a breathy sigh, my fingers tightening in the fabric of his shirt. I should stop this. I should tell him that he's the last person I should be tangled up with. That I shouldn't want him like this, not when he's trying to tear my family apart.

But I don't. Because I *do* want him. *All of him.* I slide my hands under the hem of his shirt, feeling the warmth of his bare skin, the ridges of his sculpted abs. My fingers skim over the hard muscle, over the faint raised scars scattered across his skin.

He watches me carefully, as if waiting to see if I'll stop. I don't. I pull his shirt up, pushing it higher until he lifts his arms, letting me drag it over his head. God, he's beautiful. Every inch of him screams danger, the ink curling over his ribs, the scars, the strength that comes with knowing exactly what he's capable of. And right now, he's all mine.

Max exhales sharply, his control hanging by a thread. Then, in one swift motion, he bends and picks me up, his hands gripping my thighs as I instinctively wrap my legs around his waist. I feel his strength, the effortlessness in the way he holds me, and it sends a thrill through me.

He walks us to the bed, his steps measured, deliberate, his lips finding mine again—deep this time, his tongue sweeping into my mouth in a way that makes me whimper.

When my back hits the mattress, he takes his time, hovering over me, letting his fingers trace the hem of my shirt before slowly pushing it up. The heat in his gaze makes my skin tingle. Then his hands move lower. He grips the waistband of my jeans, his knuckles brushing against my stomach as he unbuttons them one slow movement at a time.

I can barely breathe. Every touch, every drag of his fingers, sends fire racing through my veins. He keeps watching me, his eyes dark with something primal as he hooks his fingers into my jeans and pulls them down, along with my panties.

The cool air skates across my bare skin, but I don't feel exposed. I feel wanted. I feel devoured by the way he looks at me.

"Max..." My voice is a whisper, but he already knows what I'm asking for.

He leans in, his lips brushing just below my ear, his voice is molten, poured slowly and deliberately, his words meant to unravel me. "Say it." My body arches toward him, my pulse hammering. I don't hesitate.

"Yes."

I barely get the word out before Max is on me. His lips, his hands, his entire presence, it's overwhelming, consuming. He moves lower, trailing hot kisses along my stomach, his fingers gripping my hips, holding me in place as he spreads my thighs wider.

A sharp gasp leaves me as his fingers find my entrance. As our eyes lock, he inserts one finger with ease, feeling just how much I want him. Heat. Pressure. A slow, expert rhythm that makes my head spin. I arch against him, grabbing his forearm like

I could somehow have more of him when he's already everywhere.

Max groans against my neck. The sound vibrates through my body, sending waves of pleasure straight to my core. He adds a second finger curling in just the right way, coaxing me higher, higher—

My body tenses, the sensation building, consuming, building —and then I shatter. The world tilts, my breath catching as pleasure crashes through me, stealing everything, thoughts, control, the ability to do anything but fall apart beneath him.

I barely have time to recover before Max moves again. He shifts above me, his body pressed against mine, the heat of him radiating off his skin as he slides his pants down.

And then he's there, poised at my entrance, his body tense with restraint. His fingers lace with mine, pulling my hands above my head, pinning me to the mattress.

"Stay still," he murmurs, his voice dark, filled with something sinful. "Let me ruin you."

He thrusts inside, burying himself deep, stretching me, filling me in a way that has my eyes rolling back, my lips parting on a breathless moan. Max doesn't stop. His breath ghosts along the curve of my ear, every word a shadowed vow soaked in heat.

"You feel like heaven wrapped around my cock, but I'm going to make you beg for hell."

A shiver runs through me, my legs tightening around him as I tilt my head, letting him have more of me. "Then stop talking and do it."

His low chuckle vibrates through my chest, his grip tightening. "Careful what you ask for, Sparrow."

That name, Sparrow, I heard it before, but in this moment, I can't think of anything except how good this man is making me feel. Then he moves, deep, slow, controlled, his mouth brushing the sensitive skin of my throat.

"You like this, don't you?" he whispers, his voice all sin and smoke. "Being spread out under me, helpless while I take my time ruining you?"

I can barely breathe, barely think, but my nails dig into his hands holding me in place, my own need spiking with every filthy word.

"I don't do helpless, Blackwood." I manage, my voice hazy.

He nips my earlobe, his next thrust rougher, his hands pinning me completely beneath him.

"You will tonight."

A whimper catches in my throat, and he hears it. He loves it.

"I could keep you like this all night. Keep you pinned, make you take everything I give you until you can't think of anything but me."

His hips roll, pressing into that deep aching place, and I break, a soft moan falling past my lips before I can stop it.

"If you want to ruin me, Max," I whisper, breathless, my body tightening beneath him. "Do something about it."

His low growl is the only warning I get before he slams into me, his grip on my wrists unforgiving, his control fracturing.

"Say it. Tell me you want me to break you."

I gasp, my head falling back, my body spiraling, and I know, I know what he's asking for. And I want it. I need it.

"Break me."

The moment the words leave my lips, Max loses whatever restraint he had left. His grip on my wrist tightens, his thrusts turning deeper, rougher, devastatingly perfect. My body arches beneath him, every inch of me burning, unraveling, coming apart at the seams.

"That's it, Sparrow," He murmurs on my skin, his voice ragged, his control slipping. "Give in to me. Let me hear you."

I do. I can't help it. My body coils, the pressure mounting, spiraling too fast, too much. A cry rips from my throat as the pleasure crashes through me, my entire body tensing, then breaking into a million, pulsing pieces.

Max isn't far behind. With a sharp growl, he buries himself

one last time, his body shaking as he finds his own release, his name on my lips, his breath hot against my skin.

For a moment, neither of us moves. Then, slowly, heavily, Max collapses on top of me, his weight solid and grounding, our breaths tangled between us. His skin is hot, his heart hammering against my chest, his grip on my wrists finally loosening.

Seconds stretch into minutes. Neither of us speaks. We just lay there, our bodies cooling, our pulses slowing, both of us staring at the ceiling. Silent.

And completely wrecked.

Chapter Fourteen

MAXIMILIAN

THE FIRST SLIVERS of dawn creep through the floor-to-ceiling windows, casting long streaks of soft gold and muted rose across the apartment. The city is still caught in the in-between moment of night and morning, where the world hasn't quite woken up yet, and everything feels just a little more honest.

I should be somewhere else. I should be focused on the plan, on the next move, on what needs to be done. Instead, I'm standing here, watching her sleep.

Wrenley... my Sparrow.

She's curled into the sheets, her hair spilling over the pillow, the early lights catching its crimson waves. Her breathing is slow, steady, peaceful in a way that makes something twist in my chest. She shouldn't be here. She shouldn't be wrapped up in this, tangled up in me.

But she is. And for the first time, in a long time, I feel something other than rage, other than control, other than the constant weight of unfinished business pressing down on me. I don't regret a single damn thing.

I smirk to myself, tugging on a pair of sweatpants and dragging a hand through my hair as I quietly slip out of the bedroom. The living room is empty, save for the low glow of a lamp left on overnight. Elias is gone. Hugo too. I cross to the kitchen, my footsteps quiet, reaching for a bottle of water. But as I open the fridge, something catches my eye.

A note, pinned to the freezer door with a bottle opener. I pull it down, instantly recognizing Elias's messy scrawl and roll my eyes, knowing this will be some smartass note.

> Couldn't sleep. Some pretty loud, um... activity happening down the hall. Even the dog was restless. Took the Hellhound out to terrorize someone else for a while. You're welcome. P.S. If she kills you, I call dibs on your bike.

I snort, shaking my head as I twist off the cap of my water. I knew it, *Smart-ass.* I take a long sip, leaning against the counter, letting my thoughts settle, as movement catches my eye. I turn and freeze. Wrenley. She stands in the doorway, barefoot, wearing nothing but my shirt.

The hem brushes mid-thigh, the fabric to big on her but somehow perfect at the same time. The sleeves swallow her arms, her long legs bare and golden in the morning light. I should say something. I should look away. I don't. She stretches, catlike, her lips curling into a slow, sleepy smile.

"Morning." Her voice is still rough from sleep, soft and sultry in a way that makes my dick twitch.

I take another slow sip of water, watching her carefully. "Morning."

She pads across the floor, her hips swaying just enough to be distracting, stopping just in front of me.

"Got one for me?" she nods toward the bottle in my hand.

I grab another from the fridge, twisting off the cap before handing it to her.

She takes a sip and tilts her head slightly, studying me with quiet interest.

"You always wake up before dawn?"

"Force of habit."

She hums, amused, leaning on the counter. "Control issues?"

I smile. "Something like that." We're silent for a few moments, trading looks, like we are sizing each other up. She takes a drink of her water, setting the half-empty bottle down. "Well, I am going back to sleep." She turns to leave.

And I don't think. I move. Grabbing her wrist. Spinning her toward me. Lifting her onto the counter in one swift motion. She gasps, her eyes widening as she instinctively wraps her legs around my waist.

I step between her thighs, my hands firm on her hips, our bodies are so close I can feel her heartbeat on my chest. Her breath hitches.

"This," I murmur, my lips brushing just against hers, "is possibly the stupidest mistake either of us will ever make."

She exhales slowly, blinking up at me. "But you don't care."

I slide my hands lower, gripping her thighs just hard enough to make her gasp.

"No," I say, my voice low, firm, certain. "I don't."

Her lips part, her fingers curling into my bare shoulders, like she wants to pull me closer. Just as the front door swings open.

"WELL, WELL, WELL."

Elias's voice fills the kitchen, his tone positively dripping with amusement. I let out a sigh, pressing my forehead to Wrenley's. I don't turn around, but I don't have to, to know that he's standing there, arms crossed, smug as hell.

"Oh, don't stop on my account," He continues, mock-offended. "I just came back to grab my jacket. Didn't realize you two were still..." He waves a hand in the air, his grin widening. "Occupied."

I groan, my grip tightening on Wrenley's hips before I finally step back, letting her slide off the counter. Elias leans against the doorframe, far too pleased with himself.

"You know," he muses, crossing his arms, "I was wondering if I should give you guys a heads-up that the walls in this place aren't exactly soundproof."

Wrenley freezes, her entire body going rigid before slowly turning to glare at him. His smirk only grows.

"I mean, I figured a warning wasn't really necessary," he continues, "but after the noises I heard last night, I'm thinking I should've invested in earplugs."

Wrenley lets out a sharp breath, covering her face with her hands. "Oh my God, couth ever hear of it?"

Elias just grins wider, shaking his head dramatically. "Demon dog was restless, too. Had to take him out just so he wouldn't think we were under attack."

At the sound of his name, Hugo trots into the kitchen, his massive tail wagging happily. Wrenley immediately drops to her knees, running a hand down his broad back as he leans into her touch.

"Did you miss me, big guy?" she murmurs, scratching behind his ears. Hugo lets out a low, pleased rumble, nudging his massive head into her shoulder.

I watch the way she softens with him, the way her fingers move through his fur so effortlessly, like they've belonged to each other forever. Something settles in my chest. Something I don't have the time or patience to examine.

Wrenley mutters something under her breath, standing back up and shaking her head as she grabs her water bottle and stalks out of the kitchen, brushing past Elias as she goes. Elias watches her go, then looks back at me, grinning ear to ear.

He claps a hand on my shoulder.

"Well, boss," he says, far too smug. "Looks like you're officially fucked."

I don't respond. He's right. The morning stretches on, the city outside waking up slowly as I sit in the living room, elbows braced on my knees, a fresh cup of coffee in my hand. Elias slouches on the opposite couch, lazily flipping a knife between his fingers, his expression masked.

We've been sitting here for a while, going over everything we told Wrenley last night. "She took it better than I thought she would," Elias says, tossing the knife in the air and catching it effortlessly. "Didn't cry. Didn't panic. Didn't even threaten to kill us, which, you know, is surprising given the fact that we basically shattered her entire view of her family in one sitting."

I take a sip from my mug, nodding. "She's stronger than she looks."

Elias smiles, "Oh, I don't doubt that, boss."

I shoot him a look, warning. He raises his hands in mock innocence.

"What?" he asks, all fake sincerity. "Just saying. Girl walks in here like she's about to storm the gates of hell, doesn't even flinch when you start talking about the deep, dark underbelly of her parents' empire, and then, after all that—" he clicks his tongue, shaking his head, "—she lets you take her to bed like she had no other plans for the night."

I don't say anything, but I feel the smirk pull up at the corner of my mouth. Elias clocks it immediately.

"Oh my God," he groans, dropping his head back against the couch. "You're smiling. You *never* fucking smile." He points at me with his knife, eyes narrowing. "You're fucking smitten."

I take another sip of coffee, letting the silence linger between us.

Elias leans forward, his grin stretching. "Come on, man, give me the details."

I chuckle, shaking my head. "Not a chance."

"Prick," he mutters, flopping back onto the couch, still grinning. "Okay, fine, I'll settle for this—"he points at me again, "—is she ready for this?"

I don't hesitate. "Yes."

Something in my voice makes Elias's grin fade slightly. He

studies me for a beat, then nods. "Alright, then, have you told her about…"

Just as he's about to say something else, a door opens down the hall, followed by the soft padding of footsteps on the hardwood.

She's freshly showered, her wet hair pulled into a messy bun, loose strands curling at her jawline. She's still wearing the same clothes from last night, but somehow, she still looks fucking incredible, glowing in a way that makes my pulse kick up.

Elias, of course, is the first to speak.

"Well, well, well," he drawls, tossing the knife onto the coffee table. "The queen emerges."

Wrenley snorts, rolling her shoulders like she's shaking off the last remnants of sleep. "Don't get too excited, Elias. You get none of the details, yeah, I heard you, perv."

Elias clutches his chest like he's wounded. "Ouch. That hurts."

She smirks, dropping onto the couch next to me, pulling a pillow into her lap. I watch her carefully, waiting to see if she looks uncertain. If she's second-guessing any of it.

But she just leans back, stretching her legs out, looking at us expectantly. "Alright, so what's the plan?"

I shift forward, resting my forearms on my knees. "First, we need to—"

"Wait. Nope," she says.

"Nope?" I echo.

She nods, sitting up straighter. "Before we get down to business, before I drown in more family secrets, I want one night. One night where I don't have to think about any of this bullshit."

I narrow my eyes. "And what exactly does that mean?"

She grins, pulling her cell phone from the couch cushion. "It means I'm calling Margot, and we're all going out."

Elias laughs, clapping his hands together. "I like this plan."

I don't. I really fucking don't.

"That's not—"

"Oh, come on, Blackwood," Wrenley interrupts, shifting toward me. "Just one night. A little fun before things get all dark and heavy again."

Elias is already nodding, standing up, stretching. "You know what? I agree. We've been way too focused on work. Some drinking, some dancing, some beautiful women." He gestures dramatically toward Wrenley. "Sounds like exactly what we need."

Wrenley smirks at me, eyebrows raised in challenge. I exhale slowly, dragging a hand through my hair. I should say no. I should put my foot down, tell her this isn't some fucking game, tell her that letting her guard down now, especially now, is a mistake.

But then she bites her bottom lip, just barely, and I feel my restraint start to crack.

"Fine," I mutter.

Elias pumps a fist in the air. "Hell yes."

Wrenley grins, already texting. I lean back on the couch, shaking my head at myself, at all of this. This is a terrible fucking idea. And yet, I can't bring myself to regret it.

Because for one night, I'll get to watch Wrenley completely unguarded. And that? That might just be worth the risk.

Chapter Fifteen

WRENLEY

THE ELEVATOR DOORS from the parking garage glide open, spilling me and Hugo into the lobby of the hotel. As we step out, the usual reaction follows: people instinctively step back, eyes widening, wary of the massive black dog at my side.

I bite back a smirk, pretending not to notice the way the manager visibly tenses behind the front desk. With a too-sweet smile, I lift my hand and wave.

"Afternoon," I say cheerfully.

The manager says nothing, but his expression makes it very clear that if I didn't have some mystery VIP protection, Hugo and I would have been kicked out days ago. I whistle softly, and Hugo pads along beside me, completely unbothered by the stares.

Upstairs, I let him into my room, scratching behind his ears as he flops onto the carpet with a heavy sigh.

"Stay out of trouble," I murmur, watching as he rolls onto his side, already looking half-asleep. "That means no eating the furniture." Hugo lets out a low huff that almost sounds like agreement. Satisfied, I grab my phone and purse to head back out, making my way to Margot's room.

Margot swings the door open the second I knock, already looking flawless, despite it being the middle of the afternoon. Her silk shorts and oversized button-up are effortlessly stylish, her makeup impeccable, and her red lips curl into a knowing smirk as she gives me a once-over.

"You look…" she tips her head to the side, assessing me, "…suspiciously well-fucked."

I groan, pushing past her into the room. "I do not."

She grins, shutting the door behind me. "So, what's the plan? You didn't come all this way just to admire my beauty."

I plop onto the couch. "I figured we could go out, get some fresh air. Maybe hit a boutique, a nail salon…"

Margot's eyes narrow immediately. "You? *Voluntarily* shopping? For fun?"

I roll my eyes. "I can enjoy shopping."

She flops onto the armrest, studying me like I'm a puzzle she's about to rip apart. "Uh-huh. No offense, babe, but the only time you get excited about buying new clothes is when you need to attend some function you'd rather gouge your eyes out than actually go to."

I fidget, adjusting the hem of my sweater. Her smirk widens.

"Oh my God." She gasps dramatically. "Who the *hell* are we going out with tonight?"

I swallow the sudden spike of guilt. I don't want to lie to her, but I can't exactly say, *Oh, just a man who's trying to single-handedly dismantle my family's empire. No big deal.*

I keep my expression neutral. "Just someone my uncle knew," I say with a shrug.

Margot narrows her eyes, sensing bullshit.

"And?"

"And what?"

Her grin turns downright wolfish.

"And that blush on your cheeks tells me you've been thoroughly railed," she says. "So who is he?"

I groan, throwing my head back. "Jesus, Margot—"

"Don't you 'Jesus Margot' me." She slides off the armrest,

pointing at me. "When? How many times? And most importantly... how good was it?"

I cover my face with my hands. "His name is Maximilian. Once. Last night. And that is all you get."

She gasps, clutching her chest like she's offended. "Once?" That's a crime. That's a crime against humanity."

I laugh, shoving her playfully. "Can we just go?"

Margot sighs dramatically, dragging herself off the couch. "Fine. But you owe me details. And you're getting a new outfit."

I don't argue. Not because she's right. But because... maybe I want one.

The afternoon slips away quickly, lost in the buzz of a city that never stops moving.

At the salon, Margot stretches her legs out in the pedicure chair, sipping her champagne. "So," she muses, twirling a strand of hair around her finger, "you accidentally found a gorgeous, dominant man, had earth-shattering sex. And now we're going clubbing with him?"

I scowl, swirling my own drink. "It was just sex."

She snorts. "Sure. That's why you're practically glowing."

I open my mouth to argue, but the nail technician grabs my hand, inspecting my nails.

"You want them trimmed or just repainted?" She asks. Before I can respond, Margot leans over. "Give her something dark and dramatic. Black. Sexy. Sinister."

I gape at her, but the technician just nods approvingly.

Margot winks. "You have to keep up with the whole mysterious, dangerous lover aesthetic, babe."

I ignore her, but I don't argue with her either.

"So, you and mystery man..."

I narrow my eyes.

"What about us?"

She takes a slow sip, watching me over the rim. "Did he make you cum?"

I choke on my drink, coughing as I glare at her. The nail technician looks at me as well, waiting for an answer.

Margot looks completely unbothered. "What? I just need to know if it was worth it."

I throw a napkin at her face.

At the boutique, Margot flits between racks of dresses, plucking out anything that barely qualifies as clothing. She shoves an outfit into my hands mere seconds after we walk in. I turn in the mirror, admiring it. The dress is sleek, midnight black, with a hint of sparkle, hugging my curves like it was made for me. The hemline is dangerously high, accentuating my legs, while the cut in the back dips scandalously low.

Margot wolf-whistles from behind me.

"Now, that is a 'fuck-me' dress," she says, sipping her latte. "Maximilian is going to lose his goddamn mind."

I glance at her through the mirror. "You assume I care what he thinks."

She smirks, stepping closer. "Oh, you do."

I say nothing, just turn back to the mirror, smoothing my hands over the fabric. Margot grins, spinning in a slow circle in front of her own reflection. Her dress is deep red, plunging neckline, fabric clinging to every inch of her curves. The kind of dress that demands attention, but so does she.

She twirls again, then smacks my ass lightly. "Alright, let's do some damage."

And just like that, the night is set in motion.

The finishing touches, a final sweep of mascara, a touch of gloss, stepping back from the mirror, tilting my head slightly as I take myself in. The dress clings to me like a second skin, the silky fabric skimming my thighs, the delicate straps barely holding their place. The black color deepens the contrast of my pale skin, and the way the low-cut back exposes so much of me feels dangerous.

Margot lets out a low whistle, fluffing out her hair as she eyes me in the mirror. "Jesus, Wren, that's not a dress... It's a fucking weapon."

I smile, adjusting one of my earrings, "You think?"

Margot grins. "I think if Max doesn't die on sight, he's got more restraint than I give him credit for."

Before I can respond, my phone buzzes from the bathroom counter.

Maximilian: I'm downstairs.

I glance at the time, right on schedule.

"Alright," I say, tossing my lip gloss into my clutch. "Let's go."

We stride through the hotel, heads turning as we pass, the rhythmic click of our heels echoing against the marble floors. Margot hums appreciatively, then, as we step outside, she freezes mid-step.

Her eyes go wide as she breathes, "Holy fuck. That's Max?"

I glance over at him, leaning against the sleek back SUV, dressed in dark slacks and a fitted black button-down, the top two buttons undone, sleeves rolled up to his forearms. He looks sinfully good, the kind of man who could command a room without saying a single word.

He's also staring at me like he's forgotten how to breathe. His gaze slowly travels up my body, heat flickering behind those amber eyes, his fingers flexing at his sides as if he's fighting the urge to reach for me.

Margot leans in, whispering. "Ha. Yeah, that's him?"

I chuckle, tucking a loose strand of hair behind my ear. "That's him."

I walk forward, pretending not to notice the way Max's eyes darken, or how he straightens as I approach.

"Max," I say smoothly, "this is Margot."

Max pulls his eyes from me just long enough to give Margot a brief nod. "Pleasure."

Margot, still clearly processing, nods back slowly, looking between me and him like she wants to demand details immediately.

Before she can, another voice cuts in. "Holy. Fuck."

Elias steps out from around the car, eyes roaming over both of us as he lets out a sharp whistle. "Well, ladies, you look fan-fuck-ing-tastic tonight."

Margot's lips curl into a smirk. "Yeah? You don't look half bad yourself."

Elias grins, tipping an imaginary hat at her. "I do what I can."

Max, not bothering with pleasantries, places a hand on my lower back, guiding me toward the car. "Let's go."

Max ushers me into the back with him, while Elias slides into the driver's seat, Margot taking the passenger seat beside him. I try to settle next to the window, but Max grabs my wrist and pulls me into the center. His hand slides over my bare thigh, fingers pressing into my skin. I turn my head, raising an eyebrow at him.

He leans in, his breath warm against my ear. "You wore this to try and kill me, didn't you?

I click my tongue at him. "If I were trying to kill you, Black-wood, you wouldn't still be breathing."

His grip tightens slightly, his fingers tracing slow circles against my skin. "Hmm." He drags his gaze over me, his voice low, rough. "Well, Sparrow... I'm going to enjoy this."

I shiver under his touch, but I refuse to let him see how much power he has over me already. Instead, I look ahead, focusing on the road.

Elias flashes a quick smirk as he shifts gears, his tone casual but laced with mischief. "You sure you want to keep that attitude? I could make you regret it."

Margot raises an eyebrow, the corner of her mouth lifting in challenge. "I don't usually take orders from strangers," she says, her voice light with playful defiance.

Elias glances at her with a wink, his hands steady on the wheel. "Good thing I'm not a stranger, then. You've known me for at least forty minutes." Margot laughs, shaking her head, clearly amused by the banter, while the conversation shifts again, effortlessly flowing between the four of us.

I catch Max watching me again, his fingers still tracing circles on my leg, his touch casual yet possessive. This man is going to ruin me. We pull up outside a dimly lit, exclusive-looking club, the music inside thrumming through the pavement.

The line outside stretches around the building, people waiting impatiently, some already frustrated that they aren't getting in. But as soon as the car door opens, a large bouncer steps forward, giving Max a knowing nod.

"Mr. Blackwood." His voice is deep, professional, and laced with familiarity. "Good to see you again, sir. Your table is all set."

Margot's eyebrows shoot up. She leans toward me, voice low. "VIP treatment, huh?'

Before I can respond, Elias laughs, looking at Max. Who gives him a brief nod. And Elias turns back to us, grinning. "Oh, he didn't tell you?"

Margot and I glance between them.

Elias claps Max on the shoulder, still grinning. "Max owns the place."

Margot's eyes widen as she looks at me. I exhale sharply, looking at Max. His gaze is already on me, waiting for my reaction.

"Of course you do," I murmur.

He quirks his head at me, "Time to play, Sparrow. Let's see how far you're willing to go." And just like that, we step into *The Black Crown*.

Chapter Sixteen

MAXIMILIAN

THE MOMENT we step inside the club, the air shifts. The bass-heavy rhythm thrums through the floor, pulsing through my veins like a second heartbeat. The dim lights flicker between hues of deep red and electric blue, illuminating the shifting mass of bodies on the dance floor.

But none of them matter, because Wrenley is beside me. And I don't want anyone to get the wrong idea. I slide my arm around her waist, guiding her through the crowd, my touch firm, possessive. She doesn't protest.

The bouncer leads us through the club, past the swaying bodies, the velvet curtains, and up a short flight of stairs to a raised platform overlooking the chaos. A private table roped off from the rest of the club, exclusively untouchable.

The girls slide into the booth first, Margot on one side, Wrenley on the other. Elias follows, positioning himself next to Margot. I sit beside Wrenley, taking my place at her side.

The waitress approaches, all confidence and familiarity, her painted lips stretching into a sultry smile as she greets me.

"Good evening, Mr. Blackwood," She purrs, shamelessly leaning forward, ensuring I get an eyeful of her cleavage. She wants my attention. But I don't take my eyes off Wrenley.

"What do you want to drink?" I ask, tilting my head slightly.

Wrenley and Margot exchange a look, then speak in perfect unison—

"Tequila."

They giggle, and something in my chest tightens.

I glance at the waitress, disinterested. "Bottle service. Don Julio 1942."

The waitress blinks. Expensive. Exclusive. Not the kind of thing you waste on a casual night out.

"Of course," she says quickly, sending another hungry glance in my direction. "I'll be back shortly."

Margot's eyebrows shoot up as she watches her walk away. "Jesus, she might as well have climbed into your lap."

Elias chuckles, but I just lean back, sliding my hand higher up Wrenley's thigh.

"Tiffany's been trying to get at me for a while," I say, voice casual. "Not interested."

I feel Wrenley tense beside me. It's a subtle shift in her shoulder, the smallest hitch in her breathing, but it's there. I smirk, letting my thumb brush against her bare skin, a silent reassurance.

Margot kicks back in her seat, swirling the drink the waitress just placed in front of her. "So, this is how the other half lives, huh?"

Elias snickers. "You sound jealous."

Margot grins, "I'm just saying. VIP section. Top shelf Tequila. Exclusives table." She raises an eyebrow at me. "You planning on buying us all diamonds next?"

I chuckle, shaking my head. Wrenley's thigh is warm beneath my palm, her skin soft and inviting as I let my fingers graze along it absent-mindedly. She hasn't tried to move away. That's a good sign. But I can still feel the subtle tension in her body after my offhand remark about the waitress. Interesting.

I take my time, rubbing slow circles with my thumb against her skin, silently reassuring her. She doesn't say anything at first, just takes a slow sip of her Tequila, her eyes bouncing to the dance floor. Then, after a moment.

"She's pretty," she says, her voice smooth but pointed.

I bite back a smile. "Who?"

She gives me a sharp look, her brows arching. "The waitress."

I shrug, my fingers pressing lightly into her thigh. "If you say so."

She scoffs softly, shaking her head. "Come on, Blackwood." She says, lowering her head to look at me through her lashes, studying me. "I find it hard to believe that someone like you has never entertained the idea of... mixing business with pleasure."

I hum, tracing slow circles again. "I don't mix business with desperation."

Her lips twitch, and she brings her glass back to her lips. "So, what's the distinction?"

I glance toward the dance floor before meeting her gaze again, holding it steady. "I don't chase."

Her breath hitches, just barely, but I catch it. She stares at me, not breaking eye contact, and I see the way she processes my words. Slowly, deliberately, she leans in just enough for her perfume to wrap around me like a noose.

"You sure about that?" she murmurs.

My fingers flex dangerously across her thigh, every muscle in my body coiled tight. Before I can respond, Margot slams her hands onto the table.

"Okay, enough sitting around. I want to dance."

Wrenley laughs, pulling away from me, the moment between us snapping like a thread.

"Agreed," she says, already shifting in her seat.

Elias groans dramatically, rolling his neck. "I guess I can be your bodyguard for the night," he glances at me, smirking. "Because Mr. Buzzkill over there doesn't dance."

Wrenley turns toward me, that same goddamn sweet face she gave me in the car, eyes full of false innocence.

"No," I say flatly.

She pouts slightly, running a fingertip along the rim of her glass. "Come on," she coaxes. "Just one dance."

I exhale sharply, shaking my head. "Won't happen."

Margot laughs loudly, standing up. "Won't or can't?"

I shoot Margot a look, but she is already being dragged onto the dance floor by Elias. Wrenley lingers for a second longer, watching me, waiting.

I lean in slightly, voice low, rough. "I'll enjoy the show." She rolls her eyes, standing up to follow them.

The moment she's out of earshot, I turn toward the nearest bouncer, pulling him in close.

"No one touches her," I murmur. "Elias can dance with her, but no one else gets near her. You understand?"

The bouncer nods immediately. "Yes, sir."

He touches his earpiece, already speaking into a walkie-talkie as he moves away.

I watch Wrenley step onto the dance floor, the flashing lights illuminating her skin, the music pulling her into the rhythm. I feel it then, that same possessive pull tightening in my chest. She's going to ruin me. I lean back in my seat, drink in hand, eyes locked on one thing, one person. My Sparrow.

She moves with effortless grace, the bass of the music pulsing through her body as she sways between Elias and Margot. Hands in air, hips rolling, she loses herself in the rhythm, completely unaware of the effect she's having on me.

The crowd around them presses in, bodies shifting and colliding, but she's the only one I see. The way the club's low lighting kisses her skin, casting her in flashes of red and gold. The way her dress clings to every dangerous curve, teasing me with what's underneath. The way her head tilts back as she laughs, lips parting just enough to make me wonder what she'd taste like right now, slick with tequila and mischief.

Elias moves behind her, hands hovering just shy of her waist, and my grip tightens around my glass. I exhale slowly, jaw clenching. I told myself I'd enjoy the show. But then, the song changes. A slow, deep bass line rolls through the club, followed by the husky tones of Teddy Swims' "Devil in a Dress."

I swear I don't realize I've moved until I'm already on the dance floor, weaving through bodies with one single focus. Her. Wrenley. I reach her just as she rolls her hips against the music, completely lost in it. Completely unaware that I've come for her. Until my hand finds her waist.

I feel her inhale sharply as I press into her from behind, my fingers spanning her stomach, pulling her flush against me. She doesn't pull away. She melts. Her hips align with mine, her back pressing against my chest as she falls into my rhythm, letting me take control. I drop my head to the crook of her neck, my lips hovering over her skin, my voice low and rough.

"Dancing with Elias?" I murmur, my grip tightening slightly. "Bad idea, Sparrow."

She shivers, tilting her head just enough to the side like she's daring me to do more. I drag my palm slowly up her side, my fingers grazing the delicate fabric of her dress, feeling the soft, warm skin beneath. She moves against me, her body following the sultry beat, and I grind into her, matching her rhythm beat for beat. I will never let anyone touch her. But me? I'm going to ruin her. Her hand finds my forearm, nails digging in just enough to send a thrill through my spine. She tilts her head slightly, just enough for her lips to be dangerously close to mine.

"Didn't think you danced, Blackwood." She breathes, teasing.

I smirk against her ear, my voice dark and full of promise. "I don't."

She turns slightly, just enough to meet my gaze. She's playing with fire. And I'm more than happy to let her burn. The song ends, but the electricity between us doesn't fade. I don't let go of her. And she doesn't move away. For a long moment, we stand there, the music shifting to another song, the world blurring at the edges.

Then, without a word, Wrenley takes my hand. She doesn't ask. She doesn't look back. She leads me off the dance floor, weaving through the crowd as if she owns the place, as if she knows I'll follow her wherever she goes. And fuck me, I will.

Elias and Margot fall into step behind us, Margot practically bouncing with excitement, while Elias just grins knowingly. When we reach the table, Wrenley slides into the booth, and before she can move too far, I pull her close, keeping her tucked against my side. Margot collapses onto the seat beside her, Elias taking his usual spot across from us, stretching an arm lazily over the back of the booth. He shakes his head, eyes locked on me, amusement flickering across his face.

"Well, I'll be damned." He lets out a low chuckle, swirling the drink in his glass. "In all the years I've known you, I have never seen you dance."

Margot snorts, throwing a smirk my way. "What's next, Max? Gonna start writing poetry? Maybe get a golden retriever?"

Elias laughs, slapping the table. "Oh, fuck. Can you imagine?"

I roll my eyes, reaching for my drink. "I wouldn't get a retriever; I already have Elias."

Elias chokes on his drink, still laughing.

Wrenley leans into me, her fingers tracing the rim of her glass. "So, you're saying you make exceptions for certain things?"

I glance at her, my hand tightening on her thigh. "Something like that."

She smirks, but before I can say anything else, Margot grabs her hand, tugging her to her feet. "Come on, babe." Margot flicks her hair over her shoulder. "We need a trip to the ladies' room." I feel Wrenley hesitate, glancing at me before she lets Margot pull her away.

Elias grins, watching them disappear into the crowd. "So, is this a thing now?" I stay silent, taking another slow sip. Elias smiles as big as I have ever seen. "Oh, it *is*. You're fucked, man."

I don't respond. Because he's right. And that's not something I'm ready to admit. I check my watch. They've been gone too long. I don't like it.

Elias notices me tensing, his grin faltering. "Relax, man. They're just in the bathroom."

My fingers tap on the table, my instincts tightening like a

noose.   No. Something's off. I turn to the nearest bouncer, gesturing him over.

"Find her." My voice is low, controlled. "Now."

The bouncer nods sharply, pressing his hand to his earpiece, already barking orders before he disappears into the crowd. Elias leans back, rubbing his jaw, watching me carefully.

"Shit," he lets out a low whistle. "You really got it bad, huh?"

I don't answer. Because I don't have time to. I can feel it. That creeping sensation at the base of my spine. I always know when something's wrong.

Chapter Seventeen
WRENLEY

I SWIPE on another layer of lip gloss, pressing my lips together in the mirror. The bass from the club hums faintly through the walls, the steady pulse of music matching the thrill still buzzing through my veins from dancing with Max.

Margot leans against the sink beside me, grinning like a Cheshire cat, arm crossed over her chest. "Okay, but seriously." She waves a hand in the air. "Maximilian Blackwood is stupid hot. Like, illegal levels of hot. Like, I'm pretty sure he could start a cult just by existing."

I giggle, feeling the heat rush to my cheeks.

"Oh my god, shut up," I mutter, but Margot is relentless. She bumps her hip against mine. "Nope. Not happening. You danced with him like that, and you expect me to just let it slide? Uh-uh. You looked like you wanted to eat him alive."

I roll my eyes, trying not to smile. "It's... complicated," I say finally, tucking my lip gloss back into my clutch.

Margot gives me a knowing look. "Complicated?" she smiles. "That's just code for 'I wanna climb him like a tree but can't admit it yet.'"

I laugh, shaking my head. "I'll meet you outside," I say, needing a moment to breathe. "Take your time."

She gives me a salute in the mirror, still smirking, before going back to adjusting her own makeup. I push open the door, stepping into the dimly lit hallway just outside the ladies' room. It's quieter here, the music muffled, the air thick with the scent of expensive cologne and alcohol.

I exhale slowly, rolling my shoulders, trying to shake off whatever this night is turning into. Then. A hand clamps on my arm. Before I can react, I'm yanked forward, slammed face-first against the cold wall.

A sharp, familiar voice slithers into my ear, drenched in cruelty.

"Where's your savior now, little girl?"

Every muscle in my body locks up. No.

No, no, no, no.

I know that voice. I'd recognize it anywhere. The man who attacked me a year ago. The one who gave me this scar. My pulse jackhammers, adrenaline spiking so fast I almost can't breathe. His grip tightens on my arm, pressing me harder into the wall, his breath hot and rancid against my ear.

I force my voice to stay calm. "You're making a big mistake." I try to keep the tremor out of my tone. "Let me go, you sick fuck."

He laughs, the sound laced with revenge. "No one's here to save you this time, girly." He sneers, his free hand gripping my waist. "And I wanted you once... I always get the things I want."

A cold, burning rage licks up my spine. The fear is there, but I shove it down. I am NOT that girl anymore. I slam my head back, cracking the back of my skull into his nose. He grunts in pain, his hold loosening for just a second—but that's all I need.

I spin, my right fist flying, connecting squarely with his nose. There's a sickening crunch followed by his curse of pain as he staggers back, clutching his face.

"You bitch!" he snarls, blood already seeping through his fingers. "You broke my fucking nose!"

He lunges toward me again, blind with rage. I'm already moving, preparing for another hit, but then.

"WRENLEY?!"

Margot. She's standing in the doorway, her eyes wide, frozen in shock. The man snaps his head toward her, snarling. Margot screams, but I take the distraction, my fist flying again, nailing him across the jaw. He stumbles back once more, rage and confusion twisting his features.

Just as a bouncer appears out of nowhere, grabbing him by the collar, slamming him against the wall. "The fuck is going on here?" the bouncer growls.

I'm panting, my hand throbbing, my chest heaving. Margot is still wide-eyed, shaken, but something like awe flickers across her face. "Holy shit," she breathes, staring at me. "That was badass."

Before I can respond, heavy footsteps thunder down the hall. Max and Elias appear. Thank God! Max takes one look at me, at my bleeding knuckles, at the bouncer pinning the guy against the wall, and his entire body goes rigid. His jaw clenches, squeezing his fists so tight his knuckles are white, his eyes going black with pure, lethal rage. The air shifts, turning thick, suffocating, deadly.

Elias, with shock in his voice, crosses his arms. "Damn." He eyes my bleeding hand, then the groaning guy pinned to the wall. "What'd we miss?"

Max doesn't say a single word. He just stares at me, at my injuries, then turns his gaze to the man who hurt me. And in that moment, I know. Someone is going to die tonight.

Max's voice cuts through the tense air like a blade. "Basement."

The bouncer doesn't waver. He nods once, yanking the man upright by the collar. The bastard is still groaning, blood dripping from his broken nose, but no one in the hallway gives a damn.

Margot stares wide-eyed as the bouncer drags him away, his protests muffled against the sound of the music pounding through the club. My body is frozen, my mind still spinning from what just happened. Then, warm hands cup my face, grounding me back into reality. I blink, snapping my gaze up to Max. His thumbs stroke my cheeks, his stormy eyes scanning me with ferocity that steals my breath.

"Are you okay, Sparrow?" his voice low, edged with barely restrained fury, but there's something softer beneath it. I can't speak, not yet, so I nod once, swallowing hard. Max studies me for a second longer, his touch lingering, before he finally pulls back and turns to Margot.

But Elias is already by her side, his usual sarcastic demeanor temporarily gone. Margot is vomiting words at him, her hands waving as she relives every second of what just happened. "I mean, holy shit! This guy just grabbed her, and she—BAM! headbutted him! And then...." She mimes a punch, still buzzing from adrenaline.

Elias just nods, putting a hand on her shoulder. "Yeah, yeah, you're a badass by association. Come on. Let's get you both the hell out of here."

With a firm voice, Max commands, "Everyone. My office. Now." I nod again, my feet moving on autopilot as I follow him. But my eyes never leave him.

The way he carries himself. The tight coil of anger in his shoulders. The way he keeps checking over his shoulder to make sure I'm still there. And in that moment, I know one thing for certain. Whatever happens in the basement, that man will never see the outside of it again.

The office is quiet, dimly lit, and the steady bass from the club is a distant hum behind thick walls. I sit on the leather couch, my hands still trembling slightly as I rest them on my lap. Max kneels in front of me, a glass of whiskey in hand.

"Drink." He says, offering it to me.

I take it, downing the entire thing in one go, the burn of alcohol searing down my throat.

Elias and Margot settle on the couch across from us, Elias leaning back, one arm thrown lazily behind Margot as he watches me. Max waits, watching me carefully.

But I'm the first to break the silence. "It was him." My voice comes out steady, but inside, my stomach twists into knots. I set the empty glass down, meeting Max's gaze. "The man who attacked me last year. The same man you saved me from."

Max's entire body locks up. The vein near his temple pulsing. He cracks his neck as he turns to Elias, his voice low, dangerous.

"I knew I should've killed that bastard that night."

Elias exhales sharply, shaking his head. "Yeah. No shit, but the cops were already coming."

I stand abruptly, shaking off the numbness, squaring my shoulders. "It doesn't matter," I say firmly, looking straight at Max.

He narrows his eyes. "The hell it doesn't."

I step closer, my chin tilting up. "No, it doesn't. Because after that night, I made sure I was never a victim again. I learned how to fight, how to defend myself." I flex my fingers, my bruised knuckles aching, but I don't care. "And tonight? I proved it."

Max stares at me, his expression unreadable. But there's something dark and dangerous in his eyes. Like a man who just realized he's never letting me out of his sight again.

The tension in the office is thick, almost suffocating. The conversation between Max, Elias, and me moves in low, measured tones, the energy between us crackling like a live wire. Max is still on edge, his fists clenching and unclenching, his jaw so tight I swear it might crack. Elias is a little more relaxed, but I can tell he's watching and calculating the situation closely, letting Max take the lead.

Margot, however, is watching the three of us like we're a goddamn soap opera. Her arms crossed, her foot tapping lightly on the floor.

Then she tilts her head and blurts out, "Okay... but what's in the basement?"

The room goes silent.

I frown, confused by the question. But when I turn my head, both Max and Elias are looking at her now, their expressions unreadable.

Max is the first to answer, his voice flat, matter-of-fact. "That's where we hold the ones who need... reminding."

Margot blinks. "Reminding of what, exactly?"

Max shrugs, his gaze sliding to me. "Why you don't cross the wrong people."

It takes me a second to process what he's implying. Then it hits me. My stomach churns, and Margot's mouth opens wide as she covers it with her hand. That man. My attacker. He's down there right now. Max turns back to me, his voice low, calm, but firm.

"You don't have to worry about any of this, Sparrow. I'll take care of everything."

My eyes snap to his. "Take care of?"

Max just stares, letting the silence speak for itself.

Elias clears his throat. "I'll take you back to your hotel. Or if you want, the penthouse, wherever you feel safest."

I laugh, but there's no humor in it. "Fuck no."

Max's brows lift slightly, surprised at my outburst. I plant my feet, standing firm, staring him down. "If anyone gets to talk to that asshole, it's me. I am not leaving."

Max's expression darkens. "That's not happening."

"Yes, it is."

"Wrenley." His voice is sharp now, the warning clear.

I cross my arms, my jaw set. "I already told you, Max. I am not a victim. You said if I dig, if I want to know... It's my decision, *everything* is *my* decision. I've decided!"

Elias leans back on the couch, sighing heavily. "Jesus. She's got a point."

Max doesn't take his eyes off me, muscles tense, his control visibly fraying. I hold his stare, challenging him. He exhales sharply through his nose, raking a hand through his hair before muttering, "Fucking hell."

Then, finally, he nods. I've won. But before I can gloat, Elias stands up. He looks at Margot, then back at me. "Alright, badass, if you're gonna be stubborn as hell, at least do one thing right. Let me take Margot back. You don't need distractions right now."

I glance at Margot, who looks torn between wanting to argue and wanting to be anywhere but here. I squeeze her hand, offering a small, reassuring nod. "Go. Hugo needs a walk, and I don't know how long I'll be." Margot hesitates, then sighs. "Fine. But if you don't text me the second you're out of here, I swear to God, Wren—"

I nod. "I will. I promise. All the details."

Elias watches the exchange, then steps toward me, pulling me into a quick, unexpected hug. His voice is low, near my ear. "You're fucking crazy, you know that?"

I smirk. "You just figured that out?"

Elias laughs under his breath, shaking his head as he pulls back. But before he leaves, he throws Max a look, one filled with silent warning.

Max just nods once, tight-lipped. And then, Elias and Margot are gone. The door clicks shut, leaving just Max and me. I inhale deeply, steadying myself, then turn to face him.

"Alright, Blackwood," I say, my voice steady. "Let's go."

Max doesn't speak right away. He just looks at me, something unreadable flashing across his face. Then, finally, he nods once. And just like that, the real fun begins.

Chapter Eighteen

MAXIMILIAN

I LEAD Wrenley down the dimly lit hallway, the cold air thick with silence. The concrete walls absorb sound, making each step feel heavier than the last. Ahead of us, the metal-reinforced door to the basement stands like a threshold into something darker, a place most people don't walk out the same.

Just before I grip the handle, I glance at Wrenley. "If this gets to be too much, you say the word, and I'll get you out of here. No questions asked."

She doesn't hesitate. Not even for a second.

"I'll be fine." Her voice is even, controlled. Then, with an edge of impatience, "Open the door, Maximilian."

I nod once, twisting the handle and pushing the heavy door open. The room is bare, with concrete floors, exposed pipes, and a single overhead light that flickers slightly, casting elongated shadows against the walls. The stench of sweat and blood lingers in the air, metallic and sharp.

And there he is. The bastard hangs from the center of the room, his hands shackled above his head, the chains bolted into the ceiling. His feet barely touch the floor, his weight sagging against his restraints. Broken nose, the blood trailing from it dripping steadily into a dark puddle between his boots. The single overhead light casts harsh shadows over his swollen face, making him look even more pathetic than he already is.

I don't move right away. I feel Wrenley's eyes on me. She crossed her arms over her chest, her expression unreadable. Then, without a word, she turns to the bouncer standing near the door.

"Leave us."

The guy hesitates, looking at me for confirmation. I nod to him, "Wait outside." He silently slips out, the heavy door locking behind him. Silence.

The only sound is the ragged breathing of the man in front of us. I walk toward him, my movements controlled, precise. I pat down his pockets, searching for identification. My fingers brush against something, and I pull it free, a wallet.

Flipping it open, I slide out the driver's license and read the name aloud. "Anthony Voss."

Wrenley studies him like he's something stuck to the bottom of her shoe, disgusted, but not surprised. Then, she steps closer, her arms crossed tightly over her chest.

"So, Anthony, let's talk."

A slow, ugly grin stretches across his bruised face. "Talk?" his voice is hoarse, but amused, like this is funny to him. His bloody teeth glint under the light. I already don't like where this is going

"The first time you attacked me. Last year," Wrenley's voice is calm. But I hear the steel beneath it. "Tell me everything."

Anthony sniffs, spitting more blood onto the concrete floor.

"I don't remember much." He shrugs the best he can, his chains rattling. "That was a long time ago. I barely remembered your pretty little face until tonight."

I go still. Wrenley, however, doesn't react, not yet. "But then you saw me."

His grin widens, sick and self-satisfied. "And it was like fate." His voice lowers, his eyes dragging over her body like he has a fucking death wish. "Because the things I want? I always get."

The blood in my veins turns to ice. His words echoing in my

mind, 'pretty little face. The things I want? I always get.' The motherfucker is trying to taunt her. Wrenley moves first. Her hand whips out, cracking against his face so hard his head snaps to the side. A sick, satisfying sound echoes through the room.

Anthony coughs, more blood spilling from his mouth. Then, he laughs. "That all you got, pretty thing?"

A slow, black rage burns through me. I take a step forward, but she holds out her hand, stopping me. Those words again, 'Pretty thing.' He says it like he owns her. Like he's entitled to even breathe the same air as her.

"Wrong fucking move, asshole," I mutter under my breath.

But she doesn't need me to step in. Her shoulders straighten, her head tilting slightly, and I can see it in her face, this isn't fear. This isn't uncertainty. This is *anger*.

She turns to me, her gaze flicking toward something in the corner of the room. Her brows furrow slightly, and I follow her eyes to the black metal tool chest. Her gaze snaps back to mine. "What's in there?"

I let the silence stretch before I smirk. "Everything anyone could need to remind someone of who they messed with." Her lips part, but not in fear. In understanding.

I lead Wrenley to the tool chest, flipping open the heavy metal lid with a quiet clang. The hard basement light reflects off an array of tall instruments, a collection of pain and precision, neatly organized for whatever the occasion calls for.

She steps closer, running her fingers lightly over the carefully arranged tools, her nails tapping against the cold metal. Her expression remains unreadable, but there's something in the way she tilts her head, like she's considering each option carefully.

"Jesus, Blackwood, do you carry this thing around for fun?" she muses, plucking up a pair of pliers and twirling them between her fingers.

I smirk, leaning against the chest. "Never know when they'll come in handy."

She scoffs, setting the pliers back down before reaching for a box cutter. Simple. Efficient. Intimate. Anthony groans behind us, shifting in his chains.

"You two gonna fuck or kill me?" he slurs, his voice thick with blood, but still carrying that pathetic smugness. "'Cause at this point, pretty thing, I'm good with either."

My muscles coil tight. I hear Wrenley inhale deeply, exhaling slowly through her nose. The air shifts. Something sharp. Electric. She turns toward him, and when she speaks, her voice is steady, cold, unwavering.

"You really don't remember me, do you?"

Anthony's head tilts, his split lip curling in amusement. "Kitten, I've had my hands on a lot of girls—"

He doesn't get to finish. She moves fast. The box cutter flashes in her grip, slicing a precise, shallow line across his cheek. A bright, red bead appears, followed by another, trickling down in a slow, deliberate path. Anthony sucks in a sharp breath, his body jerking as pain registers.

I feel a dark, visceral thrill snake through me. My Sparrow was built for this, even if she hasn't fully realized it yet. Fuck. I shouldn't be this turned on. But I am. Watching her wield that blade so effortlessly, watching her confidence, her complete control, it's intoxicating.

I shift, crossing my arms tighter, trying to suppress the heat rising in my stomach. Anthony lets out a hiss, blinking through the sting of fresh blood. Then he laughs. It's weak. Forced. But still there.

"Fucking Bitch!" he spits, his fury igniting.

Wrenley tilts her head, her eyes settling into something slow and wicked. "That's funny. You didn't call me that when you were holding a knife to my throat."

Anthony stills. His bloodshot eyes snap to hers, and for the first time, there's something new flickering behind them. Recognition. Fear.

I smirk, pushing off the tool chest. "Now we're getting somewhere."

Anthony pants, his shoulders trembling against the chains. Then, he poises himself and changes his expression, this time into something sinister.

"You screamed that night, didn't you?" He murmurs, his voice thick with mockery. The thrill in my veins vanishes instantly, replaced by something deadly and cold. I try to take another step forward, but Wrenley beats me to it. She grips his broken nose between her fingers and twists. Anthony's scream rips through the concrete walls, raw and animalistic, his body thrashing violently.

"Fuck!" he chokes, his breath shuddering.

"Still think I don't have it in me?" she asks coolly, her fingers still digging into this ruined face.

Anthony spits blood, breathing through gritted teeth. "You're gonna regret this, kitten. YOU—"

She yanks his nose again. He screams. Louder. I watch, arms crossed, as a new kind of power settles in her shoulders. She's not the same girl from that alley. She's right. She's not a victim. Not anymore. She finally lets go, wiping her bloodstained fingers on his shirt like he's nothing but filth. Then, she turns to me, her gaze flicking to the tool chest again.

"What else you got?"

I grin, reaching in and pulling out the preloaded adrenaline syringe.

"This," I say, holding it between two fingers. "We let him pass out, and then we bring him right back."

Her eyes light up with something dark and satisfied.

"I like that idea."

I chuckle, low and approving. "I thought you might."

Anthony's head slumps forward, his breathing labored, his entire body trembling.

"Looks like we don't have to wait long," I murmur, noticing the way his eyes start to roll back.

Wrenley watches him, expression masked. "Good."

She looks at me, her dark eyes gleaming. "Then let's bring him back."

I twirl the syringe between my fingers, stepping forward. Fuck, she's dangerous. And I can't get enough of it. I grip the adrenaline syringe, letting the cool plastic roll between my fingers. The room is quiet, save for the ragged breathing of the bloodied, half-conscious man hanging from the chains in front of us.

Wrenley stands beside me, completely calm, adjusting her dress like she's about to paint a fucking masterpiece. And goddamn, if that thought doesn't make my blood heat. She's fascinating. The Wrenley from that cold, dark alley would've run from this moment. But this Wrenley? This Wrenley is stepping into the fire, her gaze blazing with purpose, her hands steady as steel.

I exhale, twirling the syringe once more, letting the moment stretch. "You sure about this, Sparrow?" I ask, my voice low and deliberate.

Her dark eyes flick to mine, challenging. "Do I look unsure?"

Fuck. That's my Sparrow.

I press my tongue to the inside of my cheek, half-smirking as I step closer, invading her space. She doesn't move.

"No, you don't," I murmur, lifting a hand to tuck a loose strand of hair behind her ear.

Her breath hitches, just slightly, but her gaze remains locked on mine. Something is thrumming between us, something wild and unstable. I'm so close to kissing her again, right here, in this fucking basement, with a half-dead man hanging in chains behind us. Jesus Christ.

Before I can act on it, a loud knock echoes from the top of the basement stairs. I grind my jaw. Perfect timing.

"If that's a goddamn interruption, I'm shooting someone," I mutter. Wrenley laughs, the sound low, breathless, intoxicating.

She likes this. She likes seeing me unravel. Before I can say anything else, the door creaks open, and Elias's voice carries down the stairs.

"You're welcome, by the way," he calls. "Margot insisted on coming back. Took up half my fucking night arguing about it. She's asleep in the apartment. With Hugo."

I sigh, dragging a hand down my face. "Of course she is."

Elias's footsteps are heavy as he makes his way down, his eyes immediately locking onto Wrenley, or more specifically, the blood dripping from her fingertips. His brows lift. Then he looks at Anthony, hanging limp, his head tilted forward, blood still oozing from his nose and cheek.

"Holy shit," Elias mutters, grinning slowly and sharply.

He looks at me. "And here you were, worried she wouldn't fit in."

I don't respond. I just watch as Elias crosses his arms, his gaze flicking between Wrenley and the half-broken man in front of us.

"Not gonna lie, Max," Elias continues, "I thought you were losing it when you got her involved in this. Figured she'd be too soft, too green. But now?"

His smirk deepens. "Looks like we've got ourselves a queen."

Wrenley doesn't react right away, just looks at him, considering for a long moment. Then, she smirks. "It's not your world I want to fit into, Elias."

Elias lets out a low whistle, nodding approvingly. "Oh, she's gonna be trouble."

I already knew that. I glance back at Anthony, the bastard, barely holding on to consciousness.

"She's not done yet," I say, gripping the syringe a little tighter.

Elias whistles again, stepping to the tool chest, looking at the array of steel instruments laid out so neatly.

"Jesus, man. You really do have everything down here, even added a few, huh?"

"Everything necessary," I mutter, still watching Wrenley.

She reaches for the syringe in my hand, her fingers brushing against mine as she takes it. I let her.

Elias lets out a low chuckle. Shaking his head. "Yep. You're so completely fucked, brother."

I drag my eyes from Wrenley to glare at him. "Shut the fuck up, Elias."

"Oh, I will." He grins, leaning against the cement wall. "But watching you try and pretend like you're not obsessed with her is the most entertaining things I've seen in years."

Wrenley arches a brow, giving me a slow, knowing smile. Yeah. I'm completely fucked. And I don't even care.

Chapter Nineteen
WRENLEY

THE SYRINGE PLUNGES into Anthony's chest with a sharp snap, and I watch his body seize, his muscles jerking violently as the adrenaline floods his system. I step back, crossing my arms as he lolls, his eyes fluttering before snapping open.

"There he is," I muse.

His breathing is ragged, a deep, ugly wheezing sound filling the small basement. His pupils are blown wide, his body fighting to keep up with what I just forced into him.

Behind me, Elias lets out a low whistle. "Jesus, that was fun."

I glance at him, smiling. "You should probably leave now."

Elias frowns, eyebrows pulling together. "What? Why?"

"Margot's upstairs," I remind him. "She's going to wake up soon, and I don't want her alone."

Elias groans dramatically, throwing his head back. "Why am I always the responsible one?"

I just stare.

He sighs. "Fine. But if she asks where you are, I'm telling her you're off committing felonies."

"That's because I am."

Elias winks. "Damn right."

He heads for the door but pauses at the foot of the stairs, his eyes shifting between Max and me, a hint of amusement curling his lips. "Try not to have too much fun without me, huh?"

Max doesn't even look at him. His eyes are on me. I barely notice Elias leaving because my pulse is beating too hard, too fast. There's a tension in the air that wasn't there before. Something dark. Something hungry.

I take a slow breath, trying to steady myself. Then I glance at Max and ask, "What's your favorite tool?

Max's brows lift, giving me a smiling frown as if he's intrigued by my question. "My favorite?"

"Yeah." I gesture toward the open tool chest. "Come on, Blackwood. Show me what you like best."

He watches me for a long, silent moment. Then, without breaking eye contact, he steps forward and reaches inside. His fingers drag over the metal, trailing over blades, pliers, and clamps. Choosing. Then he pulls out a bone saw. A small, hand-held one, serrated edges, razor-sharp and gleaming under the dim light.

I take it from him, weighing it in my palm, feeling the familiar burn of control. My lips curl as I drag a finger along the teeth of the blade. "Fitting,"

His eyes darken. Heat licks through my veins as I turn back to Anthony.

"Let's see why this is your favorite." I press the blade against his thigh, just enough for the jagged teeth to bite through the fabric. Anthony lets out a sharp inhale, his body tensing. "Wait—"

I push harder. He screams. Max lets out a low, satisfied chuckle. "Told you." I drag the saw back through the fabric, cutting deeper. Anthony thrashes, but the chains keep him suspended, helpless. His blood seeping into his jeans, dark and spreading.

I glance over my shoulder at Max, lips quirking. "I can see why you enjoy this."

Max leans in, his breath warm over my ear. Making a desire

pool at my center. "It's a slow tool," he murmurs. "Deliberate. Intimate."

A shiver runs through me, twisting it just so. "Painful." I finish for him.

Anthony is panting, his face contorted in agony. "Please!" he gasps, voice cracking. "I—I didn't—"

I tilt my head, "You didn't what? Attack me? Try to ruin my life? Think you could just take what you wanted?" He says nothing, only groans, his face pale, slick with sweat.

Max exhales through his nose. "Look at you, Sparrow," he murmurs. "A year ago, you were running. And now? You're making monsters beg."

A slow, dangerous smile spreads across my lips. "And I'm just getting started." Max laughs softly, his voice a low rumble against my skin. I turn back to Anthony, but before I make my next move, Max's voice cuts through the haze.

"Time to finish it, Sparrow." His voice is dripping with want. "I've got plans for how this night ends."

I pause, my pulse thrumming. Then, slowly, I turn to face him. He's watching me, gaze heated, expression shuttered. He holds something out to me. A knife. The same knife I was cut with. I take it from him, my fingers brushing his. The electricity between us snaps. Our eyes lock. Max nods to where Anthony hangs, waiting.

I inhale deeply, then turn back, gripping the knife tightly. And with one swift, final motion, I plunge the blade straight into his heart. I end it. The knife still in my hand, its handle warm from my grip, the blade dripping, staining the floor in slow, rhythmic drops. But I don't care.

Not about the body hanging lifeless in the chains. Not about the blood on my hands. Not about anything, except him.

Max.

He's on me in seconds, his hand fisting my hair, yanking my head back, and crushing his mouth against mine. I moan into him, my body arching, demanding more. His tongue parts my lips, his kiss devouring.

It's fire and fury, teeth clashing, lips bruising, breath mixing in heated, desperate gasps. The blade slips from my fingers, clattering to the concrete, and I don't even register the sound, not when Max is pressing into me, his hardness digging into my stomach, his hands gripping me like, he'll never fucking let go.

He grabs my ass, lifts me effortlessly, and I wrap my legs tight around his waist, grinding against the throbbing length trapped between us.

"Fucking hell, Sparrow," he rasps, biting my jaw, dragging his teeth down the column of my throat.

I shudder violently, nails raking down his back, my body completely his to ruin.

"You're soaked, aren't you?" His voice is dark, gravelly, and sin, his fingers digging into my ass as he rolls his hips, pressing exactly where I need him most.

I whimper, head thumping against the wall, my fingers clawing at his shoulders.

"You like this, don't you?" he licks up my neck, his breath hot, dangerous. "You like that you just took a life, and now you want me to take you."

I gasp, hips jerking, pushing against him, desperate for more friction.

"Say it, Sparrow." His teeth grazing my pulse, his tongue following in a slow, torturous stroke. "Say you like it."

"Yes," I breathe, my fingers threading into his thick, dark hair, yanking him closer. "I fucking love it."

A deep, guttural growl rumbles in his chest, vibrating against me. I barely have time to react before he's moving, turning us away from the wall and slamming me down onto the metal table behind us. It rattles violently, tools clanking, shifting, the cold steel biting through my skin. I gasp, arching up, but Max is already on me, his hands gripping my thighs, pushing my dress up to my waist, baring me to him.

"Fuck, Wrenley," he rasps, his gaze darkening, locked on the black lace barely covering me. "You wear this just for me?"

I smirk, my breathing ragged. "I had a feeling I'd end up in your lap at some point tonight."

His low, wicked chuckle sends heat curling in my belly. "Fucking tease," he murmurs, dragging his fingers over the damp lace, feeling exactly how ready I am for him.

I writhe beneath him, my heels digging into the table, my nails gripping his arms.

"Max—"

He tears the panties away, shoving them into his pocket like a trophy before spreading my legs wide, holding me open for him. I'm already aching, already dripping, and when he leans down, dragging his tongue between my folds, I cry out, head falling back.

"Shit—"

He groans, his grip tightening on my thighs, holding me in place as he devours me. His tongue stokes me, slow and deep, before flicking over my clit, making my entire body jerk violently.

"Max—" I gasp, fingers tangling in his hair, yanking him closer.

He just chuckles against me, the vibration sending another rush of heat through my core.

"Tastes even better than I imagined," he murmurs, voice muffled against my skin. "And fuck, I've imagined."

I whimper, thighs trembling as he devours me, his tongue stroking, circling, flicking, his fingers digging into my flesh like he'll never let go. He pushes a finger inside me, curling exactly right, and my back arches off the table, a sharp, broken cry tearing from my lips.

"That's it, be a good girl," he growls, voice dark and dripping with lust. "Make those fucking sounds for me."

I'm shaking, teetering, my body winding so fucking tight. Yep, I have a praise kink. I snap. My release slams into me, a sharp, consuming explosion of heat and pleasure, my legs tightening around his head, and I cry out his name.

But he doesn't stop. He doesn't even slow. His tongue keeps working me, riding me through it, building me up again.

"Max—" I gasp, barely able to think, barely able to breathe.

He groans into me, voice raw and hungry. "Not done yet, Sparrow." He rises, his mouth shiny with my release, his eyes wild, his chest heaving. His hand goes to his belt, his pants, and then he springs free. I swallow hard, my core clenching at the sheer size of him, the way he's thick and perfect and fucking dripping for me.

"You ready to sing for me, Sparrow?" he rasps, stroking himself, his jaw tight. "Because I'm about to fucking wreck you."

"Yes." I pant, wrapping my legs around his waist, pulling him closer, needing him now.

"Yes, Max. Fucking take me."

His eyes flash, then he thrust inside me, burying himself to the hilt in one sharp, claiming stroke. I scream, my nails digging into his back, my walls clenching hard around him.

"Fucking hell," he groans, dropping his head against my shoulder, panting. "You feel so goddamn tight."

He grabs my wrist, pinning them above my head, holding me trapped beneath him, completely at his mercy. And he moves. Hard. Deep. Brutal. I gasp, my hips lifting to meet his, taking everything he gives me.

"This is what you needed, isn't it?" he growls in my ear. "Needed me to fuck you right here, right now, with a dead man hanging ten feet away?"

"Yes," I whimper, my back arching, the table creaking beneath us.

The pleasure is overwhelming, searing. I'm spiraling again, my body tightening, coiling, ready to snap apart all over again.

"Cum for me, Sparrow," Max grits out. "Cum on my cock. Now"

I shatter, my body convulsing around him, my scream muffled against his mouth as I clench down on him, hard. Max curses, thrusts once, twice more before he groans, burying himself deep, pulsing, filling me.

And in the background, the chains creak, the sound barely a whisper in the silence. But we don't give a single fuck. I'm still catching my breath, my body boneless and spent, when it suddenly hits me. And I start laughing.

Max, still hovering over me, his forehead pressed to mine, pulls back just enough to arch a dark brow. "Sparrow, that is not something a man wants to hear after he's just fucked his woman senseless."

I shake my head, laughing even harder, my fingers still clutching at his arm. "No—it's not that." I gasp between breaths, wiping at my face with my blood-streaked hands. "It's just... oh my god, Max, how the hell are we supposed to walk through a crowded club right now? I have no panties on, and we're both covered in blood."

For a second, he just stares at me, then he laughs too, deep and rich, the sound reverberating through the room.

"Fuck." He runs a hand through his hair, still smirking. "I love that this is the part that breaks you."

I try to glare, but my own grin is unstoppable. "I'm being serious. People are going to notice. And Elias is going to lose his damn mind when he sees us like this."

Max leans in, pressing a quick, rough kiss to my lips before pulling away and helping me off the table. My legs barely holding me up, and his smirk deepened when I wobble.

"Relax, Sparrow," he murmurs, running a possessive hand down my back before squeezing my ass. "Elias will have cleared the club out by now. We're good."

I let out a breath, but then the weight of everything crashes down on me. My smile fades, my laughter dying in my throat. My gaze drifts to the bloodied corpse hanging in the center of the room.

Max notices immediately. "Sparrow," he says softly.

I swallow hard, forcing myself to meet his gaze. "How do I explain this?" I gesture vaguely, my hands shaking slightly. "Margot's upstairs. She's my best friend, but I—" I exhale sharply. "She came back with Elias, but what if she doesn't understand?"

Max watches me carefully, his expression unreadable for a long moment. Then he steps closer, lifting a blood-streaked hand to brush my hair behind my ear, his touch gentle despite the brutality we just shared.

"She's your best friend, Wren," he says simply. "A real one. She'll understand whatever you want to tell her."

I let out a slow breath, nodding once. "Yeah," I whisper, trying to convince myself.

Max gives me another long look, then glances past me to the body. "And what about him?"

I turn, staring at Anthony's lifeless form, his body slumped forward, his blood dripping in steady, rhythmic plinks onto the concrete below. For a long moment, I just stare. The *monster* who changed my life. The *piece of shit* who thought he could take something from me. The *coward* who thought he would get away with it. And now, he's *nothing*. I lift my chin, meeting Max's gaze without hesitation.

"The fucking bastard got what he deserved." My voice is cold. Steady. Final.

Max's eyes glitter with approval, but I can see the hint of something else there, too, something raw and possessive. He steps forward, his hands sliding over my waist, his fingers digging in just enough to make me feel him there. "You don't have to worry about him, Sparrow," he murmurs. "My guys will take care of it."

I nod once, "Okay."

I feel lighter, like some invisible weight that's been suffocating me has finally lifted. Max tilts my chin up, his thumb grazing my jaw. "Now, let's get cleaned up. You're a fucking mess."

I snort, shoving him lightly in the chest. "Excuse me? You're the one who fucked me on a murder table five minutes ago." He smirks. "And you fucking loved it." I roll my eyes, but my smile lingers.

"Come on," he says, guiding me toward the door. "I've got an apartment upstairs. We'll clean up there and stay the rest of the night." I sigh, exhaustion starting to weigh me down, but I nod. Because for the first time in years, I feel safe. And I have no idea what that means.

Chapter Twenty

MAXIMILIAN

AS SOON AS I push the door open, Hugo bounds toward us, his massive paws thudding against the floor, tail wagging like he hasn't seen us in weeks. Wrenley lets out a soft laugh, crouching slightly to scratch behind his ears. "Hey, buddy. Miss me?" Hugo rumbles in response, his head bumping against her thigh, his nose twitching as he sniffs at the blood on her dress.

Before I can comment, a voice from the couch shatters the quiet, a voice that's very much awake now. "Holy fuck." Margot sits bolt upright, blinking rapidly, glancing between us, her expression a mix of shock and mild horror. "What the hell happened?"

Wrenley, to her credit, doesn't miss a beat. She straightens, dusts herself off, and says smoothly. "We're fine. Just need to get cleaned up." Margot narrows her eyes like she doesn't quite believe it, but her gaze snaps to me, lingering on the smeared blood drying on my forearms, my shirt, and my hands. I expect another round of questions, but instead, she just scoffs, reaching beside her and tossing a small black bag in Wrenley's direction.

"Figured you'd need a change of clothes." Wrenley catches it with raised brows, looking at her friend with something akin to gratitude. "You're a lifesaver. Margot crosses her arms. "Don't thank me yet. I have questions. So. Many. Questions."

Wrenley grins and glances toward me. I nod toward the hallway. "Come on, Sparrow. This way." Before we can move, another voice cuts in.

"Oh, for fuck's sake."

I turn just in time to see Elias standing in the hallway, arms crossed over his chest, his sharp blue eyes raking over both of us like we're the most unbelievable sight he's ever seen. He gestures wildly between us, his lips quirking into a grin. "Let me get this straight—you two just went through all that, and you still managed to fuck each other senseless?"

Wrenley doesn't even hesitate. She tilts her head, her tone mock-innocent. "What can I say, Elias? I multi-task." He lets out a low whistle, shaking his head. "Damn. Didn't realize blood and torture got you off, sweetheart."

Wrenley flashes him a sickly sweet smile. "Didn't realize you were so obsessed with my sex life."

Elias snorts. "Not obsessed, just impressed. Terrified. But mostly impressed."

I chuckle, watching them go back and forth, enjoying the way Wrenley holds her own against him. "Alright, that's enough," I say, wrapping an arm around Wrenley's waist, guiding her toward the bedroom.

As we move, Elias calls after us, grinning, "Hey, Max—next time, warn a guy! I'll bring earplugs." I just laugh, shaking my head as I lead Wrenley inside. She smirks, elbowing me lightly. "He's an ass."

I smirk right back. "Yeah, but he's not wrong." She laughs, stepping into my room as I close the door behind us. For a moment, neither of us moves.

Then, without a word, I take her by the hand, leading her into the bathroom. She doesn't resist. And that? That might be the most dangerous thing of all. The moment the bathroom door clicks shut, Wrenley turns to me, her brows furrowed, studying me with an expression I can't quite place.

I tilt my head, leaning casually against the counter. "What?"

She hesitates for a second before huffing a quiet laugh, crossing her arms over her chest. "You usually seem so…" She searches for the right word, then smirks. "Rigid. A little uptight. But back there? In the hallway, with Elias, you looked so relaxed.

I raise a brow, stepping closer, closing the space between us. "Maybe with you, I am, and I've known Elias since we were kids."

She still looks curious, waiting for more, so I give her the truth.

"It feels natural, Sparrow." I lift my hand and trail a finger down her arm, watching the way her breath catches just so. "You feel natural."

She swallows but doesn't back away. Instead, she steps into me, looking up, something almost vulnerable lingering in her eyes before she shakes it off.

I reach past her, into the large glass show, twisting the handle until steam billows into the air, filling the space with the promise of heat.

Then, I turn back to her, my voice low. "Arms up."

Her lips parted slightly, but she complies without question, raising her arms above her head. I take my time, gripping the hem of her dress, slowly sliding it up, up, up over her soft curves before finally tugging it over her head. The dress falls to the floor, forgotten.

Now, she stands bare before me, except for the high heels still strapped to her feet.

I take a slow step back, my eyes raking over every inch of her, taking in the way the light from the bathroom casts golden highlights on her skin, the way the flush from earlier still lingers on her chest. Beautiful.

She watches me, her dark hazel eyes filled with fire, and for the first time in a long time, I feel like I'm standing too close to the sun. And I don't fucking care. Her fingers move to the waistband of my pants, popping the button open, then sliding the zipper down with agonizing deliberation.

My cock is already hard, pressing against the fabric, and she notices, smirking slightly as she shoves my pants down my legs. Before I can react, she reaches for my shirt, gripping the hem. I let her pull it up and off, tossing it aside.

Now, I'm just in my boxers, my arousal undeniable, but she doesn't rush. She hooks her thumbs into the elastic waistband and tugs them down, her eyes gaze up to meet mine as she does.

And fuck, the way she looks at me, like she owns me already. I've never wanted to ruin and be ruined by someone more. Before I can make a move, she takes one step back, ditching one of her heels, then another, taking off the other heel, until she's stepping into the shower, the steaming water cascading over her shoulders, letting the blood guide its way off, her wet hair slicked back, drops gliding over her curves.

She keeps the door open, watching me, her body half-turned, like she is waiting for me to follow. I can't wait. I step inside, the water instantly soaking my skin, my chest pressing against her back. She tilts her head slightly, letting the heat wash over us, and I run my hands down her arms, gripping her hips, pulling her flush against me.

"You were made for this, Wrenley," I murmur, my lips brushing against the shell of her ear.

And when she shudders, I know neither of us is getting any sleep tonight. Wrenley presses herself close against me, her skin slick with heat, her breath soft but steady.

For a second, I think she is going to devour me right here, but then—

"Shower first... play later."

She tilts her head back, smirking up at me, knowing exactly what she's doing. I exhale sharply through my nose, forcing myself to step back just enough to grab the bottle of shampoo from the shelf. "Bossy."

She lets out a quiet laugh but doesn't fight me when I pull her under the water, my fingers sinking into her wet hair, massaging shampoo into her scalp. Her eyes flutter shut, lips parting slightly as I work through the strands, my thumbs pressing circles into the base of her skull, sliding through soft, wet silk. She makes a small, satisfied noise, and fuck, if that doesn't make me want to drop to my knees right here.

I don't. Not yet.

Instead, I tilt her head back, rinsing the shampoo from her hair, watching as the suds swirl down her spine, before disappearing into the drain. She hums contentedly, then opens her eyes, and suddenly, the roles are reversed. She reaches for the bar of soap, lathering it between her palms before pressing her hands to my chest, slowly dragging them down.

The water glides over her fingers, over the ridges of old scars, the places where skin had been torn and sewn back together. Her brows knit together, her voice quieter now. "How'd you get these?"

I go still. For a second, I consider giving her nothing. But then, a compromise. "A long time ago, someone thought they could take everything from me." My tone is measured, controlled. "I made sure they didn't."

Her eyes flick up, searching mine. She's not satisfied with that answer. I can tell. So I give her a little more.

"I was seventeen. The Black Serpents were recruiting. I turned them down. They didn't like that." I smirk, but it's empty. "Thought they could carve me up and leave me for dead."

She draws her bottom lip between her teeth, her fingers brushing over a particularly deep scar near my ribs, her touch featherlight, but searing.

"They didn't succeed," she murmurs, her voice steady.

I shake my head. "No, they didn't."

For a second, we just stand there, water dripping between us, her fingers pressed against my past, my hands still resting on her waist. Then, her eyes darken, her fingertips dragging lower, and—

BANG. BANG. BANG.

"Alright, lovebirds!" Elias' voice thunders through the door, full of exaggerated exasperation. "There's food out here getting cold, and company waiting, so no shenanigans!"

Wrenley snorts, and I groan, tipping my head back against the tile. I swear to fucking God. I look back at her, gliding my hands down her slick skin one last time before grabbing the showerhead and rinsing her off. She sighs dramatically but doesn't fight it.

We finish up, stepping out into the steam-heavy bathroom, and I grab a massive towel, wrapping it around her before pulling her flush against my chest. Her hands press against my ribs, lingering just slightly.

"You're still staring."

Her lips curve into a smile. "So are you."

I grab another towel and dry off, keeping my eyes locked on her the entire time. She doesn't shy away. Instead, she moves slowly, unwrapping the towel, letting it slide down her body before stepping into a fresh pair of lace panties, bra, and sleek, form-fitting leggings. Then, she throws on an oversized black sweater, something soft and worn, the collar wide enough to expose one shoulder.

And fuck me, she looks better in that than she did in the damn dress.

I pull on a pair of black joggers and a fitted T-shirt, rolling my neck before leading her back out into the living room.

The moment we step out, all eyes turn to us. Margot is curled up on the couch, a drink in hand, looking entirely too pleased with herself. Elias sits at the bar, grinning like an idiot.

"About fucking time." He crosses his arms. "Was starting to think we needed to send a search party."

Margot giggles. "Or at least get a mop."

Wrenley narrows her eyes. "You're disgusting."

Elias grins. "And you're predictable."

She grabs a throw pillow off the couch and chucks it at his head.

Elias dodges, laughing. "Alright, Alright. Let's eat. Before Max decides, he'd rather eat you instead."

Wrenley glares. "You have exactly two seconds to shut up before I introduce you to my right hook."

Elias winks. "You're going fit in just fine, sweetheart."

She just rolls her eyes, but I catch the way her lips twitch, the way she leans just slightly into me as I lead her toward the table. And as much as Elias runs his mouth? For once, I think he might actually be right.

The food is spread across the table: steak, roasted potatoes, and something that looks like a high-end version of mac and cheese. Elias really went all out, not that I'm surprised. The man never does anything halfway, including making himself a nuisance.

Wrenley sits beside me, her thigh pressed against mine, warm even through our clothes. I catch the faintest whiff of her shampoo, fresh and soft, a contrast to the blood and violence from earlier. It does something to me, settles the fire, and stokes it at the same time.

Margot and Elias sit across from us, and it doesn't take long before the banter begins. "You know," Margot says, pointing her fork at me before stabbing a piece of steak. "I didn't expect five-star service after a night like this, but I gotta say, Max... you run a tight ship."

Elias scoffs, smirking as he leans back in his chair. "Yeah, well, he likes to keep people happy. Most of the time. Except me. He likes to make my life hell."

I lift a brow, taking a sip of whiskey. "Your life is an inconvenience to yourself, Brother."

Elias slaps a hand over his chest, feigning offense. "Unbelievable. The disrespect."

Margot snickers. "Oh, please, like you're not constantly trying to make his life hell."

Elias winks at her, "I have no idea what you're talking about, Trouble."

Margot pauses mid-chew. "Trouble?"

He smirks. "You just seem like the type."

Margot leans forward, her voice dripping with flirtation. "And what type is that, exactly?"

Elias doesn't blink. Doesn't hesitate. "The type that'd look real good tangled in my sheets."

Margot chokes on her drink. I groan under my breath as Wrenley stifles a laugh, watching Margot try and fail to hide the fact that Elias just threw her completely off her game.

Meanwhile, Elias just grins, eating his steak like he didn't just set the table on fire.

I dip my head slightly toward Wrenley, murmuring so only she can hear. "Should we tell them to get a room?"

She hums in agreement. "Or maybe just push them into one."

Elias throws a piece of bread at me, breaking the moment. "If you two are done whispering sweet nothings, some of us are trying to eat."

Margot scoffs, regaining some of her composure. "Elias Cade, are you implying that I'm not worth your attention?"

He leans back, a lazy smirk curving his lips. "Oh, Baby, you already have all of my attention."

Margot's brow lifts slightly, and I don't miss the way her fingers toy with the rim of her glass. This is going to be a problem.

Beside me, Wrenley twirls her fork idly between her fingers, looking between the two of them like she is watching a very interesting chess match.

I take another bite of steak, waiting. Wrenley's hand brushes against mine under the table, slow and deliberate, the light drag of her nails sending a subtle shiver up my spine. She leans in, voice low, quiet, just for me.

"It's time, Max."

I pause, looking at her.

Her expression is unreadable, but there's conviction there. Determination.

She swallows. "I want to know everything, and Margot needs to learn a few things too."

I don't answer right away. I should tell her to sleep on it, but we've already crossed the threshold, and there's no going back.

I exhale slowly, nodding. "Alright, Sparrow. No more Secrets."

I hold her gaze a second longer before I add, "But first thing in the morning. Everyone needs sleep. We'll head to the penthouse early and lay everything out for everyone."

Her fingers tighten around mine beneath the table, but she nods, exhaling softly.

The night had already taken a turn. Now, it's heading straight into the unknown.

Chapter Twenty-One

THE BED IS cold when I wake, and the space where Max should be is empty. For a moment, I just lay there, blinking against the morning light, filtering in through the curtains. The night before comes rushing back in vivid, fevered flashes, his hands, his mouth, the way he felt inside me, the blood still drying on my skin as he took me in the cold basement.

I take a deep breath, shoving the memory aside before it sends me spiraling.

The sound of a low, muffled voice coming from the living room catches my attention. Max. I slip out of bed, careful not to make a sound. He stands with his back to me, shirtless, phone pressed to his ear. His muscles shift with every breath, his body a living testament to power and precision. And then there's his tattoo. I've seen it before peeking out from beneath his shirts, curving along his ribs—but now I can *see* all of it.

A massive black raven, its wings stretching across his back in a dark, inky sprawl, each feather meticulously detailed in varying shades of black and gray. But this isn't some elegant, romanticized version of the bird. This raven is feral, mid-flight, its beak parted in a silent scream as it clutches a writhing serpent in its talons. The snake coils around its claws, sinking its fangs into the raven's leg, a single drop of inked blood trailing down Max's ribcage.

It's a battle, frozen in time, locked in eternal war. And it's fucking mesmerizing. I swallow hard as he shifts his weight, the tattoo moving with him, a living, breathing masterpiece etched into his skin.

"Make sure all their stuff is out of the hotel by noon," he says, voice calm but firm. "And stop by Gunner's."

A pause. "Food, a large bed, whatever else he needs. I want Hugo settled." Another beat, then a quiet "Good." He hangs up but doesn't turn around. Instead, his voice is laced with amusement.

"Sparrow, are you just going to stand there and eavesdrop?"

I blink, heat creeping up my neck, and step fully into the living room. Max finally turns, his eyes roving over me slowly, like he can still see every inch of my bare skin beneath his shirt. The way he looks at me is enough to make my breath catch.

I cross my arms, trying to focus. "What was that about?"

He sits at the bar facing me, elbows propped on the counter, muscles flexing in a way that makes my mouth dry. "Making sure you and Margot are out of the hotel. Your stuff will be brought to the penthouse."

I stare at him, taken aback. "You didn't think to ask me first?"

He raises a brow, completely unbothered. "Would you have said yes?"

I open my mouth, then close it. Shit. Before I can fire back a response, laughter erupts from the hallway. I glance over my shoulder just as Margot and Elias emerge from the back bedroom, both looking far too comfortable with each other.

Margot's hair is a disheveled mess, her clothes are the same as last night, and Elias looks downright smug. Max, to my surprise, doesn't even react. He shakes his head and says, "Let's get dressed, Sparrow. We've got things to discuss."

The car ride is mostly silent, except for the low bump of music vibrating through the speakers. Elias hums along quietly, his fingers drumming on the steering wheel as he navigates the city streets. I rest my head on the cool glass, letting my eyes drift shut for a moment. My legs stretch across the seat, resting over Max's lap.

He doesn't seem to notice at first, too engrossed in whatever he's feverishly typing on his phone, his brows slightly furrowed. But after a minute, his free hand finds my thigh, rubbing absent-minded circles over my skin, tracing slow, deliberate patterns.

Something about it feels natural, like he's done it a thousand times before. Like I belong here. I don't know what the hell to make of that thought. I let it sit in the back of my mind, ignoring the warmth it sends through me, and just focus on the weight of his hand against my skin as the city passes in a blur.

Back at the penthouse, we step into the open living space, the floor-to-ceiling windows casting mid-morning light across the sleek black furniture. Margot lets out a low whistle, eyes landing on the massive wall of monitors displaying various security feeds, files, and encrypted data.

"Jesus," she mutters, hands on her hips. "You're like a super spy in here."

Max doesn't react, just shrugs off his jacket and tosses it onto the back of the couch.

"Sit," he instructs.

Margo, Elias, and I settle onto the couches, the air thick with something unspoken.

I take a deep breath, looking between Max and Elias.

"Okay," I say, my voice steady despite the storm brewing inside me. "Who goes first?"

Margot frowns, confusion knitting her brows together. "First for what?" What the hell is going on?"

Elias stretches out lazily, propping one ankle over his knee, before smirking. "I think Wrenley should start."

His tone is lighter than the moment calls for, but I don't miss the knowing glint in his eyes. He leans back, arms sprawled across the back of the couch. "Start with last night... or, I don't know, maybe last year."

Margot's gaze snaps to me, the confusion shifting into something sharper. I wet my lips, sitting up straighter. "Mags.. You know I was attacked."

She nods slowly, eyes narrowing, "Yeah...You never told me many details, but I know it was bad."

I glance at Max, his face giving nothing away.

"What I never told you..." I continue, voice calmer than I feel, "...is that Max was the one who saved me that night."

Margot's mouth parts slightly, but she doesn't say anything. I keep going. I tell her everything, how Max found me, how he pulled that bastard off me, how he nearly beat him to death right there in the alley. I tell her about last night, how the man from last year came back, the fight in the hallway, even though she saw that part, and Max having him dragged down to the basement. How I killed him.

The room is silent when I finish. Margot stares at me, her expression carefully blank as she processes everything I just said. I brace myself for it, for horror, for disbelief, for judgment.

Instead, she leans back, crosses one leg over the other, and exhales a deep breath.

Then, she shrugs, "Well then," she says simply. "I'm glad you went all John Wick on his ass." Relief floods through me. I should know by now to never underestimate my best friend.

I turn to Max, meeting his gaze with unwavering expectation. "Your turn." He doesn't hesitate. Sitting with his back to the massive bank of monitors, he nods once before turning around, fingers flying over the keyboard. The screens flicker to life, pulling up the same documents, financial records, and connections he'd shown me days ago, the truth about my family's empire of greed and corruption.

The tension in the room tightens like a vice. Margot leans

forward, her brows drawing together as she scans the screens. "Are you fucking kidding me?"

Max just keeps scrolling through files, showing names tied to offshore accounts, businesses used as a front for something darker. The Ashfords weren't just wealthy elites; they were puppet masters, pulling strings in places they had no business being.

Elias, now lounging on the arm of the couch, lets out a low chuckle, but there's something dark in his eyes. "Surprise, princess. Your parents aren't exactly upstanding citizens."

Margot turns to me, her expression still processing, but there's something else in her eyes, realization. I exhale slowly, pressing my lips together before finally saying it aloud.

"This is what Benjamin was trying to dismantle."

The words hang heavy in the air. I let them sink in before continuing, my voice steady, firm. "He didn't want the Ashfords to be known for this. He wanted to cut ties, to break it all down before it consumed everything."

Max keeps his focus on the screen, his jaw tight. I can feel the unspoken weight of his knowledge, the things he isn't saying yet.

Margot shakes her head, looking at me. "Jesus, Wren. This is... It's insane." I nod slowly. "And now, it's my problem."

I look around the room, the weight of this information it's tense, the kind that presses in at every angle. No one speaks for a long moment, the gravity of it all sinking into our bones.

A sharp knock at the door sounds, shattering the stillness, making everyone in the room tense.

Hugo, who had been lying at my feet, perks up instantly, ears flicking forward. He lets out a low rumble, shifting in an alert stance. Max's fingers fly over the keyboard, killing the screens with a few swift keystrokes.

Elias motions toward the dog. "Easy, Cujo."

Max strides toward the door, his steps slow, deliberate. He swings it open.

"Hey, Boss." And the moment the man steps inside, dragging our suitcases behind him, Margot lets out a sharp gasp.

"Holy fuck!" she blurts out, staring at him like she's seen a ghost. "Noah?!"

Every muscle in my body locks up.

No. No, no, no. I groan internally, squeezing my eyes shut for a beat before covering my face with my hands. Because standing in the doorway, looking a little older, a little rougher around the edges, but still somehow the same, is Noah fucking Callahan.

His eyes sweep the room, clearly not expecting an audience. When they land on Margot, his expression flickers with genuine shock, his grip tightening around the handle of one of the suitcases.

"Margot?" he breathed, blinking at her like she was the last person he expected to see.

She stares right back, brows drawn tight, looking just as stunned. I don't have time to analyze whatever weird history is playing out, because the next second, Noah's gaze shifts to me, and the shock in his eyes morphs into something else entirely. Surprise, Smug amusement. And just the slightest hint of old heartbreak.

"Well, well," he drawls, head tilting, a slow, knowing grin creeping onto his face. "Of all the people I ever expected to find here... you were not one of them."

His words hit harder than I expected. Max, now standing beside me, goes rigid, his shoulders tensing noticeably. Elias lets out a low hum, clearly thriving off the energy shift. And Noah? He just looks at me, his dark eyes digging into mine, waiting for a reaction. I clench my jaw.

Noah lets out a breath, dragging a hand through his already messy hair. "Nice to see you, Margot," he mutters, voice clipped but polite. Then his gaze shifts to me, something sharper, more guarded, slipping into his expression. "Clearly, not good to see you, though."

Max clears his throat. "Appreciate you handling the delivery." There is a pause, just long enough to make it clear that whatever history Noah and I have doesn't interest him in the slightest. "I won't keep you."

Noah hesitates, just for a second. But then he nods once, glances at Margot again, and pulls open the door. "See you around."

The second the door clicks shut, all eyes turn to me. I groan out loud. "Oh, for fuck's sake."

Elias stretches out on the couch, grinning like he's watching his favorite sports team one point away from a win. "Well, that was fun."

Margot shakes her head, still recovering from the whiplash of that encounter. Max? He is watching me. His elbows rest on his knees, fingers loosely clasped. His expression is impassive, unreadable, but his eyes? His eyes are calculating.

"No secrets, Sparrow," he says, his voice measured, smooth. "Spill"

I cross my arms over my chest. "It was nothing."

Elias scoffs. "Sweetheart, that was a whole fucking thing."

Margot snorts. "Oh, it was definitely a thing."

I roll my eyes. "It was high school. We dated for a little over a year. I dumped him right after graduation and never looked back." I gesture toward the door. "That's it. That's the entire story."

Silence. Max's fingers tap on his knee once, twice, before he leans back in his chair. His voice is even, casual when he finally says, "He works well enough. Dependable. Competent." A small pause. "Not my favorite."

The words are innocuous, but there's something pointed, deliberate underneath them. I narrow my eyes. "That isn't necessary."

He meets my stare without hesitation. "Neither was the tension when he walked in."

Elias lets out a low laugh. "Well, fuck me. That's gonna be a fun little landmine later."

Margot sighs. "That was... a lot."

I pinch the bridge of my nose. "Can we move on?"

A beat of Silence. Then, Max exhales through his nose, nods once. "For now."

I square my shoulders, meeting his stare head-on.

"Alright, Blackwood," I say, my voice firm. "You promised no more secrets. You've shown me pieces, just enough to hook me, but now I want the full fucking story. Everything. From the beginning."

A beat. Then another. Finally, Max leans back in his chair, studying me, weighing something in his mind. Then he nods. "Alright, Sparrow." His voice is smooth, but there's an edge beneath it. "Let's talk about how I ended up in this Ashford empire of doom."

Chapter Twenty-Two
MAXIMILIAN

THE WEIGHT of Wrenley's stare is unrelenting, sharp, and expectant. She wants the truth. I exhale, leaning forward, forearms resting on my knees, rubbing my hands together before I finally look at her.

"You asked for everything, so here it is."

I was barely seventeen when they first came for me. The Black Serpents were always a problem in this city, outlaw muscle car junkies with no real loyalty, no real cause, just a hunger for money and power. They saw potential in me, a fresh recruit with sharp instincts and no family name to protect me. I told them no. Again and again.

Then, one night, they stopped asking. I had just finished working on my father's car, the garage still reeking of gasoline and sweat, when they jumped me. Six of them. I got a few good hits, but six against one was a losing battle.

They held me down. Put a knife on my ribs. Made it very clear what happened to people who told them no. The first cut was slow, deliberate, and dragged from my ribs up towards my chest. A lesson, they said. The second came faster. Third, I barely remember.

But I do remember my father finding me. He was the kind of man who didn't take kindly to threats, let alone an attempt on his only son's life. My father was a self-made man, one who built himself up from nothing and refused to bow to anyone. The serpents learned that the hard way.

I spent six weeks recovering while he burned their world to the ground. One by one, he picked them off, tore them apart, dismantled their operation from the inside. Some disappeared. Some ended up in prison. Others learned fast to fear the name Dominic Blackwood.

Eventually, he took over the club. Turned it into something more than a gang of lowlife criminals who trafficked in drugs and violence. He reshaped it into a network of people who wanted something different: power without filth, loyalty without betrayal. It was easier said than done, though. Not everyone wanted to change.

That's when Charles came knocking. Wrenley's father.

The Ashfords were used to controlling the city from behind the scenes, politicians, business deals, and corporate takeovers. But they needed people like the Serpents. They needed someone to do the things they couldn't be publicly tied to.

My father refused. And Charles Ashford is not a man who likes to be told no. For months, he tried to pressure my father into doing his dirty work, threats, bribes, and ultimatums. My father held his ground.

Then, one night, he was gone.

They made it look like an accident. A robbery gone wrong. But I knew better. I was twenty years old, and I watched the people my father fought to protect scatter like cockroaches, too afraid to stand against the Ashfords. But I wasn't afraid.

I took over the Serpents, what was left of them. And I vowed to destroy the Ashfords. But it wasn't that simple. Some of the older members, the ones who cared more about money than loyalty, sold out. They took Ashford's money, let themselves be controlled like puppets, and turned their back on the very things my father built.

The Serpents split.

A few stayed with me. The rest? They belonged to Wrenley's father. That's when Benjamin approached me. Five years ago, he walked into one of my garages, looking like a man who had already lost a war but was still fighting. He told me he needed help. Said he had been trying to dismantle what his brother built from the inside, but he wasn't strong enough to do it alone.

And I listened. Because he was the only Ashford I had ever met who wasn't drowning in greed. And now he's dead.

I finish speaking, letting the weight of the words settle over the room. Silence stretches, thick and suffocating. Wrenley's face is unreadable, but her hands are clenched into fists. I don't know if it's anger or grief or something in between.

Finally, she exhales, her voice barely above a whisper. "*This* is what Benjamin was trying to dismantle?"

I nod. "He didn't want the Ashfords to be known for this."

She stands abruptly, pacing, running a hand through her hair. "And my father—" she stops herself, shaking her head. When she turns back to me, her eyes are sharper than before.

"Then we finish what he started."

I watch her for a moment, studying the determination in her stance, the fire in her voice. And for the first time, I think she might be more dangerous than I am. Then, without a word, she turns on her heel and walks away.

Elias lets out a breath that he seems to be holding. "Well, that could've gone worse."

Margot elbows him in the ribs. "She does this with heavy news, disassociates, give her a minute, she always comes back."

I say nothing, just watching the bedroom door swing shut behind her. When I finally reach her, she's standing in my bedroom, staring at The Red Thread. Her arms are wrapped around her, head tilted slightly, and her bottom lip caught between her teeth like she's trying to hold something in. She doesn't turn.

"This painting..." she finally says, voice barely above a whisper.

I already know what she's thinking. Why is it here?

She turns to me, tears welling in her eyes, her voice breaking just slightly as she speaks. "I'm sorry."

I exhale, stepping forward, lifting a hand to brush my knuckles against her cheek. "For what?"

She swallows hard. "For what my father did. To yours. To you."

I cup her face then, thumb brushing away a single tear that escapes. "It's not your fault, Sparrow. You don't carry his sins."

Her breath shudders as she exhales, leaning into my touch. I press my forehead to hers, closing my eyes for a moment, grounding myself in her warmth. But there's more she needs to know.

I pull back, gripping her chin lightly between my fingers, forcing her to meet my gaze. "There's something else."

Her brows pull together. "What else could there possibly be?"

I hesitate for the first time all day. I force the words out before I can stop myself.

"After your attack... Benjamin asked me to keep you safe."

She blinks. "What?"

I drop my hand from her face, stepping back slightly, running a hand through my hair. "He didn't trust anyone. So I kept close by, in case I needed to step in, from the shadows."

Her lips part, shock flickering through her expression. "You... stalked me?"

I exhale through my nose, giving a single nod. "Well, yes."

She shakes her head, eyes narrowing. "Seriously?"

My jaw tightens. "Yes."

She just *stares* at me.

I continue before she can say anything else.

"I never meant to get attached to you." The confession feels heavy, raw, but it's the truth. "I was only supposed to watch, to keep you safe." I glance toward The Red Thread on the wall. "But then I saw you. Really saw you. And I..." I trail off, shaking my head.

Her expression softens just slightly, but she's still wary. "And you what?"

I meet her gaze again. "I started leaving you things."

She rears back slightly. "Leaving me things?"

I nod.

"Your apartment, I broke in one night after you left. I didn't touch anything, I just... placed a couple of cameras, left something."

Wrenley's eyes widen, her breath catching. "What did you leave?"

I take a slow breath. "The first time... a book. 'The Picture of Dorian Gray."

She inhales sharply.

"That was you?"

I nod. "It was always me."

I see the moment she starts connecting the dots. The mysterious bottle of expensive wine on her counter after a hard day. The new set of paintbrushes left by her easel when hers had worn down. The red silk scarf draped over her vanity, one she'd always assumed was a lost gift from a friend. It was all me.

I can't read her expression, and it's making me restless. "Say something."

And then, she starts laughing.

I blink. "Are you... laughing?"

She bends over slightly, hands on her knees, breathless with laughter.

I step closer, scowling. "Sparrow, this is not the reaction I was expecting."

She waves a hand, trying to breathe. "OH, no—don't—don't get me wrong, this is all very concerning." She lets out another burst of laughter. "But—Max—you literally stalked me, broke into my home, and left me presents like some twisted secret admirer—" she's still laughing.

I cross my arms over my chest, unamused. "You're not mad?"

She straightens, grinning, eyes still gleaming with amusement. "Oh, I'm mad, but this is hilarious."

Before I can respond, she turns and walks right out of the room, into the living room where Margot and Elias are lounging.

I follow, my stomach sinking. "Wrenley—" But it's too late.

She points at me dramatically, still laughing. "Mags. You will not *believe* what this man just confessed."

Margot leans forward, intrigued. "Oh, this is going to be good."

Elias grins like he's already enjoying whatever's about to happen.

I rub a hand over my face, muttering under my breath. "For fuck's sake."

Wrenley crosses her arms, still laughing, turning fully toward Margot. "So, you remember all those times I told you I thought I was being followed?'

Margot raises an eyebrow. "Yeah?"

Wrenley gestures toward me like I'm a grand Prize on a game show. "Well, it was fucking Max."

Margot's mouth falls open slightly before she turns to me, eyes wide with disbelief.

"No."

Wrenley nods. "Oh, yeah. And you remember those random gifts? The ones you swore weren't from you?"

Margot nods slowly, gears turning in her head.

Wrenley throws a hand in my direction. "Yeah, those were him, too."

Margot whips her head back to me, blinking. "Max, what the actual fuck?

I sigh, rubbing my temples. "It's not as bad as it sounds."

Margot lets out an incredulous laugh. "Not as bad as it sounds? You literally stalked her from the shadows and left presents like some Gothic sugar daddy. That is exactly as bad as it sounds."

Elias bursts out laughing from where he's sprawled on the couch, shaking his head.

"Oh, my God. I can't believe you told her."

I shoot him a glare. "Well, you knew too, so if she's going to be mad, she should be just as mad at you."

Wrenley's head snaps to Elias, her eyes narrowing. "Wait. You knew?"

Elias grins unapologetically, throwing his hands up. "Knew? Oh, sweetheart, I was there."

Margot's jaw drops. "You helped?"

Elias snickers. "Define 'helped.'"

Wrenley stares at both of us, then turns back to Margot. A beat of silence. And then, both of them dissolve into another fit of laughter.

Margot wipes a tear from the corner of her eye. "This is seriously the funniest thing I've ever heard in my life."

Wrenley leans against her, wheezing. "I know, I should be so pissed. But I just—" she wheezes harder "—Max fucking Black-wood, lurking in the shadows like a wolf, dropping off expensive wine and silk scarves like some deranged patron of the arts."

Margot snaps her fingers. "Mystery Sugar Daddy!"

Elias doubles over, crackling. "That's it. That's his new nick-name. Mystery sugar daddy."

I groan, dropping my head into my hands. "I hate all of you."

Wrenley is still laughing, but she finally meets my eyes. There's something different there, something warm, something teasing, something that tells me she's not mad.

And maybe, just maybe, she likes it.

Chapter Twenty-Three

WRENLEY

LAUGHTER STILL LINGERS in the air, wrapping around us like a veil of amusement that, for a brief moment, lightens the heavy tension of everything we've learned. I wipe at the corners of my eyes, catching my breath as I shake my head at Margot, who still looks like she is on the verge of another fit of giggles.

Max exhales, pinching the bridge of his nose before leveling a look at all of us. "Alright, now that you've all had your fun at my expense, we should discuss the plan."

Before he can launch into it, Margot tilts her head, something dawning on her. She shifts in her seat, gaze drinking in everything, her lips pursing in thought. "Wait a second," she says, eyes narrowing as she waves a hand around at the luxury surrounding us. "So, your dad worked in a garage, and I assume you took it over after he died. How does that afford...all of this?"

I glance at Max, curious about that too. I had been so wrapped up in everything else that I hadn't actually stopped to wonder *how* exactly he had built this empire of his. Max leans back in his chair, expression unreadable. "I still own the garage, several actually," he says simply. "They're fully operational, a legitimate business. But I needed more than that." His fingers tap against the armrest. "I started fighting."

I bunch my brows. "Fighting?"

"Underground fights." Elias chimes in, smirking as he folds his arms behind his head. "Big-money bets. And not just the ones he placed, people bet *on* him. He was undefeated."

Max's jaw ticks slightly, but he doesn't argue the point.

Margot's eyes widen. "Okay, so you punched people for money. That explains some of it.

Elias wags a finger at her. "That's where I came in." His grin turns wicked. "While Max was out there knocking teeth in, I started running my own little side business. Let's just say some of the biggest corporations have more money than they know what to do with. And when they're corrupt as fuck, they don't deserve to keep all of it."

I raise a brow. "You stole from them?"

Elias feigns offense. "*Stole?* No, I simply moved it to a better home."

I shake my head, lips twitching despite myself.

"But that's how this started," Max continues, his voice turning serious, grounding us back to reality. "And that's how we're going to take down the Ashfords."

And just like that, the heaviness is back. The playful ease from earlier vanishes, replaced with a sharper, more calculated intensity.

I straighten slightly. "Okay. How?"

Max and Elias exchange a look, and then Max leans forward, resting his elbows on his knees.

"We've been quietly taking over the smaller businesses that the Ashfords control. Establishing leverage in places they don't expect."

"Shady bars, Clubs, shipping yards, and private security firms." Elias elaborates. "It's not just about *owning* them, it's about turning them against the Ashfords, making their own network crumble from the inside. The moment they realize they're bleeding, it'll already be too late."

"And then," Max continues, his voice calm but laced with something darker, "we bankrupt the biggest one."

I tense slightly. "And which one is that?"

Elias grins, but there's no humor in it. "*Ashford International Holdings*"

My stomach clenches. "That's *everything*," I murmur, barely believing what I'm hearing.

Max nods. "The main empire. Your father's kingdom. Once it collapses, everything they've built falls with it."

Margot makes a small sound. "Uh, yeah, I mean, that could work, I guess."

I shoot her a look, barely suppressing a laugh at her bluntness. Max, however, doesn't look amused. His piercing eyes settle on me. "You don't like it."

I hesitate for only a second before shaking my head. "It's not that I don't like it. I just think it's not *enough*."

Max's jaw flexes, but I can tell he's listening. "Explain."

I open my mouth, ready to lay it out, but before I can, the sharp buzz of my phone cuts through the tension. I snap my head toward where it sits on the table and groan. My mother's name flashes across the screen. The room goes silent.

Margot mutters, "Of course."

Elias exhales heavily. "Fucking hell."

Max watches me carefully, his entire demeanor shifting into something unreadable. I close my eyes briefly, steeling myself, before reaching for the phone.

"I guess we're about to find out what the queen of ice and manipulation wants," I mutter before swiping to answer.

I don't know what's coming. But I already know it's nothing good. I swipe to answer, pressing the speaker icon before setting the phone in my lap. A sharp breath fills the silence before my mother's cold, clipped voice cuts through.

"Wrenley."

Not *hello*. How *are you*? Just my name, spoken like an obligation.

I roll my eyes. "Mother."

She doesn't acknowledge my tone, just forges ahead like she

always does. "The lawyers are ready to read Benjamin's will. You will be attending the meeting."

I blink. "Why do I need to be there?"

A sigh, long and heavy, filters through the line, like she can't believe I would even ask such a question. "Because Benjamin's lawyer insists on your presence," she says, her tone heavy, leaving no room for argument. "You've been named in the will."

A slow chill works its way down my spine. I sit up straighter. "Named how?"

"I guess we will find out soon enough." Another dismissive sigh. "The meeting is at 10:30 sharp, tomorrow, downtown at the office."

I clench my jaw. "Fine, I'll be there."

But of course, she's not done.

"And Wrenley," she adds, her voice turning sharp. "This is a *business* meeting in the *family* office. I expect you to dress appropriately. And do *not* be late."

Before I can snap back or tell her exactly where she can shove her expectations, she disconnects the call. I stare at the phone, my fingers flexing against my lap as frustration coils in my chest. Then, with a sharp breath, I grab the phone and toss it back onto the table with a dull *thud*.

Silence blankets the room. Max watches me, his expression unreadable, but his eyes are like fire, steady and assessing, waiting for my reaction.

Before I can speak, Elias, because, of course, it's Elias, breaks the tension.

"Well," he drawls, stretching his arms behind his head, "that was a fucking delight. Your mother sounds like an absolute ray of sunshine, Sweetheart."

Margot snorts, shaking her head. "She's worse in person."

"Oh, I don't doubt that for a second," Elias mutters. "I felt the temperature drop at least ten degrees through the damn phone."

I exhale sharply, running a hand through my hair. "Yeah, well, that's Vivian Ashford for you."

Max finally speaks, his voice steady and controlled. "What are you thinking?"

A slow, wicked grin tugs at my lips. I lean forward, resting my elbows on the table as I lock eyes with him. "I have a new plan," I say, voice laced with amusement.

Elias raises a brow. "Oh, this ought to be good."

Margot smiles big. "Oh, I *like* that face. That's our *scheming* face."

Max tilts his head slightly, watching me with quiet intrigue. "And what plan would that be?"

I sit back, my grin widening.

"First," I say, standing, "I need to go shopping."

Max sits back in the chair, arms folded across his chest, watching me with a slight look of confusion. "You need to do what?"

I smirk, grabbing my purse off the counter. "Shopping."

Margot's ears perk up immediately. "Oh, I'm coming."

But I shake my head. "Nope, you're taking Hugo to the dog park; he needs to get outside."

Margot frowns, placing a hand over her chest dramatically. "You wound me."

Elias grins. "Don't worry, I'll keep you company."

Margot scoffs. "Oh, great, just what I need, another man bossing me around."

Elias smirks, throwing an arm around her shoulders. "Boss, you around? Nah, Baby. I'm just here to make sure you don't get into too much trouble."

Margot sighs but doesn't argue.

Max stands, grabbing his keys. "Let's go," he tells me. "Wherever you want."

The boutique is dimly lit and decadent, draped in velvet curtains and racks of meticulously curated designer pieces. I trail my fingers over the fabric of another dress, pretending to examine it as I feel his eyes burning into me.

Max hasn't stopped watching me since we walked in here, his presence a weight I can feel even when I'm not looking. His voice is low, edged with that signature smirk when he finally speaks.

"Are we shopping, Sparrow? Or are we just here to torture me?"

I pause, letting his words hang in the air before turning to face him. He's lounging in a chair, arms stretched over the armrests like he owns the place, his dark amber eyes locked onto me with an intensity that sends a shiver down my spine.

I step closer, slow and deliberate, closing the space between us. His gaze shifts downward, where I rest my hand lightly on his knee, leaning in just enough so that I know he can catch the faint scent of my perfume.

I let my lips curl into a slow, teasing smile.

"Oh, Max," I purr, batting my lashes at him, watching the way his jaw ticks as I drag my nails lightly against his thigh. "If I were torturing you, you'd beg me to never stop."

His fingers flex on the armrest, his throat working as he exhales through his nose. "You sure about that, Sparrow?" he murmurs, voice lower now, rougher. A challenge.

I pretend to think, biting my lip. "Mmm, pretty sure."

His eyes darken as I let my fingers graze just a little higher, teasing, before I pull back, smirking. Max watches me retreat, a smirk forming on his lips, but his eyes give nothing away. "One of these days, Sparrow, you're going to find out what happens when you push me too far."

I toss a look over my shoulder as I slip into the dressing room, gripping the curtain with one hand. "Looking forward to it, Blackwood."

As I pull the curtain closed, I hear him exhale sharply, muttering something under his breath. I stifle a laugh. *Damn, that was fun.*

Inside the dressing room, I smooth my hands down the sleek black pencil skirt, feeling the way it clings to my hips and thighs like a second skin. The sheer white button-down is scandalously low, teasing the delicate lace of my black push-up bra beneath it. *Perfect.*

As I adjust the collar, making sure just enough of my cleavage is visible to toe the line between provocative and powerful, I call out, "By the way, you're coming with me tomorrow."

There's a beat of silence before Max makes sounds, half scoff, half dark chuckle. "Why, exactly?"

I grin, knowing he's probably sitting out there, arms crossed, that sharp, assessing gaze narrowed in suspicion. "Because I need an intimidating watchdog."

His chuckle is deep, the kind that rolls through me like a slow drag of whiskey. "I prefer the shadows, Sparrow."

"Yeah, I know. But I'm not even going to introduce you. You're just going to stand there looking all scary. My mother will hate it. My father will lose his mind. It'll be fun."

Max hums, considering. "Speaking of watchdogs, you should bring Hugo. That would send your mother over the edge, and watching your father lose his shit when he realizes you've been in Benjamin's Mansion? That would be something I'd pay to see."

I let out a soft laugh, smoothing my hands down my skirt one last time before stepping out. The moment I do, the air between us ignites.

Max is leaning forward now, elbows resting on his knees, his eyes dragging over my body so slowly, so thoroughly, it's like he's mapping every inch to memory. His jaw tightens, his lips part slightly, a flicker of hunger flashing in his expression before he turns it back into something composed.

I pretend not to notice, tilting my head playfully. "Well? What do you think, too much?"

Max stands in one smooth motion, towering over me, his smile dark and knowing. "You need one more thing." He walks past me, and I turn to watch as he scans the wall of designer heels. His fingers skim along the rows until they stop on a pair, pulling them free with a certainty that makes my pulse stutter.

My breath catches when I see them. The black stilettos are sleek and lethal, razor-sharp pointed toes, high enough to make my legs look obscene, with matte black spikes wrapping around the delicate ankle strap and down the back of the heel, and that infamous red bottom.

Oh, hell.

"Sit," he orders, his voice is low and full of promise.

I do as I'm told, lowering myself into the chair he just occupied. The second I settle, Max kneels in front of me, so close that the heat from his body seeps into my skin.

The sight of him between my legs, the way his large hands wrap around my ankle with careful possession, does something wicked to me.

"These," he murmurs, sliding my foot out of my current heels with a torturous drag, "are going to wreck them."

I arch a brow. "Them?"

His eyes turn into something predatory as he glances up at me through thick lashes. "Anyone with a pulse."

My stomach tightens, and my throat dries as he lifts my foot, trailing his fingertips along my calf, his touch barely there but scorching all the same. He slides the new stiletto on, his thumb pressing against the delicate arch of my foot before clasping the strap around my ankle, his grip firm, possessive.

His hands move to my other foot, this time even slower, his knuckles grazing along my skin before he secures the strap in place. I swear he's toying with me. And I never want him to stop. His hand stays on my legs, warm and sure, thumbs tracing small circles along my skin. He lifts his gaze, locking onto mine, and I feel it everywhere.

I wet my lips. "All done?"

Max smirks, his fingers flexing slightly. "Not even close."

The words send a delicious shiver down my spine, but before I can respond, he takes my hands in his and pulls me to my feet, the shift pressing me right against him.

I turn toward the mirror, trying to ignore the way his body brushes against mine, how his hands don't leave my hips, how he leans in, voice barely against my ear.

"You look like a whole lot of trouble..." his lips dance along the curve of my jaw. "...and a hell of a lot of fun."

My smirk mimics his as I meet his gaze in the mirror. "Good."

Chapter Twenty-Four

MAXIMILIAN

THE MOMENT WRENLEY steps back into the dressing room, she tosses me one last lingering glance before pulling the curtain closed. My jaw tightens. I should sit down, wait like a respectable man, but there is nothing respectable about the way I want her.

I take a slow breath, then move. The dressing room isn't big, just enough space for a bench and a full-length mirror, but I slip inside before she even realizes what's happening. She's mid-motion, reaching for the zipper on her skirt when she startles, eyes widening as I press the curtain shut behind me.

"Max—"

I silence her with a hand over her mouth, stepping in close, so close that I can hear the sharp inhale through her nose. "You have to be quiet," I murmur, my voice low, teasing. "We're not alone, Sparrow."

She swallows, nodding once. I let my hand brush the curve of her jaw before trailing lower, my fingers skimming the delicate fabric of her top. Her pulse is a wild drumbeat beneath my touch. She could push me away. Instead, she lifts her chin, watching me like she already knows exactly what I plan to do next.

Slowly, deliberately, I slide my hand down her side and find the zipper on her skirt. I just press my fingers into the fabric, feeling the warmth of her beneath it.

"This is reckless," she whispers, but she doesn't stop me.

I smirk, planting my lips against the shell of her ear. "Like I said, I like the shadows. Guess I'm just trying to live up to expectations."

The quiet rasp of the zipper sliding down the fabric, slow, as if every pull is stretching the moment. It fills the tiny space, loud to my ears, and then the fabric slips over her hips and pools at her feet. She's standing in nothing but that sheer, barely-there shirt and lace underwear that does nothing to hide how much she wants me.

Her breathing stutters. I don't stop.

With painstaking precision, I begin unbuttoning her shirt. One. Two. Three. I take my time, watching her expression with each slow reveal of her skin. When I reach the last button, I push the fabric from her shoulders, letting it drift to the floor, leaving her standing in nothing but black lace, heels, and temptation.

Wrenley exhales, a quiet sound of anticipation. "Max, someone could—"

I cut her off by pressing her against the wall, caging her between my arms. "Then you better be very, very quiet," I murmur, my mouth hovering just over hers, teasing, waiting.

She doesn't resist. As I drop to my knees, she braces herself against the wall, fingers curling against the cool surface.

My hands slide down the length of her thighs, my palms savoring the smooth skin before I hook my thumbs into the lace at her hips, dragging my nose along the sensitive skin just above the waistband.

I breathe her in, groaning softly. "You're already wet for me, Sparrow."

She bites her lip, trying to stay silent. I press a kiss just above the lace, then another. *Slow, patient, torturous.* "Tell me..." Pressing my tongue against the delicate fabric, making her gasp.

"Were you thinking about this when you walked out there in that outfit?"

Her nails scrape against the wall, her voice a breathy whisper. "Maybe."

I chuckle, dark and full of promise. "Maybe?"

I nip at her hipbone, making her body jolt.

"*Yes,*" she hisses, her voice barely audible.

That's all I need. The dressing room is small, and the boutique is full of people just on the other side of the curtain. But none of it matters. Right now, there's only her pressed against the wall, breathless and willing.

And me, on my knees, ready to ruin her. I lift one of her legs, guiding it over my shoulder, spreading her just how I want. Her breath hitches, her fingers tightening against the wall. My hands grip her thighs, holding her in place as I shift the lace of her panties to the side, exposing her completely to me.

I press a slow, deliberate kiss to the inside of her thigh, just high enough that she squirms. Then, dragging my nose across her slick heat, I savor the way she trembles, the way her body instinctively leans into me.

"Max—" she breathes, barely a sound.

I prod her clit with my tongue, light at first, teasing, before pressing firmer, circling slow and purposeful. She gasps, her head falling back against the wall. My name leaves her lips again, this time in a barely-restrained moan.

"Quiet, Sparrow," I murmur against her, my voice vibrating over her most sensitive spot.

She bites her lip, muffling a sound as I work her over with my mouth, alternating between long, slow strokes and quick, calculated motions. I move one hand between her thighs, slipping a finger inside her, groaning at how tightly she clenches around me.

"Fuck, you feel good," I say, my words lost between the steady strokes of my tongue. "Always so ready for me."

Her hand flies to my hair, tugging me closer, her body beginning to shake. I curl my finger inside her, adding another, pressing against that spot that makes her hips jerk into my mouth.

"Max—" she gasps.

I suck her clit between my teeth, working her faster, pushing her towards the edge. Her whole body tenses, her thighs tightening around my head, her breath hitching, coming in short, desperate pants.

And then, she falls. Her release hits her hard, her body shuddering, her back arching against the wall. She bites down on her lip, struggling to stay silent as waves of pleasure roll through her. I don't stop until she's completely spent, until she goes boneless in my grip.

I press one last lingering kiss against her before pulling back lightly, my lips still glistening with her release.

"The way you felt just now?" I rasp, my voice thick with lust. I stand, dragging my fingers up her body, over the trembling muscles of her stomach, up to cup her face. "That's what you do to me, Sparrow. Every second I'm around you, I'm fighting not to take you. My control is a very, *very* fragile thing when it comes to you."

She looks up at me, her pupils still blown, her breath still uneven.

"I like that," she whispers.

I grin, brushing my thumb over her bottom lip, before stepping back, grabbing her discarded clothes, and helping her back into them. We don't say another word as we slip out of the dressing room, but the way she looks at me, like she already wants more, tells me this isn't anywhere close to over.

The Ashford family office is everything I expected—cold, calculated, a reflection of the power and ruthlessness that built the empire inside it. The moment we step through the doors, the air shifts. Conversations hush, heads turn, eyes widen.

Wrenley doesn't falter. She walks ahead of me, her confidence radiating in the sharp click of her heels against the marble floors. Every inch of her, every precise step, every subtle tilt of her chin screams untouchable, untamable. She is a force of nature, and these people don't know whether to stare or run.

I stay a step behind, exactly where I belong right now, a shadow at her side. Not hidden, but present, silent, watching, *warning.* The suit I'm wearing is crisp, fitted, and understated compared to the ones the executives in this building wear. But I don't need expensive fabrics to command attention. The way I move, the weight of my presence, is enough.

Hugo walks in stride at my right, a solid wall of muscle and silent threat. His massive paws move soundlessly, his posture eerily disciplined for a dog of his size. He doesn't pant or wag his tail like some domesticated pet; he scans the room like he's working just as much as I am.

Good. Because I don't trust a single fucking person in this place.

The tension is thick as we pass the sea of desks and assistants who work under the Ashford name. Whispers trail behind us. Someone gasps. Someone else mutters something to the person next to them. They don't recognize me, not yet. But they will.

When we reach the double doors of the conference room, I step forward and pull them open for her. As she walks past me, she brushes her knuckles along mine, just a whisper of contact, a deliberate touch.

A quiet acknowledgment. A silent understanding. Then, she's inside, walking straight into the lion's den without so much as a twinge of hesitation.

I follow, taking my place just behind her chair, standing tall, arms at my sides, my expression unreadable.

Hugo sits beside me, his watchful stare locked on the people in front of us.

And the people? They fucking *freeze*.

Charles Ashford, Wrenley's father, sits at the head of the long table. He looks just like I remember, sharp, severe, with a presence that has always been more suffocating than impressive. His eyes narrow slightly as he takes in Wrenley, then glances over to me.

Beside him, her mother, Vivian, is poised and pristine, the picture of quiet cruelty. Her hands are neatly folded in front of her, her expression a mask of barely concealed disapproval.

The rest of the room is filled with lawyers and executives, men who have made their money through the Ashford family's reach. Their suits are expensive, their watches even more so.

But money doesn't impress me. Power does. And the only person in this room holding *real* power right now is the woman standing in front of them all.

I take my time pulling out Wrenley's chair. She lowers herself with slow precision, crossing her legs, squaring her shoulders in challenge. Her father exhales through his nose, a subtle sign of irritation.

"Wrenley," he says, his voice clipped, controlled.

She doesn't blink. "Father."

His gaze keeps coming back to me. His eyes are calculating, trying to place me. He won't find the answer. Not yet. He doesn't acknowledge Hugo at all. Mistake.

"You're late," he says.

Wrenley smiles, slow and sharp, like a blade being drawn. "No. I'm right on time."

I almost smirk... almost. But instead, I just stand there, arms loose at my sides, afraid that if I move them, I will pull the gun from my waistband and shoot him where he sits. But this is her moment. He has no fucking idea. Not yet. But he will.

Chapter Twenty-Five

WRENLEY

I LET my gaze drift from my father to my mother, lingering for a moment before finally acknowledging her. She looks over with sharp, assessing eyes before scoffing, lips curling in that signature expression of disapproval she's mastered over the years.

"Well," she says, her voice smooth but laced with something smug. "I see you've taken to... making statements with your wardrobe. Though you always did have a flair for the dramatic."

I straighten in my chair, tilting my head just slightly. "You know me, Mother. Always aiming to impress."

My father finally acknowledges Hugo, his brow furrowing as he takes in the massive dog behind me. "What is that doing here?"

Before I answer, I extend my hand in a silent command. Hugo, ever obedient, moves fluidly to sit at my side, his head easily clearing the table. His sheer size alone is enough to make the executives around us shift uncomfortably.

I let my fingers skim over his head. "I went to get him after Benjamin's funeral. I was worried he wouldn't be properly taken care of."

My father's face starts to redden, his jaw tightening.

"You had no right to be in that house," he says, his voice dangerously low.

I arch a brow, feigning surprise. "Did I not? That's interesting, considering Benjamin gave *me* a key."

Before he can snap back, a lawyer seated at the table clears his throat, eager to steer the meeting forward. "If we're all ready, I'd like to begin."

I shift my attention to him, offering him a sickly-sweet smile. "Oh, I'm ready." I glance at my parents. "Mother? Father?"

My mother rolls her eyes, exhaling as she mutters under her breath, *"I raised you better than this."*

I hear it, of course. And instead of biting back, instead of letting her get under my skin the way she's always done, I laugh. Loud. Sharp. Unapologetic. Her head jerks toward me, shocked by the response.

My father, losing what little patience he had, rubs his temples and sighs. "Yes. Let's begin."

The lawyer nods and opens a folder in front of him, pulling out a thick envelope with an embossed seal. He carefully breaks it open, withdrawing a letter. His gaze flits over the opening lines before he adjusts his glasses and begins reading aloud.

To my dear brother, Charles, and his ever-exquisite wife, Vivian,

There are very few things in this world that truly disappoint me, but I must confess, the way you raised Wrenley tops the list. You have spent her entire life molding her into a perfect porcelain doll, beautiful, poised, and silent. A pretty little thing to be placed upon a shelf and admired, but never truly free. That is the fame you call life. A game of appearances, of power built on a foundation of rot. And I, for one, find it tiresome.

Charles, you were not always the man you are

today. Once, you dreamed of more. Of better. But you let ambition twist you into something cruel, something hollow. And Vivian, well, you always did love the control, didn't you? A tightly wound string, wrapped so perfectly around your delusions that you mistook them for righteousness. I pity you both. But not enough to forgive you.

And now to you, Wrenley.

My sweet girl, my fierce and unbreakable renegade. You have no idea how proud I am of you. Not just for your strength, but for your heart. For choosing your own path, for refusing to let the wretchedness of this family blacken your soul. I should have done more for you. Should have fought harder, stayed closer, ensured you were never alone in the battles you faced. For that, I can never apologize enough.

But I hope now, you will allow yourself to trust the one person I did.

He's watching, you know. He's always been watching

My breath catches in my throat. He didn't need him to say a name; I didn't need any further clarification. I *know*. I *fucking* know. The silence that follows is thick, suffocating. I feel my mother's stare, razor-sharp. I don't look at her. I don't look at my father either, though I can feel the weight of his scrutiny pressing against me.

"Trust the one person he did?" my father finally says, a note of confusion threading through his otherwise flat tone.

My mother scoffs, irritated. "More of his theatrics. I swear, Benjamin always had a penchant for dramatics. Leaving riddles behind in death just as he did in life."

I keep my expression blank, offering nothing. But inside? Inside, my heart is *racing*. Because the man Benjamin trusted... the man who's been watching me? He's standing right fucking behind me.

The lawyer clears his throat, shifting uncomfortably in his seat as he glances down at the papers in front of him. "That brings us to the matter of the estate," He says, voice measured but cautious. "The mansion, vehicles, personal property, and all holdings tied to Mr. Benjamin Ashford."

I brace myself, already knowing where this is going.

"All of it," he continues, "has been left to Wrenley Ashford."

The air in the room turns from thick to thin like the most breakable of glass.

I blink. "Excuse me?"

The lawyer slides a thick packet of documents across the table toward me. "There are a few things requiring your signature, but as of today, the estate is yours."

My fingers hover over the papers, my mind spinning. The weight of it settles heavily in my chest. Then my father lets out a sharp, bitter laugh before slamming his hand against the table. His chair scrapes loudly as he pushes it back, his nostrils flaring.

"This is outrageous," he barks, eyes wild with fury. "That old, worn-down, *creepy* mansion should be torn down."

I snap out of my shock instantly, leaning back in my chair as I fix him with a slow, satisfied smile. "Well, it's *my* old, worn-down, *creepy* mansion, *Father*, and I plan on living in it."

My mother lets out a dramatic sigh, shaking her head with an air of exhaustion. "Of course you will."

I don't dignify her with a response, keeping my attention locked on my father. His jaw is clenched so tightly I half expect his teeth to crack. How odd to see my stone-faced father throwing a tantrum like a toddler. I turn my attention back to the lawyer, already anticipating my father's next move. And right on cue—

"And what about Benjamin's shares in Ashford International?" his voice is dangerously low.

The lawyer shifts uncomfortably in his seat, looking like he'd rather be anywhere but here. He scrolls through the documents in front of him, clears his throat, then stammers—

"Well... Mr. Ashford has left those to... Wrenley as well."

The room falls into complete silence, once again. My father's face drains of color, his fingers tightening into fists on the table.

I feel the slow burn of my mother's stare as she finally speaks. "This can't be right," she murmurs, voice sharp with disbelief. "He wouldn't."

The lawyer pushes his glasses up the bridge of his nose, visibly sweating. "It's all in order, Mrs. Ashford. The documents are legally binding."

My father's eye twitches, his whole body radiating barely contained rage. He looks like he's about to lose control, and I prepare myself for the inevitable explosion.

But before he can say a word, Max leans in. His voice is low, a whisper meant only for me. "Stay strong. Show no fear."

The lawyer shifts uncomfortably in his seat again. "Miss Ashford, you'll need to sign a few more documents to finalize the transfer."

I force myself to stay steady as I sign each one. The moment I'm done, I hold my copies behind me without looking, wordlessly passing them to Max. His fingers brush against mine as he takes them, his touch solid and steady.

The lawyer exhales in relief, clearly eager to be done with this. "This concludes the reading of the will. On behalf of my firm, we extend our deepest condolences for your loss."

I rise from my chair, smoothing my hands over my skirt before shaking the lawyer's hand with a wicked smile, my eyes never leaving my father.

"Well," I say, voice syrupy with false warmth. "I guess we'll be working together now."

He practically sneers, his voice razor-sharp as he spits out, "I guess so."

I arch a brow. "Try not to sound so excited."

His eyes darken, but before he can say anything else, my mother cuts in with a pointed glare. "I would suggest you take this seriously, Wrenley. The business of this family is not something to play with."

I smile at her, all teeth. "Oh, trust me, Mother. I take it very seriously."

Her eyes narrow, suspicion marring her expression. She doesn't trust me. *Good.* I turn on my heel and stride toward the door. Max is already there, holding it open.

Before stepping through, I call over my shoulder, "Hugo, *heirher komman.*"

My father flinches as Hugo immediately moves to my side, his massive frame casting a shadow over the table. Max and I exchange a look before walking to *my* office in perfect stride.

The moment the door swings shut behind us, I let out a slow breath, tension still curling in my stomach. Max watches me, eyes unreadable. "Are you okay?" he asks, his voice low.

I nod, glancing up at him. "Yeah," I say, barely above a whisper. "But I think I just declared war."

Before I can think twice, Max is on me. His hand tangles in my hair as his lips crush against mine, his kiss urgent and unrelenting. I gasp, and he takes advantage, deepening it, his tongue sweeping against mine in a way that steals the breath right from my lungs.

I press into him, fingers grasping the front of his shirt, pulling him impossibly closer. His hand slides down my waist, gripping just tight enough to make me feel owned. Heat pools low in my stomach, and I'm ready to lose myself in him completely.

A sharp knock at the door rips through the moment like a blade. Max lets out a low, frustrated growl but doesn't step away immediately. His forehead rests against mine, his breathing ragged. "You've got to be fucking kidding me," he mutters.

I laugh breathlessly. "Welcome to my life."

Another knock, louder this time. Max exhales harshly and steps away, smoothing down the front of his shirt before striding to the door. He swings it open, revealing the last person I want to see right now.

My mother.

She barely spares Max a glance before sweeping into the office with the confidence of someone who owns the place. Her sharp gaze scans the room, finally settling on Hugo, who lifts his head from where he's lying by the front windows.

"This is an office, Wrenley," she says, her voice clipped. "That *animal* should not be coming back here with you."

Before I can open my mouth to argue, Max steps in. "Where Wrenley goes, Hugo follows," he says, in a smooth, even but firm tone.

My mother turns to him, finally taking him in. Her gaze is assessing, cool, and then dismissive. Like she has already decided he isn't worth her attention.

She turns back to me. "And who, exactly, is this man? And why is he here?"

I pause, holding her stare for a long second before slowly smiling. A knowing, dangerous little grin.

"Oh, him?" I say, tilting my head. "He's my personal bodyguard."

Her eyes narrow slightly, and she turns to Max again, her expression unreadable. Max, to his credit, meets her gaze head-on and gives her a full-on shit-eating grin. "Where Wrenley goes," he says, his voice laced with dark amusement, "I follow."

My mother purses her lips like she has just tasted something bitter. She doesn't argue, doesn't acknowledge him further, just turns back toward the door.

But before stepping out, she pauses. "The dog," she says coldly, "will be a conversation for your father."

Then she's gone, leaving behind a trail of tension thick enough to choke on. The second the door clicks shut, I let out a long, slow breath.

Max walks to the desk, crossing his arms over his chest, watching me. "Personal bodyguard?"

I smirk, walking up to him. "You didn't expect me to introduce you as my stalker-turned-lover, did you?

He smirks. "I think I prefer obsessive shadow lurker."

I nudge him with my hip, and he steps back, shaking his head with amusement. "Come on, there is nothing to find, but let's search this place anyway."

I start with the desk and file cabinets. Max goes to the bar cart, running his hands along the wood panels. He crouches, inspecting the bottom.

"Found something," he mutters. He presses on one of the panels, and it shifts. A hidden compartment clicks open.

"Let's see what Benjamin was hiding," I say.

He pulls the panel open, retrieving a leather-bound notebook. It's thick, and the pages are slightly worn. I grab my purse and shove it inside without opening it. "Let's go." Max looks like he wants to protest and read it now, but just nods in agreement.

We step out of what is now *my* office, walking toward the elevators. Hugo keeps pace beside me, his hulking presence a comfort in a place that still reeks of my parents' control. The tension in my shoulders finally starts to ease when—

"Wrenley."

I stop. My stomach tightens, and my fingers flex at my side. I exhale slowly before turning around. My father stands a few feet away, his expression unreadable, but his gaze heavy. His tailored suit is sharp, his stance controlled, but something is lingering beneath the surface, something I can't quite place.

Max shifts beside me, his presence solid and unwavering. He doesn't touch me, doesn't speak, but he's there, a force just waiting to be unleashed. My father's eyes narrow as they drift to him.

His lips curl into something that isn't quite a smile. More like a knowing smirk. "You're Maximilian Blackwood."

I tense, but Max remains relaxed, his face unreadable.

He nods once. "I am."

"The fighter, right?" my father continues, his voice dipping slightly like he's savoring the words.

Max meets his gaze without hesitation. "Yeah. Once upon a time."

A long beat of silence stretches between them, something unspoken. My pulse pounds in my ears, but Max doesn't flinch, doesn't react, just watches my father with the same controlled ease he carries like armor.

My father exhales through his nose, looking between us, then shakes his head slightly, as if amused. "Interesting."

That single word feels like a loaded gun.

He turns to me next, his expression hardening. " Princess, you made quite the entrance today."

I tilt my head, forcing a pleasant expression. "It was a lovely meeting."

His jaw tics. He doesn't acknowledge the sarcasm. Instead, his gaze drops to Hugo, who stands beside me like a living shadow.

"This," he says, nodding at the dog. "It's not happening. That animal does *not* belong in the office."

Hugo lets out a low chuff, almost like he's laughing at the absurdity of the statement.

I school my features, falling into the same cold, detached expression my mother has mastered. My voice is calm, clipped, and perfectly measured.

"Father," I say smoothly, my fingers curling around the edges of my purse. "The dog is not the problem here."

His nostrils flare, but he doesn't argue. He only holds my stare for a moment longer before nodding, something unreadable flashing through his eyes.

I don't wait for him to speak again. I turn on my heel and step into the elevator. Max follows without hesitation, and Hugo moves in beside him, his shoulder brushing Max's leg.

Just before the doors close, I meet my father's gaze one last time.

"See you soon."

The doors slide shut, cutting off whatever response he might have had. A long silence fills the elevator as we descend. Finally, Max lets out a low chuckle, shaking his head.

I glance at him. "What?"

His lips twist into a smirk, but there's something darker beneath it. "You really don't give a damn what he thinks, do you?"

My mind wanders back to a time when my father's voice wasn't laced with bitterness. I'm small again, running through the sprawling gardens of the estate, my laughter ringing out like music. He's there, tall and strong, with a smile that could warm even the coldest corners of the mansion. His hands are always steady when he lifts me up onto his shoulders, the scent of his cologne mixing with the fresh air. "Come on, Princess," he'd say, his voice light and full of affection as he pointed out the world around us. "You're the only one who can catch the sun." I would giggle, my tiny fingers gripping his hair as we raced through the fields, the sound of my heartbeat syncing with his every step.

But that warmth faded as quickly as it had come. I remember the cold distance growing between us as I got older, each opinion I voiced, each question I asked, pushing him further away. The adoration in his eyes evaporated, replaced by a look of disdain. He started calling me "Princess" less like a term of endearment and more like a mocking reminder of who he once thought I should be, an obedient, compliant little girl. It became clear that the more I grew into myself, the more he resented me for it.

My chest tightens at the memory, the sting of that lost connection still raw, even after all these years. And now, standing before Max, I realize how much I truly distanced myself from the man I once tried so hard to please.

I lift my chin, "Not anymore."

He watches me for a long moment, his gaze unreadable. Then, without warning, he reaches over, threading his fingers through mine, squeezing just once. I squeeze back. And we don't say another world the whole ride down.

Chapter Twenty-Six

MAXIMILIAN

THE PENTHOUSE IS QUIET, save for the soft rustle of paper and Wrenley's steady breathing. The city sprawls beyond the floor-to-ceiling windows, glowing with a million lights, but inside, the world has narrowed to just the two of us.

She's perched on my lap, one leg draped over the arm of the oversized leather chair in my bedroom, her back resting against my chest. Her body fits against mine like I was made to hold her. My arms rest loosely around her waist, fingers idly tracing patterns over the silky material of her shirt. She's stolen another one of mine, unbuttoned enough to keep my attention locked on the exposed skin beneath.

The small, worn, leather notebook we found at the office rests between us, pages filled with Benjamin's elegant but hurried handwriting. She flips through it, her fingers ghosting over the ink. "I still can't believe this was just sitting there, in the bar cart of all places," she murmurs

I smirk against the shell of her ear, inhaling the faint trace of her perfume. "Ben always did like to keep things hidden in plain sight."

She exhales sharply, shifting slightly. My grip tightens instinctively, fingers splaying across her waist, keeping her against me.

The feel of her warmth grounds me in a way I don't have the patience to unpack.

Her voice lowers, barely above a whisper. "It's all here, isn't it?" She doesn't look at me, but I can hear the weight of the realization in her tone. "Everything my father has been doing, everything he was trying to pull Benjamin into."

I lean forward, resting my chin on her shoulder as I turn the page. "Looks like Benjamin was documenting everything. Either as insurance... or as a warning."

She scans the list of names again, some familiar, some unknown, but all connected in a way that reeks of corruption. My gaze follows hers, settling on the one name that appears more than any other. *Charles Ashford.*

"He knew," she murmurs, her fingers clenching slightly. "He knew exactly what they were doing. He just didn't know how to stop it."

I tighten my grip on her waist, my voice steady. "And now we do."

She nods, but I can feel the tension humming beneath her skin. Wrenley has always been fire, but this... this is something else. A quiet storm is rolling in, ready to burn everything down.

And so help me, I will stand at her side while she strikes the match. Her fingers continue to glide over the inked pages again before she finally speaks.

"We could ruin them."

I smirk. "We *will.*"

She's quiet for a moment and then shakes her head. "No, Max... that won't stop them." She turns her head, her lips dangerously close to mine, eyes dark with something I've never seen in them before. "They need to be taken out." A pause. *"Permanently."*

A slow, dark grin spreads across my lips. "Careful, *Sparrow.* Say things like that, and I might think you deserve a crown."

She tilts her head, her voice unwavering. "Maybe I do."

That sends something dark and possessive curling in my chest. I press a kiss just below her ear, my voice a low murmur. "That's dangerous shit to admit."

She exhales sharply, but she doesn't pull away. Instead, she leans into me. She's quiet for a long moment, closing the book and absently running fingers over the notebook's spine. When she finally speaks again, her voice is steady, but there's something deeper beneath it.

"My father doesn't like to lose."

I smirk against her skin. "Neither do I."

She studies me for a beat like she's weighing my words, deciding if she truly believes them. Then slowly, a smile curves her lips to match mine.

"Good."

The air shifts between us, the weight of everything momentarily forgotten in the thick, magnetic pull. Her body shifts, her legs adjusting in my lap. She's not oblivious to the effect she has on me. I tilt my head, my nose grazing the column of her throat. "You should be in bed, Sparrow."

She turns just enough so that her lips nearly brush mine. "I am."

Damn her. My fingers tighten on her waist, my pulse hammering beneath my skin. Her body presses just a little closer, her breath warm against my lips. "You keep looking at me like that, Wrenley, and I won't be able to stop myself."

She flutters her lashes, feigning innocence. "Who said I want you to?"

Fuck.

A low growl rumbles in my throat as I capture her lips, my hand threading into her hair, tilting her head to deepen the kiss. She melts into me, fingers sliding into my hair, tugging, pulling, pushing me closer.

The notebook slides from her lap, forgotten, as I lift her effortlessly, her legs wrapping around my waist. *For tonight,* I tell myself as I walk us to the bed, *we take what we want.* War can wait until morning.

The world outside fades away, reduced to nothing but the warmth of her skin beneath my hands and the way her lips move against mine, slow, deliberate, consuming. This isn't like before. It's not a firestorm of desperation or unchecked fury.

It's different. *Deeper.* I lay her down, taking my time, my weight settling over her like a promise. She sighs against my mouth, fingers threading into my hair, pulling me closer, melting into me, becoming a part of her.

My hands explore the curves I've already committed to memory, but tonight, I take my time. I need her to feel this, to understand what she's doing to me. I break the kiss, my lips trailing down her neck, lingering over her collarbone. Her skin is warm and fevered. I can feel the way her pulse jumps beneath my mouth.

"You're dangerous, Sparrow," I murmur against her skin.

A shiver runs through her, and she arches into me, offering me more. "I thought you were the dangerous one," she whispers back, her voice teasing, breathless.

I chuckle, low and dark, dragging my teeth lightly over her shoulder. *She has no idea.* "I think we both are."

My fingers slip beneath the hem of her shirt, dragging it up inch by inch, exposing the soft skin of her stomach. I lift it over her head, tossing it aside before kissing her again, slow and deep, like I have all the time in the world.

She tries to push for more, her hands sliding under my shirt, nails scraping against my abs, but I pull back, smirking.

"You're trying to rush me," I murmur.

A breathless laugh escapes her lips. "Maybe."

I slide my fingers down her ribs, my touch light, teasing. "Not tonight, Sparrow." Then my mouth is on her breast, my tongue tracing a slow, maddening circle around her nipple before I suck it into my mouth. Her back arches, her moan soft, but needy.

I slide my hand lower, over her stomach, my fingers dipping

beneath the waistband of her panties. I take my time, running a single knuckle over the slick heat between her thighs, teasing.

"Maximillian," she breathes, already trembling beneath me.

I groan against her skin, the sound rough. "Say it again."

She threads her fingers through my hair and tugs, her voice laced with frustration and desire. "Maximillian."

My restraint snaps. I grip her panties and drag them down her legs, my mouth following, leaving a trail of open-mouthed kisses along her hip bones, down the inside of her thigh. I settle between her legs, my breath hot against her center, before I press a slow, lingering kiss right where she needs me most.

She gasps, her hips jerking, but I hold her down, keeping her exactly where I want her. I run my tongue over her, slow and torturous, tasting her, savoring her.

"Fuck, Sparrow," I groan, flicking my tongue against her clit.

She moans, her fingers tightening in my hair, her body already trembling beneath me. I keep going, pushing her closer, dragging her higher, until she's writhing, panting my name like a plea.

Then she shatters. Her thighs tense, her back arches, and she comes apart on my tongue, her release coating my mouth, her moans breaking into breathless gasps. I give her one last, slow stroke before moving back up her body, pressing my lips to hers. She's still trembling, still catching her breath. I love the way she tastes, love the way her body responds to me.

Her hands are already moving, fumbling with the waistband of my sweats, pushing them down. I help her, lifting my hips, letting her free me completely. Her fingers wrap around my cock, stroking me in slow, teasing pulls.

I groan, resting my forehead against hers, my control slipping. "You're killing me."

She smirks, her thumb circling the head of my cock, dragging her nails lightly along the underside. "I thought you didn't break so easily."

I growl, grabbing her free arm and pinning it above her head.

"Oh, Sparrow," I murmur, my voice rough with need. "You have no idea what you do to me."

But she proves me wrong. Because in the next breath, she pushes against my chest, catching me off guard as she rolls me onto my back. My brows lift in amusement, but my smirk is pure hunger.

"You think you're in charge now?" I murmur, watching her with dark, hooded eyes.

She straddles me, her slick heat rubbing against my cock, teasing us both. She leans down, her lips barely grazing mine. "I *know* I am."

My hands slide up her thighs, gripping her hips. I'm barely holding myself back. She drags her nails down my chest, her touch sending fire through my veins. "Feels good, doesn't it?" She whispers, rolling her hips, letting my cock slide through her wetness.

"Fuck, Wrenley," I growl, my fingers digging into her skin. "You're playing a dangerous game."

She smirks, her hand bracing against my chest. "And what are you going to do about it?"

I don't get a chance to answer. Because she sinks down onto me, taking me inch by inch, stretching around me in the most intoxicating way. A guttural moan rips from my throat as she starts to move, rolling her hips and finding her rhythm.

"Fucking Christ, Sparrow." My control is slipping. My restraint is gone.

I thrust up into her, matching her movements, taking us both higher. She gasps, moans, leans forward, and captures my lips with hers, swallowing both of our sounds.

I slip a hand between us, my thumb pressing against her clit, rubbing slow, firm circles.

"Max—" My name is a breathless moan, a plea, and I know she's close.

"Cum for me, Sparrow," I rasp, thrusting into her harder.

She does. Her body tightens, her release hitting her in waves as she cries out my name. I follow a second later, burying myself deep as I spill inside her, my head falling back against the pillows, my breath ragged.

For a long moment, neither of us moved. She collapses against my chest, our heartbeats pounding in sync, our bodies still trembling with the aftershocks of pleasure. I wrap my arms around her, holding her close, pressing a slow, lingering kiss to her shoulder.

"Fucking *hell,* Sparrow." I breathe, my voice hoarse. "You're going to ruin me."

She smiles against my skin, pressing a kiss to my jaw. "Good."

We stay like that for a while, tangled in each other, the world outside forgotten. Eventually, I roll us onto our side, keeping her pressed against me as I pull the blanket over us.

Neither of us speaks. We don't have to. Because for the first time in a long time, everything feels exactly as it should.

By morning, the warmth beside me is gone.

I reach out instinctively, my fingers brushing against the cool sheets where Wrenley should be. My eyes snap open, and for a second, I listen, searching for any sign of her.

The faint hum of voices filters in from the living room. I exhale, scrubbing my hand down my face before throwing the covers off. My body still hums from last night, my muscles sore in all the best ways. Wrenley is a force, one I never saw coming, one I don't think I'll ever be able to walk away from.

I pull on a pair of sweats, followed by a black t-shirt, and step out of the bedroom, following the sound of her voice. As I round the corner, I find her standing behind Elias, a steaming cup of coffee in her hands. She's barefoot, wearing my shirt, her long legs exposed, and her hair a little messy from sleep. I cross my arms over my chest and lean against the wall, watching.

"Not hard at all," Elias is saying, his fingers flying across the keyboard as multiple screens flicker with feeds I don't recognize, "I could have it set up in a couple of days, tops."

Wrenley sips her coffee, considering. "And no one would know?

Elias snorts. "Please. You're talking to a professional, princess—"

"*Don't* call me that," she interrupts, her tone sharp. Of course, she doesn't like her father's nickname for her.

Elias grins but doesn't correct himself. "No one will have a damn clue. I'll make sure of it."

I decide to make my presence known then, stepping up beside Wrenley and plucking the coffee cup right out of her hands.

She startles slightly before turning to glare at me. "Excuse you."

I take a sip, black, strong, exactly how she likes it, before arching a brow. "You're really going to move into that place?"

She shrugs, stretching her arms above her head. The movement lifts my shirt higher on her thighs, making it incredibly hard for me to focus.

"Well, my apartment is three hours away." She points out, "And that's a hell of a commute."

I take another slow sip of coffee, considering. Then, casually, I say, "You could always move in here with me."

Silence. Elias stops typing. Wrenley blinks. I feel the weight of Elias's stare before I even turn my head. He's gaping at me like I just suggested we take Hugo skydiving.

He finally finds his voice. "Wait. *Wait.*" He shoves back from the desk, twisting in his chair to face me fully. "Did you just—*did you just invite her to move in?*"

Wrenley recovers before I do, smirking into her now-empty hands. "That's what it sounded like to me."

Elias looks between us, then back at me, his expression torn between amusement and pure, unfiltered disbelief. "This is happening. This is *really* happening. The great Maximilian Blackwood—the same guy who once told me, and I quote, 'people are liabilities, and attachments are distractions'—is now offering *cohabitation* like it's a casual Tuesday."

I roll my eyes, shoving the coffee cup back into Wrenley's hands. "Don't be so dramatic, Brother."

Elias throws his hands up. "Oh, I'm sorry, am *I* the dramatic one here? Because I just watched you go full domestic over here like we're in a goddamn rom-com."

Wrenley giggles, sipping her coffee again as she watches us like this is the most entertaining thing she's ever seen.

I arch a brow at her. "You haven't said no."

She tilts her head, studying me, then a slow, devious smile spreads across her lips.

"Or..." she muses, dragging out the word, "*you* could move into my big, creepy mansion with me."

Elias snorts, slapping a hand against his thigh. "Oh, now *that* I would pay to see. Big bad Max lurking through the dark hallway, making every floorboard creak." He leans back in his chair, shaking his head. "You know what? I'll even come too. I can be the live-in IT guy. We'll turn that Gothic hellhole into the most well-surveilled haunted house on the East Coast."

Wrenley hums, pretending to consider it. "That's true. I *could* use someone to monitor the cameras. But that means you'd have to move out of your little hacker cave here, Elias. Do you even *own* a bed?"

Elias gasps, clutching his chest. "Wow. *Wow.* First, Max goes soft, and now you're coming for *my* lifestyle? This is a dark day, Wrenley. A dark, *dark* day."

I shake my head, reaching out and tugging her against me. She stumbles slightly, laughing into my chest as I curl an arm around her waist.

"I'm not moving into your haunted house," I murmur against her hair.

She grins up at me. "Not even if I ask nicely?"

Elias groans loudly. "Oh, for fucks sake, just marry her already and put me out of my misery."

I shoot him a glare, but Wrenley just laughs, taking another sip of coffee as if she's thoroughly enjoying watching me squirm.

"Careful, Sparrow," I murmur. "You keep pushing, and I just might."

Her breath hitches, and that smug grin falters, just for a second. I grin. Yeah. She's not the only one who can play this game.

Chapter Twenty-Seven

WRENLEY

TWO WEEKS.

That's how long it's been since I stood in my family's office and changed everything. Since I looked my father in the eye and let him know I wasn't going anywhere. Since I decided to take the fight directly to them.

And now, here I am. Standing in the grand foyer of *my* mansion, something I once ran from. The air feels heavier here, charged with the ghosts of the past and the weight of the present. But this time, I'm not alone. I square my shoulders and welcome the smile.

I convinced Max to move in first, though, if I'm being honest, it didn't take much effort. He pretended to grumble about it, saying something about preferring the penthouse, but I saw the way he watched when I first brought it up. Like he was already planning where he'd position the security cameras before I even got the full sentence out.

Elias, on the other hand, had required a bit more convincing. He's convinced the place is haunted, which, considering the creaks and occasional unexplained noises, might not be too far from the truth. He said, *and I quote*, 'I don't fuck with ghosts, Wrenley,' which sent me into a full-blown fit of laughter. But in the end, he relented, mostly because he knew Max wasn't going to let me live here alone.

And Margot? Margot took the most effort. "This house is going to eat me in my sleep," she muttered under her breath as she hauled her suitcase up the stairs.

I turned to her with a smirk. "Hugo will protect you."

She shoots the massive dog a wary look. "He'd probably help."

I just laughed, rolling my eyes before throwing an arm around her shoulders. "You'll be fine."

She sighed dramatically, "I swear to God, Wren, if I see a single Victorian-era ghost child, I'm burning this place to the ground."

A few hours later, I stand in the center of the grand hallway, taking it all in: the dark wood paneling, the vintage chandeliers, the eerie paintings that Benjamin curated over the years, and I feel something settle in my chest. This is mine now. It doesn't feel real yet. Benjamin is gone, his home is now my home. It will feel real soon enough.

Max walks in from the study, rolling up the sleeves of his Henley, looking at home despite his earlier grumbling about "living in a goddamn museum."

"Cameras are set up," he says, coming to stand beside me, his shoulder brushing mine. "Elias is finishing the wiring in the basement."

I glance at him, arching a brow, "And Margot?"

He smirks. "Last I checked, she was measuring the wine cellar for a mini-bar."

I chuckle, shaking my head. "Sounds about right."

His finger brushes against mine, a small, fleeting touch that still spikes that fiery energy between us. "You okay?"

I exhale, scanning the vast space in front of me. "Yeah, I am ready to get started," I say, rolling my shoulders back, already shifting into focus mode.

Max turns to me, one brow quirked as he crosses his arms over his broad chest. "First food, then we plan.

I open my mouth to argue, but he just levels me with a look, the kind that brooks no argument.

I sigh dramatically. "Fine, I'll cook."

A smirk tugs at the corner of his lips when Elias walks up, clapping his hands together. "Fucking finally, domestic Wrenley has entered the chat."

I roll my eyes, already making my way toward the kitchen. "Go get food before I change my mind."

Max chuckles, and Elias grumbles about why we can't just order something as they head out the front door. Once they're gone, I take a moment to re-familiarize myself with the kitchen. It's massive and outfitted with every high-end appliance imaginable, but I wouldn't expect anything less from Benjamin. He loved to cook when he wasn't busy scheming against the family empire, that is.

I'm opening cabinets, trying to find the right pans, when I hear the telltale sounds of feet tapping across the marble floor.

Margot saunters in, balancing four bottles of wine against her chest like she just made the haul of the century. She slams them onto the counter with a grin. "I come bearing gifts."

I glance at the labels and let out a low whistle. "Jesus, Margot. You just went straight for the top shelf, huh?"

She smirks, "Obviously."

I pick the bottles up one at a time and turn them over in my hand. Château *Margaux 2015, Opus One 2018, Domaine de la Romanée-Conti, and Screaming Eagle Cabernet Sauvignon.*

I blink. "You do realize these bottles cost more than some people's rent, right?"

Margot shrugs, already reaching for glasses. "And, doesn't living here make us the 1% now?"

I just shake my head, laughing as I pull out a Bluetooth

speaker from the center island. "Fine. But if we're doing this, we're doing it right." Margot chooses her 'badass playlist', the music blares to life, and Margot lets out an excited whoop, spinning in place before pouring us both full glasses of wine.

By the time the guys return, Margot and I are already onto our second bottle, dancing around the kitchen. "Little Girl Gone" by Chinchilla fills the kitchen.

Max and Elias step inside, grocery bags in hand, only to stop dead in their tracks.

Margot and I don't notice at first, too wrapped up in the song, singing at the top of our lungs, moving in sync with the music.

"I like your blood on my teeth just a little too much."

Margot grabs my hand, twirling me dramatically before flipping her hair over her shoulder like she's performing for a sold-out crowd. Max just stares, blinking like he can't quite process what's happening.

Elias, on the other hand, whistles low under his breath. "Well. I guess we missed the pregame."

Margot clocks them in the doorway and immediately marches up to Elias, yanking one of the bags out of his grip and placing it on the counter. Then, without warning, she grabs both his hands and *forces* him to drop the rest.

"Margot—" Elias barely has time to protest before she drags him into the middle of the kitchen.

"Nope," she declares, pointing at him with a manicured finger. "You are dancing, it's house rules."

Elias groans but lets her pull him in any way, and within seconds, they're moving to the beat, Margot grinding against him while Elias just throws his hands up like *What the fuck is happening?*

I'm laughing so hard I nearly spill my wine. Max steps beside me, crossing his arms, watching the scene with an expression torn between amusement and utter disbelief.

I turn to him, grinning. "You look like you have something to say."

His lips twitch like he's fighting a smile. "I was just going to ask if I should be worried about the kitchen."

I smirk. "Oh, you should definitely be worried."

He shakes his head, leaning against the counter as Margot yells. "*Faster, Cade!*" before dramatically dipping herself in Elias' arms.

Elias just sighs, shooting Max a look, "Kill me."

Max chuckles, finally grabbing one of the bags and setting it down. "Not before a last meal."

I take a long sip of wine, laughing as I watch Margot spin Elias again, feeling lighter than I have in weeks. The kitchen is warm with the lingering scents of dinner, the air still carrying the hum of laughter from earlier. We've worked our way through almost all of Margot's ridiculous wine collection, and I'm feeling pleasantly buzzed, my limbs loose but my mind sharp.

I reach for the last unopened bottle, holding it up with a smirk before popping the cork. "Alright," I say, pouring myself a glass, "I have a plan on where to start."

The mood shifts in an instant. Max, Elias, and Margot straighten in their seats, all traces of humor melting into focus. Max leans back, elbows resting on the chair's arm, his dark eyes locked onto mine with quiet intensity.

Elias, on the other hand, kicks his feet up onto the chair next to him, swirling his glass of wine like this is about to be some casual business meeting.

Margot, though still perched on the counter, sets her drink down, her curiosity piqued.

I take a breath and lean forward, my fingers tapping the stem of my glass. "When I was doing some digging into one of the names in the notebook—Carter Moretti— I traced some assets back to a warehouse on the outskirts of town. Minimal security. No big paper trails leading back to it, but just enough bread-crumbs to make me suspicious."

Elias immediately pulls out his phone, already typing. "Address?"

I nod, rattling it off from memory. "I think it's one of the places they're using to house illegal weapons before they distribute them."

Max's expression darkens, his fingers tapping against the table. "What kind of weapons?"

"I don't know yet," I admit. "Could be anything. Small firearms, military-grade equipment, we won't know until we get inside."

Max tilts his head, considering. "And what exactly do you want to do with this warehouse, Sparrow?"

I meet his gaze head-on, my tone steady. "Hit it. Take every-thing. Then go after the ones who own it."

Elias turns, glancing at Max with a grin. "Have I mentioned how much I like her?"

Max doesn't look away from me. "This is going to put a target on your back."

I smirk. "I already have a target on my back."

Margot clears her throat. "Okay, just for clarification, we're talking about *stealing* an entire warehouse full of illegal weapons and, what? Just keeping them?"

I shake my head. "Yes. I want to make it a liability for them. If we take it, they're going to scramble to cover their tracks. It's going to put pressure on the supply chain, which means they're going to start making mistakes. And mistakes are what we need."

Elias gives a full smile. "Oh, yeah. I *really* like her."

Max exhales through his nose, shaking his head slightly, but there's something in his eyes, a glint of admiration. "And you think it's just going to be that easy?"

"No," I say simply. "But it's the first step."

A charged silence fills the space.

Max finally leans forward, resting his forearms on the table. "Alright, Sparrow. Let's plan a heist."

I set my glass down, the weight of what we're about to do settling over me. "We don't have a lot of time. If we hit it on Sunday, we should be able to get in and out before they have a chance to move anything."

Max nods, considering. "Sunday gives us two days to prepare. It'll be quiet—most shipments don't go out until Monday morning."

"Exactly," I say, glancing at Elias. "I need you to get inside their security systems. I want eyes on that place before we set foot near it. How many guards are scheduled, what their rotations look like, *everything*."

Elias smirks. "Already ahead of you, sweetheart." He thumbs through his phone, pulling up something on his screen before sliding it toward me. "Pulled the satellite images earlier. It's got standard perimeter fencing, cameras, and two entry points. If it's anything like other warehouses, there'll be a guard inside the control room. I can loop the feeds, but we'll still have to deal with anyone physically there."

Max taps a finger against the screen, eyes sharp. "I can get some guys to help with that. We'll need to keep it quiet. No unnecessary noise, no unnecessary bodies."

I nod, then turn to Margot, "Mags, I need you up the road, dressed like *sin*, pretending your car broke down. If someone gets too close or something seems off, you let us know and distract them."

Margot raises a brow, unimpressed. "So you want me to be the bait?"

I smirk, "I want you to be a distraction. There's a difference."

She rolls her eyes but grins. "Fine. But I'm picking my own outfit, and it's going to be dangerously short."

Elias hums. "Damn, this just became my favorite part of the plan."

Max gives him a deadpan look. "Focus."

Elias sighs. "Fine, but if she's part of the plan, I'm sticking with her. No way she's out there alone if someone actually shows up."

I shoot Margot a knowing glance. "Good luck getting him to shut up for an entire stakeout."

Margot smirks. "I've got ways."

Elias raises a brow, intrigued. "I'd love to hear them."

Max groans. "Can we get back to the *actual* plan?"

I laugh but refocus. "Okay. Here's how it plays out. Elias loops the cameras, and we go in quietly. If the guards inside are minimal, we take them out non-lethally. There's no need to raise alarms. Max, you get your guys with some trucks in position before we breach."

Max nods. "Once we secure the warehouse, what's next?"

I meet his gaze. "We take everything. Every last weapon, every crate. We move it before they can."

Elias grins. "And where exactly are we moving an entire warehouse full of illegal weapons?"

I smile. "We keep what we want for a rainy day, and destroy the rest."

Max watches me carefully, his fingers drumming against the table. "This is bold, Sparrow."

I tilt my head, "Is that concern I hear?"

He leans in slightly, voice low. "It's admiration."

A slow, knowing smirk curves my lips. "Good. Then let's make some chaos."

Chapter Twenty-Eight

MAXIMILIAN

"WE ALL NEED to get some sleep," I say, pushing back from the table. "The next two days are going to be long as hell."

Wrenley stands, but the moment she does, she wobbles slightly on her feet. I'm at her side before she can stumble, my hands firm on her waist.

She giggles, the sound light and unguarded, her fingers clutching at my forearms for balance. "Whoa. Okay, maybe the wine finally hit."

I smirk. "Yeah, no shit."

Elias leans back in his chair, grinning. "I'd say some of us need sleep more than others."

Margot swirls the last of her wine in her glass, eyeing Wrenley with amusement. "Or maybe just some water first."

Wrenley waves them off, but when she leans into me, her body warm and pliant, I tighten my hold, steadying her.

"I've got her," I say, cutting off whatever smart-ass comment Elias is about to make.

Elias shrugs, his smirk widening. "Hey, I wasn't gonna say anything."

Margot snorts. "Liar."

I shake my head and guide Wrenley toward the stairs, her steps slow but deliberate as we make our way to the room. She's tipsy but not wasted. Just loose, flushed from the wine, her guard lowered in a way that makes her look softer than usual.

And maybe a little too damn tempting. When we reach the door, she looks up at me through heavy-lidded eyes, her lips slightly parted.

"Alright, bedtime, Sparrow."

She pouts but doesn't argue as I push open the door. Once inside, she moves to strip off her jeans, but her fingers fumble with the button. She lets out a frustrated sound.

I huff a laugh, stepping in. "Here, let me."

She rests her hands on my chest for balance, looking up at me as I undo the button and slowly slide the zipper down. Her breath hitches. Mine does too.

My fingers graze her hip bones, my knuckles skimming the soft skin of her stomach as I ease the denim down her legs. She steps out of them, her bare thighs brushing against mine.

Fuck.

She's standing there in nothing but her top and panties, looking at me like I'm the only thing in the world worth looking at. I swallow hard. This was supposed to be me getting her *to* bed, not me getting her *into* bed.

I clear my throat, stepping back. "Alright. Lie down."

She smirks. "You're bossy, you know that?"

I cross my arms. "And you're drunk."

She giggles and flops onto the bed, her hair fanning out over the pillows. I pull the blankets over her, but when I step back, she blinks up at me.

"What are you doing?"

I pause at the door. "Making calls."

She frowns. "Now?"

I nod. "Need to get some guys in place for the warehouse job."

She shifts onto her side, tucking her arm under her head. "You trust them?"

I hesitate. "They are the Serpents that stuck with me, I trust them with my life."

She sighs, studying me, her gaze searching for something. Then, softer, quieter, she asks, "Maximilian... this is going to work, right?"

The way she says my name, careful, unsure, but trusting, it does something to me. I move back to the bed, crouching so we're eye level. I run my knuckles down her cheek, watching the way her lashes flutter at the touch.

"Yes, Sparrow," I say, voice steady. "It's going to work."

She searches my face, looking for something, certainty maybe. Whatever she finds there seems to ease the tension in her shoulders.

She nods. "Okay."

I press a soft kiss to her forehead, lingering for just a second longer than I should.

Then I stand and force myself to step away.

"Sleep," I say. "Tomorrow, we get to work."

She hums, her eyes already slipping shut. I watch her for a moment longer, something tight coiling in my chest, before I slip out of the room. I rub a hand over my jaw, exhaling. There's still so much left to do. And not much time to do it.

The study is quiet, the kind of silence that settles deep in the bones, heavy with thought. Benjamin would be so proud of Wrenley, taking this all in stride, finishing what he started.

I lean back in the leather chair, phone in hand, flicking through contacts, mentally sorting who I can trust to watch my back, watch Wrenley's back, and not ask too many damn questions. I already know who they are.

I exhale sharply, dragging a hand down my face before tapping the call button to one of the few people who won't fuck this up.

The phone rings twice before a familiar gravel-rough voice answers. "Didn't think I'd be hearing from you this late, Boss."

A smirk tugs at the corner of my mouth. "Yeah, well, figured you could use something to do."

"Depends. Is it a beer run or a bloodbath?"

I huff a quiet laugh, "Bit of both."

Riot, his real name long buried, has been with me since the Black Serpents split. Loyal, lethal, and crazy enough to follow me through hell if I asked. If I need someone to pull a trigger without blinking, it's him.

"I need the crew," I tell him, all business now. "All four of you. Tactical gear, full comms. Cargo trucks. And we need guns, big ones."

There's a pause before he lets out a low hum. "Planning a fuckin' war, are we?

"Something like that."

I hear the rustling of movement on his end, picturing him already getting to work, probably grinning like a lunatic because he's been itching for something like this.

"You want clean or messy?" Riot asks.

"Clean... for now."

He chuckles darkly. "That's no fun."

I smirk. "Yeah, well, I'd rather not set off alarms before we even start."

He hums in agreement. "Fine, clean it is. I'll have everything ready. When do we move?"

"Sunday, I want to hit this warehouse before they have a chance to relocate."

"Done. I'll send you the details soon." He pauses, then, in a tone that's both half-amused and half-serious, he says, "You sure about this, Brother? Ashfords don't play fair."

I never had to tell him who we were going after; he always knew this day was coming. I glance toward the closed door, thinking about the woman currently sleeping upstairs, completely unaware of the war we're about to start.

The anger that's been simmering inside me for years coils tighter, ignited by the thought of Charles Ashford still thriving off the backs of the people he's crushed under his polished shoe. "I'm sure."

Riot exhales a short laugh, but there's steel beneath it. "Then let's burn these motherfuckers to the ground."

I barely pull the phone from my ear before he asks, "Where do you want the gear?"

"Benjamin Ashford's mansion."

Riot lets out a low chuckle. "Well. Well, that's a fuckin' choice."

I don't explain, I don't have to. "I need everything there by tomorrow afternoon."

"No later than noon," he confirms easily. "I'm always ready."

That much is true, Riot lives for this shit. The line clicks dead, and I set my phone down, dragging a hand over my jaw. This is it. No turning back. The next forty-eight hours. They'll decide everything.

The soft glow of the monitors lights up the study, shadows stretching across the walls as I sit back, scrolling through the satellite images Elias pulled up earlier. I've been staring at them for over an hour, mapping out every possible scenario, every weak point in security, every potential blind spot.

This must go perfectly. If we fuck up even a little, the Ashfords will know we're coming for them. I zoom in on the warehouse, noting the placement of the security cameras and the routes leading in and out. It's set back off the main road, with minimal coverage and no heavy patrols, exactly like Wrenley predicted.

"They got lazy," I mutter to myself

They don't expect someone to come for them. Not yet. I start placing the team in my head. I'll take the point with Riot. Elias will handle overwatch from the van, hacking into the security feed in real time. Wrenley will ride with me. There's no way in hell I'm letting her out of my sight.

And we'll be on my bike. A fast exit is always a smart move, and if shit goes south, we'll be gone before anyone knows what hit them. I can't risk the Ashfords knowing she is involved yet.

A soft ping breaks through the silence. I glance down at my phone.

Riot: Got your crew, boss. Handpicked for a proper fucking party.

I smirk, shaking my head before clicking the attachment.

Four names. All men I trust. And every single one of them is just as dangerous as they are insane.

-**Riot**: A demolition expert and combat psychopath with a taste for explosives and violence. Never seen a fight he didn't love.

-**Reaper**: Former military, a sniper so good he could thread a bullet through a needle at 800 yards. Quiet. Deadly. Doesn't miss.

-**Wrecker**: Built like a fucking wrecking ball, hence the name. Specializes in hand-to-hand combat and making people disappear.

-**Torque**: Best damn driver I've ever met. Can handle any vehicle, make any getaway look easy, and has a love for high-speed chaos.

I let out a low chuckle. It's a solid crew.

I type back.

Me: Good, I'll send the final layout soon. Noon tomorrow at the mansion.

The reply comes almost instantly.

Riot: You got it, Boss. Let's raise some hell.

I smirk and set my phone down, looking back at the screens. The weight of this is finally settling in. *Two more days.* It's tight, but it will work. And then we make our first real move against the Ashfords.

The final layout is set. The plan is solid. Every detail is accounted for. Still, I keep double-checking, staring at the screens, making sure nothing has been overlooked. I should go to bed, but my mind won't shut off. Too much is at stake.

That's when I hear it. Soft, almost distant at first, like a whisper carried through the halls.

A piano.

My head tilts, listening harder. The melody is familiar, haunting, slow, full of something aching. Then her voice joins it.

It's low and smoky, a little rough around the edges, but so fucking beautiful it stops me cold.

I push back from the desk, moving toward the sound.

The library. The door is cracked open, a sliver of warm light spilling into the hallway.

Inside, Wrenley sits at the grand piano, facing the massive floor-to-ceiling window that overlooks the garden. Moonlight washes over her, making her hair look like red ink, her body framed against the dark night beyond the glass.

Her fingers move effortlessly over the keys, each note resonating through the room, filling the space with something that feels almost too intimate to witness.

"What a wicked game you play..."

Her voice is quiet but drenched in emotion, the words curling around the music like smoke. Not just singing, feeling every word. I lean against the door frame, crossing my arms as I listen. I don't move. Don't interrupt. I just watch.

The song is slow, aching, a confession of want, loss, and inevitability. And fuck if it doesn't hit something deep in my chest. She plays through the entire song, lost in it, eyes closed as she sings the last lines. The final note lingers, fading into silence.

Before she can start another song, I push the door open farther. "That was hauntingly beautiful."

Wrenley jumps slightly, her fingers freezing on the keys.

She turns toward me, eyes wide with something close to

embarrassment. "Jesus, Maximillian, how long have you been standing there?"

I smirk, stepping into the room. "Long enough to know I need to hear it again."

Her lips press together, cheeks heating. "I don't... I don't sing in front of people."

I raise a brow. "Why?"

She shrugs, looking down at the piano keys. "I don't know. It just feels too... personal, I guess."

I tilt my head. "And your paintings aren't personal?"

She exhales a quiet laugh, shaking her head. "It's different?"

"How?"

Her fingers glide absently over the keys, not playing but moving as if they need something to do. "With painting, I can hide behind the canvas, I can say everything I want without ever having to speak it out loud."

I watch her closely, the way her eyes flick toward the window like she's still half-lost in the song.

"But when I sing..." she trails off, biting her lip. "There's no hiding."

I nod, understanding more than I probably should. Because I know what it's like to hide behind something, a name, a reputation, a carefully constructed wall built to keep people at a distance.

She must see something in my expression because she gives me a small, self-deprecating smile. "It's stupid, right?"

I step close, resting my hand against the top of the piano. "No, it's not."

Her lips part slightly, surprise flickering across her face.

"Why are you awake?" I ask, shifting the conversation.

She huffs out a soft laugh, rubbing her temples. "Well... I assume Margot is currently showing Elias exactly how she plans on distracting people..."

My brow furrows for half a second, then realization clicks.

The corner of my mouth lifts. "Thin walls?"

Wrenley groans, covering her face with her hands. "Solid house. *Thin* fucking walls."

I chuckle, shaking my head. "Guess their chemistry finally boiled over."

She peeks at me through her fingers. "You mean you didn't already hear it happening?"

My smirk deepens. "I was focused on something else."

Her blush darkens, but she holds my gaze, something unspoken crackling between us. An allure we both know won't go away.

Chapter Twenty-Nine

WRENLEY

"SING FOR ME AGAIN." Max's voice is low and rough in the quiet of the library.

I glance at him from where he's sitting beside me on the piano bench, his arm draped along the back, his body turned slightly toward mine. He's close, too close, and the warmth of him seeps into my skin, making it hard to think straight.

I shake my head, giving him a small, teasing smile. "Not a chance."

He leans in, his breath warm against my jaw. "Why not?"

I shrug, my fingers running over the keys, not pressing down. "Because I don't perform on demand."

Max hums, his fingers tapping lazily against the wooden bench. He leans in, his breath warm against my ear. "That's fine, I'll just have to *make* you sing on my demand."

My pulse stutters. I turn my head just enough for our lips to brush, and just like that, the air between us shifts, full of electricity like we've both been waiting for this moment.

Max doesn't wait any longer. His hand moves, trailing up the outside of my thigh, fingers teasing at the edge of my sweatshirt. His touch is slow, controlled, but I can feel the tension in him, the barely leashed restraint, the hunger simmering just beneath the surface.

I let out a shaky breath, my lashes fluttering as I meet his gaze. "You want to hear me?" I murmur, my voice laced with challenge. "But I would rather see if you can keep me quiet."

His lips curl into a dark smirk. "Oh, Sparrow. You're going to regret that."

And in one fluid motion, he grips my waist and lifts me onto his lap, turning me to straddle him on the piano bench. His hands slide beneath my sweatshirt, his palms warm against my bare skin as they press into my lower back, pulling me closer.

I can feel every inch of him beneath me, hard, wanting, and that explosive need that's been there since day one ignites into a wildfire. I shift in his lap, grinding against him just enough to pull a groan from his throat. His hands tighten.

"Wrenley," he growls, his voice a warning. But I just smirk against his mouth, threading my fingers into his hair as I kiss him deeper, harder. I don't care that we're in the library, I don't care that anyone could walk in. I don't care about anything except him.

Max grips my ass and crashes it onto the piano keys. The piano protests beneath me as Max presses me against the keys, a tangled mess of sharp, broken notes ringing out through the library. But I barely notice because his mouth is on mine, hungry, demanding, like he's been starving for this.

I barely get a breath in before his lips move down my neck, nipping, sucking, marking. My head falls back against the piano, and his hands are everywhere, gripping my waist, sliding under my sweatshirt, fingertips teasing the underside of my breast.

A shiver runs through me as his mouth follows the curve of my collarbone, his teeth grazing over sensitive skin. He's teasing me. Winding me up. And he knows it.

"You always have to be in control, don't you?" I murmur, my nails scraping down his back.

Max lifts his head, his eyes blazing as he looks at me. "And you don't?"

I smirk, pushing against his chest, just enough to make him

lean back. Challenge accepted. In one quick motion, I shove the sweatshirt over my head, leaving me in nothing but my thin lace bralette. His eyes darken as they rake over me, but before he can reclaim control, I push against his shoulders until he's the one sitting back on the piano bench. His brows lift, that smirk playing on his lips, like he's curious to see what I'll do next.

I don't hesitate. I slide off the piano, dropping to my knees between his legs. His breath catches, and for the first time since I met him, I have him at my mercy. I run my hands up his thighs, feeling the tension in his muscles, the way he's holding himself back. I take my time, dragging my fingers over the band of his sweats, teasing, taunting.

His hands are fists at his side. "Wrenley." His voice is rough, barely controlled.

I glance up at him through my lashes, my fingers hooking into the waistband. "I thought you wanted to hear me."

His jaw clenches. I pull his sweats down just enough, freeing him, and fuck, he's already thick, hard, waiting. I wrap my hand around him, dragging my thumb over the tip, and his head falls back with a low, guttural curse. I smile, leaning in, trailing my tongue up the length of him, slow and deliberate. His hips jerk, just slightly, but I catch it. I know what I'm doing to him.

When I finally take him into my mouth, his hands immediately tangle in my hair, his fingers gripping just enough to send a spark of heat through me.

"Fuck, Sparrow," he groans, his voice wrecked. "You have no idea—"

But I do. I feel the way his body shakes, the way his breath stutters, the way his grip tightens when I take him deeper. I love that I can do this to him. I set a slow, torturous pace, hollowing my cheeks as I suck him deeper, my tongue flicking just right. He shudders, his control unraveling, his hips lifting to meet me.

His fingers tighten in my hair, guiding me, but never forcing. Just needing. And then, in one brutal, desperate motion, he pulls me off him. His chest heaving, his eyes wild, his hand shaking as he drags me back up his body.

I don't even get a word out before he silences me with his mouth, his kiss deep, consuming, claiming. The taste of him on my lips and the low growl he lets out tell me exactly how much that turns him on.

"Bedroom. Now." His voice is dark, commanding.

A thrill runs through me, but I smirk, lifting a brow. "I thought you wanted to hear me sing."

Max lets out a low chuckle, but there's no humor in it, just heat, just desperation. "Sparrow," he murmurs, dragging his lips along my jaw. "You're about to fucking scream."

Max's words are still a wicked promise in my ear when he leans in even closer, his breath hot against my skin.

"Run."

My heart stutters. Then, I bolt. Laughter bursts from my lips as I tear away from him, my bare feet flying across the smooth wooden floor of the library. I don't know where I'm going, only that I must move, must get away, must make him chase me.

Because I want him to catch me. I hear the low growl of amusement behind me, the scrape of the piano bench as he stands. Then, footsteps. Heavy. Measured. Closing in fast.

I barely make it to the grand staircase before his fingers graze my waist, missing me by an inch. I gasp, take steps two at a time, adrenaline and heat pumping through my veins.

But I don't make it far. At the top of the stairs, he catches me. One arm wraps around my waist, yanking me back against him, my breath leaving me in a sharp gasp. His other hand grips the banister beside me, caging me, his body pressing flush against mine. I'm trapped.

And I don't want to escape. His lips brush my ear. "Got you."

A shudder rips through me. Max spins me in his arms, and before I can take a breath, his kiss finds its way back, like home. It's desperate, searing, all-consuming, his tongue coaxing, taking, devouring, his teeth nipping at my bottom lip before soothing the sting with another deep, damning kiss.

My back hits the banister as he presses closer, his hands possessive as they grip my waist, sliding beneath my bralette, exploring, memorizing, claiming.

I break the kiss long enough to catch a breath, my hand clutching at his shoulders, my nails digging in as his mouth moves down my neck, kissing, sucking, teasing.

"Max—"

"I know." He mutters against my skin. His voice is wrecked, his hands shaking as he slides them up my thighs, lifting me in one fluid motion. I wrap my legs around his waist, my hands tangling in his hair, pulling his lips back to mine.

He moves with purpose, his steps measured as he walks a few feet until my back is pressed against the smooth, cold marble column at the top of the stairs.

We're in the middle of the mansion. Out in the open. And neither of us cares.

"Tell me you want this." He murmurs on my lips.

I tighten my legs around him, my nails scraping down his back, my lips brushing his ear as I whisper. "I want you."

Max growls, actually growls, his hands shoving my bralette over my head, tossing it to the floor. His mouth finds my collarbone, then lowers, dragging heat and fire in its wake.

I arch into him, feeling the hard length of him pressing against my already aching core, and I'm so goddamn ready I can't think straight.

"I need you inside me," I breathe, my fingers already tugging at the waistband of his sweats.

Max doesn't hesitate. He frees himself, hot and thick and pulsing against me, and then, he's there. He drags the head of his cock through my center, teasing me until I'm shaking, pleading, desperate.

"Max," I whimper, my forehead falling against his.

He positions himself, his breathing uneven. His hands tighten on my hips, holding me steady. As he thrusts inside me. Deep. Hard. Completely.

A choked gasp leaves my lips as I stretch around him. My nails bite into his shoulders, his groan low and guttural as he stills inside me for a moment, like he's trying not to lose himself too soon.

"Fuck, Sparrow." He groans, his forehead pressing to mine. "You feel...so fucking perfect."

I lift my hips, urging him deeper. "Move," I whisper.

And he does. His pace starts slow, deep, and deliberate, his thrusts hitting every right spot inside me. But patience has never been our virtue. It builds between us, faster, harder, his hands gripping my waist, my legs tightening around his hips, his mouth crushing against mine as he drives into me.

Every movement, every thrust, every gasp, and moan is hungry and desperate and raw.

And then, he says it. "I'm falling for you, Wrenley."

Everything inside me shatters and reforms all at once. I go still in his arms, my chest rising and falling rapidly, my eyes locked onto his, those sharp, dark, dangerous eyes that have always made me feel like I was standing on the edge of something life-changing.

And I don't wait. I cup his face, my fingers brushing the apples of his cheeks, and whisper, "I'm falling for you, too, Maximilian."

His lips claim mine, a promise, a vow. Then, he fucks me harder. I clutch onto him, letting him take, consume, and ruin me, and I give him everything in return.

We fall apart together, the world around us fading as we crash, shatter, and burn. When it's over, when we're nothing but breathless, trembling bodies tangled together, he doesn't let me go.

He holds me against him, our foreheads touching, our hearts pounding in sync. Max exhales, breathing warm against my lips. "Mine." He whispers.

I smile, pressing a soft kiss to his lip. "Yours." I breathe.

The mid-morning air is still crisp against my skin as I lounge on the wide stone steps of the mansion, sipping my coffee while Hugo bounds through the grass, chasing a butterfly far too small for his massive paws. The sun is starting to peak over the large oak trees, the estate is alive with sound, the distant chirp of birds, the rustle of leaves in the breeze, and the faint creak of the old house settling behind me.

I stretch, feeling the dull ache in my muscles, a reminder of last night. A smirk tugs at my lips just as the front door swings open. Margot steps outside, barefoot and still looking half-asleep, her blonde waves a tangled mess from what kept her busy last night. She holds something between two fingers, dangling it in front of me like an offering. My bralette.

"Well, well, well," she muses, flopping down beside me. "Looks like one of us had an eventful night."

I pluck the delicate scrap of lace from her fingers, twirling it absently. "You're one to talk," I shoot back. "From the sounds of it, you and Elias were having your own little... adventure."

Margot gasps dramatically. "Me?" she asks, feigning innocence. "I would never."

I arch a brow. "Thin walls, Mags." She giggles, looking at me, "Yeah, we heard."

She groans, burying her face in her hands. "You know what? Let's just both agree to never speak of last night again."

I snort. "Not a chance. I want some details."

We're still laughing when my phone vibrates beside me, the sharp ping of a security notification cutting through the light-hearted moment. My stomach drops as I glance at the screen.

ALERT: FRONT GATE OPEN.

The casual amusement drains from my body in an instant. I snap upright, already scanning the long driveway stretching beyond the property's gates.

"Margot, get my bag," I say quickly, voice tight.

She blinks at me, not yet processing the shift in tone. "What—"

"NOW!"

She darts inside without another word. Too late. A black SUV rolls up, tires crunching against the gravel, moving with a purpose that makes my blood simmer.

"Hugo, Ferse," I command in German.

The massive dog abandons his play instantly, trotting to my side, his posture rigid and alert. Margot rushed back, tossing my bag to me, breathless. I rip it open, fingers closing around the cool metal of my gun, checking the chamber in one fluid motion.

Four large men step out tattooed, muscled, and exuding an energy I don't like. Hugo lets out a low, deep growl, stepping forward on command.

The driver stands out, built like a brawler, swirling tattoos on his biceps, his green eyes sharp with amusement, like he's already decided I'm not a threat.

I tighten my grip on my gun. Wrong move.

Everything shifts in a blink. The bastard pulls his gun and aims it straight at Hugo. My blood ignites. I fire a warning shot near his feet. "You even think about pulling that trigger," I say, voice cool and razor-sharp, "and I promise you, it'll be the last thing you do."

Silence. Then, the driver smirks.

"Fiery little thing, aren't you?" he drawls. "I like that."

"Hugo Geh..."

Hugo lunges forward, a growl ripping from his chest.

The man doesn't flinch; instead, he cocks the gun.

"Back the fuck off, mutt," he warns, his voice losing all humor.

Fighting the urge to squeeze the trigger again.

"Riot!"

Max's voice cuts through the standoff like a blade. Heavy footsteps thunder behind me as he and Elias burst from the front door, both armed and ready. The energy shifts violently. Max strides forward, shoving himself between me and Riot's gun.

Hugo is still bristling with tension, his growls rolling deep and deadly.

"Lower them," Max tells both of us.

I don't move. Neither does Riot.

"I said, *lower* them."

I finally shift my gun just slightly, but I don't put it away. Riot does the same, though his smirk doesn't fade.

"Jesus," Elias mutters, rubbing a hand down his face. "Two fucking seconds and you're already trying to kill each other?"

Max turns to Riot, his voice cold. "What the fuck was that?"

Riot shrugs, unapologetic. "I don't trust things that can eat me in one bite."

I narrow my eyes, zeroing in on the man who just threatened my dog. "That's funny," I say sweetly. "Because I don't trust men who point guns at innocent animals."

Riot raises an eyebrow. "We can work on that."

Max exhales through his nose, rubbing his temple. I can tell he's torn. He trusts Riot, but he also knows I'm one second away from making an example out of him.

"He's with me, Sparrow," Max murmurs low, so only I can hear. "Let it go."

I don't like it. Not at all. But I trust *him*. So, slowly, I lower my gun. Hugo, sensing my command, backs up a step, still watching Riot like he'd love nothing more than to rip him apart.

"Good boy," I murmur, running my fingers through his thick fur. "Bleib."

Riot finally slides his gun into his waistband, shaking his head. "Jesus, didn't think I'd have to dodge bullets before breakfast."

"Well," Elias deadpans. "You shouldn't have pointed a gun at her fucking dog."

"Yeah, thanks for that observation, Captain Obvious." Riot huffs before his eyes turn to Max. "Anyway, I assume you didn't bring me out here to get shot at. So, let's go inside."

Max doesn't answer right away. Instead, he looks at me, gauging my reaction.

I take a slow breath, forcing myself to nod. "Fine."

"Let's go," I say over my shoulder. "We've got work to do."

Chapter Thirty

MAXIMILIAN

THE ROAR of the bike beneath us is a steady hum, vibrating between my thighs as I weave us through the backroads near the warehouse. Wrenley's arms are wrapped tight around my waist, her body flush against my back, but I can still feel the tension thrumming through her. We're close.

Margot is in position up the road, her car parked at just the right angle to look convincingly broken down. She'll flash some leg, bat those lashes, and pull any stray eyes away from where we need to be. Elias is in a black SUV nearby, hunched over his laptop, already working his magic on the warehouse's security feeds. The cargo vans, our ticket out, are stashed out of sight.

The rest of the team is already waiting. Riot, Reaper, Wrecker, and Torque. Six of us against who the fuck knows how many. The plan is simple: In. Load up. Get the hell out.

The voice crackles through the comms. Elias's tone is clipped and sharp. "We've got a problem."

I slow the bike, taking us to a quiet stop behind the line of trees, cutting the engine. Wrenley is already slipping off, her gun in hand.

"What kind of problem?" Riot asks, already sounding pissed.

"The kind where our easy in-and-out just turned into a fucking bloodbath."

I clench my jaw. "Be specific, Elias."

"The warehouse is full."

Silence hums over the comms for a beat.

"Security?" I ask.

"Oh, yeah," Elias mutters. "Armed to the fucking teeth. And guess who's paying a little visit to his favorite Ashford weapons stash?"

Wrenley tilts her head, waiting.

"Carter Moretti."

My stomach turns to ice. Riot swears under his breath, Reaper mutters something dark. Carter Moretti is not some nameless grunt. He's one of the most brutal enforcers on my shit list, a man with no soul, no loyalty, and no hesitation to put a bullet in someone's skull for looking at him wrong. And he's here. I look at Wrenley, expecting hesitation.

Instead, in true Wrenley fashion, she fucking laughs. "Nothing my family does is ever easy," she murmurs, shaking her head. Then, deadpans: "So, new plan, we kill them all."

Silence. Torque lets out a low whistle over the comms. "I might love her." Reaper chuckles. Riot just mutters "holy fuck" under his breath.

I smirk. "Alright then, Sparrow," I say, turning to the rest of the team. "Let's make some noise."

We kill them all.

The words hang in the air, and Riot chuckles lowly through the comms. "Well, boss? What's the call?"

I grip the handlebars of my bike tightly, my eyes scanning the warehouse perimeter.

"We go in fast. Quiet. We get the job done."

"And Moretti?" Reaper asks.

"If we can take him alive, we do." My gaze flicks to Wrenley, who's already checking her ammo, focused and ready. "But if he makes it difficult—"

"We put him down," she finished, her voice calm.

A smirk tugs at my lips.

"Alright, team. Move in."

We move in, splitting into teams. Riot, Wrecker, and Torque circle to the back entrance while Wrenley, Reaper, and I take the side door.

Elias's voice crackles in my ear: "Three guards patrolling near your entry, moving left."

I glance at Wrenley, who holds up three fingers, already anticipating the fight.

She moves first. The first guy never sees her coming, a silenced shot straight to the temple. He's dead before he hits the floor. The second manages to turn, raising his rifle, but I get to him before he can pull the trigger. A quick, brutal slice across his throat, and he drops, gurgling. The third man bolts, but Reaper is faster. One pop. A headshot. The guy crumples.

"Warehouse is crawling," Elias mutters. "They know you're here."

"Let them come," Wrenley says. We push forward.

As soon as we breach the main floor, all hell breaks loose. Gunfire erupts, bullets pinging off metal crates as we take cover. Riot takes a hit to the shoulder, cursing before barking, "Fucker!" and unloading his shotgun into the guy who clipped him.

Torque, always the reckless one, gets grazed along his thigh but keeps moving like he doesn't feel it. "Damn, that stings," he mutters before snapping a guy's neck.

The air is thick with smoke and the metallic scent of blood. Moretti's men are dropping fast. Wrenley moves like a goddamn assassin, ducking behind cover, popping up to land clean head-shots. At one point, she presses her back against mine, and both of us reload.

"You showing off, Sparrow?" I murmur.

"You keeping up, Blackwood?" she quips back, her smirk sharp.

The last guard standing makes a run for it, but Wrecker shoots him in the leg, sending him sprawling onto the concrete.

Then, Silence.

"That's it?" Riot asks, rolling his shoulder.

"Not yet."

A single figure steps forward from behind a row of crates.

Carter Moretti.

"Blackwood," Moretti sneers, his voice thick with arrogance. "Heard you were sniffing around places you don't belong."

I keep my gun trained on him, stepping forward. "Funny, I was just about to say the same thing to you."

"This warehouse belongs to the Ashfords." He says smoothly. "You know how they are about people touching their shit."

Wrenley steps beside me, gun steady, eyes cold. "It's not theirs anymore."

Moretti laughs. "Ah. You must be the little princess causing all the fuss with your family." His eyes trail over her in a way that makes my fingers twitch on the trigger.

"Call her that again," I warn, my tone deadly.

Moretti grins, daring me. "What, Blackwood? You playing the white knight now?"

I take another step closer; my gun leveled at his head.

"This doesn't have to get ugly," he says. "You take what you came for, and I pretend I never saw you."

"You think this is about the weapons?" Wrenley scoffs. "You're dumber than I thought."

"Oh, honey," Moretti smirks. "You've got no fucking idea what you've stepped into."

Then, out of the corner of my eye, movement. A gunman, half-buried behind a crate, rifle aimed directly at me. Wrenley sees it first.

"NO!"

She moves before I do, lunging at me just as the shot rings out. The impact is immediate. A sharp crack. The sound of flesh tearing. She collides with me, the force sending us both staggering back. I barely catch her before she hits the ground.

A dark red bloom spreads across her chest, the bulletproof

vest having slowed the shot but not completely stopped the damage.

Her eyes go wide. Her lips part, and then she crumples.

Unconscious.

"WRENLEY!"

Something in me snaps. The world slows. My pulse pounds in my ears. Carter Moretti is smirking, thinking he's won something. That smirk disappears when my bullet tears through his fucking knee. He drops. Screaming. I don't stop. I unload three more shots into his leg, his arm, and his hand.

Torque and Riot are already ripping through the last standing gunmen, making sure no one else gets a second chance. Reaper moves beside me, covering our backs, but my focus is singular. Moretti is writhing on the floor, blood pooling beneath him.

I press my gun to his head. "I'm fucking ending you right now." He's shaking, gasping in pain.

"Blackwood—" he chokes out. "Please—"

"You don't get to beg." Just as I pull the trigger, splattering Moretti's brains across the concrete, I hear it.

"Max," Elias's voice cuts in over the comms. "We need to move. NOW!"

I look down at Wrenley's still body.

"Boss, we've got incoming." Riot's voice is urgent.

Fuck.

I shove Moretti's bleeding body aside, scoop Wrenley up into my arms, and turn.

"Move, NOW!"

We haul ass out of the warehouse, and Elias is already pulling the SUV up fast. Reaper and Riot cover us as we load Wrenley in, Torque shoves Elais out of the driver's seat, peeling out as gunfire erupts behind us.

My hand presses against Wrenley's vest, feeling the warmth of her blood seeping through the fabric. I can hear Elias barking orders through the comms. I don't care.

All I can hear is her shaky, shallow breathing.

"Hold on, Sparrow," I murmur against her temple. "Just hold on."

The ride is hell. Wrenley is crumpled against me, pale and too still, her chest rising and falling too shallow beneath the vest. My hands won't stop shaking as I press down on the wound, trying to feel how bad the damage is.

"Fucking drive faster!" I snap at Torque, my voice raw.

"I'm going as fast as I can!" Torque yells back. "This isn't exactly a goddamn ambulance!"

Reaper is kneeling across from me, his hands steady as he tries to assess the injury. His face is tight, controlled, but I see the flicker of concern in his eyes.

"We need to get this vest off her," he says, reaching for the straps.

I nod, my throat so tight I can barely breathe. I help carefully lift Wrenley forward as Reaper unclasps the buckles, peeling them off slowly.

The vest is ruined, a gaping tear where the bullet hit, the fabric charred and shredded. Beneath it, her white tank top is soaked in red.

"Shit," Reaper mutters under his breath. He grabs a knife, cutting through her shirt so we can get a better look.

And then—

I see it.

The bullet didn't fully penetrate, but the impact was still devastating. There's an ugly bruise already forming around the torn skin, blood oozing where the metal is still embedded in her side.

"Reaper?" My voice is hoarse, desperate.

"She's lucky," he mutters, pressing a cloth to the wound to slow the bleeding. "If the vest hadn't slowed it, this would've gone straight through her lung."

"She needs a hospital." The words rip out of me.

"NO HOSPITALS!" Riot barks over the comms. "You know we can't, not with heat on us."

"I don't give a fuck about the heat, Riot!" I roar, my hands tightening around Wrenley's limp form.

She stirs, her fingers twitching against my thigh.

"M-Max?"

My heart stops.

Her eyes flutter open just barely, glassy and unfocused. Her lips part, her breathing is too shallow, too weak.

"I'm right here, Sparrow," I murmur, leaning closer, my hand cupping her cheek.

She tries to smile, but it's barely there.

"Did we... win?" Her voice is so faint, so weak.

"Yeah, baby," I whisper, pressing my forehead to hers, desperation clinging to every inch of me. "We won. But you need to stay awake, okay?"

Her hand lifts weakly, gripping the front of my shirt.

"Hurts," she breathes.

I squeeze my eyes shut, biting back the fear clawing at my chest.

"I know, Sparrow," I whisper. "Just hold on. We're getting you help."

"Max..." Her breath catches. She blinks slowly, like it's a struggle to even keep her eyes open. "If I don't wake up again... re-remember—I was always yours. Do-Don't follow me yet, Max. Not yet." And then, she goes limp.

"NO. No, no, no, no—Sparrow, stay with me!" My voice breaks.

"FUCK!" I slam my fist against the side of the SUV, rage and panic warring in my chest.

"Torque!" I shout. "Get us the fuck there NOW!"

"Hold on, I'm pushing this bitch to the limit!" Torque grits out, the tires screeching as he takes a sharp turn.

I look down at her, my whole world shrinking. "Come on, Wrenley," I whisper, brushing my fingers against her jaw. "I need you to open your eyes. Just look at me, baby."

Nothing. She's so still. Reaper curses under his breath,

checking her pulse. "She's out, but she's still with us. Just barely." Barely. That word sends cold fucking terror slicing through me.

"Torque, how much longer?" I demand through clenched teeth.

"Less than five minutes," Riot answers for him over the comms. "The safe house is prepped. Doc is already there."

"She better be, or I'm going to start breaking necks," I snap.

Reaper gives me a look, but I don't give a single fuck about staying calm. Not when Wrenley is bleeding out in my arms. Not when I could lose her. Not when I realize that if she dies today, so does every single person responsible.

I swallow down the rage, pressing my lips against her cold forehead. "Hold on, Sparrow," I murmur. "Just hold on."

The SUV comes to a shrieking halt, I jump out, dragging Wrenley with me.

I burst through the doors of the safe house, Wrenley limp in my arms, her skin too pale, too fucking cold.

"DOC!" My roar echoes off the walls, raw and frantic.

She's already moving before I finish yelling, ripping on gloves, and clearing the steel table in the center of the room. Black hair pulled back, eyes sharp as blades, Doc is all business.

"Put her here! NOW!" she barks.

I lay Wrenley down carefully, but fuck does she look bad. The wound is still oozing, her chest barely rising and falling.

"Jesus," Doc mutters, grabbing the gauze and peeling back the soaked fabric around the bullet wound. "She lost too much blood. Reaper, help me get the rest of her clothes off. We need to check her for internal damage."

Reaper is already moving, knife in hand, slicing away at what remains of her top. His face is grim, but steady.

"Max, backup." Doc's voice is tight, impatient.

I don't move. "She needs me here," I grind out.

"No, she needs *me* to stop her from bleeding out on my table. BACK. UP."

I shake my head, reaching for Wrenley's hand, but Elias is suddenly there, Riot beside him.

"Come on, man," Elias says, gripping my shoulder.

"I'm not leaving her," I snarl, my entire fucking body shaking.

"You're not helping!" Doc snaps. "You're in the goddamn way. Elias, GET HIM OUT!"

Arms clamp around me. "Fuck OFF!" I lash out, but Elias and Riot drag me back, their grips iron-tight.

"Max! Fucking STOP," Riot grits out. "Let them work!"

The door slams shut, locking me on the other side. I stand there, fists clenched, chest heaving, my heart slamming like a battering ram against my ribs. And then, Wrenley screams. It's raw, pain-laced, the kind of sound that twists something vicious and unbearable inside me.

I lunge for the door, slamming my fist against it. "Let me the fuck back in!"

No response. I start dragging my hands through my hair, pacing like a caged animal.

"She's strong," Elias murmurs, but I barely hear him.

Because fuck that. Strength doesn't mean shit against a bullet wound. "She shouldn't be in this life," I mutter, voice low, more to myself than to them.

Riot exhales, arms crossed, "She's here now."

"Yeah," I grind out, my jaw tight, my head pounding. "Because of me. I should've protected her better. Should've kept her out of the fucking crossfire."

"And how the fuck were you supposed to do that?" Elias challenges. "She's not some delicate thing you can shove in a cage. She made her choice and proved she can handle it."

I don't answer. Because I know he's right. And I still fucking hate it. Minutes tick. Hours stretch into what feels like an eternity. Then, finally, the door swings open. Doc steps out, sweat on her brow, gloves stained red. I can't breathe.

She pulls off her gloves with a snap, her gaze locking onto

mine. "She lost a lot of blood," she says evenly. "But we got the rest of the bullet out."

My stomach drops. "And?"

Her expression softens, just slightly. "She's alive, Max."

The air rushes from my lungs. I brace a hand on the wall, exhaling hard, my head dropping forward. "She's alive," I murmur, the words sinking into my bones.

"Yeah," Doc nods, arms crossed. "She'll need rest. Pain meds. No running into fucking bullets again anytime soon."

I let out a breathless half-laugh, half-growl. "Can I see her?" My voice is hoarse, raw. Doc sighs. "Yeah, but keep it quiet. She needs to sleep." I don't need another word. I'm already pushing past her.

Chapter Thirty-One

WRENLEY

DARKNESS SURROUNDS ME, the only light in the room coming from a single lamp in the corner, casting a warm glow over the walls. My body feels heavy, sore, but alive. The dull ache in my chest is manageable, though a reminder that I took a bullet today.

I blink, my vision adjusting, and take in my surroundings. I'm in a bedroom, probably a safe house, based on the unfamiliar and impersonal feel of it. The air smells faintly of antiseptic and something else...leather and whiskey.

Max.

My gaze shifts, and there he is, asleep in a chair beside the bed, his upper body leaning over my legs, his hand wrapped tightly around mine. His dark hair tousled, his normally sharp, commanding presence softened by sleep. Even in unconsciousness, his grip on me is firm, like he refused to let go even in his dreams.

I glance further around the room, my chest tightening at what I see. They're all here. Elias is sprawled out in an armchair, arms crossed over his chest. Margot curled into a ball on the couch, her head resting on Riot's shoulder, who is snoring quietly. Wrecker is half-sitting, half-lying on the floor, and Torque has one leg slung over the arm of another chair. Even Reaper, who seems cold and distant, leans back against the wall, arms loose at his sides.

A soft smile tugs at my lips. They're safe. We all are. I shift slightly, trying to sit up, and immediately regret it when a sharp pain shoots through my chest. A small gasp escapes me.

Max jerks upright instantly, his hand still clutching mine. His eyes snap to mine, dark with concern, his other hand coming up to cup my face, his thumb brushing over my cheek.

"Sparrow," he breathes, voice thick with sleep but filled with relief. "You're awake."

I blink up at him, offering a small, tired smile. "Where am I?"

His shoulders relax a fraction, but the tension is still there. "Safehouse," he murmurs. "Doc patched you up here. We couldn't risk a hospital."

I nod, my head foggy, but the memory of earlier today rushes back. The warehouse. The fight. Carte Moretti. The gun. Me pushing Max out of the way. The bullet slamming into my chest.

Max must see the realization on my face because his jaw tightens, and his grip on my hand firms. "You scared the hell out of me, Wrenley."

Before I can answer, movement around the room draws my attention. The others are waking up. Margot stretches, groaning as she sits up, her eyes going wide when she sees me.

"Holy shit, you're awake!" She's immediately at my side, brushing hair from my face, her touch gentle but frantic. "How are you feeling?" Are you in pain? Do you need anything?"

I huff out a small laugh. "You sound like a worried mother."

"Yeah, well," she mutters, shooting Max a look before turning back to me. "We've been watching you like a damn hawk. I swear, if you almost die again, I'm gonna kill you."

Before I can respond, one of the guys, Wrecker, I think, mutters, "I'll get Doc," as he disappears out of the room. I glance around at everyone, taking in their relieved yet exhausted faces.

Then I look at Max again, his hand still warm on mine. And I smirk. "Who are *you*?" I ask, keeping my face perfectly serious.

Max goes rigid. His spine straightens, his eyes go wide, and for a split second, I see something I have never seen before.

Fear.

Margot gasps, Elias snaps awake, and I bite the inside of my cheek to keep from grinning. Max stares at me, his grip on my hand tightening. "You don't know who I am?" I press my lips together, holding back a giggle, but I can't do it for long. His face starts to pale. I finally break and let out a weak laugh. "I'm kidding," I say, wincing slightly as my chest protests the movement.

Max exhales, his entire body sagging with relief, before he levels me with a look. "Sparrow, I swear to God—"

I laugh again, though it's softer this time. "Sorry, I couldn't pass up the opportunity." He shakes his head, running a hand down his face, but there's a smirk there now, hidden beneath the exasperation. "Only you could almost die and turn it into a fucking joke," he mutters. "You've been spending too much time with Elias."

Elias, who is now wide awake and grinning, leans forward. "Finally, someone else sees my contributions." I roll my eyes as the door opens, and Doc walks in, her sharp gaze locking onto me immediately.

She crosses the room in three quick strides, her no-nonsense demeanor taking over. "Alright, let's see how much damage you've done to yourself." Max reluctantly steps back, though he hovers nearby as Doc checks me over.

"How bad is it?" I ask, wincing as she presses against my side.

She doesn't answer right away, just keeps examining me. Then she nods. "You're stable. You lost a lot of blood, but the bullet's out, and nothing vital was hit. You'll be sore as hell for a while, but you'll live."

I let out a breath I didn't realize I was holding. "So when can I leave?" Doc gives me a sharp look. "You *should* rest her for a least a few more hours. But since you're stable, you can go home. No strenuous activity for a week. You need to let your body recover. No running, no fighting, no lifting anything heavy."

She pauses, then looks pointedly at Max. "No sex."

Silence.

Then Elias, ever the asshole, burst out laughing. "Oh, this is gonna be fun." Max glares at him. "Shut the fuck up, Elias."

But I can't help it, I laugh too, even as pain shoots through my ribs. Margot shakes her head, muttering something about how this will be a miracle if we listen to Doc's orders. Max sighs, rubbing a hand over his jaw before looking at me. "Home?" he asks softly. I nod, exhaustion tugging at my limbs again. "Yeah," I murmur. "Let's go home."

The drive back to the mansion is quiet, the weight of exhaustion settling over all of us. Torque is behind the wheel, Riot riding shotgun, while Max holds me against his chest in the back seat. The others follow in another vehicle, their headlights trailing behind us on the dark road.

The motion of the car and the steady beat of Max's heart under my cheek lull me into a half-asleep state, my body aching but warm in his embrace. His arms are wrapped tightly around me, one hand absentmindedly tracing patterns along my hip. It's comforting.

But then, out of nowhere, I blink up at him and mumble, "I want a chocolate milkshake." Riot nearly chokes on his own breath, twisting in his seat to look at me. "You killed a bunch of assholes, got shot, almost died, and now you want a fucking milkshake?"

I shrug sleepily, "Yeah."

Max lets out a soft, amused huff, and Riot shakes his head, grinning. "This might be the craziest girl you've ever had, Blackwood," Riot says, laughing. "But, honestly, she's good for you." Max just smirks, pressing a kiss to my temple. "I know."

Despite the teasing, Torque pulls through a drive-thru, and a few minutes later, I'm sipping on my milkshake, humming in satisfaction while the guys shake their heads in disbelief.

By the time we pull up to the mansion, my body feels ten times heavier than it did before. I slide out of the SUV, tossing my empty cup into a nearby trash can before heading toward the front doors.

The moment we step inside, there's a blur of black fur barreling down the stairs straight for me.

Hugo.

Before I can react, Max's voice cuts through the air, sharp and firm. "Nein. Sitz." Hugo instantly skids to a stop, dropping his massive body into a sit. His golden eyes locked on me, ears twitching forward.

I huff a quiet laugh and step toward him, lowering myself to his level. "It's okay, buddy," I whisper, stroking my hand through his thick fur. His big head leans into my chest, his body vibrating with contained excitement. "I missed you, too."

Pressing a soft kiss to the top of his head, I straighten and turn back to where the others are standing. The exhaustion in the room is tangible, but so is the determination.

I take a breath. "Okay, it's time to make the next plan. We can't let up. We need to—"

"No," Max cuts in, his tone leaving no room for argument.

I blink at him. "No?"

He steps close, his expression firm. "Shower. Bed. Now. You can work in the morning."

I want to argue, but as I glance around the room, I take in the sight of all of us, clothes stained with dried blood, dirt smudged across faces, exhaustion hanging heavy in the air. Even I can't deny that we need rest.

I sigh, reluctantly nodding. "Fine." I look at the guys. "There are plenty of spare rooms and showers. Get some sleep."

Elias smirks. "You heard her, boys. Try not to fight over the best rooms."

I roll my eyes and turn toward the stairs, but before I can take a step, Max scoops me up effortlessly. I yelp, immediately protesting, my hands pressing against his chest. "Max! I can walk!"

He keeps walking, completely unfazed. "I don't care."

I glare up at him, but there's no real heat behind it. "You're impossible."

He half smiles and winks, his grip tightening around me. "And you love it."

I huff, crossing my arms as he carries me up the stairs, my body betraying me as I melt into his warmth. And even though I won't say it just yet... He's right.

Max sets me down gently in the bathroom, his hand lingering on my waist like he's afraid to let go. He turns away, reaching to turn the shower on, allowing the hot water to heat the space. Steam rises almost immediately, surrounding us in thick tendrils.

I exhale, reaching for the oversized shirt they had put me in at the safe house. The moment I try to pull it over my head, a sharp, searing pain lances through my side. I gasp, my body tensing as my arms instinctively drop back down. Max turns instantly, his brows drawing together in concern. "Here, let me help." His voice is softer now, careful.

I nod, letting my hands fall away. He steps in close, fingers brushing my skin as he carefully lifts the hem of my shirt, peeling it away from my body with slow, deliberate movements. His eyes darken as they flick over the bruising along my ribs, the faint traces of blood still on my skin. His jaw clenches, but he doesn't say anything.

Next, he kneels, his hands gliding down my hips as he hooks his fingers into my pants and slides them down my legs. My balance wavers for a second, but he steadies me effortlessly, his hands warm and sure against my skin. When I'm standing bare before him, he looks up at me, his gaze lingering on mine, searching.

He stands and steps back, leaning on the counter, arms crossed as he watches me step into the shower. The hot water cascades down my body, washing away the blood, the dirt, the exhaustion. My muscles loosen under the steady stream, but there's still a tightness in my chest, an ache that has nothing to do with my wound.

I turn around, meeting his gaze through the steam.

"I thought you were going to help me," I say, my voice carrying over the sound of the water.

His lips twitch. "I didn't want to push my luck."

I raise my hands in surrender. "No funny business. I promise."

His expression shifts, something unreadable flickering across his face before he exhales and pushes off the counter.

He pulls his shirt over his head, revealing the carved lines of his torso, and steps out of his pants. The second he steps into the shower, his warmth surrounds me, his presence wrapping around me like a second skin.

He reaches for the bottle of body wash, squeezing some into his hands before smoothing his palms over my shoulder, down my arms, carefully and deliberately. Neither of us speaks at first. His hands move over me with an aching kind of tenderness, his touch reverent as he works his way down my body. I shiver as his fingers skim over my ribs, over the bruises, his jaw flexing as he forces himself to stay gentle.

"I was scared," I whisper.

His hands pause for a fraction of a second before continuing. "Me too."

I swallow hard, tilting my head back to let the water fall over my face. "I thought... I thought that was it. When I hit the ground, I couldn't breathe. I couldn't move. And all I could think about was—" I cut off, shaking my head.

Max steps closer, his hands cradling my face, thumbs brushing over my cheeks. "Say it."

I look up at him, my throat tight. "All I could think about was you." Something cracks in his expression, something raw and unguarded. His fingers slide into my hair, tilting my head up as his lips brush over mine. "Sparrow," he murmurs, the name weighted with something deeper than before. "If you had died—"

I press a finger to his lips, shaking my head. "I didn't."

His eyes burn into mine, his hands gripping me tighter like he needs to reassure himself that I'm real. That I'm still here. I slide my hands up his chest, feeling the steady, solid beat of his heart beneath my fingertips. "I need you to promise me something."

He exhales, his hands sliding down to grip my waist. "Anything."

I meet his gaze, steady and sure. "If something happens to me—"

"No." His grip tightens. "Don't."

"Max."

His jaw clenches. "You are not dying on me, Wrenley."

I press my hand against his chest. "If something happens," I continue, my voice softer, "promise me that you'll burn everything they've built to the ground."

His eyes darken, a slow exhale leaving his lips. "I was going to do that anyway."

A small, bittersweet smile tugs at my lips. "Then promise me you won't stop."

His hands grip my waist firmly, his gaze unyielding. "I promise."

I let out a slow breath, nodding. Then, Max tilts my chin up, his lips on mine in the softest, most deliberate kiss he's ever given me. It's not desperate. It's not frenzied. It's a vow. He deepens the kiss, his fingers threading into my hair, his body pressing flush against mine. And just like that, the weight of the world fades away. Because at this moment, in the warmth of his arms, I know, I'm exactly where I'm supposed to be.

Max has been holding me hostage in bed for two days, his arms wrapped around me like an unyielding fortress. His warmth, his steady breaths against my hair, should be enough to lull me back into sleep. But it isn't. I stare at the clock on the nightstand, the dim numbers glowing back at me. **3:57 AM.**

I can't sleep anymore. My mind won't let me. The conversation in the shower, the way Max held me like I was the only thing keeping him tethered to this world, it's all still circling in my head. And now, an idea is forming, one I can't ignore.

Slowly, carefully, I shift out from under his arm, his grip tightens briefly, a small sound rumbling in his chest, but I press a soft kiss to his temple, and he relaxes again.

I slide out of bed, reaching for the silk robe hanging on the chair, slipping it on as I pad across the room. My fingers barely make a sound as I twist the handle, pulling the door open just enough to slip through before clicking it shut behind me.

The hallway is quiet, the whole house still except for the faint rustling of the wind outside. I move quickly, my bare feet silent on the hardwood, making my way toward the room Elias has claimed.

I push the door open without hesitation, stepping inside and shutting it behind me. The room is dimly lit by the lights outside, casting soft shadows over the furniture. Elias is sprawled out on the bed, one arm thrown over his face, the other resting on his stomach. I am grateful he is wearing boxers. He looks peaceful, for once. I walk to his side, leaning down until my lips are close to his ear.

"Elias," I whisper. "Get up." He doesn't stir. I poke his arm. "Elias."

Still nothing. Rolling my eyes, I press a hand against his chest and shake him lightly.

He groans, blinking awake, his face scrunching up in confusion. "Wren?" His voice is thick with sleep. Then, suddenly, he's upright, fully alert, eyes scanning me like he's expecting the worst. "What's wrong? Are you okay?"

I shake my head quickly. "I'm fine."

He exhales heavily, running a hand down his face. "Jesus

Christ, woman, you can't just wake a guy up like that after what happened the other day. Thought we were under attack or some shit."

I smile wickedly. "Not yet."

His eyes narrow. "What do you mean by 'not yet'?"

I take a step back, crossing my arms. "I have an idea. And I need your help."

Elias groans, flopping back onto the pillows. "It's four in the goddamn morning, sweetheart."

I grin. "Exactly. The perfect time to get to work."

He lets out a long, exaggerated sigh, staring up at the ceiling for a moment before glancing at me. Then, shaking his head, he swings his legs over the side of the bed, sitting up.

"This better be good," he mutters, rubbing his temples.

"Oh, trust me," I say, my grin widening. "It's going to be very good. I'll start coffee."

Chapter Thirty-Two

MAXIMILIAN

THE BED IS COLD, and my body is instantly alert. My eyes snap open, and the sight of the vacant side of the bed has me sitting up, scanning the room. The bathroom door is open, and the soft glow of morning light filters through the curtains.

She's not here. I throw the blankets off and push out of bed, not bothering to grab anything but the gun from the nightstand as I stalk toward the door. My pulse pounds, and each step down the hall is sharpening my focus.

Then I hear it. Voices. Muffled, low conversation coming from the living room. I descend the stairs quickly, taking them two at a time, my bare feet silent against the wood. The second I round the corner, I take in the scene, my pulse slowing, but my irritation spiking.

Wrenley is curled up on the couch under a thick blanket, her fire-red hair a wild mess, a half-empty mug of coffee resting on the arm of the couch. Elias is on the floor next to her, his legs crossed, the coffee table pulled against him with three laptops open, screens flickering with lines of code, security feeds, and documents I don't recognize.

Riot is perched on the arm of a chair nearby, nodding as he listens, adding in his own thoughts here and there. And Wrenley? She's deep in conversation, pointing at one of the screens, her brows furrowed in determination, completely unaware that I'm standing there, in only my underwear and ready to kill someone.

A silent shadow moves in the periphery, and I barely have time to react before Reaper appears beside me, pressing a hot cup of coffee into my hand. I raise an eyebrow at him. He shrugs. "You're gonna need this."

I glance back at the scene, eyes landing on Wrenley as she gestures toward the screen. "How long have they been at this?" I mutter, keeping my voice low.

Reaper chuckles lightly. "Since about four-thirty."

I inhale deeply, trying to control the mix of relief and frustration.

"She woke up, pulled Elias out of bed, and started plotting." Reaper folds his arms, glancing over at them. "Riot came in about an hour later. They're putting together something... creative."

I blow out a slow breath, rubbing my hand over my jaw. I should have known. Of course, she couldn't just sleep off getting shot. No, she had to be up before dawn, whispering in Elias's ear about some brilliant, half-crazy idea that would probably make my life hell.

She shifts then, her head tilting towards Elias as she smiles at something he says. And something in me tightens. I take a slow sip of coffee before making my presence known.

"What the fuck is going on?"

Elias just looks up at me, unbothered, grinning like the asshole he is.

"Good morning, Sleeping Beauty." He glances at my bare chest. "Or should I say, Sleeping Beast?"

Riot chuckles, Reaper shakes his head, and Wrenley, finally, turns to look at me. Her smile falters just a little as her eyes rake over me, taking in my state of undress. "Maximilian," she says, all innocent. "You're up."

I arch an eyebrow. "No shit. You wanna explain why you weren't still in bed when I woke up?"

She lifts her coffee, taking a long sip before responding. "I had an idea."

I set my cup down on the table beside me, crossing my arms. "And that required waking Elias up at an ungodly hour?"

She grins. "Yes."

Elias smirks at me. "She's very persuasive."

I shoot him a glare before turning my attention back to Wrenley. "Sparrow." My voice is low, warning. "You were shot two days ago."

She waves a hand. "And I'm not dead. So…" she gestures to the screens. "We keep going."

I pinch the bridge of my nose, exhaling sharply. "Explain. Now."

She leans forward, wincing slightly, reaching past Elias to one of the laptops. "I couldn't sleep. My mind kept spinning with everything, and I realized, we've been focused on taking down their businesses, their money, their weapons." She looks up at me. "But what if we go for something deeper?"

I narrow my eyes, intrigued despite my frustration. "Go on."

She taps the screen. "There's something else my father values even more than his empire."

I tilt my head. "And what's that?"

Her lips curl into a slow, wicked smile.

"His legacy."

I take a seat on the arm of the couch, rubbing my hand over my jaw, my mind already spinning. Wrenley's words hang in the air, electrified with something I can't quite place yet.

His legacy.

She sits up straighter, shifting the blanket off her shoulders as she types something into one of the laptops in front of her. Elias leans in, scanning the screen, his expression shifting from amusement to something more serious.

Riot, still perched on the chair's arm, stretches and nods, eyeing me. "I like where this is going."

I take a slow sip of my coffee, watching them all. "Alright, Sparrow. What exactly are we talking about here?"

She meets my gaze, her expression fierce and determined. "We burn everything," she says, voice smooth, unwavering. "Not just the businesses, not just the money. We dismantle the entire foundation my father built. His name, his influence, his power. We don't just take what he owns, we take his reputation, his alliances, his ability to ever claw his way back to the top."

I feel a slow smirk tug at my lips. "Alright," I murmur. "I'm listening."

She leans forward, her fingers dancing over the keyboard as she brings up files, images, and scanned documents.

"Elias and I started digging through the names we pulled from the Ashford holdings. We knew the money was being funneled through a series of shell companies, offshore accounts, and black-market deals. But I found something else last night, something personal."

She clicks a folder open, and the screen fills with a list of high-profile names. Politicians. Business moguls. Judges. All people in her father's pocket.

Elias grins, tapping the screen. "Turns out, dear old daddy keeps *receipts*."

I exhale sharply, my grip tightening on my mug. "What kind of receipts?"

Elias clicks a few keys, pulling up a string of encrypted messages. "Bribes. Blackmail. Extortion. The kind of shit that, if leaked, could topple careers, ruin families, and send people running for cover."

Wrenley tilts her head. "And the best part? He's been keeping a *ledger*, a personal record of every deal, every payment, every person who owes him."

I let out a low whistle. "Fuck me."

Riot leans in. "So we're talking total annihilation. Exposing him publicly?"

Wrenley nods. "But not just him. Everyone who's been

involved. The men who took his bribes, the ones who've been laundering money through his businesses, the ones who look the other way when he moves weapons or traffics drugs."

Reaper, still quiet in the corner, finally speaks. "That kind of move won't just make enemies of the Ashford's. It'll put a target on all our backs."

She doesn't even hesitate. "I know."

I study her, watching the way her fingers curl into fists on her lap, her jaw tight with controlled fury. "You *really* want to do this," I murmur.

She lifts her chin. "Benjamin was already trying to take them down this way. He knew my father was powerful, but his real power isn't in his money, it's in the people who owe him." She gestures to the screen. "If we take them out, he's just a man with a crumbling empire."

I tap my fingers against my knee, considering. She's right. Cutting off the money hurts him. Taking his businesses cripples him. But if we expose him? If we rip out his connections, his safety net?

He's done. Wrenley looks around the room. "If anyone wants to walk, I get it, no hard feelings." Everyone sizes each other up, and they all start to smile. Reaper speaks first, "I'm in, I'm curious to see how you play this out." The rest nod in agreement.

But there's one problem.

I glance at Elias, "How secure is this information?"

Elias sighs, cracking his knuckles. "Right now? Pretty fucking secure. But if we're planning to use it, we have to be careful. If we release everything at once, your father will know where it came from, and he'll start plugging holes."

Wrenley nods. "Then we don't dump it all at once. We leak it. Slowly. Just enough to create chaos, to make people panic. If the right people start getting nervous, they'll turn on him before he even knows what's happening."

Riot grins. "Divide and conquer."

Reaper nods approvingly. "It's smart. You turn his allies into enemies. Make them desperate. Make them afraid."

I look at Wrenley again. She's sitting there, still wrapped in the blanket, her hair messy, her face a little pale from everything she's been through, but fuck, she's a goddamn force.

I reach over and curl a finger beneath her chin, forcing her to look at me. "You're not just taking his empire, Sparrow." My voice is low, rough. "You're going to dismantle his soul."

She holds my gaze, her pulse fluttering beneath my touch. "Yes," she whispers. "I am."

I lean in, brushing my lips over hers, feeling the fire between us ignite. And then Elias clears his throat loudly. I pull back slowly, cutting him a glare.

"Jesus Christ," Elias groans, rubbing a hand down his face. "Can we not do this right now? I'm trying to destroy a man's life here, not watch you two eye-fuck each other."

Wrenley laughs, leaning back into the couch, her eyes still locked on mine.

I smile. Then I sit up, cracking my neck, my focus snapping back to the plan. "We need to move fast," I say. "We need to start leaking this shit before he catches on."

Elias nods. "Give me a few hours, and I'll set up encrypted accounts to start the drip feed."

Riot grins, flexing his knuckles. "And if anyone needs more hands-on lessons in betrayal, I'll be happy to oblige.

Reaper smiles. "Just say the word."

I look at Wrenley. This is it. The beginning of the end for Charles Ashford. And the rise of something new. I lower to sit next to Wrenley's grabbing her chin again, my thumb brushing along her jawline as I search her eyes. She's serious.

Not just about dismantling her father's empire, not just about exposing his sins to the world. She wants to end him. And not in the figurative sense. I can see the fire burning behind those hazel eyes, the absolute certainty, the purpose.

She's not just taking everything from him. She's going to kill him. Wrenley leans in, her voice barely a whisper, but her words carry more weight than anything else we've said this morning.

"When this is over, when he has nothing left, I'm going to be the one to pull the trigger."

The entire room goes silent. Elias stops typing, Riot stops grinning. Reaper even looks up from where he's leaning. But I don't flinch, I don't try to talk her out of it. Because I get it.

I know the kind of hatred that sits in your chest like a live wire, burning through your veins, turning you into something colder, harder, more relentless. I know what it's like to want revenge so badly that it consumes you. I've been there. I am there. And now, so is she.

I tighten my grip on her chin, just enough to make her focus on me. "Then we make sure you get that chance."

Reaper exhales sharply, rubbing a hand over his face. "Fuck me, you two are a match made in hell."

Riot lets out a low whistle. "You are terrifying, a God-damned Crown-less Queen."

Wrenley pulls back slightly, her lips twitching at the nickname, but she doesn't take her eyes off me. I let her go, sitting back, my mind already racing ahead.

This changes things. I was already committed to bringing down the Ashford's. Already willing to burn their empire to the ground. But now? Now it's personal for her, too. And I'm going to make damn sure she gets what she wants.

I look around the room, at the people who have become more than just allies in this war. They're family. And we're about to destroy everything the Ashford's have built. One piece at a time.

I glance back at Elias. "You said you'd have the accounts ready in a few hours?"

Elias shakes his head like he can't believe this is happening. "Yeah, yeah. I'll get it done."

Riot cracks his knuckles. "And when do we start sending people personal invitations to their downfall?"

Wrenley tilts her head, her voice like silk-wrapped steel.

"Now."

Chapter Thirty-Three

WRENLEY

I PUSH OFF THE COUCH, stretching as much as I can before turning to the group. "I need to change." Max, who has been watching me like a hawk since I first started talking, narrows his eyes. "For what?"

A slow, wicked smile spreads across my lips. "Because I want to see the look on my father's face when the first piece falls into place."

Max watches me for a long moment, assessing me. Then he nods once. "I'm coming with you."

I don't argue. I wanted him there anyway. But I glance at Reaper, who has been leaning against the wall, arms crossed, silently observing the whole conversation. "You too."

His head tilts slightly. "Why me?"

"Because you're good at standing there looking scary as hell," I say with a smirk. "And you're about the same size as Max. You can borrow one of his suits."

Elias snorts from his spot on the floor, where he's still sifting through endless amounts of data. "Damn, Reaper. You finally get to dress like a real person." He gives him an unimpressed look but doesn't argue.

Elias claps his hands together and stands. "I'll get the SUV pulled around, and I'll load up Hugo." Riot, who has been

231

lounging on the armrest of the chair, chuckles. "You're seriously taking the dog into an office?" Max and I exchange a knowing glance before I turn back to Riot, my smile deepening. "Yes. It kills my mother slowly." Riot throws his hands up. "Say less."

With that settled, I head upstairs with Max at my heels. In the bedroom, Margot is already waiting for me, sitting on the vanity stool with her legs crossed. She holds up a curling iron like a weapon. "I figured you'd want to look devastating while ruining your father's life."

I grin. "You know me too well." I strip out of my pajamas and pull a sleek black dress from the closet. It's tailored to perfection, hugging my curves, with high-slit, long lace sleeves, and a plunging neckline that is just shy of scandalous. Power drips from the fabric, and as I slide into it, I know it's the perfect choice.

Margot gives me a wolf whistle. "Holy shit, Wren. That's an empire-shattering dress." I laugh. "Exactly the reaction I want."

She sets to work on my hair, curling it into sleek waves. As she works, she catches my gaze in the mirror. "I know you, Wrenley. And I know this isn't just about business. It's personal. You're going for blood."

I meet her eyes, unflinching. "Damn right, I am. You have been quiet about all this. Do you want to leave?"

Margot hums, twisting a curl around her finger before letting it fall. "Hell no! I want to watch you burn them, make sure you enjoy it, babe." I smile, knowing she is low-key enjoying this just as much as I am.

Meanwhile, across the room in the closet, Max is tugging on a black suit, his movements quick and precise. He glances at Reaper, who is adjusting the cuffs of his borrowed one.

"Feels weird," Reaper mutters.

Max smirks, straightening his own jacket. "What? Looking respectable?"

Reaper gives him a look. "I don't do respectable." Max chuckles but doesn't argue.

When I step away from the vanity, both men turn, their eyes

raking over me. Max's gaze darkens immediately. His jaw tenses, and he takes a slow step toward me. "You're going to kill me." He mutters under his breath.

I arch a brow, pretending innocence. "Is it too much?" His fingers graze my hip, and his voice drops lower. "No. It's just enough." Reaper clears his throat. "Yeah, so... I'm just gonna pretend I'm not here."

I laugh, stepping back. "Come on, boys. Let's go make my father sweat." As we head downstairs, Hugo is already waiting by the door, tail wagging. I snap my fingers, and he falls in line beside me as we step outside, ready to burn the first piece of my father's empire.

✦

The elevator doors slide open, and a hush falls over the office floor of Ashford International. Heads turn. Whispers ripple like wildfire. I keep my chin lifted, my pace unhurried as I step forward, Hugo walking obediently by my side. His massive frame radiates power, his every step perfectly in sync with mine. Behind us, Max and Reaper move like twin shadows, silent and imposing, a step behind on either side of me.

I can feel the weight of their presence. The tension coils tight in the air, pressing against the walls of the sleek, modern space that my father built as his kingdom. It's always been a place meant to intimidate, to command obedience with glass walls, polished floors, and the ever-present, suffocating scent of power.

But today? Today, I am the one commanding the room. Every single pair of eyes locked on us knows something is different. They can feel the shift. They can sense the storm coming.

I don't break my stride. I don't acknowledge the gasps or the murmurs of employees who have spent their careers cowering under my father's rule. Instead, I move with purpose, heading straight for the large glass door of the conference room at the end of the hall.

Inside, I can see them already gathered. My father. My mother. A handful of board members and legal advisers. I don't bother knocking.

Max and Reaper step forward in perfect unison, each grabbing one of the doors and pulling them open with force. The heavy glass swings wide, the sound reverberating through the space like the first strike of war drums.

The meeting grinds to an abrupt halt.

I step through the threshold, the heels of my Louboutin's clicking against the pristine floor, my nails, polished obsidian black and filed to a perfectly sharp point, dragging slowly across Max's chest as I pass him. Not the subtle touch like the last time we were here, but deliberate. Purposeful. Possessive. Max's eyes darken, his jaw ticking ever so slightly. I don't stop. I don't falter.

Hugo strides in beside me, massing and unwavering, as if he, too, understands the gravity of this moment. Across the long table, my father leans back in his chair, his fingers steepled together as he watches me with barely concealed irritation. My mother, seated primly beside him, barely turns her head, though the flicker of her gaze over my appearance is unmistakable.

Of course, she notices the outfit. The plunging neckline. The high slit of the dress. The undeniable confidence I wear like armor. She exhales sharply, unimpressed, before looking away. My father, however, studies me for a long, silent beat before finally speaking.

"To what do we owe this... unexpected visit?"

His voice is smooth, measured, like a man who thinks he still holds every card in the deck.

I smile. It's slow. Sweet. And filled with venom. "Oh, don't mind me," I say, sauntering forward. "I just figured I'd drop in to see what I've inherited."

A muscle jumps in his jaw. "You're disrupting a private meeting."

"Private?" I feign a pout. "That's strange. Because, as far as I'm aware, my shares of Ashford International make me a significant part of this little gathering."

A few of the board members shift uncomfortably in their seats. My mother, still refusing to look directly at me, simply sips from her delicate crystal glass of water, as if I'm nothing more than an inconvenience she is forced to tolerate.

"You have no business here," my father says, voice clipped. "This is not a place for you to play whatever game you think you're playing, Princess."

I tilt my head, my smile never failing. "Oh, but it is, Father. You see, I'm not playing." I set my hands flat on the table, leaning forward just enough to let the glint of my nails catch the lights. "I own a seat here. And you," I let my voice rise just a little, making sure the whole room can hear. "You should start getting used to that."

Silence. Thick. Heavy. Delicious. Max, standing just inside the door, adjusts the sleeves of his suit jacket. I don't need to look at him to know that he's barely restraining the smile I can practically feel radiating off him.

Reaper, on the other hand, remains impassive, watching. Calculating. I straighten, letting the moment stretch just long enough to watch my father's fingers tighten around the polished wood of the table.

Then, finally, he exhales. "You don't belong here, Wrenley."

I chuckle. "See, that's where you're wrong. Because the difference between now and last time I sat at this table—" I slide into the empty chair across from him, placing my hands in my lap with a perfectly practiced grace that I stole from my mother's own playbook. "—is this time, I *do* belong here. And you can't do a damn thing about it."

My father's eyes darken. My mother sighs through her nose, finally setting down her glass and casting a glance toward Hugo, who has planted himself at my side like a well-trained soldier.

"Wrenley?" she murmurs, disapproval dripping from every syllable. "The *dog*... again, I told you."

I rest my elbow on the table, propping my chin against my fist. Before I can say anything. Max, whose presence has been a silent storm brewing behind me, finally steps forward. His voice is calm, controlled, but it cuts through the tension like a blade.

"Where Wrenley goes, Hugo follows."

The entire room shifts. It's subtle, but I catch it. The way my father's eyes narrow toward Max. The way my mother sits is just a little straighter in her chair. The way the board members glance between them, suddenly realizing that something is happening here, something they don't fully understand.

I smile. Sitting back, relaxed. "You can add that to the list of things you'll have to accept, Mother."

Her lips press together, thin and taut. My father studies me for a beat longer before his gaze slides to Reaper, his eyes still narrowed. Max, they know. Reaper, they don't.

"And who, exactly, is *he*?"

Reaper remains silent. He doesn't move. Doesn't react. He just stares back at my father, expression unreadable.

I, however, don't miss a beat. "This?" I say smoothly, gesturing toward him. "Oh, this is my other personal bodyguard."

My father's eyes widen for a moment before smoothing them. My mother exhales sharply, muttering something under her breath. And Reaper? Reaper finally smirks.

My father knows better than to push for an answer. He won't get one. And just like that, the first domino begins to fall.

I settle into my chair at the conference table, legs crossed, fingers idly stroking over Hugo's massive head as he sits obediently beside me. My father's voice drones on, the conversation at the table weaving through projected earnings, asset holding, and supply chain concerns, words that used to be meaningless to me. But not anymore.

Not now that I own a piece of this corrupt empire. I don't contribute to the discussion, not yet. I just listen. Watch. Let them get comfortable. Then, casually, I extend a hand without looking. Reaper steps forward immediately, placing my phone in my palm. I unlock it with a quick swipe, typing out the simple words.

> Do it now.

I press send. A few moments later, my phone pings. I turn it over, glancing at the message from Elias.

> Done.

Perfect. I place my phone face down on the table and lean back in my chair, fingers steepling beneath my chin. I can feel Max's gaze on me from behind me, but I don't turn to meet it just yet.

A heavy sigh from across the room draws my attention.

"Wrenley." My mother's voice is clipped, sharp with impatience. "Are you even paying attention?"

I smile sweetly. "Of *course* I am, Mother."

She purses her lips, eyes gawking toward my nails, polished, sharp, and black as night. A silent disapproval lingers there, but I don't give her the satisfaction of reacting.

Silence stretches. Then, almost at the same time, several phones start ringing. Not just ringing—blaring. A ripple of unease rolls through the room as executives shift in their seats, exchanging glances as they fumble for their devices. One by one, their expressions morph from mild confusion to outright horror.

Then there's my father. His eyes widen, his face turning a blotchy shade of red as he grabs his phone, barking a sharp, "WHAT?" into the receiver.

The tension in the room thickens, the kind of suffocating, electric energy that tells me exactly what Elias has just pulled off.

My father shoves his chair back so forcefully that it scrapes loudly against the floor, rattling the table. "We're done here," he growls, ignoring me entirely as he storms from the room. Several board members practically scramble to follow, some of them still pale and stiff as they hold their phones to their ears, whispering urgent orders.

I stand slowly, smoothing my hands down the fabric of my black dress before turning to Max and Reaper. No words are needed. I nod once.

They move instantly, flanking me as I stride out of the conference room, the power in my step matching the chaos I've just unleashed. By the time we make it to my office, the first domino has fallen. And I'm just getting started.

Chapter Thirty-Four

MAXIMILIAN

WRENLEY LEANS against the edge of her desk, arms crossed, her expression one of pure satisfaction. The smug little smirk on her lips tells me she's enjoying every second of this. And she should. That was a goddamn power move back in the board-room, and watching her father's face turn ten shades of red had been *beautiful.*

I step toward her, close enough to see the excitement still burning in her eyes. Reaper lingers near the door, hands clasped behind his back like the ever-silent sentinel he is. "You pulled that off perfectly," I say, dragging my fingers along the edge of the desk beside her. "Almost like you've been playing this game a lot longer than you let on."

Her smirk deepens. "What can I say? I learn fast."

Reaper exhales sharply through his nose, something like amusement flashing across his normally unreadable face. "I'll be outside," he says, snapping his fingers for Hugo to follow. "Try not to make too much of a mess in here."

Wrenley snickers, and I roll my eyes as Reaper leads the dog out, shutting the door behind him.

The second it clicks shut, I turn to her, bracing a hand on the desk beside her hip. "So," I murmur, voice dropping an octave, "that thing you did back there, where you practically castrated your father in front of his board—*that* was sexy as hell."

She tilts her head, her polished fingernails tapping against the dark wood of the desk. "Oh? You like watching me tear my family apart, Blackwood?"

I hum, trailing a finger along the hem of her dress. "I like watching you *win*, Sparrow."

Her breath hitches, barely noticeable, but I don't miss it. She places her hands on the desk behind her, arching just enough to subtly push her chest forward. It's a dare. One, I have every intention of accepting.

"You know," she says, voice syrupy sweet, "I think you just like watching me, *period*."

I chuckle, my fingers tracing up the inside of her thigh, stopping just shy of anything truly wicked. "You say that like it's a bad thing."

She hums, shifting ever so slightly, her knee brushing my hip. "It could be," she muses, her voice barely above a whisper, "depending on what you plan on doing about it."

I grip her thigh suddenly, fingers tightening just enough to make her gasp. "Oh, Sparrow," I murmur, leaning in until my lips nearly brush hers, "you have no idea the things I plan on doing to you."

Her breath stutters, but she doesn't pull away. If anything, she leans in, her lips parting slightly. Her eyes zero in on my mouth, and fuck, that look alone is enough to make my self-control hang by a thread.

But I don't kiss her. Not yet. Instead, I slide my hand higher, the tips of my fingers grazing the heat between her thighs through the flimsy barrier of lace.

Her breath catches. "Max," she warns, but her tone betrays her; it's not a warning at all.

I smirk. "What is it, Sparrow?" My fingers stroke once, light as a whisper, and she shudders. "You were saying?"

She grips the desk like she needs to steady herself, her chest rising and falling faster now. "You're a menace," she breathes.

"And yet," I murmur, pressing my lips just below her ear, "you're not telling me to stop."

Her head tilts back slightly, giving me more access to the soft skin of her neck. I kiss the spot just beneath her jaw, slow and lingering, before nipping at it lightly. She inhales sharply, her fingers tightening on the desk.

"Max," she whispers, more of a plea than anything else.

I pull back, breathing hard, forcing space between us even though every cell in my body is screaming at me to take her. To bend her over this desk and remind her exactly who she belongs to. But I can still hear Doc's voice in the back of my mind—*No sex. She needs rest.*

I exhale sharply, my grip on her thighs tight, before I drop my hands entirely, dragging them through my hair. "Doc said no sex, Sparrow," I rasp, as if saying it out loud will make it easier to walk away from this.

Wrenley tilts her head, her smile all wicked with delight. "Well," she breathes, trailing her fingers up my chest, "I've never been one to follow the rules." Fuck. My restraint shatters.

"Fuck it."

Before she can say another word, I grip the back of her thighs and hoist her onto the desk, sending papers flying to the floor. She gasps, her legs wrapping around my waist, her hands tangling in my hair as our mouths crash in desperation.

She moans into the kiss, arching against me, and it's pure fucking heaven. My hands roam her body, pushing up her dress, palming her ass, dragging her flush against me so she can *feel* what she does to me.

Her fingers make quick work of the buttons on my shirt, pushing it off my shoulders before she moves to my belt. "You're taking too long," she mutters, frustration lacing her voice.

I chuckle darkly, grabbing her wrists and pinning her to the desk. "Patience, Sparrow."

She glares, but the effect is ruined by the way her breath hitches when I drag my teeth down the column of her throat, sucking a mark just beneath her jaw.

I release her hands, and the second I do, she shoves my belt free, popping the button of my pants and pushing them down just enough. My fingers slide beneath the lace of her panties, tearing them away in one swift motion.

She gasps, half outraged, half arousal. "Those were my favorite."

"I'll buy you a thousand more," I growl, already positioning myself between her legs.

Her nails dig into my shoulders as I grip her hips and pull her close, teasing her entrance with the tip of my cock. She whimpers, shifting against me, but I hold her still.

"Say it," I murmur against her lips. "Tell me how bad you want it."

She tips her head back, exposing her throat, her breath coming in short, desperate gasps. "Max, please."

That's all it takes. I drive into her in one deep thrust, swallowing the cry that escapes her lips as she clutches at my back, pulling me deeper.

"Fuck," I groan, burying my face in the crook of her neck. "You feel so fucking good."

Her legs clench around me, her heels digging into my ass, urging me on. "Then *move*," she commands, her voice ragged.

I smirk against her skin before obeying, setting a punishing pace, gripping her hips as I fuck her right there on the desk.

The room fills with the sounds of our pleasure, ragged breathing, the sharp slap of skin against skin, her breathless moans, and my deep guttural groans.

She drags her nails down my back, marking me, claiming me, and it only spurs me on.

"You like this, don't you?" I murmur against her ear, nipping at the sensitive skin. "You like knowing anyone could walk in and see you like this, see you coming apart for me."

She lets out a strangled moan, her walls clenching around me.

"*Max*," she gasps. "I'm—"

I slide a hand between us, circling her clit in tight, meticulous strokes. "Cum for me, Sparrow."

Her body tenses, her breath catching, and then she shatters, crying out my name as she falls apart in my arms. The sight of her completely wrecked, completely *mine*, pushes me over the edge. With one final thrust, I spill into her, groaning her name against her lips as I claim every inch of her.

For a long moment, neither of us moves. Her head rests on my shoulder, our breathing tangled together, her fingers tracing mindless patterns on my skin.

Eventually, I press a lingering kiss to her temple, smoothing her hair back. "So much for following the rules."

She laughs breathlessly, tilting her head to look up at me. "Rules are meant to be broken."

I smile, brushing my lips on hers one last time before reluctantly pulling away, helping her straighten her dress as I tuck myself back into my pants.

As I pick up the scattered papers, I shake my head. "This desk is never going to feel the same again."

Wrenley smirks, hopping down and smoothing her hands down her clothes. "Good." I chuckle, grabbing her by the waist and pulling her back in for one more slow, deep kiss before stepping back and nodding toward the door.

"Come on, Sparrow," I say. "Let's go see what kind of chaos Elias has cooked up while we were in here." She laughs. "Well, let's go see if anyone heard all that."

I smirk. "*If*?"

She rolls her eyes, grabbing my hand as we head for the door. And for once, I don't even try to stop her. The second Wrenley and I step out of her office, Reaper is standing there waiting, a knowing smirk on his face as he glances between us.

"Stitches still intact?" he asks, deadpan.

Wrenley presses a hand to her side, her lips twitching as she exhales. "Yeah... I think so?"

Reaper shakes his head, crossing his arms. "I'll check when we get back to the house. Try not to fuck them up any worse before then, yeah?"

I shoot him a glare, but he just grins wider, already walking toward the elevator.

Back at the mansion, Reaper doesn't waste any time. He goes to grab his bag of supplies. "Come on, let's see what damage you did," he mutters as he walks to the kitchen. "If they're loose, they'll need to be redone."

Wrenley sighs, pushing off the couch. "Fine. I need a drink first."

I follow her into the kitchen, watching as she grabs a bottle of whiskey, pours herself a glass, and knocks it back in one go. Then she hops up onto the counter, legs swinging as she gestures at Reaper. "Alright, do your worst."

I'm still standing there, arms crossed, staring at her like she's lost her damn mind. "Uh, Sparrow... you *do* realize you're naked under that dress, right?"

Reaper, already pulling on a pair of gloves, shrugs. "I helped perform her surgery. I've seen it all already."

I shoot him a murderous look. He holds up his hands in mock surrender. "*Not* that I was looking."

Wrenley just rolls her eyes, reaching for the sleeves of her dress. "Oh, for fuck's sake, you're all acting like a bunch of schoolboys."

She pulls the top half of her dress down, exposing herself without hesitation, as Reaper grabs his supplies. I try, *really fucking try*, to be supportive and mature about this, but every primal instinct in me is screaming that no one should be seeing her like this except *me*.

And then, just as Reaper sets to work, *of course,* Elias and Riot stroll into the kitchen, mid-conversation.

"Yeah, so I had to reroute the system twice—" Elias starts, but then freezes. Riot walks straight into his back, not paying attention, before he looks up, and his eyes go wide. Silence.

Then my growl fills the kitchen. "Turn. The fuck. Around." They both do. Immediately.

But Elias, being Elias, still must run his damn mouth. "I mean... technically, we already saw—"

"Elias," my voice is a warning.

"Right, right. Eyes closed, head down. *Definitely* not thinking about your girlfriend's tits."

Wrenley, unbothered as ever, just shakes her head. "You two are like twelve-year-olds. They're just boobs."

I narrow my eyes. "*My* boobs." Reaper, still working, doesn't even look up. "This is *so* weird for me."

Wrenley smirks, then looks at Elias. "You were saying?" Elias, still facing the wall, clears his throat. "Uh, yeah. So. We set everything in motion. First steps are done, and it's spreading like wildfire. Your father's phone is probably melting as we speak."

Riot, unable to resist, leans a little toward Elias and whispers loud enough for me to hear, "Can we turn around yet, or is Max still looking like he's going to kill someone?"

Reaper snorts. Wrenley just laughs. And me? I run a hand down my face, *seriously* considering murder. Just as I'm about to throw Elias and Riot out of the kitchen *physically,* Margot bursts in from the opposite side, holding a laptop in one hand, her eyes glued to the screen.

"Oh, hey. Boobs," she says absentmindedly, barely sparing Wrenley a glance.

Elias groans. "What the *fuck?* Why does *she* get to look?"

I shrug, deadpan. "Well, she has some, so it's fine."

Margot pauses mid-step, brow furrowing. "Wait, *what?*"

Still sitting on the counter, Wrenley sighs dramatically. "Oh, my God. *Everyone, get over it already.*"

Margot just shakes her head and waves the laptop. "Anyway. While you all were dealing with *that,* I was doing some digging into Vivian, because you guys were focused on her father, and let's be honest, that woman is *terrifying.*"

Elias hesitates but finally steps forward, still very clearly trying not to let his gaze drift anywhere inappropriate. "What did you find?"

Margot plops the laptop down on the counter next to Wrenley. "I think I found something big."

Wrenley straightens, wincing slightly as Reaper finishes up her stitches and steps away. "*What* is it?"

Elias, now leaning over the laptop, squints at the screen, his brows knitting together. He mutters a distracted *hold on* before shifting to Margot, "How the hell did you even find this?"

She shrugs, a sly smile tugging at her lips. "Eh, I know some *basic* hacking stuff."

Elias glares at her. "Baby. This is *not* basic hacking."

Margot grins and nudges him with her elbow. "Don't be jealous, baby, I'm just more talented."

Elias groans, but his eyes remain locked on the screen, his complexion paling slightly.

Wrenley narrows her eyes. "*Elias.* What the fuck is it?"

Elias swallows hard, looking like he might pass out. His mouth opens, but nothing comes out.

"*Elias!*" He quickly shakes his head and mutters, "Nope. Not doing it. *You* tell her."

I stiffen at that. Whatever is on that screen is *bad.*

I step forward, my voice low. "Tell her *what?*"

Margot, uncharacteristically serious now, slowly turns the laptop toward Wrenley. "You might want to stay sitting down for this one, babe."

Chapter Thirty-Five

WRENLEY

I STARE at the laptop screen, my breath caught somewhere between my lungs and my throat. My mind barely registers Elias and Margot continuing to talk, their words tangling together like static. I can't move. Can't blink. The words in front of me burn into my brain, repeatedly, as if saying them enough time will somehow make them untrue.

Vivian killed Benjamin. Not my father. Not the empire itself. My *mother*. The emails are time-stamped, spanning months, private exchanges between Benjamin and my mother, ones that should have never seen the light of day. The words are acidic, seething with venom, each line more damning than the last.

> VIVIAN: I KNOW WHAT YOU'RE DOING, BENJAMIN. I WON'T LET YOU TEAR THIS FAMILY APART.
>
> BENJAMIN: THE ASHFORDS DESERVE TO BURN, VIVIAN. YOU KNOW IT AS WELL AS I DO. IF YOU WEREN'T SO BUSY PLAYING QUEEN OF THE DAMNED, YOU MIGHT HAVE FOUND YOUR SOUL BY NOW.
>
> VIVIAN: YOU THINK YOU'RE SO CLEVER? YOU THINK YOU'RE UNTOUCHABLE? YOU FORGET WHO YOU'RE DEALING WITH. I MADE THIS FAMILY, BENJAMIN. I MADE CHARLES. YOU'RE NOTHING BUT A PETULANT CHILD WHO NEVER LEARNED HIS PLACE.

BENJAMIN: I LEARNED IT. AND NOW I INTEND TO
DESTROY IT.

VIVIAN: YOU WON'T LIVE LONG ENOUGH TO TRY.

The next message is the final nail in the coffin.

VIVIAN: YOU WON'T FEEL A THING, LITTLE
BROTHER. CONSIDER IT A KINDNESS.

My stomach turns violently, nausea rising so fast I feel like I might be sick.

"I'm gonna be sick," I murmur.

Margot's head snaps up. "Hey, hey, breathe, okay? Just breathe, Wren."

My hands are shaking so hard I have to clench them into fists to keep from reaching for something to break.

"She—" I try to swallow, but my throat is bone-dry. I shake my head. "She *killed* him."

Silence grips the room like a vice, the weight of realization pressing down on everyone.

Elias scrubs his hands down his face. "Yeah. She did."

Max hasn't said a word, but I can feel his presence like a live wire beside me. He's tense, barely keeping himself in check, watching me with dark, careful eyes. I can hear the quiet pop of his knuckles as he curls his fingers into a fist, but he stays still. Waiting.

For *me*. For *my* reaction. And it doesn't come. Not yet. Instead, I just... stand.

Pushing off the counter, moving slowly, methodically, as if my body is acting on some kind of muscle memory I don't even recognize. I don't look at anyone. I don't trust myself to speak. I just walk. Up the stairs. Away. I hear Max shift behind me, instinctively following.

Then Margot's voice, soft but firm. "No. Let me."

Max doesn't argue. At least, not out loud. I feel her presence before I hear her footsteps. She's quieter than I expected, or maybe my pulse is too loud in my ears. Still, I don't stop walking until I reach my bedroom. I step inside, but I don't close the door.

I sit on the edge of the bed, staring at the floor, my mind reeling. Margot leans against the doorway, crossing her arms. "You wanna talk about it, or should I just stand here until you finally stop pretending you're okay?"

I let out a breath that's more of a laugh than anything else, except it's hallowed. Empty. "I don't know what to feel." My voice sounds foreign to me. Detached. Margot steps inside, slow and careful, like she's approaching a wild animal that might bolt at any second. She sits next to me, nudging my legs with hers.

"That's okay," she says softly. "You don't have to know what to feel. Not yet."

I exhale through my nose, staring at my hands in my lap. "It was supposed to be him. My *father*. It was *always* supposed to be him."

She doesn't correct me. Doesn't offer empty reassurances. She sits and waits. Because she knows me better than anyone. And she knows what's coming. A storm. A war. And this? This was the final fucking straw.

"I need to change," I murmur, standing from the bed.

Margot watches me carefully, as if she's afraid I might collapse at any second. "You sure you don't want to talk more?"

I shake my head. "Not now. Meet me downstairs?"

She hesitates but nods, standing as well. "Alright. I'll be in the kitchen."

I don't wait for her to say anything else before I slip into my closet, grabbing a pair of worn jeans, a black tank top, and sneakers. I move quickly, stripping out of the dress I'd been wearing and yanking on the new clothes with methodical precision. I pull my hair into a loose bun at the top of my head, not bothering to check the mirror before I step out and make my way downstairs.

I hear them before I see them. "She didn't say anything?" Torque asks his voice lower than usual.

"No," Elias answers, "Margot says it's like a trauma response or something."

Max is silent. I round the corner into the kitchen, and all conversation stops. All eyes shift to me.

I meet each of their gazes before exhaling slowly. "I want to paint."

Silence.

Elias blinks. "You—what?"

"I'm going to Aether Art Supply." I grab my keys from the counter. "I need canvases. Paint. Charcoal. Whatever else calls to me."

Max stands. "I'll drive."

I nod, pocketing my keys. "Alright."

No one questions it. Elias and Riot exchange a look but don't press. Margot watches me, her expression unreadable.

Max grabs his keys from the island, following me out the front door.

❦

The drive is silent. Not uncomfortable, just quiet. Max doesn't push. He knows that if I want to talk, I will. And if I don't... well, he'll wait. It's something I never realized I needed before him, the space to just *be* without expectations. Without someone demanding answers, I'm not ready to give.

He drives through the city, his fingers tapping against the gear shift absentmindedly. I stare out the window, watching the world move around me, detached from it all.

By the time we pull up to Aether, I feel like I can breathe again. Inside, I let my fingers skim over the rows of paint tubes, the familiar scent of canvas and linseed oil settling something deep inside me. I grab what I need without overthinking: deep red, blacks, blues, and a few neutrals. A few oversized canvases, fresh brushes, and some charcoal.

Max follows behind me, saying nothing, but I can feel his presence like a tether grounding me in place.

He tosses his credit card on the counter. "You don't ha—"

"I know," he says, grabbing the bags and leading me back to the car.

The drive back to the house is the same comfortable silence, the weight in my chest not quite gone, but manageable.

I step out of the car, grab my things, and head toward the back garden. Max follows. I don't tell him to. He just does. He settles into one of the wrought-iron chairs nearby, pulling his phone out, fingers moving swiftly over the screen. He doesn't have to say it; I know he's texting Elias, telling him to be ready whenever I decide the next move. I set up my easel, stretching the canvas into place before I take a deep breath.

Then, I start.

The first strokes are chaotic, slashing through the blank space with charcoal, dragging shadows across the canvas, shaping something dark and twisted, beginning to form. My hands move faster, colors bleeding into one another, frantic and raw.

Minutes stretch into an hour before I finally speak. "My mother was never warm," I say, my voice calm despite the raging inside me. Max doesn't look up from his phone. "No?"

I shake my head, dipping my brush into deep crimson. "Not even when I was little," I pause, watching the paint drip down the canvas before continuing. "She wasn't cruel, exactly. Just... cold. *Always disappointed in me.*"

Max looks up at that, watching me closely now. I let out a short, humorless laugh. "You know what she said to me the first time I showed her one of my paintings?"

He shakes his head.

I look at him. "She told me that art is for people who have nothing better to do."

His jaw clenches, but he stays quiet.

"She wanted me to be like her," I continue, layering darker shades onto the canvas. "Perfect. Polished. Someone who could smile at charity galas and sip champagne without saying a single *real* thing. She called it 'maintaining appearances.'"

Max exhales through his nose, rubbing a hand along his jaw.

I shake my head, adding streaks of black. "Benjamin was the only one who ever really saw me. He let me be who I was. Encouraged it. And she *hated* that."

Max's voice is quiet, steady. "And now you know she's the one who took him from you."

I don't respond right away. I just stare at the stroke of red seeping into the canvas, smearing under my fingertips. Then, finally, I nod. Max doesn't say anything else. He just watches. And for the first time in a long time, I don't feel alone in it.

The final stroke of black smears across the canvas, jagged and heavy, as if my own hands refuse to soften it. I drop the brush, my chest rising and falling unevenly as I take a slow step back, tilting my head to study the image in front of me.

It's her. Or rather, how I *see* her.

My mother's face is there, distorted, half consumed by darkness. Her porcelain skin fractured, cracked like an old doll's with lines creeping up her cheeks, her forehead, her throat. Her eyes, hollow, empty, devoid of warmth, swallowed by the same shadows that spill out behind her, stretching like poisoned ink bleeding. The colors are sharp, violent, a mix of black, gray, and deep reds that seem to pulse with something insidious.

Her lips are curled, not quite a snarl, not quite a smile—just... *wrong*. In her hands, she holds a pair of golden shears. The blades gleam, polished and sharp, handles elegant, delicate, deceptively beautiful. But they are open. Ready to sever.

The ribbons tangled around them are frayed at the ends, twisting and curling around her fingers, some barely hanging on by a thread. But others have already been cut, falling lifelessly at her feet, nothing more than remnants of something once whole.

A chill rolls down my spine. "This is how I see her," I

murmur, my voice quiet, but steady. Max stands, his boots silent against the stone as he moves behind me, his hands sliding around my waist before he gently pulls me into his lap as he settles back into the chair.

I let him. His warmth seeps into me, grounding me as I lean against his chest. His fingers skim up my back, tracing soft lines over my spine.

He studies the painting for a long time before he finally speaks. "It's haunting." His voice is low, reverent. "But it's fucking *brilliant.*"

A humorless laugh leaves me, my fingers gripping his shirt. "It's her."

"Yeah." He nods, his chin brushing my temple. "It is."

I swallow hard, my throat tight. "Benjamin always told me that I had a way of pulling truth out of things most people didn't even notice."

Max is quiet for a moment, then, "He was right."

I squeeze my eyes shut. The weight of everything I've been holding back, everything I've been *avoiding,* crashes down on me all at once.

I grip his shirt tighter, my breath hitching. "I miss him," I whisper.

Max's hold on me tightens.

"He was the only one who encouraged me to find and follow my passion," I continue, my voice trembling. "The only one who ever believed in me. In what I wanted. Who I wanted to be." A shaky breath. "And she took him from me."

Max doesn't interrupt. He just listens. His fingers trail up my arms, slow and reassuring, his other hand resting firmly on my thigh, keeping me anchored to him.

I don't know how long we sit there, minutes, maybe hours, but the tension in my body slowly unravels as his presence steadies me.

Then, softly, he speaks. "I didn't know him as long as you did," he murmurs. "But I knew enough." He exhales, leaning his head back against the chair. "Benjamin wanted something better for this city, for you. He wasn't afraid to take risks, and he knew how dangerous it was. He still tried anyway."

I nod, pressing my face into his chest.

"He used to say the same thing about you," Max continues, his voice quiet. "That you were *his* risk. That you weren't supposed to turn out the way you did, not with the parents you had." I choke out a small, watery laugh.

"He told me once that you were the only good thing to come from your father's bloodline," Max says, pressing a kiss to the top of my head. "And that he'd die before he let them ruin you."

A sharp pang spears through my ribs, my breath catching. And just like that, the dam breaks. A soft, broken sob escapes me as I curl tighter against him, my fingers dipping into his shirt, my body trembling from the weight of it all. Max just holds me. He doesn't say anything else. Doesn't try to tell me it's okay, or that I need to be strong, or that I need to move on.

He just *stays*.

His arms stay locked around me, his hands gentle as he strokes soothing circles into my back. The tears keep coming, silent and steady, until exhaustion starts to pull at me, my breathing slowing, my body going slack against him. He shifts slightly, adjusting so I'm more comfortable, and I feel the soft press of his lips against my temple before everything fades to black. And for the first time since Benjamin died, I let myself really rest.

Chapter Thirty-Six

MAXIMILIAN

THE AFTERNOON SUN HAS SHIFTED, casting long golden streaks across the garden. Wrenley is still curled in my lap, her breathing soft and even against my chest. Her body is warm, relaxed, and completely trusting. It's a dangerous kind of trust, but *fuck* if I don't crave it.

Movement from the house catches my attention. Wrecker and Torque step onto the stone path leading toward us, their boots crunching over the gravel. Wrecker stops short when his gaze lands on the painting Wrenley left propped up on the easel. His expression shifts, something between awe and disbelief washing over his normally unreadable face.

I feel Wrenley stir against me, the shift of her body subtle, but enough for me to know she's waking. I press a soft kiss to the top of her head before brushing her hair back. "Sparrow," I whisper. "If we sit in the sun much longer, you're gonna burn."

She blinks up at me, her lashes heavy with sleep. There's a moment where she looks so damn peaceful, it makes something in my chest squeeze tight. But then she follows my line of sight and notices Wrecker standing in front of her painting, looking like he's just seen some sort of divine intervention.

"Holy fuck," Wrecker mutters, shaking his head slightly as if trying to snap himself out of whatever trance he's in. He glances back at her, his brow furrowed. "You're fucking brilliant, you know that?"

She stretches slightly before shifting in my lap, rubbing her eyes. "You think so?" Her voice is laced with exhaustion, but there's a hint of amusement there, too.

Wrecker scoffs, still staring at the canvas. "Yeah, I think so, can I keep this?"

Torque crosses his arms, giving the painting a quick glance before Wrenley can answer, and says, "Elias called. Said some new plan is coming."

I don't respond right away. Instead, I turn to Wrenley, watching her closely. She tilts her head slightly, lips pressing into a thoughtful line before shrugging one shoulder. "Yeah," she replies simply. "I guess it is."

I push to my feet, pulling her up with me, making sure she's steady before brushing my knuckles along her cheek. Then, because I fucking need to, I cup the back of her neck and pull her into a slow, lingering kiss. It's not desperate. It's not frantic. It's something deeper.

She sighs into my mouth, her hands pressing against my chest, and for a moment, I think about forgetting the entire world again. But there's work to do. Plans to finalize. I pull back, letting my lips hover over hers before murmuring, "Come on, Sparrow. Let's go fuck up your family."

She smirks, slipping her hand into mine as we turn toward the house, leaving behind the painting, the garden, and any last piece of hesitation about what we're about to do.

The moment Wrenley and I step into the study, the energy shifts. The house has felt charged all day, but now it feels like the moment before a storm, heavy, waiting to break.

Elias is perched at the table, the three laptops open in front of him, the glow of multiple screens reflecting off his face. Riot is leaning against the wall near the bar cart, arms crossed, while Torque and Wrecker are sprawled across the couch, looking like two men who are ready to destroy anything at a moment's notice. Reaper stands near the fireplace, as silent and imposing as ever, watching everything with a careful eye. Margot sits on the edge of an armchair, her legs tucked under her, a half-finished glass of wine in her hand.

They've been waiting.

Elias is the first to break the silence. "Glad you two could finally join us," he says, arching a brow. "I was starting to think we'd have to burn this place down just to get your attention."

Wrenley smirks, brushing past me as she approaches the table. "Patience, Elias," she says smoothly. "I'm here now."

I take the chair next to hers, keeping close, my knee brushing against hers beneath the table. No one comments on it, but I don't miss the way Reaper glances between us before returning his attention to the screens.

"We're making progress," Elias says, tapping a few keys. The images on the monitors shift, showing back records, security footage, and a scrolling list of names. "Between the warehouse hit and the financial bleed we started, your dad's been scrambling. He's been calling in favors, but the well is running dry."

Riot chuckles darkly. "Seems like the Ashfords are finally feeling the pressure."

"Not enough," Wrenley mutters, eyes scanning the data in front of her.

Elias smirks. "That's why we keep pushing. Your father's got too many loose ends, and we've got receipts for all of them."

Reaper speaks up, his voice low. "We took their weapons. We hit their finances. But that's just the surface. If we really want to dismantle them, we need to keep going."

Torque leans forward, rubbing a hand over his stubbled jaw. "We need a bigger hit. Something that sends a message."

I nod. "The goal isn't just to weaken them. It's to ensure they never recover."

Margot sighs, swirling the wine in her glass before looking at Wrenley. "Optics matter too. Your father thrives on control,

Wren. If we strip him of that, if you destroy the illusion... he's finished."

Elias taps on the keyboard again, pulling up another set of documents. "Which is where I come in," He says smugly. "I've been gathering evidence, transactions, offshore accounts, and internal communications. The moment we drop this, the world will see the Ashfords for what they are."

Silence stretches for a moment. Wrenley leans back in her chair, exhaling slowly. I can tell she's thinking, piecing it all together, mapping out every possible outcome.

Then, finally, "This isn't enough."

All eyes snap to her. Elias blinks. "Excuse me?"

She straightens, her voice calm but laced with something sharp. "Taking down my father is a priority. But if we stop here, we're only cutting off the head of the snake. The body will keep moving."

I lean forward, studying her. "What are you saying, Sparrow?"

Her eyes find mine, burning with something lethal. "There's one more thing we need to plan." A pause. Then, "My mother's death."

The room stills.

Elias lets out a breath. "Damn, sweetheart. You don't fuck around."

Reaper's expression remains unreadable, but he nods once in silent agreement.

Wrenley's voice is steady, controlled. "She killed Benjamin. She has just as much blood on her hands as my father, maybe more. And if I don't stop her, she'll find a way to destroy me, too."

I exhale, my jaw tightening as I watch her. She doesn't hesitate. Doesn't waver. She means every word.

Reaper speaks first. "Then we plan it. We make sure it's clean. Undeniably."

I nod, pushing down the protective instinct that rises in my chest. "Alright," I say, voice firm. "Let's put an end to the Ice Queen."

Margot sits up straight, tossing back the last of her wine. "Alright, we need something stronger than this if we're gonna plan a goddamn assassination."

Wrenley smirks, standing with her. "Come on, Mags. Let's raid the bar."

Two of them disappear into the kitchen, leaving the rest of us sitting in charged silence. The weight of what we're planning settles over the room like a storm cloud, thick and inevitable.

Elias exhales loudly, rubbing his face. "Jesus Christ. First, we take out half their operations, and now we're planning a hit on Mommy Dearest. This escalated fast."

I lean forward, bracing my elbows on my knees. "She's already said she's pulling the trigger on her father, too."

Elias looks at me, his expression unreadable, before he leans back, folding his arms. "So we're really doing this. We're talking full-scale *execution* of the Ashford family."

Reaper, who's been silent for a while, finally steps forward, his sharp eyes locking onto me. "Are you sure about this?"

I glance up at him, my jaw tight. "You think I'd let her do this alone?"

He shakes his head, unimpressed. "That's not what I asked."

The tension crackles between us like a live wire. I push up from my chair, pacing across the room as I drag a hand through my hair. The weight in my chest grows heavier with every step, but it's not uncertainty; it's conviction.

"If she wants to take the throne of a corrupt empire, I'll place the crown on her head. If she wants to tear it down and disappear into nothing, I'll follow her into the abyss. And if she wants to set the whole world on fire, I'll be right there beside her, handing her the goddamn matches and watching it burn."

The silence that follows is thick and unmoving. The weight of my words lands like a blow, even though every single person in this room already knew where I stood.

Reaper stares at me, his expression hard, assessing, then something shifts. His lips twitch at the corners, his smile slow and knowing.

"If you don't marry this girl, you're the biggest dumbass I know, and I will."

The room erupts in low chuckles, tension bleeding away just enough to let us breathe. But I don't laugh. Because for the first time since all of this started... the thought doesn't scare me. It feels inevitable.

Riot snorts, shaking his head. "I mean, she did survive a bullet for you, and you two have been screwing each other across half the city. Just saying, at this point, you'd be stupid not to lock it down."

I don't confirm or deny it. Because the truth is... I think he might be right. The conversation is still hanging in the air when the girls walk back into the room. Wrenley and Margot are carrying a pitcher of margaritas and a full bottle of tequila, looking pleased with themselves.

"What's so funny?" Wrenley asks, setting the drinks down on the table before pouring herself a glass. Wrecker opens his mouth to say something, but freezes when his gaze locks onto mine. He seems to decide against it, shaking his head quickly.

I smile, pouring a drink. "Nothing. We're just acting like a bunch of twelve-year-olds, right?"

Margot and Wrenley exchange a look before grinning. At the same time, they both say, "Boobs."

Torque groans. "For fuck's sake."

Laughter fills the room again, the dark cloud that had settled over us temporarily lifting. Torque sits up straighter, his brows furrowing. "Hey, shouldn't we make sure Wrenley's name isn't tied to any of this? I mean, she does own part of the business now, right?"

The room goes still. All eyes shift to Elias, who looks genuinely offended. "Are you fucking kidding me? You don't seriously think I didn't already scrub her name from every goddamn traceable document and remove her from everything that needed removing, do you?"

Riot grins, handing him a shot. "God bless our hacker prince."

Elias lifts the glass, lounging back on the couch. "Damn right."

With that settled, the planning continues. The afternoon shifts into night, and we go over every detail, tightening every loose end. Shots of tequila are passed around. Margaritas disappear at an alarming rate. Somewhere along the way, Margot starts dramatically reenacting one of Wrenley's inevitable confrontations with her mother, complete with her best "ice queen" impression.

But my focus keeps slipping back to Wrenley. The way she looks when she's scheming, her sharp mind cutting through every obstacle like a blade. The way she laughs easily despite the weight of everything pressing down on her shoulders.

The way she meets my gaze from across the room with something dark and looming behind those striking eyes. Fuck. I'm so screwed.

Suddenly, she stands and grabs my hand, pulling me up from my seat with a sultry look in her eyes...

"C'mon, Maximilian," She murmurs, tugging me toward the stairs.

The room erupts into catcalls and whistles.

"Atta boy, Blackwood!" Wrecker laughs.

"Get it, Boss!" Riot hoots.

Margot claps dramatically. "Make good choices!"

Elias just sighs, shaking his head. "Or bad ones. Whatever."

Reaper is smiling, only says "Stitches."

I shoot them all a middle finger over my shoulder as Wrenley leads me upstairs, laughter chasing us the whole way. I don't know what the hell I did in another life to deserve this woman. But I sure as hell am not letting her go.

Chapter Thirty-Seven

WRENLEY

I DON'T STOP until we reach our bedroom, my pulse a steady thrumming in my ears as I lead Max inside. As soon as he clicks the door shut behind us, I launch myself at him, legs wrapping around his waist, arms around his neck, my mouth crashing into his like I need him to breathe.

Max groans against my lips, catching me effortlessly, his grip bruising as he cups my ass, pulling me impossibly closer. Walking us toward the bed without breaking the kiss, his tongue tangling with mine in a frenzy of heat and hunger.

Then, suddenly, he wrenches me away from him, only to throw me onto the mattress. I barely have time to register the loss before his hands are on my jeans, undoing the button in one swift motion. He yanks them down my legs, his fingers skimming over my skin with a mix of impatience and possession.

I sit up just enough to grab the hem of my tank top, popping it over my head, and toss it aside. Max exhales sharply, his eyes darkening when he sees that I'm not wearing a bra.

"Fuck, Sparrow," he rasps, his hands trailing up my ribs, over my breast, his thumbs running over my already hardened nipples.

A smirk tugs at my lips. "Something wrong?"

He growls in response, shoving me back against the bed as I reach for the button of his pants, making quick work of it. I push them down over his hips, along with his boxers, freeing his cock, thick, hard, and already leaking at the tip, loving what I do to this man.

I bite my lip, dragging my fingers over him, teasing. Max grabs my wrist and pins it above my head, his other hand gripping my jaw as he presses his forehead against mine, his breath coming hot and uneven.

"You have no fucking idea how bad I need you," he growls, his voice rough with restraint.

"Then take me, hard," I whisper, my lips brushing his, my body arching into his like belonging to him. His eyes flash with something primal, and he's flipping me onto my stomach, his large hands gripping my hips, pulling me onto my knees.

A sharp smack lands on my ass, making me gasp.

"Impatient little thing," he mutters, running his fingers through my center, groaning at how ready I am for him.

Without warning, he thrust into me, stretching me with one deep, punishing stroke. I cry out, fingers clutching the sheets, the burn of him filling me, igniting me raw and desperate inside. Max doesn't ease up, he fucks me hard, relentlessly, his grip tightening on my hips, dragging me back against him with every thrust.

"This is what you wanted, Sparrow?" he grits out, his voice a mix of hunger and possession.

"Yes," I moan, meeting his thrust, taking everything he gives me.

His hand snakes up my spine, tangling in my hair, pulling my head back. "Say it."

I shudder, my body already on the verge of breaking. "Fuck me, Max." I breathe. "I want all of you."

A deep growl vibrates through his chest as he slams into me harder, the headboard rattling against the wall, our moans and heavy breathing filling the room.

His hand slips between my legs, his fingers finding my clit, rubbing tight, merciless circles.

"Cum for me," he orders, his voice a command, a demand I can't disobey.

Pleasure rips through me like lightning, sharp, blinding, and impossible to contain, my walls clenching around him as I scream his name. My vision goes white. Max curses, his rhythm faltering, his grip turns bruising as he thrusts deep one last time before he finds his release, spilling into me with a guttural groan.

We're nothing but tangled limbs and heavy breaths, our bodies still trembling from the aftershocks. Then Max collapses beside me, pulling me against him, his lips pressing against my damp skin, whispering something against my shoulder. Something I feel more than I hear. Something I already know to be true. We're completely, irrevocably, and utterly ruined for each other.

The adrenaline has finally settled, leaving nothing but warmth and the steady sound of our breathing filling the room. My head is on Max's chest, tracing lazily over his skin as he absently runs his fingers up and down my spine. It's peaceful in a way I never imagined possible.

"Do you ever sleep?" I murmur, pressing a soft kiss to his collarbone.

He hums, his chest vibrating under my cheek. "With you in my bed? Apparently not."

I grin, dragging my nails lightly across his stomach, feeling him shiver. "Poor thing. I must be exhausting."

"You are," he says, tipping my chin up, his lips caressing mine. "But I wouldn't trade it for anything."

I sigh, letting my eyes close for a moment, savoring the heat of him against me. "Tell me something about you I don't know." Max's fingers continue their slow path down my back, his voice low. "I was a terrible kid."

I snort, looking up at him. "No way."

"Swear it." He smirks, rubbing his thumb over my bottom lip. "I once stole a pack of gum from a convenience store just because the guy at the register wouldn't sell me a beer; I was twelve."

I laugh, shifting onto my side, propping my head up with my arm. "And here I thought you only stole weapons and beat people half to death."

"I'm a man of many talents," he teases, his eyes glinting with something softer as he watches me. "What about you, Sparrow? Tell me something."

I pretend to think for a second. "I used to want to be an actress."

He raises a brow, interested. "Really?"

I nod. "When I was little, I used to act out scenes from movies in my bedroom. I even made Margot play supporting roles."

Max grins, brushing a stray strand of hair from my face. "And what changed?"

I shrug, glancing at where our fingers are tangled together. "Life. I found my passion in painting instead."

He studies me for a moment, then kisses the top of my head. "You'd have made one hell of an actress, Sparrow."

A small smile tugs at my lips. "Maybe in another life."

The silence stretches between us again, comfortable and easy. I close my eyes, listening to the steady hum of his heartbeat beneath my ear. Eventually, drifting off, cocooned in his warmth.

When I wake, it's still before dawn, and I feel an entirely different kind of hunger curling in my stomach. Max is still asleep, his arm draped lazily over my waist, his face relaxed in a way I rarely see. He looks so damn perfect like this, unguarded, peaceful.

But I want him awake. I press a kiss to his chest, then another lower. Max shifts but doesn't wake. I trail my kisses down the ridges of his stomach, my tongue tracing against the dip of his hip bone. His breathing deepens. Smiling, I move lower. The second my mouth wraps around him, a sharp breath hisses through his teeth, his hands flying to my hair.

"Fuck," he groans, his hips shifting slightly.

I hum, taking him deeper, my fingers digging into his thighs as I move slowly and deliberately. His grip tightens in my hair, a broken sound escaping him as he wakes fully, his body going tense. "Sparrow—"

I lift my eyes to him, keeping my pace slow, torturous. Before I can finish what I started. Max curses, his jaw clenching as he pulls me up, rolling me onto my back. His lips crash into mine, his kiss searing, desperate.

He settles between my legs, his hands framing my face, his breath ragged.

"You drive me fucking insane," he mutters against my mouth.

I grin, dragging my nails down his back. "That's the goal."

Max lets out a low chuckle, his eyes lock on mine with an intensity that makes my breath hitch. The humor fades, something deeper settling in the space between us.

"I love you," he says, the words slipping out rough, unpolished, but real.

I go still, my heart pounding. But I don't hesitate. "I love you, too."

Max exhales, like he's been holding it in, like some part of him wasn't sure I'd say it back. Then he kisses me, slow, deep like he's memorizing the way I taste. And when he pushes into me, it's not just sex. It's something so much more.

The warm glow of morning filters through the mansion, casting long golden streaks along the hallway as Max and I head downstairs. My silk robe flutters against my bare legs, the satin sleep shorts underneath barely covering anything. Max, dressed in only sweats, looks as effortlessly rugged as ever, his muscles still taut from the way I had woken him up earlier.

He presses a kiss to my temple as we reach the bottom of the stairs, his hand resting possessively on the small of my back. I glance toward the living room, pausing mid-step at the sight before me.

Margot and Elias are sprawled across the couch, completely naked. Riot is knocked out across from them, wearing only his boxers, one leg dangling off like he lost a battle with gravity. I tilt my head, narrowing my eyes at the scene. I'm... not entirely sure what happened here last night.

Max, on the other hand, takes one look, sighs heavily, and promptly turns on his heel. "Nope." He walks straight into the kitchen without a second glance.

Margot shifts groggily, her hair a mess, a lazy smile curling on her lips as she spots me.

"Morning, sunshine," she croons, stretching like a satisfied cat.

I arch a brow, crossing my arms. "Mags, put your toys away when you're done playing with them."

Elias, barely lifting his head, groans. "You weren't supposed to be up yet." His voice is gravelly with sleep, dripping with smug amusement.

"Margaritas were strong, huh?" I quip, already walking toward the kitchen. Behind me, I hear Riot groggily chuckle, muttering something about needing to reassess all his life choices.

I push through the kitchen door to find Max at the counter, already starting a pot of coffee, his broad back facing me. Reaper walks in just as I hop onto the counter, his medical bag slung over his shoulder, eyes already assessing me.

I sigh, shaking my head as I undo the tie to my robe. "Alright, let's get this over with."

Max clears his throat pointedly. I blink at him. "I have something on under here, you big baby."

Reaper snorts, tossing his bag onto the counter. "Shame.

Think I got a glimpse of Elias's bare ass last night, might as well round it out with yours."

I laugh, but Max scowls, grabbing his coffee, muttering under his breath, "I will murder all of you before noon."

Reaper just grins. "Sounds like a you problem, brother." I tilt my head at Reaper as he works, his fingers precise as he checks over my stitches. Despite the early house and his usual stoic demeanor, there's something soft about him today.

"You know," I say, watching him closely, "you started off all scary and broody, but you're actually coming out of your shell a bit."

He snorts, shaking his head as he finishes and starts packing up his kit. "Yeah, well... I think we're a bit alike, you and I." He glances up, and for the first time, there's something more open in his expression. "I feel comfortable with you, I guess."

I grin. "I have that effect on people."

"You have *some* effect on people," Max mutters, sipping his coffee. Before I can shoot back a retort, the kitchen doors swing open, and the rest of the house filters in, everyone in various states of undress and pajamas.

Margot, still looking pleased with herself, slides onto one of the barstools and snags the coffee pot right out of Max's hand to pour herself a cup. Elias shuffles in right after her, stealing a piece of toast straight off the counter.

Riot leans against the fridge, stretching like a man who spent the night on the floor and regrets all of his life choices. "Well, we survived another night in the madhouse."

"I don't know if I'd call last night *survival*," Elias says, smirking at Margot.

Before she can fire back, the kitchen door swings open again, and Torque steps inside, pausing just past the threshold. He slowly takes in the scene, disheveled hair, half-dressed bodies, coffee cups clutched like lifelines, and finally just shakes his head.

"If I were a stranger walking into this," he drawls, "It looks like one hell of an orgy just went down in this house..." he lets his words hang, arching a brow before adding. "And from the *sounds* we all heard, some very loud noises came from upstairs."

Silence stretches for half a beat before I turn to Max, my expression completely unrepentant.

"I regret nothing."

Max chuckles low and dark, pulling me against him with an arm around my waist. "Good. Because if I have my way, those *loud noises* aren't stopping anytime soon."

Margot lifts her mug in a mock toast. "Too loud noises."

Elias smirks. "And regretless decisions."

Wrecker, who has been silent, sighs. "This is why I drink."

Reaper just shakes his head, already retreating with his coffee in hand. "I fucking hate this house."

"You love it here," I shout at his back. He turns and gives me a wink before rounding the corner. I just smile. Because *this*, madness, this chaos, this makeshift family, is everything I never knew I needed.

Chapter Thirty-Eight

MAXIMILIAN

IT'S BEEN a week since Wrenley and I decided to officially bring Riot, Reaper, Wrecker, and Torque into the house. They didn't even put up a fight about it, just threw their duffel bags in whatever rooms were available and acted like they'd lived here for years. It made sense. They were always here anyway, and if we are going to finish what we started, we needed them close.

But today? Today was the day we finally put the nail in Charles Ashford's coffin.

I stand next to Wrenley, dressed in a dark suit, hands folded in front of me as we step off the elevator into Ashford International. Reaper is at my other side, wearing one of my suits again, except now he owns the look like it was meant for him. Riot and Wrecker follow behind us in a show of force, their presence alone enough to make employees turn their heads, whispers spreading like fire.

And then there's Wrenley. She walks between us like she owns the entire fucking city. She's a vision in an all-black ensemble, a fitted blazer with nothing but a silk bralette underneath, a tailored skirt that hugs her body in all the right places, and heels sharp enough to kill a man. Her nails, polished black as ink, tap idly against her thigh as she steps forward. Hugo walks at her side, the trained protector he is, drawing equal parts fear and admiration from the office staff.

We don't stop. Not when security tries to subtly alert the upper floors. Not when her mother's assistant practically stumbles out of her chair at the sight of us. And certainly not when the double doors to the boardroom come into view.

Reaper opens them without a word, and Wrenley strides in like she's been running this place her entire life.

Charles Ashford and the board are already seated, discussing whatever the hell they think is important—until they see us.

Silence. A single heavy breath from her father.

Her mother, seated perfectly poised, sets down her pen. "Wrenley, dear," Vivian says smoothly, though there's a slight tension around her mouth. "To what do we owe the pleasure?"

Wrenley doesn't acknowledge her.

Instead, she turns her cold, calculated gaze directly on her father.

"We need to talk."

Her father scoffs. "You think you can just waltz in here like you run the place?"

"I don't think," Wrenley says, voice like silk-wrapped steel. "I know."

The board members shift uncomfortably, murmuring among themselves.

"Enough," Charles barks at them before looking back at his daughter. "Say what you came to say or get the hell out."

Wrenley steps forward, her expression unreadable. She takes her time, deliberately placing a single manila folder on the conference table before sliding it toward him.

"You might want to read that."

Charles hesitates, eyeing us before he finally flips it open. His face pales instantly.

The entire boardroom watches in stunned silence as his fingers tighten around the papers inside, documents, bank statements, and internal memos that expose just how deep his corruption runs. Offshore accounts. Fraudulent contracts. Illegal business dealings are woven so tightly into Ashford International's fabric that there's no untangling them without a complete collapse.

"What—" his voice catches, his grip so tight his knuckles go white. "Where did you get this?"

Wrenley just smiles.

"Doesn't matter," she says, her tone almost amused. "What does matter is that this has already been sent to every major financial regulatory board and law enforcement division that would be interested."

A pin could drop in that boardroom, and it would sound like a gunshot. The members exchange frantic glances, some already reaching for their phones. Vivian's fingers twitch where they rest on the table, but her expression remains eerily calm. Charles, on the other hand, looks like he might stroke out right here. His chest rises and falls heavily, his eyes wild with fury.

"You think you can do this to me?" he spits the words through gritted teeth, standing so abruptly his chair screeches back. "I built this fucking company! You ungrateful little—"

"I think," Wrenley interrupts, tilting her head, "that you're done, Father."

The doors burst open behind us as security rushes in, called by some desperate fool on the board. Hugo instantly moves to Wrenley's side, a low growl rumbling in his chest. One of the guards steps forward, but before he can say a single word, Reaper blocks his path, adjusting his cuff like he's debating how badly he wants to break someone's bones today.

Riot sighs dramatically. "Now, now, let's not make a scene."

"We already made a scene," Wrecker points out.

"I know," Riot grins, "I just like saying it."

"Enough." Charles' voice is a harsh rasp, the weight of his downfall pressing down on him like lead.

I step forward now, placing myself at Wrenley's side, staring him down.

"You don't want to make this harder than it already is," I say, my voice calm but laced with warning. "There's no getting out of this one, Charles."

His furious gaze snaps to me, and for a moment, I almost expect him to lunge. But then, his shoulders drop. The fight bleeds out of him. And then he does the one thing I didn't expect. He laughs. It's a bitter, humorless sound as he shakes his head, looking around the room at the people who have suddenly distanced themselves from him.

"You all really think this is over?" he scoffs. "You think I don't have contingencies?"

"I don't care what you *think* you have," she says smoothly. "Because by the time you try to play whatever pathetic little game you have left, it's already checkmate."

For the first time, I see something in his eyes that almost looks like fear. He exhales sharply, schooling his features. Then, he fixes his suit jacket, straightens his cuffs, and walks toward the door, the others hot on his heels.

But not before pausing beside his daughter. He leans in just slightly, voice low enough for only the two of us to hear.

"You've made a mistake, *Princess*," he murmurs. "One that you can't take back."

She doesn't flinch. She just meets his gaze, completely unfazed.

"No, Father," she whispers back. "I just finished what Benjamin started."

His jaw clenches, nostrils flaring. But instead of saying another word, he turns and strides out of the boardroom. We watch them go.

The moment he's out of sight, Wrenley exhales, smoothing down the front of her blazer before turning back to us.

"Well," she muses. "That was fun."

Reaper chuckles under his breath. "You're fucking terrifying."

"I try," she smirks.

I shake my head, stepping closer, brushing my knuckles along hers. "We should go before your mother *tries* to have us removed."

Wrenley nods, turning on her heel. The moment we step out of the boardroom, my hand ghosts over her lower back, guiding her through the stunned office. But as we make our way toward the elevators, she leans in just slightly, her voice barely a whisper.

"There's still one more thing left to do."

I already know what she's talking about. The final move. The one that will end this. For good. The moment the elevator doors close, sealing us away from the hushed whispers and the weight of what just happened in that boardroom, I move.

Before Wrenley can even process it, I push her back against the cool metal wall, my hand wrapping around her throat, not too tight, just enough to remind her that she's mine. That she belongs right here, against me, with her pulse thrumming under my palm.

"That," I growl, my voice thick with something dark and unhinged, "was the hottest fucking thing I've ever seen."

She barely gets a breath out before I kiss her, desperate for it since we entered this hellhole, kissing her like I need to brand her, like I need to carve my name into her soul. She gasps against my lips, her fingers gripping in my shirt, pulling me impossibly closer.

I don't care that we're not alone. I don't care that Reaper, Riot, and Wrecker are standing two feet away, pointedly staring straight ahead as if this isn't happening. All I care about is the woman in my hands, the woman who just burned her family empire to the ground with nothing but a smile and a well-placed dagger to his back.

When I finally pull back, leaving her breathless, I stare at her. And then I say the one thing I never thought I'd say to anyone.

"Marry me."

Silence.

The kind of silence that carries weight. That holds an entire room hostage.

Riot coughs. Wrecker makes a noise in the back of his throat.

And Reaper? Reaper turns his head so fucking slow, it's

almost painful, eyes wide like I just announced I was about to sacrifice a baby goat in the middle of this damn elevator.

Wrenley blinks at me, lips parted, her breath coming in short little bursts. I watch as realization dawns, as the words sink in, as if something flickers in her wicked, hazel eyes. And then she does the most Wrenley thing imaginable. She laughs. Tilts her head ever so slightly, her nails dragging over my chest.

"Maximilian Blackwood," she murmurs, amusement lacing her tone. "Are you seriously proposing to me in a goddamn elevator?"

I don't hesitate. "Yes."

Riot lets out a strangled noise that sounds suspiciously like a laugh. Wrecker mutters something under his breath. Reaper, still wide-eyed as fuck, shakes his head. "Man, you are *so* far gone."

I don't take my eyes off her. "Say yes, Sparrow."

She studies me, her smile turning softer at the edges, something raw flickering behind her playful exterior. And then she tugs me down by my collar, brushing her lips against mine.

"Ask me again when we've finished this," she whispers. "When they're all dead."

The hunger in my chest burns hotter. Because I already know her answer. And fuck, if I won't move heaven and earth to get us there. The elevator dings. My hand stays wrapped around her throat for just a second longer. A promise.

As we step out into the underground parking garage, Riot exhales sharply, shaking his head. "Well," he mutters. "That was a hell of a ride."

Wrenley just winks at him. And we slide into the SUV, Torque revs the engine, the war already burning in our veins, I know one thing for certain: by the time this is over, Wrenley Ashford will have my ring on her finger. Even if I must kill every one of these bastards to make it happen.

The second we pull into the driveway, everyone moves to exit the SUV, but before I can even reach for the handle, Wrenley's hand presses against my chest, stopping me.

"Stay," she murmurs, dark eyes glinting with something wicked.

I arch a brow. "Sparrow, we *live* together. You can't wait to get inside?"

She grins, the kind of grin that makes my blood run hotter. "Nope."

She moves, climbing over the middle seat and into my lap, straddling me like she owns me. Fuck.

A growl rumbles in my chest as my hands find her hips, fingers digging into the fabric of her skirt. "Can't even make it out of the car, huh?"

She hums, trailing her fingers over my jaw, her nails scraping just enough to make me shiver. "That little *hand necklace* moment in the elevator?" Her lips brush against mine. "Pretty fucking hot."

I let out a low chuckle, dragging my hands up her back. "Yeah?"

She nips at my bottom lip before pulling back, eyes flashing. "Yeah. And out here? I can be *loud.*"

Fuck me. My grip tightens as I pull her closer, kissing her with the same feverish hunger that's been riding me since she walked into that boardroom and set the world on fire. She shrugs off her blazer, letting it fall somewhere onto the floorboard, and I shove my own jacket off my shoulders, desperate to get closer, to feel more.

I slide my hands beneath her bralette, fingertips skimming the soft skin of her back, just as her fingers start working the buttons of my shirt.

Before we can take this any further, a sharp knock rattles the window. We both freeze. I snap my head to the side, my jaw clenching as Reaper stands there, arms crossed, looking *done* with our shit.

"Get inside," he says, voice flat. "Now."

I glare at him. "Reaper—"

"Elias needs something," he cuts in, his tone leaving no room for argument.

Wrenley leans back, taking a deep breath before letting out a little laugh.

"Cockblocked by our own damn security," I mutter.

She smirks, rolling her hips against me once more before slipping off my lap. "Don't worry, *watchdog*," she teases, straightening her clothes. "I'll make it up to you later."

I groan as I rake a hand through my hair, watching her smooth her skirt, adjust her bralette, and grab her blazer from the floor.

Reaper knocks again, this time harder. "Now, *Blackwood.*"

Yeah. *Definitely* killing him later. I sigh, readjusting myself before stepping out of the SUV, shooting Reaper a pointed glare.

He just smirks. "Took you long enough." Wrenley saunters past him, tossing a smug glance over her shoulder. "Sorry, I was busy."

Reaper snorts, and I shake my head, watching her disappear into the house. Already counting down the minutes until I can get her alone again.

The moment we step inside, I feel it, like the air pressure begging to be snapped. I follow the murmur of voices down the hallway, my body still humming from the near-miss in the SUV. The second I step into the study, I know whatever's waiting for me here is about to kill my mood entirely.

Elias stands near the monitors, arms crossed tightly over his chest, his jaw set like he's bracing for impact.

"What?" I demand, my voice cutting through the silence like a blade.

Elias exhales sharply, "We can't find them."

I narrow my eyes. "Who?"

He looks at Wrenley, who's just walked in behind me, her heels clicking against the hardwood.

"Your parents," he says. "They disappeared."

The air shifts instantly.

Wrenley stills beside me. "What do you mean by *disappeared?*"

Elias runs a hand through his hair, clearly reluctant to explain. "I mean, their phones stopped transmitting an hour ago. No activity. No security footage of them anywhere since they left Ashford International."

A heavy silence follows. Wrenley presses her fingers against her temples, muttering, "*Fuck, fuck, fuck,*" under her breath before inhaling sharply.

"There's a tunnel," she says, voice tight.

Elias and I both turn to look at her. She lifts her chin, eyes flashing. "Under the building. I found it once when I was sixteen."

My jaw tightens. "And where does it go?"

She exhales. "I don't know. I only found the entrance. After that, there was always security near it. I could never get back in."

Elias curses under his breath, already typing furiously on his laptop.

"Can you pull up blueprints?" I ask.

"I'm already trying," he mutters. "But if this thing was built under the building, it was probably done off the books. It's not going to be easy to find."

I turn back to Wrenley, placing a hand on her lower back. "You sure about this?"

She nods once. "Positive."

I glance at the others who are all standing by, waiting for orders.

"Then we don't stop until we find it," I say, voice cold, lethal. "Because I refuse to let those fuckers slip through our fingers."

Chapter Thirty-Nine

WRENLEY

SEVERAL HOURS HAVE PASSED, and still, nothing. Elias is hunched over his laptop, fingers flying over the keyboard with an intensity I rarely see outside of his usual cocky demeanor. Margot sits beside him, just as focused, murmuring things to him in a shorthand that sounds like another language. Their heads are close, their whispers urgent, their movements perfectly in sync, like they've been doing this for years.

Wrecker and Torque brought in another couch at some point, settling in like they knew no one would be leaving this room until we had answers. The tension is suffocating.

I sit back in my chair, staring at the screen but not seeing anything. The glow of the monitors, the quiet tapping of keys, and the low murmurs of conversation all blur together, forming a restless energy that presses against my ribs.

Riot walks in, dropping several pizza boxes on the table like an offering. "Figured no one wanted to cook," he says, voice casual, though there's an underlying concern there. "Can't take over the fucking world on an empty stomach."

No one moves for the food, though, least of all me. My focus drifts back to Margot and Elias, their quick-fire exchanges escalating, both of them speaking in some cryptic tech-speak I barely understand.

Elias lets out a sharp breath, shaking his head. "Baby, I already checked that."

Margot snorts, smacking his arm. "Then check it again, *Big Shot.*"

I blink, slowly turning to Max, who's sitting beside me, watching them with a similar expression of disbelief.

"What the fuck is happening?" I ask under my breath. "Are they... a thing now?"

Riot chuckles from where he's leaned against the desk. "Well... we might be."

Max grunts, his gaze flicking from Elias and Margot to me, looking almost offended by the possibility. I should laugh. Should be teasing Margot and demanding answers. But I don't. Because something is pressing down on my chest.

I shove back from my chair suddenly, my movements sharp and jerky. Max's head snaps toward me immediately, concern flashing across his features. I don't wait for him to speak, I just move, my feet carrying me quickly out of the study, and down the hallway, my breath coming shorter and shorter with every step.

The walls are closing in. The air is too thin. My lungs feel tight, and my heartbeat is erratic. Footsteps echo behind me, heavier than my own.

Max.

I hear him get up. Feel the way his presence chases after me, ready to step in. A hand lands on my wrist, stopping me before I can get too far. Not Max.

I whip around, and Reaper is standing there, his expression unreadable but his grip firm.

I can't catch my breath. My throat is tight, my vision tunneling. "Reaper—" I start, my voice barely a whisper.

"It's a panic attack," he says calmly, his voice steady and grounding. "I've got you, little warrior."

Behind him, Max slows to a stop. For a second, it looks like he wants to argue, to shove past Reaper and take me into his arms.

But after a long beat, his jaw clenches and he nods once before stepping back.

Reaper keeps his hold on me, his other hand bracing my elbow. "Come on," he murmurs, steering me gently toward the nearest wall and guiding me to sit down. "You're okay. Just breathe."

I do as he says, focusing on the cadence of his voice, the weight of his hands anchoring me, trying to pull myself out of the spiral. But all I can think about is the fact that my mother and father have disappeared. And I have no idea what that means

I can't breathe.

The wall feels too close, the air too thin, and no matter how hard I try to focus on his voice, on the solid weight of his hands bracing me, I'm spiraling deeper.

"Come on, little warrior," he murmurs, his grip steady but not forceful. "Just breathe with me."

I try. I really do. But my chest is locked up, my pulse erratic, and no matter how much I focus on the inhale-exhale rhythm he's giving me, it's not working. My hands shake. My skin feels too tight. The air in my lungs turns to cement as I start clawing at my neck and jacket.

Reaper watches me carefully, his jaw tightening. He exhales sharply before standing and pulling me up with him.

"Max," His voice is firm, commanding.

Max is already there, closing the space between us in an instant, his gaze zipping between us with barely contained worry. "What do I do?"

Reaper doesn't hesitate. "We need to get her out of these clothes first."

Max's brow furrows, tension rolling off him. "What? Why?"

"She's overheating. And she needs pressure. Deep, grounding pressure from both sides. It'll bring her back down."

Max stares at him for half a second before looking at me, his expression torn between concern and understanding.

"Okay,' he says, voice softer now, his hands moving to my jacket first, slipping it off my shoulders.

Reaper helps, both of them are careful, calculated. When my skin meets the cool air, it does help, just a little, but it's not enough.

Reaper looks at Max. "Hold her."

Max doesn't hesitate this time. He kneels in front of me, his arms wrapping around my back as Reaper moves behind me, pressing his own weight against me. It's overwhelming at first, and I try to fight it. But after a moment, the pressure starts to register differently. Grounding. Secure.

I focus on the sensation of Max's warmth, on Reaper's steadiness, on the way their combined strength makes the panic in my chest shift, just slightly.

"Breathe, Wrenley," Reaper murmurs behind me.

Max presses his head to my chest, his thumb stroking slow circles against my back. "I've got you, Sparrow."

I cling to his voice, his presence, letting it pull me out of the storm inch by inch. Minutes pass, long, slow minutes, before the tension in my muscles finally starts to ease. My breath evens out, my heartbeat slowing to something steadier.

Reaper is the first to step back. He moves carefully, like he's making sure I won't collapse the second his support is gone. He watches me for a beat before bending to pick up my discarded clothes, handing them to Max.

"She's coming out of it," Reaper says, voice softer than usual. "But get her into something comfortable. Keep her close."

Max nods, standing and taking the clothes from him. "Thank you."

Reaper gives him a look before walking away, leaving the two of us alone in the hallway. Max turns back to me, his expression full of something heavy and unreadable. "Come on," he says gently, wrapping an arm around my waist. "Let's get you showered and into something comfortable."

I don't argue. I nod, leaning into him as he leads me upstairs.

Because right now, the only thing I need is to be in his arms. The moment I step into the shower, I let the hot water cascade over me, washing away the tension still coiled tight in my muscles. My hands press flat against the wall, my head bowing forward as steam engulfs me. I feel the ghost of the panic attack lingering in my chest, but I shove it down.

I don't hear him enter. But I feel him. Max steps into the shower behind me, his heat wrapping around me even hotter than the water. For a moment, he doesn't touch me, just stands there, letting the weight of his presence settle into my bones.

Then his hands skim up my sides, slow and firm, grounding me. He pulls me back against him, my spine meeting the solid warmth of his chest.

I sigh, leaning my head back to rest on him.

"Please distract me," I murmur, voice barely audible over the rushing water.

Max doesn't respond at first, but I can feel his lips pressing on the curve of my neck. His fingers trace up my arms, then slide back down, teasing over my ribs before his left hand wraps around my throat, tilting my head further back.

His other hand skims down my stomach, over my hip, then lower, parting me with slow, calculated strokes.

"Is this what you need, Sparrow?" he rasps against my ear, his voice dark and teasing as his fingers slip between my thighs. A sharp gasp escapes me as he strokes over my clit, soft at first, then with just enough pressure to make my knees weaken.

"Yes," I whisper, gripping his wrist at my throat, anchoring myself to him.

He hums approvingly, the sound vibrating against my skin before his teeth graze off my jaw. "Then let me give it to you."

His fingers slide lower, teasing at my entrance, pressing just enough to make my breath hitch. His grip on my throat tightens, his lips burning a path down my shoulder as he sinks one thick finger inside me. I moan, rolling my hips into him.

"That's it," he murmurs, pumping his finger slowly, tortuously, before adding another.

The stretch, the pressure, it sends fire licking up my spine.

I pant, rocking against his touch, and then, breathless, desperate, I say, "Ask me again."

Max stills. For half a second, I think he's going to stop, but then his hand at my throat tightens possessively, his mouth brushing against my ear as he growls, "Marry me."

At the same time, he strokes deep, curling his fingers just right, and I shatter. My body bows against him, a strangled moan spilling from my lips as my orgasm crashes over me like a tidal wave. He holds me through it, his fingers still working me, milking every last tremor.

As my breathing evens out, I whisper, "Yes."

Max stiffens behind me, his whole body going rigid. Slowly, he turns me in his arms, his eyes burning into mine. "Yes?" he repeats like he's making sure he heard me right.

I nod, my hands stretched across his heart, which belongs to me, my lips parting as I breathe, "Yes."

The word barely leaves my lips before he growls, gripping my waist as he lifts me effortlessly. My legs cocoon around him, and he steps out of the shower without a second thought, both of us dripping wet as he carries me to the bed.

He lowers me onto the sheets, hovering over me, his eyes drinking me in like I'm the only thing that matters in the world.

And then his mouth is taking all of mine. The kiss is deep, consuming, tongues clashing, teeth grazing, breaths tangling as hands roam, nails dig, bodies press closer.

His mouth trails down my neck, over my collarbone, leaving wet, open-mouthed kisses that have me writhing beneath him.

"Mine," he growls, sucking a bruise into my skin, marking me.

A shiver rolls down my spine, my nails raking down his back. "Yours."

His hands grip my thighs, spreading me open as he settles between them. The hard length of him presses against my slick heat, teasing, taunting. He watches me as he lines himself up, dragging the head of his cock through my wetness, making me gasp.

"Max," I whimper, hips lifting, seeking more.

His eyes darken, his control fraying. "You're fucking perfect, Sparrow."

Then, with one deep thrust, he sinks inside me. I cry out, my back arching, my fingers clawing at his shoulders as he fills me, stretching me in the most devastating way.

He groans, his head thrown back, his breath ragged. "Fuck," he grits out, barely holding himself together. "I'll never get over how damn good you feel."

He starts to move, long, deep strokes that send pleasure spiking through me, pushing me higher with every roll of his hips. I meet him thrust for thrust, my body molding to his, our rhythm perfect, effortless. The tension coils, tighter, hotter, burning just beneath the surface.

Max's hand slides down my body, his thumb finding my clit, circling in time with his thrusts. I gasp, my body tensing, the edge rushing toward me fast and hard.

"Sparrow, cum for me," he demands, his voice pure sin.

His words, his touch, push me over. I fall, shattering around him, my orgasm ripping through me in violent waves. Max curses, his hips steady, his grip tight as he thrusts once, twice more before he follows me over the edge, groaning my name as he spills inside me.

For a long moment, we just lay there, tangled together, both of us still trembling, our breaths ragged. Max presses a slow, lingering kiss to my shoulder, his arms wrapping around me, holding me close. He pulls back just enough to look at me, his gaze soft but intense.

"I love you," he murmurs, his voice raw, full of conviction.

My heart clenches. I cup his face, my thumb brushing over his cheekbone as I whisper, "I love you, too." His expression darkens, his grip on me tightening.

"Say it again," I smirk, dragging my nails down his back. "I love you, Maximilian Blackwood."

He groans, burying his face in my neck. "Fuck, Sparrow. You're going to be the death of me."

I laugh, pressing a kiss to his temple. "Not today."

We fall asleep tangled, limbs entwined, hearts still racing, our world finally feeling like it's exactly where it's supposed to be. Mostly.

Chapter Forty

MAXIMILIAN

THE SOFT BUT firm knock at the door stirs me from sleep, and my body is instantly on alert. Wrenley shifts beside me, the weight of her head slipping from my chest as she blinks awake. She clutches the sheet to her bare chest.

"Come in," she calls, her voice still husky from sleep.

I don't move yet, keeping my body stretched out beneath the sheets, watching as the door cracks open and Reaper steps inside. He's standing there, looking as unreadable as ever, but there's something softer in his stance this morning.

"Just wanted to check in," he says, his deep voice quiet, as if not wanting to disturb the peace of the room. His gaze flickers over Wrenley like he's assessing more than just her physical state.

Wrenley exhales, then points to the chair in the corner. "Sit."

He does, his usual military posture relaxed but still controlled, always aware of his surroundings.

"I'm okay," she says, but I can hear the weight behind it. The exhaustion. The lingering unease.

I stay quiet, watching as her gaze lingers on him. Her brow pulls together slightly before she asks, "How did you know what was wrong with me? How to calm me down like that?"

Reaper doesn't answer right away. His fingers tap against his thigh in slow rhythmic beats. "You learn things in the military." A pause. "I had some panic attacks when I got out, too."

I glance between them, watching as something unspoken passes between them. A mutual understanding. A connection between two people who rarely lose control, who are always the ones holding it together.

Wrenley tilts her head slightly, studying him. "You don't seem like someone who loses control."

Reaper gives a humorless smile. "Neither do you."

She huffs out a quiet laugh, but there's something deeper in her expression. Something she understands now.

They keep talking, voices low and even. She asks him a few things about his time in the military, and he answers in clipped but honest responses. It's rare for Reaper to open up, and I get the feeling that Wrenley is one of the few people who can get him to do so.

I listen for a while before I finally huff, unable to help myself. "Who are the twelve-year-olds gossiping now?"

Wrenley turns her head to glare at me, but Reaper just smiles as he stands. "I'll leave you two to get dressed."

As I pull on my jeans and shirt, I wait until the bathroom door closes behind Wrenley before slipping out, catching Reaper in the hall.

"I need to run an errand," I say, my voice low.

He stops, glancing over his shoulder.

"Keep an eye on her while I'm gone." My tone makes it clear I don't want Wrenley knowing about it. "If she has another panic attack, please handle it before it gets bad."

Reaper nods once, his face unreadable. "I've got her."

I give him a firm nod before turning toward the stairs, my mind already racing through the next few hours. I need to head to my father's garage.

There's something there I need to get. Something that's been waiting for the right moment. And now? Now is the time; I have an important piece to set into motion before the final act begins.

I pull into the gravel lot of my father's old garage, the hum of my bike cutting out as I kill the engine. I just sit there, gripping the handlebars tightly. This place is more than just steel and oil; it's the last piece of my father that I can still hold onto.

With a slow exhale, I climb off the bike, my boots crunching through the gravel as I make my way inside. The garage still smells the same: gasoline, metal, the faint trace of the cigars my father used to smoke in his office.

I weave through the clutter, past old muscle cars in various states of repair, and push open the door to the office. It's exactly as I left it, neat, minimal, but weighted with memories.

I kneel in front of the old safe in the corner, my fingers spinning the dial with muscle memory alone. A few clicks, a final turn, and the heavy door swings open.

Reaching inside, my hand closes around the small black box.

I pull it out, flipping it open with my thumb. The ring inside is everything I envisioned for her. The band is dark silver, sleek yet heavy, embedded with sharp black diamonds that catch the dim light. But the one thing that ties it all together is the deep crimson rubies set into the band.

They aren't just any rubies. They're from my mother's wedding ring. I had them carefully removed, reset into this, something new, something worthy of Wrenley. A piece of my past, of my family, is now bound to my future.

To her.

Snapping the box shut, I slip it into my pocket and stand, already moving with purpose. I don't waste any time getting back on my bike, kicking up gravel as I take off back toward the house.

Halfway there, I hit Reaper's number on my phone in the stand on the handlebars.

He answers on the second ring. "Yeah?"

"I need you to get Wrenley out of the house for a couple of hours."

There's a pause on the other end before Reaper's voice lowers. "What? Why?"

I glance at the road ahead, weaving between cars. "Just do it. No questions."

Reaper exhales sharply, but I hear the subtle rustling in the background like he's already moving. Then he speaks quietly, like he's covering his mouth. "She's sitting right next to me."

I roll my eyes. "Hand the phone to Margot."

There's a muffled noise before Margot's voice chimes in. "What's up, boss man?"

I take a breath. "Listen carefully. Reaper is taking Wrenley out of the house, and I need your help. What I'm about to tell you, you cannot react to."

Silence. Then a suspicious hum. "Go on..."

"I already proposed."

A sharp inhale. A gasp.

"Margot," I growl.

"I know, I know, I just—" I can hear the excitement threatening to explode from her. "You're serious?"

"Dead serious."

She exhales, lowering her voice. "Alright, what do you need me to do?"

"I need flowers. A lot of them. But not that pastel shit, not that soft, romantic crap. Deep colors, muted blacks, blues, purples, reds. Make it look like something she'd like."

Margot makes a thoughtful sound. "Yeah, yeah. I got you. I know her style. Gothic fairy-tale shit. Don't worry, I'll make it perfect."

"Good. I'll be home soon." I hang up, pressing harder on the throttle.

When I pull up to the house, everything is already in motion.

Riot and Wrecker are hauling in massive floral arrangements, their arms full of dark roses and black calla lilies. Torque and Elias are placing candles around the living room, dimming the lights to a moody glow. Margot is standing in the middle of it all, directing traffic like a tiny dictator, her phone in one hand and a clipboard in the other.

As I step inside, I scan the room, my chest tightening. It's exactly what I envisioned. Muted, elegant, dark, just like her.

Elias pauses, holding a deep red bouquet up with an unimpressed expression. "Damn, these look kinda dead."

Margot whips her head around so fast that he leans back. "You absolute moron," she hisses. "This is exactly what she likes. Have you not noticed that we live in a giant haunted mansion? She didn't change a single thing about it."

Elias shrugs, clearly unaffected. "Yeah, but—"

"No buts," Margot snaps, yanking the flowers from his hands and adjusting their placement. "Trust me, this is perfect."

I smirk, watching them bicker as I step further inside, taking it all in. My fingers brush over the small box in my pocket, my mind already imagining the way she'll look when I slip the ring onto her finger. The way she'll react when she sees the rubies, when she realizes what they mean.

This is it. This is the moment she deserves. Now, all I have to do is wait for her to come home.

I'm taking one last look around when Wrecker steps up beside me, clapping a heavy hand on my shoulder. "Gotta say, man," he muses, "this is way better than the elevator."

I smirk, shaking my head. "Yeah, no shit."

Margot, who has been obsessively adjusting a bouquet, whips

around. "Wait—what? Elevator?" Her eyes narrow. "Did you *propose* in an elevator?"

I look at my feet and mumble. "And the shower."

Margot looks at me like I've committed a felony. "Maximilian, you wound me," she gasps, clutching her chest.

I sigh, rubbing my forehead. "She already said yes." Then I gesture to the room. "But this... she deserves this."

Riot, leaning against the back of the couch with his arms crossed, chuckles. "Look at you," he drawls. "Losing yourself over a girl."

I glance at him. His grin widens. "Bout damn time."

Before I can respond, my phone buzzes in my pocket. I pull it out, glancing at the screen.

Reaper: We're back.

I exhale sharply, tucking my phone away and turning to the group. "Alright. Everyone out."

Margot instantly groans. "Oh, come on! I helped put this together—"

Before she can protest further, Elias and Riot each grab an arm, practically dragging her toward the hallway.

"Elias! Riot!" she yelps. "You traitorous sons of—"

The door swings shut behind them, muffling whatever insult she's trying to hurl my way.

The house falls silent. I stand there, shifting my weight, the small black box burning a hole in my pocket. That's when I hear it. Her laugh. That warm, infectious sound that hits me in the chest like a damn sledgehammer. She's home.

The front door swings open, and I hear her and Reaper talking, something about the drive, about how she's a terrible influence.

I step toward the archway. "Living room, Sparrow."

There's a pause. Then, her heels click against the hardwood as she makes her way in. She steps through the doorway, her expression shifting from amused to something unreadable as she takes in the space.

The dim glow of the candlelight. The deep, muted floral arrangements stretching across the room. The way the entire space is transformed into something intimate, something beautiful, something *hers.*

She stares, silent, her lips parting slightly. Finally, her gaze finds mine.

"Max..." she breathes, something almost fragile in her voice.

I take a slow step forward, closing the space between us.

"I wanted to give you something real," I say, my voice low. "Not a rushed proposal in an elevator. Not a half-choked-out question in a shower. I wanted *this*—" I gesture around us. "Something worthy of you."

She blinks rapidly, like she's trying to hold something back.

I reach into my pocket, pulling out the small black box. Her breath catches. I drop to one knee. For the first time, I see her *truly* speechless. I flip the box open, revealing the black diamond ring embedded with the rubies from my mother's wedding ring.

Her hand covers her mouth.

"I love you, Wrenley." My voice is steady, firm, and *certain.* "I will stand beside you, fight for you, burn the world down *with* you if that's what you want. So, Sparrow..."

I hold the ring out to her. "Marry me."

Chapter Forty-One

WRENLEY

MAX IS STILL on one knee, his intense gaze locked onto mine. But I can't take it. I can't just stand here and stare at him like I'm not bursting at the seams. With a delighted giggle, I throw myself at him. Like a crazed schoolgirl, I swore I would never be.

Max barely has time to brace himself before I crash into him, knocking us both onto the floor. His surprised grunt is muffled by my laughter as I straddle his waist, cupping his face between my hands.

"Yes," I breathe, pressing my lips to his. "Of course, yes."

Max lets out a deep, full-bodied laugh, *a real one,* the kind I don't think he even realizes he's capable of. He shakes his head, amusement lighting up his features. "You're going to be the death of me, Sparrow."

"Good," I tease, sitting up. "I'd hate to be the only one suffering."

He grins, sliding the ring onto my finger before wrapping an arm around my waist and pulling me down into him. His lips meet mine, and the kiss is soft at first, sweet, reverent, before turning into something deeper, something that makes my whole body hum with warmth.

For a moment, it's just us. The world outside of this moment ceases to exist.

Until—

"Oh my God!" Margot's excited screech practically shatters the air.

Max groans as my head jerks up. I turn toward the door just as Margot barrels in, Riot on her heels, his expression torn between exasperation and amusement.

"Sorry, brother, she's out of control," Riot mutters, hand in the air as if he tried to stop her.

Margot completely ignores him, her eyes locked on the ring on my finger. "Let me see! Let me see!" she demands, vibrating with excitement.

Still giggling, I lift my hand, showing off the black diamond and rubies gleaming in the dim light. Margot lets out a dramatic gasp, clutching her chest like she might faint.

"Holy *fuck*, Wren. This is, is insane. *Look at it!*" She waves a hand wildly toward Riot, who just smirks.

"Told you the guy lost himself in her," Riot comments, arms crossed over his chest. "Finally."

I glance back down at Max, still lying beneath me on the floor, his hands lazily gripping my hips. His eyes are filled with something I can't quite describe, something raw, something real.

I bite my lip, my heart pounding as I lean down and whisper against his lip, "You're stuck with me now, Blackwood."

His grip tightens. "Wouldn't have it any other way, Sparrow."

Margot clears her throat loudly, ruining the moment. "Okay, as much as I love this entire vibe, Max on the floor looking thoroughly *wrecked*, you being all loved-up and glowing, we have *so much* to do."

I arch a brow. "Like what?"

"Like wedding planning, obviously!"

Max groans beneath me again. "Jesus fucking Christ."

Margot gasps, eyes wide with faux betrayal. "Excuse you, Mr. Broody Boxer, but we are planning *the* wedding of the century, and I will not have you dragging down the energy."

Max looks up at me, deadpan. "This is your best friend."

I sigh, giving him a sarcastic grin. "I know. Isn't she *great?*"

Max sighs, shaking his head, but the smirk tugging at his lips gives him away. "Guess I'd better marry you fast before she turns this into a three-day event."

Margot perks up. "Oh my God, three-day wedding? That's brilliant—"

"NO!" Max and I say at the same time.

Margot pouts, but before she can argue, Elias limps in with Torque and Wrecker trailing behind him, all three looking suspiciously smug.

Elias rubs his shin. "She kicked me to get out the door... So, how does it feel, fiancées?"

I beam, holding up my hand. "Feels fucking amazing."

Riot snickers. "Yeah, yeah. But do you *love* her?"

Max sighs, but when he looks at me again, all the sarcasm is gone.

"Yeah," he murmurs, fingers tracing circles against my hip. "I really do."

And just like that, the teasing stops, replaced by something warm. Margot sighs again, pressing a hand to her heart. "Ugh. Fine. I guess I can settle for a one-day wedding if you two are going to keep being disgustingly perfect."

Elias smirks. "Oh, don't worry. I'll start taking bets on how long it takes them to sneak off and defile some unsuspecting piece of furniture."

Max narrows his eyes. "I *will* kill you."

The entire room bursts into laughter, and I just shake my head, knowing without a doubt, I have everything I ever wanted, almost. As the laughter dies down and everyone starts talking amongst themselves, my gaze drifts to the corner of the room.

Reaper stands there, leaning on the wall, one ankle crossed over the other, watching the whole spectacle with a knowing grin.

I push off Max's lap and march straight over to him, hands planted on my hips. "So this is why we had to go run useless errands?"

Reaper grins. "Yeah. But I got you a milkshake."

I let out a laugh, shaking my head before throwing my arms around him. "I say we make weekly milkshakes a thing." He stiffens for half a second before sighing and wrapping me in a firm hug.

As he leans in, his voice drops so only I can hear. "You know... if you don't want a big wedding, I *am* ordained."

I pull back sharply, eyes narrowing in playful suspicion. "You are *full* of surprises."

He shrugs, completely unbothered, while the guys in the room exchange confused glances.

"What the hell are you two whispering about?" Elias asks, eyeing us like we might be plotting a crime he's not in on.

"None of your business," I say smoothly, but Reaper laughs, walking over to Max and shaking his hand.

"Congrats, brother," he says, nodding. "You are a *lucky* bastard."

Max chuckles, squeezing his hand in return. "Yeah, I know."

After the excitement settles, we all end up lounging in the living room. The drinks are flowing, the tension from the past few weeks finally lifting as the conversation drifts between jokes and wedding talk.

I'm curled up in Max's lap, legs tucked beneath me, when curiosity finally gets the better of me. I hold up my left hand, my thumb running idly over the settings in my ring. "So... why black diamonds and rubies?"

Max's fingers trace slow patterns on my thigh. "The black suits you."

I smirk. "Obviously."

His lips twitch, but then his expression softens. "The rubies... were my mother's."

My breath catches. I look up at him, feeling the emotion tighten in my chest. "Max... you never talk about your mother."

He exhales, rubbing a hand over his jaw like he's trying to figure out where to even start.

"She was an amazing woman," he says finally, voice quieter now. "Strong. Kind. The only real softness I ever knew growing up. She had this way of making my father, who was the hardest, most stubborn man I've ever known, completely *melt* just by looking at him."

A lump rises in my throat.

"She died when I was a teenager," he continues. "She didn't tell me how bad it was. Just kept smiling, like she didn't want me to be scared."

From across the room, Elias raises his glass. "To Eloise Blackwood," he says, his voice rougher than usual. "She was a *hell* of a woman."

Max looks towards him, something tight in his expression, but then he nods. "Yeah. She was."

Elias takes a slow sip of his drink before muttering, "Cancer took her. We were barely fourteen."

I glance between them, the weight of their loss squeezing my chest. I reach for Max's hand, weaving my fingers into his.

"I hated my father for a long time after that," Max admits, staring down at where our hands are linked. "Not because he did anything wrong, but because he was alive and she wasn't. It wasn't fair. He wasn't soft, wasn't warm like she was. He was hard and distant, and I didn't understand why."

I squeeze his hand, silently urging him to continue.

"It took me years to realize... he was grieving. He just didn't know how to show it."

His finger tightened around mine, his thumb brushing over my knuckles.

"She was the only thing in his life that was untouchable," he says. "And when she died, everything *broke*."

I swallow against the thickness in my throat. "Max..."

His gaze finally lifts to mine, and his expression is unreadable. "The rubies were hers," he murmurs. "The only thing I had left of her. I wanted them to be yours."

Tears well in my eyes before I can stop them. I bite my lip, shaking my head. "You *asshole*," I whisper, voice breaking. "You can't just *say* things like that and expect me not to cry."

A slow, almost shy smile tugs at his lips. "I'd rather you cry over this than what we've been dealing with."

I let out a weak laugh, swiping at my damp lashes before cupping his face.

"I love it," I whisper. "I love *you*."

Max's jaw tightens, his throat working as he holds my stare. "I love you, too, Sparrow."

I kiss him, slow and deep, and when we pull away, he rests his forehead on mine.

"God help the rest of the world," Elias mutters, rolling his eyes from across the room. "They *are* disgustingly perfect."

Margot clicks her tongue, throwing a pillow at him. "Let them have their moment, you heartless troll."

Max just smirks, wrapping his arm tighter around my waist. For the first time in my life, I don't just feel safe. I feel at home. The low hum of conversation and laughter starts to fill the room again, but attention is only on Max. His hand rests lazily on my thigh, his finger tracing light circles on my skin, a quiet possessive touch that sets my whole body on edge.

I lean in, brushing my lips against his ear, my voice just low enough for only him to hear. "I'm going to the kitchen..." I pause for dramatic effect, letting my breath fire over his skin before adding "...if you oh, you know felt like stalking me some more.."

His hands tighten on my thigh, his fingers digging in slightly. He doesn't speak, just gives a small, almost imperceptible nod. I stand slowly, stretching a little as I do, and begin walking toward it without another word. I don't look back, but I don't have to; his presence is a weight behind me, a slow-burning heat I can feel without even seeing him.

The moment we step into the kitchen, Max moves. His hands are on me before I can turn around, gripping my hips, pulling me back against his chest. "Sparrow," he whispers, his breath warm against my neck, "you're dangerous."

I smirk. "You love it."

His fingers slide beneath my shirt, his palms flat against my stomach as he lifts the fabric higher. "Yeah," he says, voice low. "I really fucking do."

I barely have time to brace myself before he spins me around and lifts me onto the counter. His mouth crashes into mine, his hands gripping my thighs and spreading them apart as he steps between them.

It's not slow. It's not gentle. It's desperate, all-consuming, hands roaming, mouth devouring, bodies colliding in a feverish need neither of us even tries to resist.

He unbuttons my shorts, lifting me with one hand as I help him slide them over my hips and drop them to the floor, his fingers teasing before he unbuttons his own pants, pulling himself free and thrusts into me in one swift motion. I moan against his mouth, my nails digging into his shoulders as he grips my hips, anchoring me in place as he moves.

"Max—" I gasp, my head falling back against the cabinets.

"I know, baby," he growls, biting my neck, "I know."

The pace is relentless, my heels digging into his back, his name falling from my lips like a prayer. The sharp edge of the counter digs into my thighs, but I don't care. All that matters is the way he feels, the way he fills me, the way his hands grip my skin like he never wants to let go.

It doesn't take long. We're both already on edge, the tension from the past few weeks coiling tight in our bodies. When I shatter around him, he follows right after, groaning my name like it's the only thing keeping him tethered to this world. We stay there for a moment, both breathing heavily, my head leaning back on the cabinet, and his head finds my chest.

Then—

"Ah, man," a familiar voice groans. "We eat in here."

Max tenses immediately, but I just smirk, tilting my head toward where Wrecker is standing in the doorway, looking thoroughly unimpressed.

"You couldn't make it upstairs?" he continues, shaking his head in disbelief.

I grin. "No, I couldn't."

Max groans, pulling back slightly, his hands still gripping my hips. "You're impossible."

"You love it."

Before Wrecker can say anything else, the sounds of Elias shouting, "FUCK!" echoes from the other room, followed by the sudden commotion of chairs scraping, voices yelling, and hurried movement.

Max and I exchange a look. Shit. We rush to redress, barely getting ourselves together before we bolt back into the living room. Whatever's happening, it's big.

Chapter Forty-Two

MAXIMILIAN

THE STUDY IS HUMMING, the blaring alarm from the computers rattles through my skull. The room is thick with tension; Elias and Margot hunch over their screens, their fingers flying over the keyboards in perfect synchronization. The monitors glow, reflecting in their eyes as data scrolls, images flicker, and multiple feeds pull up security footage from all over the city.

Margot's mouth is set in a firm line, her voice razor-sharp as she mutters, "Baby, pull up all the pods and follow that fucking car. I got this one."

"Already on it," Elias says without missing a beat, his eyes darting around screens as he rapidly clicks through footage.

I step up behind them, my chest tight. "What the hell is going on?"

Elias's hands don't stop moving, his focus locked on the screens. "I found where the tunnel comes out." His voice is clipped and controlled. "Your in-laws took two different cars and went in opposite directions. I'm tracking one, Margot has the other."

I look to Wrenley, standing just beside me, her body rigid with tension. Her fists are clenched at her side, her breathing sharp and measured. She knew they'd run, hell, we all did, but we didn't expect them to split up like this.

"Where are they going?" she asks, her voice dangerously steady.

Margot shakes her head, her fingers still flying over the keyboard. "Nowhere familiar. They aren't going back to the Ashford estate, that's for sure."

Elias grits his teeth, clicking between screens with practiced speed. "They have to be running to someone. We just need to figure out who."

I press a hand to the small of Wrenley's back, grounding her. She doesn't move, her focus locked on the monitors.

A fragment of movement catches my attention on one of the feeds, a black sedan weaving through traffic. Elias zooms in, his expression darkening.

"Your father," he mutters. "Heading west, fast as fuck."

Margot exhales sharply. "Vivian is taking back roads, heading toward the outskirts of the city. What, that woman hates anything that is not the city?"

I catch Wrenley's eye. This isn't frantic scrambling; it's calculated.

"They knew we'd come after them," she says quietly. "They knew they needed to separate."

Elias exhales through his nose, leaning back for half a second before jolting forward again, his eye narrowing at the screen.

"Oh, you've got to be fucking kidding me."

"What?" I snap, already feeling the tension coil in my spine.

"They aren't just running," he growls, tapping a few keys. The image shifts, showing an overhead view of an industrial complex. "Your mother just entered an abandoned textile factory."

Wrenley's face hardens. "She's meeting someone."

Margot's fingers fly over the keys again, pulling up the blueprints of the location. "And this place has been owned by a shell company that, surprise, surprise, traces back to Ashford International."

Wrenley doesn't hesitate. Her voice is sharp, unyielding. "We go now."

But Elias turns in his chair, shaking his head. "Sweetheart, this isn't live. This is where they went. I'm running timestamped data, this is from yesterday, after you left the office." His voice is calm, but firm. "We need to wait. Let me keep digging, figure out where they are now."

Wrenley's jaw tightens, frustration flashing across her face. But Elias isn't wrong; charging in blind could cost us everything. I glance at her, watching the war in her eyes, the desperate need to move, to act, battling against logic.

She exhales sharply, running a hand through her hair before finally nodding. "Fine. But we don't wait long."

I lock eyes with Elias, and he nods once before turning back to his screens. "We won't."

Hours pass, agonizing, silent hours. The study is dim, the glow of the monitors casting eerie shadows against the walls. The tension in the room is thick enough to choke on. Wrenley had fought it as long as she could, but exhaustion finally won. She's curled against Reaper's shoulder on the couch, her breath slow and even. Holding on to Hugo's massive head.

I can't sit still. Pacing the floor, I rake a hand through my hair, my jaw clenched tight.

"This is taking too damn long," I mutter.

Torque, slouched in one of the chairs with his boots kicked up on the coffee table, raises a brow. "Patience is a virtue, brother."

I level a glare at him. "Not one I give a fuck about."

Wrecker, sitting beside him, chuckles. "You've been in constant motion for the last three hours. If you keep pacing, you're going to wear a hole in this fancy-ass rug."

Elias, still hunched over the screens, doesn't look up. "Let him wear the rug out, it's ugly anyway."

Margot snorts from her place beside him, eyes scanning data

as fast as she can process it. "Says the man who dresses like a 90s hacker stereotype."

Elias gestures vaguely at the monitors. "I am a 90s hacker stereotype."

Their back and forth doesn't break the tension, not really, but it's enough to keep the room from imploding.

I glance at Wrenley. She hasn't stirred. Reaper sits as still as stone beside her, but his sharp eyes meet mine. "She needed the sleep," he says, his voice low enough that only I hear it. I nod. I know she did. But every second that ticks by is one we could be using to move, to hunt, to put an end to this once and for all.

Margot suddenly sucks in a breath, her fingers flying over the keyboard. "Oh, fuck. I found them."

Every head snaps toward her. She clicks a few more keys, pulling up a grainy security feed.

"What the hell is this?" Elias mutters, his brows furrowing as he leans in.

Margot zooms in on a section of the footage. "That's them. Charles and Vivian. But... who the hell are these guys?"

Torque and Wrecker straighten, their eyes narrowing at the figures surrounding Wrenley's parents. Margot pulls up another angle, and my stomach drops. The patch on the jackets. The ink on their skin.

Black Serpents.

The room goes deathly silent. Every single one of them turns to look at me. I stare at the screen, my blood running cold before settling into something darker. Every eye in the room is on me, but I don't flinch. I draw in a steady breath. Then, low and steady, I say, "Wake her up."

Reaper gently shifts, his voice low as he nudges Wrenley's shoulder.

"Time to wake up, little warrior."

Wrenley stirs, blinking against the dim light of the study. She looks around, her sleep-heavy eyes sweeping over the tension in the room before landing on me.

She straightens immediately. "What's happening?"

I exhale, my voice tight. "We found them."

She pushes her hair back, already alert. "Where?"

I hesitate for a second. "With the Black Serpents."

Her lips part slightly, shock written across her face, before her brows knit together. "I thought they were gone."

Wrecker scoffs, shifting in his seat. "All but us, yeah. But these guys? The one with your parents? These are old-school fuckers, who left when Dominic took over. The ones who only care about money and power. Just like your family."

Elias doesn't look away from his screens. "They're moving again." His fingers fly across the keyboard, shifting between cameras and satellite feeds. "They're splitting up. This time, we're following them live."

Margot mumbles, "Thank you, facial recognition, even if hacking it gets me on a watchlist, this is worth it."

Everyone watches in heavy silence as the feeds track both vehicles. Minutes stretch on into an hour.

Then, Elias sits back and points at the screens. "Two different locations. Both remote, both should be accessible, but we won't have long once we get there."

Wrenley shifts closer, staring at the maps. Her father's location is closer.

She doesn't hesitate. "We need to split up. Hit them at the same time."

My jaw clenches. "No."

"If we don't, we could lose the other one," she presses. "If my father gets hit first, my mother will run. If we go for her first, my father will disappear. We have to move at the same time."

Her voice is strong, unwavering. I already know where this is going. I hate it. "No fucking way," I snap.

"If you go after my father," she says, her voice softer now, "this is the moment, Max. You need this. For your father. For what the Serpents did to you. You deserve to be the one to end it."

I cross the room in three steps and grip her face, forcing her to meet my eyes. "Are you insane? I am *not* leaving you."

Her hands come up, wrapping around my wrists, squeezing tight. "You have to."

The room is so goddamn quiet I can hear every breath, every shift of fabric as the others watch.

"I don't like this," I grit out.

Reaper steps forward, steady as ever. "I'll stay with her." I snap my eyes to him, jaw tight. "I've got her," he says evenly.

Silence stretches. Everything in me wants to say no, to grab her hand, to keep her near where I can protect her.

But she's right.

I release a heavy breath, letting my forehead press against hers for the briefest second. "I don't like it," I repeat.

Her hand tightens around my wrist. "I know."

I pull back, turning to the others. "We move within the hour."

Riot jumps to his feet, grinning. "Hell yeah, let's do this shit." Making Hugo jump off the couch and start pacing around everyone in the room.

Wrecker cracks his knuckles. "Been waiting for this."

Torque just smirks, stretching like he's warming up for a fight. I look back at Wrenley one last time, every muscle in my body resisting the decision I just made. She gives me a small nod. Determined. Strong.

I clench my jaw.

"I want Doc here on standby," I add, scanning the room. "I don't want to take any fucking chances."

Elias nods, grabbing his phone. "I'll make the call."

I exhale through my nose, forcing down the tension crawling through my chest. I pray to whatever god exists that I don't regret this. The tension from the study follows us upstairs like a shadow, pressing against my back with every step.

Wrenley moves with quiet efficiency, stripping down to

change, her movements smooth, practiced. Like she's done this a hundred times before. I know better. This is different.

I watch her for a moment before stepping into the closet, pulling my own gear together. When I return, she's tugging a tight black long-sleeve shirt over her head, her dark jeans already slung low on her hips.

She looks up as I approach, silent as I lift her new bulletproof vest in my hands. "Arms up," I murmur.

She obeys without hesitation, letting me slide the heavy vest over her head. I adjust the straps, tightening them against her body, brushing my fingers over the curve of her ribs, the small dip in her spine.

Her gaze stays locked on mine the entire time.

When I finish, I grip the straps at her shoulders and pull her closer. "Stick close to Reaper," I say firmly. "No pushing people out of the way of flying bullets."

She smirks. "But I like pushing people."

I don't smile. "Wrenley."

She exhales through her nose. "Fine. I'll be careful."

I tighten my grip. "Promise me."

Her expression softens. "I promise."

Satisfied, barely, I nod and step back. She tugs on the straps of my own vest, securing them properly before smoothing her hands down my chest.

"Don't take any stupid chances either," she says, her voice quieter now. "And make sure my father feels *everything*."

A dark smile pulls at my lips, "Oh, I will, Sparrow."

She nods, stepping back, and we finish gearing up in silence.

Outside, the air is thick with anticipation. Hugo is pacing like he doesn't want to be left behind. Wrenley commands him back inside the house, patting his head before shutting him in.

Two SUVs wait, engines humming low, headlights casting sharp beams through the dark. Doc is already here, unloading medical equipment from the back of her own vehicle, Reaper helping her without a word. Wrecker and Riot check their weapons beside the SUVs, Torque murmuring something under his breath as he double-checks ammo.

The others move with quiet efficiency, like a well-oiled machine. This is it. As I move toward the vehicle, Wrenley's voice cuts through the noise.

"Wait."

I stop immediately, turning to face her, slightly panicked. "What is it?"

She doesn't look at me. Instead, she turns to Reaper, and a small smile tugs at the corner of her lips.

She lifts her chin slightly. "Do it now."

Reaper stills. Everyone else does too. Silence stretches between them, and a slow, knowing grin spread across his face. "You sure?" he asks.

Wrenley nods. "Before this all goes down. Do it."

My brows pull together. "What the hell are you two talking about?"

Reaper's smile deepens as he reaches into the front pocket of his jacket, pulling out something small, something silver.

A thin chain. And at the end of it, a small, simple pendant in the shape of a dagger.

Recognition slams into me just as Wrenley steps forward, dipping her chin so Reaper can slip the chain around her neck.

I watch as he fastens it, his finger quick and steady. The chain settles against her collarbone, the tiny dagger gleaming against her skin.

Reaper steps back, tilting his head. "Perfect fit, like I knew it would be."

I stare at the pendant, my jaw tightening. It's a Serpent's

mark. A symbol of blood, of loyalty, of an oath that can't be broken.

Wrenley catches my expression and smirks. "What? You didn't think I'd go into this war without wearing the crown, did you?

Fuck. She just swore herself to this life. To me. To all of it. And she did it willingly. The others are watching now, waiting for my reaction.

I exhale slowly. Stepping forward, I curl my fingers around the pendant. Twisting the cool metal between my thumb and forefinger, I drag my gaze back to hers.

Her smirk hasn't wavered. Neither has my grip. I tug the chain just enough to make her stumble toward me, my other hand coming up to cradle the back of her neck.

"You realize what this means, don't you?" My voice is low, rough.

She lifts her chin. "I do."

I let the silence stretch between us. Then, without another word, I place a lingering kiss on her forehead, inhaling deeply.

"Let's finish this," I murmur.

She nods once, stepping back. I release the chain, letting the dagger settle back on her chest. Reaper watches us with quiet satisfaction before finally saying. "Alright then. Let's raise some hell."

A chorus of agreement echoes around us as we load into the vehicles. And I slide into the front seat, my knuckles tightening around the wheel. I realize something. By the end of tonight, the Ashfords won't just be ruined.

They'll be erased.

Chapter Forty-Three

WRENLEY

THE SUV HUMS along the darkened roads, the city lights fading in the distance as we close in on the secluded location my mother is hiding. Margot's fingers flying across her laptop, the faint glow illuminating her focused expression. She and Elias split up so they could keep constant communication between the two teams, making sure we stay on top of any surprises.

From the driver's seat, Riot shifts slightly, drumming his fingers on the wheel. "So... does this mean the Serpents are back?" Though his voice is light, it carries an edge, a tension that settles in my chest like a stone.

From the passenger seat, Reaper turns, his dark eyes finding mine in the back. "Well, little warrior," he says, voice calm yet filled with curiosity. "What does this mean?"

I let out a slow breath, my grip tightening on my thigh as I meet his gaze. "Of course, we're fucking back," I say, voice steady, resolute. "But this isn't about power for power's sake. I've got plans, quiet ones, sharpened at the edges. Think less Robin Hood, more *reckoning*. I wear the crown, but don't expect me to play by any rules. I make my own, and I *don't* play fair."

Margot snorts, "So, I should start practicing my curtsy... or loading a gun. You say 'plans', but I hear 'felonies with extra steps.'" Riot lets out a low whistle, grinning. "Pretty sure that's the new motto. Should get it stitched on the back of our jackets."

Reaper just shakes his head, murmuring. "God help *them.*"

I smirk, but don't deny it. "We're ten minutes out, the others are already in place," Margot announces, her tone shifting back to serious.

The car falls silent again. The only sounds are the low hum of the tires against the road and the occasional beep from Margot's laptop. The anticipation coils tight in my chest, my pulse a steady thrum in my ears.

I reach into my vest pocket, fingers brushing over the weight of my gun, reassuring myself of its presence. My mother always thought she could control everything. She manipulated. She poisoned. She *killed.* But tonight, I take my power back. I take *her* life back.

Reaper's voice cuts through the quiet. "You sure you're ready for this?"

I exhale slowly, my fingers flexing once before I meet his gaze. "I've never been more sure of anything in my life."

The SUV rolls to a stop under the cover of darkness, the thick canopy of the trees swallowing us whole. The engine cuts off, leaving the soft rustling of leaves and the distant chirp of crickets.

I reach for my gun, my fingers wrapping tightly around the grip as I exhale slowly. My heart pounds in my chest, but my hands remain steady.

The comm crackles to life, and Max's voice fills my ear. "Sparrow, let's do this."

A breath leaves my lips, one last moment of stillness before I step into the storm. "Agreed," I whisper back.

"Go, go, go," comes Reaper's urgent command.

We move as one, slipping through the trees like shadows, the cabin coming into view. It's as rundown as I expected, wood rotting, the porch sagging, a single light flickering from inside. But something about it feels *off.* Too quiet. Too still.

A sick feeling pools in my gut.

Then—

BOOM! The world detonates.

A blinding light swallows the night, and the air splits with a roar that drowns thought. Fire and debris erupt outward, a violent shockwave slamming into me like a freight train. My feet leave the ground, and I fly. And then, impact.

The earth punches the breath from my lungs. Pain rockets through my spine, each vertebrae screaming as I skid across the gravel and dirt. My ears ring, a high-pitched shriek that tunnels everything else.

Smoke. Dust. The copper tang of blood. I blink against the haze, coughing as my chest spasms. Something warm trickles down my temple. The world spins. The edges go dark... and I almost let it take me.

For a moment, I let it. It's *quiet* here. Max is here. I smell him: cedar, leather, whiskey, and safety. His arms curl around me. I want to fall into him.

NO! NO!

I wrench myself back to consciousness with a guttural breath. My skull pulses with searing pain. Vision blurs, then sharpens.

The cabin is gone. Obliterated. Nothing remains but twisted wreckage, fire licking at the blackened skeleton of wood and metal. Flaming debris rains from the sky. The air is thick with smoke, ash, and the scorched stench of gasoline and singed hair.

Something groans nearby, a splintering crunch.

Reaper. I spot him crumpled against a toppled tree, a beam pinning one leg beneath it. Panic claws up my throat as I scramble toward him.

"Reaper!" I shout, my voice raw. I drop to my knees, hand scrabbling against the debris.

He coughs, lifting his head with a grimace. "Still alive," he croaks. "Not loving it, though."

"Hold on." I brace and shove against the beam with every ounce of strength left. It shifts with a crack, enough for him to drag his leg free. Blood stains his thigh, his pants torn and soaked.

A sharp scream breaks the air. It's Margot.

"Get back to the SUV!" She cries, her voice frayed with terror.

Through the smoke, I see Riot, limping, his shirt torn open, a gash slicing from his ribs to his hip. His arm presses tight against his side, blood streaming through his fingers.

"Shit," Reaper grits out, staggering to his feet. He reaches Riot first, slinging his arm over his shoulder and taking the weight without complaint.

Then I see it, shrapnel. A jagged piece jammed deep into Riot's calf. His jeans are soaked, crimson darkening the fabric to near black.

"Riot!" I cry, rushing to his side. He gives me a tight, pain-laced smirk. "Still pretty, aren't I?" he huffs. "I'll live."

The ringing in my ear intensifies. Beneath it, a cold certainty forms. They knew we were coming. "She's not here." My mother isn't here. This was set up.

Margot's voice breaks through my earpiece, fear crackling through the static. "The others are offline. I can't contact anyone."

My heart *stops*. I whip toward Reaper, panic clawing at my throat. Max. I can't reach Max.

"Get in the damn car, Wrenley!" Reaper barks, shoving Riot into the backseat.

Everything is happening too fast. The bitter bite of smoldering wood fills my lungs, the remnants of the explosion painting a fiery image behind my eyes. My ears are ringing, the adrenaline surging through my veins, making it feel like the whole world is moving at warp speed.

I climb in after Riot, my hand already reaching for his leg. His entire body jerks when I press down on the wound, a deep, guttural groan ripping from his throat.

"Shit—" he grits out, his fingers digging into the seat.

"Keep pressure on it!" Reaper growls from the driver's seat as he slams his foot on the gas. The SUV lurches forward, speeding down the back roads so fast the trees blur into streaks of darkness outside the windows.

"We need to stop the bleeding," I say, my voice tight with focus.

"Yeah? No shit," Riot groans. His head falls back against the seat, sweat beading along his brow.

Just as a sharp ringtone cuts through the chaos. Riot fumbles with the blood-smeared burner phone, pressing it to his ear. The second he hears whoever is on the other end, his whole body tenses. His face drains of color.

"Fuck."

A single word. But it's enough.

A sinking feeling slams into my gut. "What? What is it?"

Riot doesn't answer. His grip tightens around the phone until his knuckles turn white. Then he hangs up, tossing the phone to the floor with a loud thud before slamming his fist against the door.

"Riot! What the fuck is going on?" My voice is sharper now, panic laced through it.

His jaw is locked, his eyes burning with something dark. "We have to get back. Now."

Reaper doesn't ask questions. He only slams his foot down harder.

By the time we screech into the mansion's driveway, the entire house is lit up. The front door flies open before we even stop, and Doc is already storming out, her eyes scanning and assessing.

Reaper jumps out, barely putting the car in park before he's yanking the back door open.

"Riot?" Doc demands before Reaper even has time to explain.

"Injury to the leg, shrapnel, the cut on his abdomen seems superficial. The rest of us are okay, just thrown around." Reaper says, urgency clear in his voice.

Doc nods. "Get him inside."

Riot stumbles out of the SUV, throwing an arm around Reaper's shoulders as they haul him toward the house.

The sound of another roaring engine has Reaper setting Riot on the front steps. I whirl around just as the second SUV comes tearing up the driveway.

The doors slam open before it even comes to a full stop

"DOC!" Elias yells, voice hoarse with panic. Doc is already running toward them when the back doors swing open.

And that's when I see him. Wrecker. Covered in blood. Barely conscious. My stomach plummets. She is already barking orders, pressing her fingers against his neck, checking his pulse.

Then, Elias turns to me. His wild eyes lock onto mine. His hands dig into my shoulders, grounding me in place, but I barely feel them. His voice is a distant echo, distorted by the roaring in my ears.

"Max is gone. They took him," his voice strained, almost disbelieving. "We were ambushed after the cabin exploded. The Black Serpents took him."

Something inside me shatters.

A deep, guttural scream rips from my throat, raw, feral, slicing through the night air like a blade. The kind of scream that comes from a place so deep inside, it feels like it's dragging my very soul out with it. It's pure, unfiltered agony. I barely register the way everyone flinches at the sound. The way Hugo starts barking wildly from inside the house. The way Doc freezes, her hands hovering over Wrecker like she's afraid to move.

The way Margot's head snaps up from her laptop, her eyes wide with shock. The way Riot mutters a quiet, "Jesus fucking Christ." I don't care. I. DON'T. CARE.

The Black Serpents and my parents have him. They have Max. I wrench myself out of Elias' grip, stumbling back, my breath fracturing into sharp, ragged gasps. My hands claw at my chest, as if I can dig out the ache tearing through me. It's too big, too deep.

This can't be happening. Not him. Not now.

My head snaps to Elias, my vision tunneling as I grab onto his arms, nails biting into skin. My voice shakes, but my words slice like broken glass.

"*Where?*"

Elias swallows hard, his Adam's apple bobs, but no sound comes.

"Where did they take him?!" I shove him, weaker than I want it to be, but rage fills in the cracks.

His jaw clenches. "We don't know yet—"

"Then *FIND OUT!*"

I whirl toward Margot. She's already at her laptop, fingers flying, her face pinched in a storm of focus and fear.

"I'm trying, babe, I swear." Her voice is tight, brittle, like it'll shatter if she lets her emotion slip.

Reaper moves toward me, instinct, comfort, but I flinch back violently, shaking my head. "Don't touch me."

I'm not in control. One hand on me and I'll break apart. I'll shatter. Riot and Torque exchange a glance, dark, unreadable. Their silence says everything..

Elias steps closer, voice low, steady, urgent. "Wrenley, we'll find him. We will. But you have to let us work. You have to *breathe.*"

Breathe?

How the hell am I supposed to breathe when Max is out there? Alone. With the same people who carved his skin. With the ones who killed his father and left him for dead.

"I'm not breathing until he's back," I whisper. My voice is raw. Poisoned with grief.

Elias meets my eyes. He doesn't argue. He just nods. He gets it. But that doesn't stop the pressure building in my chest, tight, *crushing*. A cold sweat breaks out down my spine. My hands go numb. Everything spins. My knees buckle, just slightly, but it's enough. I can't breathe. I can't breathe. I can't--

Reaper moves so fast. I don't even see him coming. Before I can collapse, arms close around me from behind, unyielding, solid. They lock me in place, pinning my arms to my sides as my body tries to fold in on itself.

"Breathe, little warrior," Reaper murmurs against my hair. His voice is calm. Too calm. A tether I want to sever.

I scream. It tears from my throat, raw, broken, furious. Reaper doesn't flinch. He doesn't let go. He tightens his grip, pressing his chest to my back, forcing me to feel the weight of him, anchoring me, dragging me back from the edge one heartbeat at a time.

I thrash, wild and desperate. My elbows slam into him, my nails clawing at the air. I want to hurt something. I want to be free. But he's stronger.

"I've got you," he says again, low and steady. "Just breathe, Wrenley."

I gasp, lungs refusing to fill. My heart pounds like it's trying to escape, battering against my ribs with animal panic. I don't know how long I fight him. Seconds. Minutes. A lifetime. But his grip never falters. His voice never wavers. And slowly, so slowly, the pressure in my chest loosens its grip. Not gone. Never gone. But no longer devouring me whole.

My body slumps in his arms, spent. My cheek rests against the hard line of his forearm. My breathing is still ragged, but deeper now.

Reaper lifts me easily, cradling me like I'm made of fire and glass.

"We're going inside," he says, voice like steel wrapped in velvet. No one argues.

Elias steps forward, worry etched across his face. But Reaper shakes his head once, sharp and final. A silent *don't*. Torque moves first, pushing the front door open as Reaper carries me past them. I don't protest. I don't fight anymore. I just hold on to the ache in my chest and the rage boiling beneath it.

Because if I let either one go, I'll fall apart again. And then, so soft I almost don't hear it, Reaper leans in and whispers, "I'll bring him home for you."

He pauses. Just for a breath. Like there's something else he wants to say. Something was sitting heavy on his tongue, unsaid.

But instead, he exhales slowly, tightening his grip just enough to let me feel it. "Even if it kills me."

Chapter Forty-Four

MAXIMILIAN

THERE'S SHOUTING. Gunfire cracks through the air, sharp and vicious. Wood splinters nearby. Smoke rolls in thick and suffocating, clinging to my lungs. I'm disoriented, the explosion still ringing in my bones. My body's sluggish, limbs refusing to obey as I try to push myself up

BOOM!

Another blast. Not an actual explosion, a flashbang. A searing white detonation behind my eyelids. My ears scream. My thoughts scatter. And then, hands. Rough. Panicked. Too Many. They grab me, yank me upright. I lurch forward instinctively, elbowing one of them in the gut. A grunt and a retaliatory blow slams into my ribs, knocking the wind clean out of me. Pain bursts behind my eyes as they wrench my arms back. Cold steel bites into my wrists, tight. Too tight.

I snarl. Thrash. Useless. A black bag slams over my head. Darkness. I'm shoved forward, knees slamming into rough ground, boots dragging through gravel and dirt as they haul me like dead weight.

Voices slice through the chaos, clipped, urgent. "Get him in the van." "Fuck, he's heavier than he looks." "Doesn't matter. Move."

My shoulder smashes into cold metal. I'm tossed in like trash.

The door slams, the engine growls, the van lurches forward. I don't know how long we're driving. Minutes. Hours. My head throbs, deep, pulsing pain behind my eyes. My ears are still ringing. Everything's blurred. Disconnected.

I'm out of the van and strapped to a chair now. I fight the pull of unconsciousness, but it drags me under like an undertow. I lose. Darkness takes me. Wrenley's laugh, warm and reckless, her hand in mine. The way she kissed me was like she wanted to start fires. NO! I bite down on the inside of my cheek, hard. I need the pain. I need it to stay present.

I roll my shoulders, testing the give of the restraints. Too tight. Where is Wrenley? Is she safe? Did they hit her, too? Riot, Margot. Reaper. Elias. Are they even alive?

A soft scuff of movement draws my attention. There's someone in the corner. Watching. The figure steps forward, into the dim glow of a single, flickering lightbulb. He's older, maybe mid-fifties, his salt and pepper hair slicked back, deep lines cutting through his weathered face. But there's power in his stance, the kind that comes with years of being feared.

I don't recognize him, but I know this type. He stops just a few feet away, tilting his head as he studies me. Then, his mouth curves into a slow, mocking smirk.

"Maximillian." My entire body locks up at the name.

Only one man has ever called me that. My father. I grit my teeth, my muscles straining against the restraints. "Who the fuck are you?" The man tsks, shaking his head as if disappointed.

"Now, now," he muses, taking a slow step closer. "That's no way to greet an old friend."

"I don't know you."

"Oh, but I know you." His eyes gleam with something dark, almost reverent. "You were just a boy last time I saw you."

I say nothing, waiting.

"You don't remember, do you?" he chuckles, low and amused. "It's been what, twelve years maybe more?"

I stay silent, my mind working overtime, twelve years ago, I was—what? Sixteen? Seventeen? Just before my father was killed. Something twists in my gut, but I don't let it show.

He sighs, feigning disappointment. "What a shame. But I suppose I shouldn't be surprised. You always were *so* stubborn."

My jaw clenches. He steps closer, his presence looming in the light, casting sharp shadows over his face. "Things could have been so different tonight, Maximillian," he murmurs. There it is again. That fucking way he says my name. My hands curl into fists, even as the cuffs bite into my wrists.

He smirks like he sees the anger bubbling under my skin, like he's waiting for it to spill over. "You should have taken my offer all those years ago." He sighs, feigning regret. "You could have had everything. Power. Wealth. A name that meant something."

I bark out a sharp, humorless laugh. "Yeah?" I tilt my head, eyes dark and daring. "And what... ended up just like you? A washed-up relic with a God complex?"

His smirk falters. For a second. Then, his fist slams into my jaw. Pain explodes through my skull, rattling my teeth. But I grin through the blood, licking it from my lip.

"Touched a nerve, did I?" I taunt, rolling my shoulders despite the restraints. "Guess that means I'm right."

He exhales sharply, straightening his jacket, his mask of control sliding back into place. "You always were a fighter, weren't you?" he muses, shaking his head. "But tell me, Maximilian."

He steps closer, his voice dropping into a dangerous whisper. "How much fight will you have left when I bring you her head?"

Everything inside me goes still. Not rage. Not yet. This is something worse. Colder. The kind of stillness that comes just before a storm rips the earth apart. I lift my gaze, locking onto his, letting him see exactly who he's dealing with.

And when I finally speak, my voice is calm. Deadly. "Try it."

He leans in, his breath hot and taunting against my face. "Oh, I intend to."

The stench of damp concrete and rot clings to the air, thick and suffocating. I don't know how long I've been tied to this fucking chair, but my arms ache, my shoulder burning from the tension of my wrists being bound behind me.

I shift slightly, testing the restraints. It's still too tight. The man in here before said his piece and then slithered out, leaving me alone in the suffocating silence.

But I'm not alone for long. Footsteps. Slow. Unhurried. Controlled. Whoever is coming wants me to hear them. I exhale through my nose, keeping my expression blank even as the door creaks open and a familiar smell fills the room.

I don't have to look to know who it is. Charles Ashford. The devil wrapped in a custom suit. He descends the final step effortlessly, his polished shoes tapping roughly against the concrete floor. Smug as ever. Not a single hair out of place, his tailored navy suit pristine, as if he didn't just lose his entire empire to his own daughter.

He smiles at me. "Maximilian."

I stare. I say nothing, letting the silence stretch between us. I know men like him. They hate silence. And I am happy to let him stew in it.

He sighs, shaking his head like I'm some kind of disobedient child instead of the man who is going to put him in the fucking ground.

"It's been a long time, hasn't it?" I say, looking at him incredulously.

He lets out a mock sigh, tilting his head. "Oh, don't look at me like that, I just wanted to talk."

I exhale through my nose, my patience already razor-thin.

"Talk?" My voice is gravelly and venomous. "I'd rather rip your fucking throat out with my teeth."

His smirk deepens. "Now, now," he muses, pacing in front of me, hands clasped behind his back. "That's no way to greet the man who gave you such a... lucrative opportunity."

I bark out a sharp laugh. "Lucrative?" I shake my head, amused despite the ache in my skull. "That's cute, Charles. But I don't work for you. Never have, never will."

He stops, eyeing me with a critical gaze. "No, you don't." His voice is smooth, controlled. "But my daughter? Well, she certainly seems to be quite... involved."

I go still. The room feels colder. Tighter. Like all the air has been sucked out of it. "What the fuck did you just say?"

He smirks. "You and Wrenley," he says smoothly. "I want to talk about it. About how you convinced her to go along with this... crusade of yours."

A slow grin pulls at my lips. I chuckle, shaking my head, because this man is even more clueless than I thought. "Convinced her?" I repeat, raising a brow. "That's adorable. You think I had to *convince* her?"

Charles' expression flinches briefly, but before he can respond, another pair of heels clicks against the stone floor. Cold. Controlled. Calculated. I glance to the side just as Vivian Ashford steps into the dim light, her expression as sharp as a blade.

"He's right, Charles." The Ice Bitch herself.

My lips pull into a slow, taunting grin. "You two *really* have no fucking idea, do you?"

Vivian's gaze sharpens, something flickering behind her eyes for just a moment before she smooths it away. Charles tilts her head, ever the smug bastard. "Why don't you enlighten us, then?"

I lean back, settling into the chair like I'm perfectly comfortable despite the cuffs biting into my skin. "She hates you both."

Charles's jaw ticks. "She always has." I shrug, smirking. "She was just going to ruin your business. Tear it down, piece by piece."

I let the words settle, my gaze fixed on Vivian, watching for any sign of a reaction. Nothing. Not yet. So I go for the kill.

"But when she found out what *you* did to Benjamin?" I nod toward Vivan. "She snapped."

Vivian's nostrils flare just slightly. Charles' fingers twitch. There it is, a slight shift in posture. I let out a mock sigh, shaking my head.

"It's funny, really." I chuckle. "You two spent years trying to turn her into your perfect little porcelain doll. But the second she figured out how to shatter the glass cage you built around her? She decided to use the shards to slit your fucking throats."

Charles exhales through his nose, arms folding to hide the fists he's making. Vivian stays silent. But I see it. The way her lips press into a razor-thin line. The way her fingers flex at her sides. She's cracking. And I can't fucking wait to see her break.

Charles recovers first. "Wrenley always was... emotional."

I grin, sharp and cruel. "Oh, you don't know the half of it."

I lean forward as much as my restraints allow, my smirk stretching wider. "I mean, the way she completely loses her mind when I make her cum? Fuck, Charles, it's a thing of beauty."

And there it is, Vivian's lips recoil in disgust. Charles visibly stiffens. I chuckle, slow and dark, watching them with amusement. "She's so fucking needy. Always begging me—"

"Enough." Charles's voice is sharp. Clipped. I just laugh.

"What? Uncomfortable?" I sign dramatically. "If you knew the things that came out of your little princess' mouth when I'm buried inside her—"

"I said enough!"

There it is. His calm control fractures. I grin wider. Vivian turns her head just slightly, eyeing me with mild disappointment. "Touch a nerve, Charles?" I mock, my voice dripping with amusement.

He exhales sharply, regaining his composure, but I can see the tension in his jaw.

"This isn't about her." He straightens, smoothing his hands down his suit like I didn't just get under his skin. "This is about you, Blackwood. You could have had everything. Instead, you chose... this."

I laugh again, sharp and humorless.

"This?" I shake my head. "You *don't* get it."

I roll my neck before, my eyes lock onto his. "She'll be the one to end you." He doesn't move. Doesn't even blink. But I can feel the shift. The weight of the words is sinking in.

"Not me." My voice is low, lethal. "Not your enemies. Not your so-called allies. Wrenley will put you in the fucking ground."

His eyes darken. My smirk turns razor-sharp. "And the best part?" I let the silence stretch. "She's going to enjoy every second of it."

Vivian's nails tap once against her arm before stilling. Charles breathes through his nose, his jaw so tight he might crack a tooth. Good. I hope he fucking chokes on it. Vivian finally steps forward, her gait seeming unsure.

She looks calm. Amused, even. Like this is just another business meeting, and she's simply negotiating a contract. I watch her carefully as she tilts her head, eyeing me like I'm a puzzle she's already figured out.

"I have a proposition for you, Maximilian."

I raise a brow, my lips twitching.

"Oh, this should be good."

She smiles. Like a fucking viper. "You're strong. Ruthless. Resilient." She glances at Charles, then back at me. "You could still be useful."

I blink once. Then I bark out a laugh. "You're joking."

Her expression doesn't waver. "Not at all."

She takes a slow step forward. "When she hears of your death, she'll break."

"She will," Charles finally says, voice calm, composed, absolute. "She'll grieve, scream, maybe even kill someone. But she'll come back to us. Because when the pain fades, we'll still be here. And you?"

He steps closer, expression still smooth. "You'll just be another mistake she regrets."

I don't blink. "She doesn't regret me. She regrets *you*. Every fucking day."

His jaw tightens, just barely. Hit.

Vivan cuts back in. "I don't love her, you know." She says it like she's talking about the weather. "She's not something you love. She's something you shape. And if she breaks under the weight of you, that only proves she wasn't strong enough to carry what we gave her."

I laugh, bitter and guttural. "You didn't give her anything but a legacy soaked in blood and lies."

Vivian leans in. "And you're just a wolf in the shadows she mistook for a savior."

My head spins. Vision flickers. Wrenley appears, barefoot, furious, golden hazel eyes gleaming in the dark. She crouches in front of me, cupping my bloodied jaw with both hands. "You're not done," she whispers. "You don't get to leave me. Not like this."

My chest seizes. I try to focus.

Vivan frowns. "Is he... smiling?"

I laugh, raw and cold. I lift my chin, even as blood trickles from my mouth. "She already wears a crown. She forged it in fire and ash while you weren't looking."

Vivian's expression tightens. Charles's eyes narrow. Calculating.

"You didn't raise a daughter," I sneer. "You tried to raise a weapon. But she chose to become a queen."

Vivian leans in, too close. "When your mutilated body is returned to her doorstep, this pathetic crusade of hers will fall apart. She'll come back where she belongs."

"She's right," Charles adds. "She will come home. To us."

I smile, slow and savage. "She *is* home. Where she chooses to be, that's her kingdom. And when I die?" My eyes lock with Vivian's. "She won't run. She'll *reign*."

There's a pause. A breath. Vivian's voice, cold as the grave.

"We don't like getting our hands dirty, Maximillian. That's never been our style."

Charles adjusts his cufflinks again. "We prefer professionals."

Vivian straightens, her eyes gleaming. "So we brought someone in. Someone who wants you to suffer. Someone who's been waiting."

She turns to go, but I speak one last time, my voice hoarse but steady. "You really don't get it, do you?" I whisper, "I don't fear death." They pause. "I'd die for her a thousand times over. Because that woman you tried to break?" I grin through bloodied teeth. "She's not just some crown-bearing queen."

I lean back against the chair, a smile curling at the edge of my split lip. "She's my wife." Vivian freezes mid-step. Charles's jaw ticks. And in the silence that follows, I give them nothing else.

Chapter Forty-Five

WRENLEY

REAPER CARRIES me up the stairs, his grip firm but gentle. I'm barely aware of the way he lays me down in the bed, the familiar scent of the sheets surrounding me. The room is dim, but even in the low light, I see him drag a chair over from the corner and sink into it with a heavy sigh. His arms cross over his chest, and his head tilts back slightly, but his eyes never fully close. He's guarding me like he told Max he would.

Tears still slip down my face, silent and endless. The door creaks open. Footsteps. Doc. She moves around the room, setting something down on the nightstand. I don't have the energy to look at her, but she speaks anyway. "This'll help, Wrenley," she says softly. "It'll take the edge off. Let your body rest."

A cool prick on my arm. Relief seeps in almost instantly, dulling the raw, jagged pain threatening to consume me whole.

Doc keeps talking, though her voice seems further away now. "Wrecker's stable," she says. "Grazed by a bullet on the side of his head, but didn't do too much damage. Some broken ribs, but he's alive. Riot's leg is fine, didn't hit bone, he's stitched up and pissed about the cane."

Reaper nods from his chair, his jaw tight. He says nothing. Time slips in and out, my mind drifting somewhere between awake and unconscious. The door opens again. This time, it's Elias. "Everything's packed," he says. "It's time to go."

Reaper stands immediately. I hear the legs of his chair scrape against the hardwood floor.

"She's barely awake," Doc murmurs.

"I've got her."

Then, weightlessness. I realize I'm being picked up again, Reaper cradles me against his chest like I weigh nothing at all. The world outside is a blur. Cool air. The sound of doors opening. A car ride that I barely register.

FOUR DAYS LATER

I stir, my body feeling... hollow. Heavy. The softest warmth near my feet. Hugo. I hear his deep breaths, the occasional twitch of his paws on the bed.

There's a faint creak of a chair shifting. I force my eyes open. Reaper is slumped in the seat next to me, arms folded, eyes closed, but I know better than to think that he's truly asleep.

"Where are we?" My voice is hoarse, scratchy from disuse.

He jerks awake instantly, blinking at me like he wasn't expecting me to speak. He drags a hand over his face before sitting forward. "Safe house," he says simply. "We didn't think staying at the mansion was a good idea. They have Max. We're a bit beat up to defend ourselves."

I nod once. A slow, tired movement. I turn over, away from him. I hear him sigh.

The days bleed together. People come and go from the room, updating Reaper on the progress of finding Max. I don't listen. I don't care. I feel... empty. The fight has been drained out of me.

I don't eat. I don't drink. I barely move. I know this isn't me. But I can't find my way back. I hear Doc talking near the door. "It's been too long if she doesn't eat or drink something soon, I'm going to have to start an IV and possibly put in a feeding tube," she says, voice sharp. "Other than drugging her, there's not much else I can do."

"No," Margot snaps, firm and unwavering.

The mattress dips slightly as she sits beside me. I don't move. Can't. She brushes my unruly hair from my face, gently, patiently. But her hand lingers a second too long; she's worried.

"I know this is how you deal, Wren," she says softly. "You shut down. Go quiet. Float out of your body so you don't have to feel it." I blink, eyes still fixed on the ceiling.

"But Max doesn't need a ghost of you," she whispers. "He needs you. Whole. Awake. Breathing." Her voice cracks, just slightly. "And I need you, too."

The words slice through the fog. She shifts beside me, clearing her throat. "Come on, babe,' she murmurs. "Let's get a shower, yeah? You don't want to still look like *this* when Max comes back."

Max. The name crashes into me. My chest tightens, painful and sharp. I turn my head. Really look at her. The sheen of tears in her eyes. The way her voice shakes, but she's still holding me together. And finally, I nod.

Relief floods her expression. "Reaper," she calls over her shoulder. "Run a bath."

There's a pause before footsteps fade. Margot helps me sit up, her arms solid around my shoulders as my legs tremble beneath me. I lean against her without shame.

Reaper reappears a few minutes later, leaning against the doorframe. His eyes skim over me, guarded, unreadable. But something flickers beneath.

"Bath's ready."

Margot doesn't give me a chance to second-guess. She walks me into the bathroom, stripping away the clothes someone must have changed me into at some point. My body feels distant, fragile, like it belongs to someone else. She eases me into the water, kneeling beside the tub. Her fingers work through my hair with slow, deliberate care. She's done this before, for herself, for me, after *other* things.

When she's done, she glances toward the doorway. "Reaper," she calls, "Help me get her out."

I hear him hesitate. The air tightens. "Reaper," Margot sighs, "I need help getting her dressed."

Another pause. Then a low grumble. "If Max kills me for seeing her naked, I'm haunting your ass."

A laugh bubbles up in my throat, small, cracked, but real. "I won't let him hurt you." I catch the flickers of a smile on his face. "Well, now there's my little warrior."

He kneels, carefully wrapping the towel around me before lifting me out of the tub. His arms are strong, steady, but not cold. His grip is careful, almost too careful. Like he's holding something back. I catch a shift in his jaw, a flicker in his eyes when I lean against him, unsteady.

It's nothing obvious. Just... a pause. Like he wants to say something but doesn't. Maybe I imagine it. Maybe not. But I feel it. Something just beneath the surface. I don't know what it means. I'm too tired to figure it out. He carries me back to the bedroom in silence.

Margot is already laying out clothes, but she stops when she sees us. Her gaze lingers, for just a second too long. "Can you help her dress? I'm going to get food."

Reaper silently nods and begins to help.

The hum of conversation surrounds me, a quiet kind of comfort that I hadn't realized I needed. Wrecker and Riot are sitting across from each other, both leaning back on the couch, sharing stories about old battle scars like they're trading baseball cards.

Wrecker lifts his shirt slightly, revealing a jagged scar across his ribs. "This one? Took a bullet from my old club president. Fucker still owes me."

Riot snorts, shaking his head. "That's cute. This one," he points to a faint scar near his hairline, "was from a broken beer bottle in a bar. Never let a drunk asshole convince you he throws a better punch than you."

I giggle, shaking my head at their ridiculous stories, keeping my mind from spiraling, and for that, I'm grateful. The front door swings open, and Torque and Margot walk in, bags clutched in their arms, the scent of greasy food filling the room instantly.

"Salvation has arrived." Torque announces, dropping the bags onto the table.

Margot grins, holding up a white cup with a straw. "And, of course, your milkshake, madam."

I beam at her as she tosses it to me, catching it with ease before taking a sip. The moment the icy sweetness hits my tongue, I groan in satisfaction. "You guys might be my favorite people."

Everyone digs in, the sounds of unwrapping paper and munching filling the room. Elias is still at his station, hacking away with one hand while he shovels fries into his mouth with the other. The occasional muttered curse tells me he's still deep in whatever he's trying to track down.

Riot wipes his hands off on a napkin, eyeing me as I reach for another burger. "Jesus, Wrenley, you just out-ate all of us."

I pause mid-bite, lifting a brow. "No, I didn't."

He tilts his head, pointing at the mess in front of me. "You just ate two and a half burgers, at least two things of fries, and you're still sucking down that milkshake like it's your last meal."

I smirk, setting the burger down and flipping him off. "You mad you got taken down by a girl?"

Riot says with a grin, "Oh, honey, if you wanted me to take you down, all you had to do was ask."

Reaper clears his throat, shaking his head at Riot. We all laugh. But before he can fire back, there's a knock at the door. Everything goes quiet. Eyes dart around the room, shoulders tensing, like we're all counting heads to see who else is missing.

Torque pushes away from the table, already reaching for the gun in his waistband. He moves toward the door, carefully, glancing at Elias. Elias nods, signaling that the cameras don't show an immediate threat. Torque unlocks the door and pulls it open.

Noah.

I blink, my stomach twisting. Elias is already on his feet, his chair scraping loudly against the floor. "What the fuck did you find?"

Noah steps inside, shaking the rain from his jacket, but his eyes are locked on me.

Waiting. I glance between Elias and Noah, my chest tightening. Why is he here?

"What the hell is happening?" I demand, my voice sharp, my pulse kicking up.

Noah's jaw tightens as he exhales, shaking his head. Then he lifts his gaze to mine and says. "We need to talk."

I sit forward, my stomach already twisting into knots. "Then talk," I say, my voice steady despite the cold dread running through my veins. "They're all going to hear it anyway."

Noah exhales sharply, rubbing a hand over his face before locking eyes with him. "I found where they're holding Max."

The entire room is still. My fingers tighten around the cup in my hands as I wait for the next words to leave his mouth. I already know they're going to wreck me.

"And?" I push, my voice quieter now.

Noah hesitates for half a second before finally saying it.

"Your parents are there. It's bad, Wrenley... he's being tortured."

The words slam into me like a freight train, sucking the air from my lungs. The milkshake cup slips from my hands, dropping onto the table, its contents spilling over the table in a forgotten mess.

A sharp ringing fills my ears, drowning out the sound of Margot's sharp intake of breath, the way Riot mutters, "Motherfuckers."

I see the way Elias clenches his fists before slamming them against the table. "Tell me everything," he growls.

Noah doesn't hesitate this time. He launches into the details, telling us how he tracked down the location, how the Black Serpents, still loyal to my father, have set up camp there, how they've kept Max alive, but barely.

The more I listen, the more something inside of me burns. A vicious, consuming fire, fueled by rage, guilt, and the bone-deep certainty that I wasted too much time lying in bed when I should have been finding him.

No more.

I push up from my chair so fast it scrapes against the floor, the noise sharp in the heavy silence.

"Okay," I say, my voice firm. "We move at nightfall."

Elias looks at me. "Wren—"

"We don't go quietly." I cut him off. "We kill everyone, but my parents—" My lip curls, my voice dropping into something lethal, "leave them for me."

No one speaks for a moment. Then Elias nods. Noah releases a breath and takes a step back as if he's physically distancing himself from the weight of what he just delivered.

Elias narrows his eyes at him. "You're done here. Go."

Noah tenses. "I can still—"

"No," Elias snaps, already turning towards his computers. "We don't need you for this part."

Noah's jaw flexes, but he doesn't argue. He knows better and walks out the door.

I watch him for a second before shifting my attention back to Elias. "What the fuck?" I snap. "You got *him* involved?"

Elias exhales, pinching the bridge of his nose like he's already exhausted. "I needed someone on the ground working contacts, and these four fuckers refused to leave with you the way you *were*." He flicks a glance at them, who all shrug unapologetically.

"He's right." Torque adds, crossing his arms.

"And," Elias continues, looking at me again, "Noah's a puppy. People tell him things."

Riot smirks. "It's true, we scare people, he's like a golden retriever."

Margot snorts, and even though my heart is still slamming against my ribs like it wants to break free, I feel a small flicker of something like relief.

I turn to Wrecker, the fire in my veins burning hotter with every second that passes. "What can you get your hands on that'll make a big impact first? Let's send them scrambling."

A slow, wicked smile spreads across Wrecker's face. "Oh, sweetheart, it's already in the car."

Elias is already pulling up blueprints on his screen, his fingers flying over the keyboard. "The location's an old factory," he says, bringing up the schematics on the massive monitors. "Security's most concentrated on the perimeter, but there's a secondary building here—" he zooms in, pointing, "—which they're using as barracks. My guess? That's where most of the men are stationed when they're not guarding."

"So we hit that first," I say.

"Exactly." Elias nods. "Make them panic, send them into defense mode, and while they're scrambling, we move in on the main building."

I stare at the screen, my pulse pounding as the reality of this sets in. "We're doing this."

"We hit here next," Elias continues, tapping a different part of the blueprint. "Max is in the basement."

Reaper folds his arms over his chest. "That's where your parents will be, too. They're expecting us to hesitate with Max down there. They think we won't go in guns blazing because of him."

I don't hesitate. "Then we prove them wrong."

He nods. "I'll throw a concussion grenade before we go in, disorient them. It won't kill them, but it'll give us an opening."

"Good," I say, my hands clenching into fists. "Let's gear up. We leave as soon as it's dark, and we all come back *alive*."

Everyone moves at once, chairs scraping, weapons being checked, armor being pulled from duffel bags. The air in the room shifts, no more joking or teasing, just deadly, quiet determination.

We're coming, Max. And nothing will stop us.

Chapter Forty-Six

MAXIMILIAN

THE DOOR GROANS OPEN, and I don't bother lifting my head. Pain radiates from every inch of my body, a constant, gnawing ache. My wrists burn where the cuffs bite into my skin, my ribs throb from the last beating, and my mouth is thick with the taste of blood.

Shoes scuff against the cold concrete, slow, deliberate steps. Then, that voice. Luca Moretti.

I force my head up just enough to meet his eyes. He's polished, too polished. A neatly tailored suit, not a hair out of place. Like he's just about to step into a high-rise meeting, not stand over the man responsible for putting his father in the ground.

"Maximilian," he drawls, crouching in front of me. "How are you holding up?"

I let out a slow breath. "Oh, you know. Five-star accommodations. You should consider opening a bed and breakfast."

Luca chuckles, but there's no humor in it. "You always did have a mouth on you." He reaches out, tapping a knuckle against my jaw like he's testing how much fight I have left. "I wonder how much longer you'll be able to use it."

I jerk my head away from his touch, ignoring the sharp protest of my muscles. "I don't know, Moretti. Your father didn't like my mouth much either, especially when I was telling him exactly how I plan to put him six feet under."

His jaw flexes, and there it is, the hidden rage I was waiting for.

"You don't get to speak of him," he states, voice low and sharp.

I slowly grin through the pain. "Yeah? And I made sure he knew exactly why before I pulled the trigger."

The hit comes fast. His fist slams into my ribs, sending white-hot pain ripping through my torso. I grunt, shifting in the chair, but I don't break eye contact.

Luca exhales, shaking out his hand like the impact hurt him.

"You think this is funny?" he sneers.

I tilt my head back, smirking through the blood on my lips. "I think it's fucking pathetic."

His nostrils flare. "You're tied to a goddamn chair, Blackwood. Bleeding, broken. And yet, you still think you're in control.

I chuckle darkly. "I know I am."

Luca narrows his eyes. "How do you figure that?"

I shift slightly, testing the tightness of the restraints. "Because you're talking to me instead of killing me. That means you're scared. Not of me—" I let the words sink in before I add, "Of *her*."

Luca stills. And that's when I know. I laugh, deep and rough. "Yeah. You should be."

His lips press into a thin line. "Your little Wrenley can play pretend all she wants, but she's nothing. She's not a soldier, she's not a killer. She doesn't have what it takes to go through with it."

I smirk. "That's where you're wrong."

Luca shakes his head, standing to his full height. "It's a shame, really. I wasn't even looking for this war. But after discovering what happened to my father, I struck a deal with the Ashfords. Seemed only fair that I get my revenge before I help them disappear."

I stare at him, my blood running cold.

Luca smiles, "Oh yeah, Blackwood. Once I'm done with you, I'm putting a bullet in that *bitch* of yours. Then, I'm ensuring your little gang of misfits never sees the light of day again."

A slow, dangerous grin spread across my face. "Yeah?" I rasp, shifting in my chair. "That's a solid plan, Moretti. Except for one little problem."

Luca raises an eyebrow. "And what's that?"

I lean forward as much as my restraints will allow, my voice dropping to a deadly whisper.

"She's already coming."

Luca laughs like I've just told him the punchline to a joke he wrote. It's sharp and smug and way too confident.

"She's not coming," he says with a cocky grin, shaking his head. "No one knows where you are. You've been off-grid for *days*. We scrubbed everything, even the security pods. No signal, no trace."

He steps closer again, tugging the sleeves of his suit jacket like he's preparing for a performance. "Let's get started with finishing this, shall we?"

He moves to the black metal case, opens it with a deliberate snap, and rolls it open like a fine piece of art. Tools gleam under the harsh overhead bulb: scalpels, clamps, a branding iron, a blowtorch, a knife that's too curved to be anything but cruel.

He chooses a scalpel first. I roll my eyes. Predictable. The blade glides across my chest, shallow, but it burns like hell. He doesn't go deep. Not yet. He's just getting warmed up again.

I grunt. Not from pain, but from boredom. He slices again, a clean line down my rib cage. Another across my thigh. He's tracing a pattern, one I can't see, but I can feel.

Blood trickles, warm and steady, down my skin. Dripping off my fingertips, pooling beneath the metal chair I'm anchored to. Still, I don't scream. I don't even flinch.

He growls. "You like to play tough guy? Fine."

He drops the scalpel, grabs a pair of pliers, and steps in close. "Let's see how long you hold out."

The first finger bends, then *snaps*; the sound is sick and sharp. Lightning bolts of pain shoot through my arm and up my spine, but I bite down hard enough to taste copper and say nothing. The second comes with a twist. He wants me to break. Wants me to cry, to beg, to plead.

But all I do is laugh. "Come on, Luca," I rasp. "You can't do better than that?"

He slams the pliers down and picks up the blowtorch next, igniting the blue flame with a hiss that echoes around the basement.

"No nerves in your fingers?" he snaps. "Let's try something more sensitive."

He presses the flame near my side, not touching the skin, just close enough to *sear* the air. Then he burns me.

The second burn lands on my shoulder, branding deep, and that one nearly takes me out. But I stay quiet. I won't give him the satisfaction.

I'm fading, though. I can feel it. The edges of my vision blur. My heart pounds against cracked ribs. My head slumps forward.

Then Luca leans in close and whispers. "I'm going to keep you alive, you know. Just enough to watch us take everything from her. Piece by piece."

There's a *click* upstairs.

Then a **BOOM!**

The floor trembles beneath my chair. Dust sifts down from the ceiling, and the light overhead sways.

Luca stumbles before another explosion. Closer. Harder.

"What the fuck was that?" Luca shouts, spinning around.

The basement door bursts open. Charles Ashford rushes down the steps, panic in his eyes, Vivian right behind him, looking frantic but composed in that cold, calculating way she always does.

"We have to go," Charles barks. "We're under attack."

Luca steps toward them. "You said we were secure!"

Vivian's eyes dart to me. I'm bloodied and broken, but not beaten.

"Which enemy of yours is it?" Luca asks again, grabbing her arm.

Vivian opens her mouth to respond, but I beat her to it.

Head still hanging, I laugh. It's dry and hoarse and laced with blood, but it builds. Charles freezes. Vivian narrows her eyes.

I lift my head. My smile is cracked and cruel. "My *wife*.... Is here."

Charles's face drains of color. Vivian takes a half-step back, something that almost looks like *fear* growing in her eyes. And Luca? He just stares, stunned, as I start to laugh harder, even through the pain, even through the broken fingers and scorched skin and blood coating every inch of me.

They thought she wouldn't come. They thought they could break me. They forget what happens when you corner a storm. And my *Sparrow* is fucking hurricane.

The basement erupts into chaos.

Charles is barking into a phone, spit flying as he demands updates. Vivian is pacing like a caged animal, her perfectly polished facade cracking with every echo of gunfire above us. Luca is pacing too, his knife back in his bloody hand, eyes wild with panic as the building shakes again.

"You said this place was locked down!" Luca snarls at Charles.

"I was told it was!" Charles fires back.

"You were *wrong*." Vivian snaps, turning on them both. "We should've run when I said to!"

The basement door slams open. A canister rolls down the stairs. It hisses for half a second before it explodes. The flash sears through the room, white-hot and immediate. I throw my head down, squeezing my eyes shut in time, but the sound is disorienting. My ears ring. My vision blurs.

Vivian screams. Charles swears. Luca dives behind a metal support beam, shielding himself from a follow-up that doesn't come.

I blink hard, trying to clear my vision as footsteps thunder down the stairs. Then I hear the voice.

"CLEAR!"

Reaper.

My lungs seize.

"Basement secure!" he yells. "I've got eyes on the target, Max's in sight!"

Another voice, sharper, colder, cutting through the smoke and shouting like a damn dagger—

"Get away from him, or I swear to God I'll end you right here!"

Wrenley.

My chest clenches, pain, relief, *love*. I try to lift my head, but the muscles don't cooperate. Still, I manage to turn slightly, blinking through the afterimages of the flashbang.

More shadows storm the room, Elias, his rifle up and steady, expression stone-cold.

"Hands where I can see them!" he barks, moving like a man possessed.

Reaper is at my side in seconds, his gloved hands already working on the restraints. "I got you, brother," he mutters, voice tight. "Just hang in there."

My throat is raw, but I can't stop myself. "Took... you long enough."

He huffs. "Drama queen."

I try to laugh, but it comes out like a broken cough. Reaper grits his teeth, shaking his head.

Wrenley's voice again, closer this time, low and lethal. "Max."

I blink up, and she's there.

Red hair is wild. Face smudged with soot. Black tactical gear hugging every curve like it was made just for her. And those eyes, burning, furious, and so fucking *beautiful* I forget about the blood crusted to my skin.

She lowers her gun for only a second, just long enough to reach out and cup my face.

"Hey, Sparrow," I rasp.

She doesn't cry. Doesn't shake. Just leans in, her forehead pressing against mine

"You're okay," she breathes. "You're okay. We've got you."

Behind her, Reaper is already checking my injuries, shouting over his shoulder, "Get him out to Doc—now!"

Charles, Vivian, and Luca are corralled together by Riot and Elias, rifles trained on them, their screams drowned out by the roaring in my ears and the fire in my chest.

Because *she came for me*. She walked through hell to get here.

And if I wasn't already in love with Wrenley Ashford, this would've done it. But I am. God help anyone who tries to keep us apart again.

Chapter Forty-Seven

WRENLEY

THE METALLIC GROAN of chains and Reaper's gritted curses fill the space, as he and Wreck haul Max up from the chair, trying to move through to the door. Blood soaks what's left of his shirt, his face battered and bruised, and his lip split in more than one place. He hisses, the sound slicing through me sharper than any bullet.

"No."

The word is raw. Absolute. They freeze.

Reaper, hand gripping Max under one arm, glances over at me. "What?"

Max's bloodied head turns toward me, and even half-broken, his eyes burn with resolve. "Not until we end this, Sparrow."

I nod once. Reaper's voice is cool and steady. "How do you want to handle this?"

I don't hesitate. **CRACK!** Luca Moretti's neck snaps beneath my hands, clean, brutal, final. His head jerks sideways with a sickening twist, eyes wide in shock, he never gets to process.

His body crumples, limp and useless, hitting the concrete with a heavy thud. I stare down at him, heart pounding but steady. No regret. Just silence, and satisfaction of knowing this one won't hurt anyone ever again.

"Holy fuck." Riot murmurs.

The silence that follows is shattered only by Charles's startled gasp and Vivian's quiet, cold breath.

"Bring them," I say

The air in the basement feels heavier than it did before. It's thick with smoke, blood, fear, and something else I can't name. Riot and Elias have both stepped back after dragging my parents to the center of the room, leaving them kneeling in front of me like the traitors they are.

My hands still ache from the force it took to snap Luca Moretti's neck. He never got the chance to beg, like his father.

My father is already trying to talk. "Princess, please... whatever you're thinking, just listen to me. I know I've made mistakes, but I've always loved you. You're my *daughter*."

"Shut up!" I snap. My voice echoes off the concrete walls. It's cold, even in my own ears.

My mother, of course, remains calm, composed, and cruel. She lets out a humorless laugh, the sound somehow louder than my father's desperate pleading. "You really should have died last year." She says, looking at me like she's already won something.

Every muscle in my body goes rigid. "Explain."

She shrugs one shoulder like she's discussing the weather. "Your little attack. It wasn't random. I arranged it. A few broken ribs, a little fear... I thought it would be enough to make Benjamin fall in line. I underestimated how much he cared about you. Then that one—" she gestures to Max with a curled lip. "—showed up and ruined everything."

Max's body tenses beside me, Reaper keeping him upright on his left. His eyes are burning, locked on her.

"I couldn't get close again after that. Not with *him* always watching. Always protecting you. And then, what do you do? You go and marry him." She sneers. "You always had a flair for dramatics, Wrenley."

I don't correct her. I don't even flinch. If she wants to think Max is my husband, let her. It seems to cut deeper that way. That she failed in every way that mattered. That Max, the man she never saw coming, became the one thing she could never control. Let her choke on it.

"Enough," I whisper.

She blinks. But I'm not talking to her anymore. Max is at my side now, helped there by Reaper and Wrecker, barely standing, but present *with me.* His chest heaves under the weight of pain and fury, but his hand steadies when I reach for him.

They kneel before us. My mother, stone-faced, unblinking. Regal to the bitter end. My father, trembling. Tears streak his cheeks, his breath hitching as the barrel points between his eyes. He tries to speak. A plea. A whimper. But it's already too late.

"Finish it," I say, my voice low, steady. Final. "Let's end this... *My Shadow.*"

Max's hand moves beneath the folds of my shirt, sure and smooth. He draws a spare gun from the small of my back. "Together," He whispers. I nod.

And in perfect silence, we raise our weapons. My mother meets my gaze. Unmoved. Unapologetic. My father sobs. A broken man. A coward, finally seeing his own ending.

Two shots, two bodies, no hesitation. The sounds echo across the dust and stone. Then... silence. The Ashfords are no more.

Because I am a Blackwood.

Max groans out. "Sparrow—" The sound slices through the haze of smoke and finality. I turn my head sharply just in time to see his eyes roll back, his body beginning to slump.

"No," I whisper, my gun slipping from my hands as Reaper and Wrecker lunge to catch him.

"Max!" I cry, rushing to his side, grabbing his arm like I can hold him together with just my touch. Reaper's voice breaks through the chaos, firm and laced with panic.

"Get him out. NOW!"

Everything becomes a blur. The smell of fire, of blood and smoke, the sharpness of gunpowder still lingering in the air, none of it matters. Not with Max unconscious being drug out of the basement. I chase them out, stumbling over the bodies littering the ground, the world warped in that strange, disorienting way that only comes after the storm.

The SUV doors are thrown open, Reaper and Wrecker lifting Max inside. I scramble in after them, barely aware of the heat radiating off the burning building behind us.

"He's not waking up!" I scream, my hands searching his chest like I might find the answer beneath his torn shirt and bruised skin. "Why isn't he waking up?"

Reaper leans in, fingers pressing to Max's neck. His jaw tightens. "He's alive," he says, but his tone is grim. "Barely. He should be unconscious right now. If he wakes, the pain will push him over the edge."

I press my lips to Max's and whisper, "Don't you dare leave me."

"Drive, Torque!" Reaper shouts from the back. "Get us the hell out of here."

The SUV tears through the trees and down the back roads that are nothing but dust and dirt under the tires. My hands are sticky with Max's blood as I cradle his face, kissing his temple, whispering everything I never got to say.

"We're almost there," Reaper mutters, checking Max's pulse again. "Doc's waiting."

Back at the mansion, the gates are already open. I spot Margot and Doc standing on the porch, eyes wide, gurney ready.

I don't even feel the car stop before I'm yanking the door open and screaming. "He's losing blood!"

Doc doesn't hesitate. "Inside!" she barks, and the chaos begins all over again.

Only this time, it's not about vengeance. It's about saving the man I can't live without.

Doc is screaming. Not yelling, *screaming,* orders at Reaper, who's got blood up to his forearms as they cut away Max's clothes. The floor is slick, and the air smells like iron and antiseptic. The moment I see the full extent of Max's injuries, I freeze.

There's so much blood. Too much.

His torso is mangled, deep gashes, angry bruises, and one side swollen and blackened. His shoulder is twisted wrong, and his lip is busted so badly I can't tell if it's still bleeding or just split wide open. His body looks like something out of a nightmare.

I can't breathe., My vision narrows, and a buzzing sound builds in my ears.

"Wrenley!" Elias's voice cuts through the fog, sharp and direct. Then his face is right there, nose to nose with mine, his hands gripping my shoulders.

"Look at me. You don't get to check out again. Not now. Not with him lying on that table. He needs you. You hear me? He. Needs. You."

I blink hard. The tears fall anyway. But I nod. Just once.

Doc's voice breaks through next. "I need blood! NOW! Everyone not helping, get out. This isn't going to be pretty."

I try to move. I can't. My legs won't work, and my feet feel like concrete. My body is screaming to stay, to go to him, but I'm stuck in place like I've been glued to the floor.

Elias doesn't wait. He scoops me into his arms and carries me out, back into the kitchen. I don't fight him. I can't. I'm still frozen in the worst kind of fear. The moment he sets me down, I start looking around like a madwoman.

Margot watches from the counter, her brows furrowed. "What are you looking for?"

"I don't know," I breathe. "Booze. A joint. Something. *Anything* to dull this... this—" I wave a hand at nothing and everything, the ache inside me clawing its way out.

"No drugs," Torque says, pouring a shot of whiskey. "Just one."

I nod, throwing it back.

Time drags. The minutes turn into hours, into eternities.

We take turns pacing the floor. Margot. Torque. Elias. Even Riot, still bandaged, limps back and forth like he can't sit still. I don't remember how long it's been, but the door creaks open.

Reaper walks in, and the moment I see his face, I feel like I might throw up. It's grim. Flat. Worn out. And too quiet.

"Reaper?" I whisper, but my voice breaks halfway through.

He doesn't say anything at first. Just walks toward me, slow and steady. And then he's right in front of me, gently cupping my face in his calloused hands.

"There was a lot of damage," he says softly. "Internal bleeding. He was close, too close. He stopped breathing at one point, but Doc got it under control. She's finishing the last of the stitches now."

My knees give out. I fall into him, sobbing as he pulls me close. His arms wrap around me like armor, grounding me even as the floor falls away. I can't stop crying, can't stop shaking, but it doesn't matter.

He's alive. He's still mine. Reaper doesn't say anything more. Just holds me through the storm until I start to breathe again. Until the ache in my chest becomes bearable.

Until I can open my eyes and see something beyond the horror. And when I finally pull back, wiping my face with the sleeve of my shirt, I look him in the eye and say, " I want to see him."

Reaper's voice is calm. "He's stable," he says, eyes on me. "But he's gonna be out for a while. We need to move him upstairs, somewhere quieter. More comfortable. You can sit with him there."

I nod, because it's the only thing I can do without breaking again. Margot moves to my side, replacing Reaper without a word. Her hand slips into mine, grounding me just enough. She leans close and whispers, "He'll wake up. He loves you too much not to." I squeeze her fingers tightly, unable to say anything back.

Reaper and Torque head out, and I listen to the rustle of movement down the hall, Max being carried carefully, reverently, like something sacred. Elias and Riot release almost synchronized sighs of relief, as if now, finally, they can believe he's going to make it.

That's when Wrecker walks in, his usually casual expression more subdued. "Okay," he says, rubbing the back of his neck. "This might not be the moment, but... I handled the thing with your parents." He glances around before his eyes land on me. "They're gone. Buried in unmarked graves out near the old factory. No one's ever going to find them."

I take a slow breath. My chest tightens, not with grief, but with strange, cold acceptance. "Good," I murmur.

Elias, still standing near the counter, adds, "It already hit the news. Explosion, collapsed structure, accidental detonation during demolition work." He lifts a brow. "Someone was careless with explosives."

The smallest giggle escapes me before I can stop it, surprised and sharp-edged. "Well?" I say, brushing a hand beneath my eyes, "That's one way to explain it."

Reaper reappears, silent as always, and jerks his chin toward the stairs. "You can see him now."

I don't wait. He walks just behind me as I climb the stairs, my legs heavy and trembling with each step. At the bedroom door, Reaper opens it for me. Inside, Max is lying on the bed, pale and bandaged, but breathing. The monitor on the table beeps steadily, a rhythm that fills the silence like a lifeline.

Reaper moves a chair beside the bed. But I don't sit. I walk around to the other side, my fingers shaking as I slip out of my boots and climb onto the mattress as carefully as I can. I curl into Max's uninjured side, my head resting gently on his shoulder, my hand lying over his heart like I'm trying to will it to keep beating.

Doc appears in the doorway, arms crossed, already frowning. "Wrenley," she starts. "He needs rest. You all do."

"I know," I say softly, not lifting my head. "I just... I just need to be close to him. That's all."

There's a pause. Then Doc gives a small, reluctant nod and jerks her head to Reaper to follow her out.

Once the door clicks shut, the quiet returns, just me and Max and the soft sound of machines humming in the background.

The tears come with warning, falling onto his chest as my fingers tighten around his. "I'm so sorry," I whisper. "I'm sorry I didn't find you sooner. Sorry, I let them—" My voice breaks, shattering around the words.

"I should've protected you better."

His chest rises and falls steadily, but there's no movement. No reply. Still, I press my lips to his jaw, to the edge of his mouth, to the bruise at his temple.

"You're my heart," I whisper. "You're my shadow, Maximilian. You've always been there, even when I didn't see you. So please... come back to me."

And then I lay still, curled around him like armor, and close my eyes. I will wait for as long as it takes.

Chapter Forty-Eight

MAXIMILIAN

THE FIRST THING I register is the low hum of breathing, multiple people, soft and steady. The second is the warmth pressed into my side, as the weight of a small hand resting over my heart. My eyes crack open slowly, and the room comes into focus in a dim wash of light from a nearby lamp.

There are chairs scattered around the bed. Every one of them is occupied. Elias is slumped with his arms folded across his chest, Margot curled up in an armchair with a blanket draped over her. Torque, Riot, even Wrecker, each one asleep but close, like they've refused to leave.

But it's her hand I see first. Her fingers splayed gently across my chest, her ring catching the faint glow of light. That ring. My ring.

The one I had made her before I even understood that she'd save me in return. I wrap my hand around hers. Lacing our fingers together and bringing her knuckles to my lip.

"I had this made the night I pulled you from the alley when I knew you would be mine," I murmur, my voice rough and cracked from disuse. "Back when I thought I was just saving you. I didn't realize then... You were going to save me, too."

She stirs beside me slowly, lifting her head just enough to meet my eyes, her movements careful like she is terrified I'll shatter if she moves too fast.

"Yours," she whispers, voice thick with emotion as tears start to roll down her cheeks.

The look on her face breaks something wide open in me. My Sparrow.

I shift slightly, pain flaring deep in my ribs, but I ignore it. "You've been here the whole time?" I ask, though I already know the answer.

She nods, brushing tears away with the back of her free hand. "You stopped breathing for a minute, Max. I thought I'd lost you."

"I'm not going anywhere," I say, tightening my grip on her hand. "Not now. Not ever."

There's movement in the room, Elias jerks awake first, blinking like he's not sure if he's dreaming. When he sees me looking back at him, he practically falls out of his chair.

"Holy shit," he breathes, loud enough to wake the others.

Margot bolts upright. "Max?'

Wrecker leans forward in his chair. Riot blinks once and mutters, "Well, hell. About damn time."

Wrenley doesn't move from my side, but her head drops to my shoulder, and I feel her exhale against my neck.

Reaper walks in a second later, holding a mug of coffee. He stops dead in the doorway when he sees me awake.

"Well, I'll be damned," he mutters, setting the mug down on the nightstand. "You scared the hell out of us, brother."

"I scared myself," I rasp.

"You're awake," Margot says with a grin, blinking back her own tears. "Which means Wrenley doesn't have to burn the world down after all."

"She still might," Elias mutters. "She's been keeping it all in for you."

Wrenley sniffs and presses a kiss to my shoulder. "It's okay now. You're okay."

I squeeze her hand again and glance around at the people crowded in this room, my family, my people, and I know exactly where I belong. With her. Always.

It's been over three weeks since everything went to hell and back. Since Wrenley and the crew tore down an empire and saved me from its rubble. Recovery has been a bitch, slow, painful, humbling. Every inch of me was bruised or broken, stitched together by Doc's careful hands and the unwavering presence of the woman who never once left my side.

Nights have become our sanctuary. Wrenley and I wrapped around each other, voices low as we lay in the dark, talking about everything, her childhood, my past, our future. There's a softness to her now that wasn't there before, one that mirrors my own. And still, the fire hasn't dulled; it's only burned hotter.

It's early now, the sky still painted in shades of navy and charcoal. I slide quietly out of bed, careful not to wake her. My body aches with a dull reminder of what I've been through, but I move with purpose.

Downstairs, the house is silent. I walk into the kitchen and fire up the coffee maker, the familiar smell grounding me as I lean against the counter. The hum of the machine is the only sound until Wrecker steps in, rubbing the sleep from his face, hair sticking up in every direction.

"You're up early," he mumbles, stretching before dropping into a chair.

"Yeah," I say, pouring two cups. I hand him one and take a sip of mine. "I need a favor."

He arches a brow over the rim of the mug. "What kind of favor?"

I level him with a look. "I need all of you to leave the house."

Wrecker chokes on his coffee. "What? Now?"

I nod once. "Yeah."

He grins like an idiot, setting the cup down. "Ah, I see. Doc cleared you, huh? Time to get it in."

Before I can respond, Wrenley walks in, barefoot in one of my shirts, and nothing else, sleep still clinging to her eyes. "Go find your own sex life to keep out of mine, Wrecker." She says, not missing a beat.

Wrecker chuckles, giving her a wink and mutters, "Yes, you're terrifying majesty," as he walks out of the kitchen, already shouting for the others to get moving.

She steps into my space, sliding her arms around my waist. "You're kicking everyone out?"

I glance down at her, lips curving into a slow, rakish grin. "It's time."

Her eyes darken slightly, a knowing spark in them. "You sure?"

"I've been cleared for a few days," I murmur, brushing my knuckles along her jaw. "And I've been planning every second of what I'm going to do to you."

Her breath hitches just slightly, and she smiles up at me. "Well, then," she whispers. "What are you waiting for, my shadow?"

I lean down, lips brushing hers. "Nothing, Sparrow. Not a damn thing."

The second the front door clicks shut and silence settles through the mansion, I don't waste a second. My hands are on her, my mouth taking her with everything I've been holding back since I was pulled out of that fucking basement.

She meets me with the same feral need, her fingers already dragging at the hem of my shirt, her breath ragged and wanting. I let her pull it over my head, toss it aside, then I lift her up onto the counter like she weighs nothing, spreading her thighs so I can stand between them.

"I've been planning this," I growl into her neck, kissing,

biting, marking every inch of the skin I couldn't get to while healing. "Since the second I woke up and saw you curled against me in bed."

She lets out a breathless laugh that turns into a moan as I slide my hands under her shirt, lifting it, watching it pool beside us. "And what exactly did you plan, my shadow?"

I sink to my knees in front of her and grin up at her. "Every. Damn. Detail." She's not wearing anything underneath the shirt, something that makes me groan like I'm in pain. I take my time, tongue and hands worshiping her until she's writhing on the counter, crying out my name, my hands gripping her thighs tight enough that I know she'll have bruises.

I scoop her up, carry her like she's the only thing that's ever mattered, taking her upstairs. The moment we're in our bedroom, I throw her onto the bed, crawling over her with hunger I can barely keep contained. Our mouths crash together again, raw and desperate.

And when I flip her over. I freeze.

My breath catches as I trace the ink etched into her back. The sparrow mid-flight, wings spread wide. It's Unapologetically her. And behind it, woven into shadow and strength, is the unmistakable silhouette of a black wolf. Me. But it's the words that stop my heart entirely.

Where you go, I follow.

My handwriting. My words. I remember scribbling it in the book I left her, something I'd never known she saw. But she'd kept it. And now she wears it on her skin.

"You got this…" My voice is thick, reverent. "You put this on your body."

She shifts under me, her cheek pressing into the mattress as she glances over her shoulder. Her hair is a curtain of red silk across the bed, rich as sin, her lips swollen from our kiss, and there's a softness in her eyes that wrecks me.

"I drew it while I was waiting for you to wake up," she says, voice low and tender. "I couldn't sleep, I just kept drawing. Those weeks you were healing after you came back to me... I knew it had to be permanent."

I stare at her, completely undone.

"You marked yourself with me." I run my fingers along the inked line of the wolf's silhouette, my chest aching with something deeper than love.

"I didn't need ink to be marked by you, Maximilian," she whispers. "But I wanted it. I wanted to carry you with me... always."

I don't think. I act. I flip her gently onto her back, kissing her like I'm trying to memorize the shape of her mouth all over again. My hand slides down the curve of her waist, gripping her thigh as I press between her legs. She's still warm and slick from before, still aching for me, and God, I'm gone.

"I'll never get enough of you," I rasp against her lips. "You understand that, right?"

Wrenley wraps her legs around my waist, nails digging into my shoulders. "Then don't stop."

I push into her slowly, deliberately, watching her eyes flutter closed as he arches beneath me. Her mouth opens in a silent moan, and I press kisses along her jaw, her neck, the hollow of her throat.

I move inside her, every thrust worshipful, reverent, desperate to match the permanence of what she's done. She gave me her body, her heart, and now... her skin.

She is mine. And I am hers. And as her name leaves my mouth like a prayer, and her nails claw at my back, and her legs tremble around me, I know. There will never be anyone else.

She's draped over me, skin damp and flushed, breath slowing against my chest. I hold her there, one arm looped lazily across her waist, the other resting in her hair, fingers slipping through the strands over and over like I can keep her tethered to me that way.

The storm has passed, the fire, the chaos, and now we're floating in the quiet after. The kind of silence that only follows something this consuming. She's warm. Bare. Still trembling from what we had just given each other.

She fits against me like she was carved for this spot. I tilt my head and press my lips into her hair, breathing her in. Lavender and sweat and paint, her.

Her fingers start to move slowly, grazing over the lines of my chest, drawing absent patterns in my skin. Every once in a while, she drags her nails just enough to make me twitch. I know she's not doing it to tease, not this time. This time, she's grounding herself.

"You're quiet," I murmur into her hair.

She shifts, cheek sliding against my shoulder as she presses a kiss to the hollow just beneath my collarbone. "I'm thinking."

"That's always dangerous," I say with a crooked smile.

She huffs a laugh against my skin. "You love it."

I close my eyes, soaking her in. "Yeah. I really do."

There's a weight in her now, not heavy, but full. Settled. It's like something inside her clicked into place, and I feel it. Every time she breathes. Every time her touch slows, softens.

We've both been clawing toward something since the moment we collided. Maybe... this is it. We lie there for a while. No ticking clock. No plans. Just skin on skin and the sound of her breath syncing with mine.

Then she says it. Soft. Steady. Absolute.

"It's time for a wedding."

It doesn't feel like a question. It feels like gravity. I turn my head to look at her. She's watching me, eyes darker in the low light, lips curved in that half-smile she always gives me when she's about to change everything.

My chest tightens. Not from panic. From awe. Because I've never heard a more certain promise in my life. I reach for her hand

and lace our fingers together, pulling them to my lips. "You sure?" I ask, my voice rough.

Her smile widens. "Max... I've been sure since the moment you pointed a gun at me, told me to trust you, and get in the car."

I laugh quietly, shaking my head. "Hell of a beginning."

"Maybe. But the ending." She slides on top of me, resting her hands flat on my chest, her hair falling like a cascade of blood-red waves around us. "That's ours to write."

I study her for a long beat, heart thudding under her palm. Then I sit up just enough to cup her face, holding her in that soft, still space between everything we were... and everything we're about to be.

"Then let's write the whole fucking thing," I whisper. "You and me, Sparrow."

She kisses me, slow, lingering. A promise in the dark. And I know it in my bones.

We survived the fire. Now we build something that lasts.

Chapter Forty-Nine

WRENLEY

IT'S NEAR MIDDAY, golden light streaking through the bedroom window, casting long shadows across tangled sheets and bare skin. Max is on his back, arm behind his head. A lazy smirk tugging at his lips. I'm draped across his chest, fingers tracing the fading bruises on his ribs, not tender anymore, just reminders.

We haven't moved in hours. Not since we said it. It's time for a wedding. I'm not even sure how long we stayed wrapped in each other afterward, talking, kissing, planning pieces for a future we never thought we'd get to build.

And then— *Crash. Slam.*

A door opens downstairs. Loud voices echo off the hallway walls.

"Hugo, no! Down!" someone yells.

Max tenses beneath me, just as the sound of paws thundering up the stairs grows louder. A second later, our bedroom door bursts open and Hugo launches himself onto the bed, right between us, all tongue and wagging tail.

I squeal, laughter bursting from my chest as he plants a slobbery kiss on my cheek. Max groans, half-laughing, pushing the massive dog off his chest.

"Ab!" he barks in German. "Runter, Hugo. Runter!"

Hugo gives one of those deep, offended huffs before dropping into a proud sit between us, his tail wagging like he's just saved the world.

From the hallway, Riot's voice drifts up, breathless: "Sorry! He doesn't listen to me. Ever. I'm just decoration at this point."

Max sighs, chuckling as he runs a hand over his face. I collapse back into the pillow beside him, eyes wide, still giggling.

"Well," I say, brushing hair out of my face, "so much for a quiet day."

We throw on some clothes, bare minimum effort, and make our way downstairs. Everyone's already filtering in: Reaper and Torque in hushed conversation. Wrecker and Riot are arguing over a half-eaten bag of chips, Elias pouring coffee like his life depends on it. Margot is sitting cross-legged on the counter, scrolling through something that probably doesn't concern any of us.

It's loud. Unruly. Messy. It's *home.*

Max slides a hand down my back and nods to me. I draw in a breath.

"Alright," I say loud enough to pull every eye to me, "time to stop putting this off."

Margot's head snaps up. "Oh shit, *what* are we doing now?"

Max smiles. "She means the wedding."

There's a pause.

"Oh my GOD!" Margot shrieks.

Riot laughs. "Honestly thought they'd elope in the middle of a shootout or something."

"That's still on the table," Max deadpans, and I elbow him.

Reaper gives Max a sideways look and mutters, "I'm not wearing a tux."

Margot is already halfway across the room, pulling her bag off a chair, rifling through it like a woman possessed. "I knew this day was coming, and I am prepared. I have at least seven bridal magazines here somewhere. Maybe eight. Where's the mood board? We need themes. Colors. Cake tasting, oh! Do we want rustic? Whimsi-goth? Do we want—"

"No." I laugh, holding my hands up to stop her.

Margot freezes.

"This isn't going to be a big affair. No catered five-course meal. No designer gowns flown in from Paris."

"But—"

I cut her off gently. "*This*—" I look around at every single one of them. "This is all I need. Right here. You guys. Max. Hugo. The *weirdest* little family I never asked for and now couldn't live without."

Margot crosses her arms. "Fine," she mutters. "But do we at least get to go dress shopping? I'm not letting you get married in one of Max's T-shirts, I will *literally* die."

I smirk. "Yes, Mags. We'll go dress shopping...But I am wearing black."

She squeals and throws her arms around me, almost knocking me backward. I laugh against her shoulder, catching Max's gaze over her head.

He looks at me like I'm his whole damn universe. And maybe... I am.

WRENLEY

MAX'S HAND finds mine the second I reach him. His thumb grazes the inside of my wrist, gentle, grounding. "Hi," he whispers. I swallow.

"Hi." The officiant's voice is a blur. I barely hear it. My world has narrowed to the space between Max's eyes and mine, to the heat of his hand, the rhythm of our breathing.

When he says his vows, they're poetic. They're not rehearsed. They're real.

"I don't have the right words for this," he says. "For you. I just know I was nothing until you saw me. Until you didn't run." He pauses.

"And if you ever burn the world down, Wrenley, I'll be the one standing beside you... handing you the matches."

Laughter breaks softly through everyone. My eyes sting.

My vows are just as messy. "You were never just my shadow,' I say. "You were the reason I survived mine."

When we kiss, the applause is thunderous, but all I hear is him. All I *feel* is him. His lips on mine. His hand is around my waist. And for the first time in my life, I feel whole

SIX MONTHS LATER

The mansion is never quiet. Someone's always yelling, laughing, swearing, or blasting music through the halls at an ungodly volume. There's a dent in the kitchen wall from when Riot and Elias got into a screaming match over laundry, and Wrecker swears the upstairs chandelier is haunted after Torque's last late-night *training* session. But somehow... it feels like home.

Max and I live in the east wing. Margot took over one of the guest suites across the hall, though she spends just as much time sneaking between Riot's and Elias's rooms. No one talks about it. Not because they are hiding it, just because no one knows what the hell it *is*.

"We're a triangle," Margot had said with a shrug. "Or a disaster, probably both."

Torque is dating someone now. No one's met her yet, but the consensus is: "She's nice, a bit shy, might run for the hills once she realizes she's surrounded by lunatics." Wrecker gives it a month, I give it three.

Reaper and I have weekly milkshake runs. Just the two of us. No matter how busy things get, we *never* miss them. We don't talk about Max on those runs. Or the past. Or what we are.

But lately... I've started to notice the way his eyes linger when I laugh. The way he hesitates, like he wants to say something but doesn't. He hides it better now. Keeps his distance. But I'm not stupid. I feel it. And I don't know what to do with it. Not yet. Max doesn't seem to mind. He trusts me. Trust *us*. He never asks what Reaper and I talk about. (We mostly argue about toppings. He hates whipped cream. He's wrong.)

This morning, the house is unusually quiet. Which is suspicious. I gather everyone into the study, which has been turned into a war room. One by one, they file in, half-dressed, groggy, arguing about coffee. Riot's shirtless. Elias is wearing Margot's sweatshirt. Margot is smirking like she knows exactly what kind of chaos is about to unfold.

Max leans against the far wall, arms crossed, eyes only on me. Reaper's already seated, coffee in hand. When they're all finally seated, I step forward, a large envelope in my hands. The room is still.

"Now then," I say, smiling like a woman about to ruin everyone's day, slamming a folder onto the desk.

"Long live the Black Serpents. Let's begin."

Acknowledgments

To anyone who's ever wanted to set fire to the story they were told to live, this one is for you. Writing *Vows of Vengeance* was cathartic, brutal, and wildly personal. There were plot holes, panic attacks, and late-night scenes fueled by caffeine and spite, but somehow, this world came alive.

To my husband, Brandon, when I first said, "I think I want to write a book," you didn't hesitate. You said, "Hell yeah. Do it. Make it a bestseller." You've believed in my every single step, even when I doubted myself, even when I was sleep-deprived, overstimulated, and talking about fictional trauma like it was gospel. You listened when I needed to talk through a scene that made no sense out loud, and you reminded me to *step away* before I gave myself a migraine and couldn't write for a few days. You gave me the space to chase this story down, to get lost in it, and to fight for it. You've always been in my corner, and I don't have the words big enough to thank you. But just know, every page carries a piece of your faith in me. I love you more than Max loves Wrenley. (And we both know that's saying something.)

To my best friend, Alyssa, thank you for listening to every unhinged rant, crying with me over scenes that broke us both, and magically finding the plot holes and missing chapters I *swore* I'd already written. You are my ride or die, and my Margot. Literally, your strength, humor, and loyalty shaped her from the beginning. This book wouldn't exist without you, and neither would she.

To my editor, Roxana, thank you for pushing me to cut deeper, dig harder, and helping me sharpen every scene until I bled on the page. My amazing cover designer at Asterielly Designs who was able to decipher the vibes and elements I wanted throughout the cover and create something dark and beautiful. Also, a HUGE thank you to fellow indie author S.B. Ellie for helping format this beast of a book. I was at the edge of a cliff, and you pulled me back and helped me out.

To the readers, especially the ones who live for morally gray chaos, blood-stained loyalty, and love that hurts before it heals: you are my people. You rooted for the girl with rage in her bones and the man who watched her from the shadows. You stayed through the fire, the heartbreak, and every sharp-edged moment in between. You saw beauty in the broken, power in survival, and softness in violence. Thank you for giving this story a home. Thank you for letting Wrenley bleed. Thank you for letting Max love. This book was written for you.

To Wrenley and Max, you didn't make this easy. But you made it worth it.

And finally, to Reaper, my silent sentinel. She was never supposed to see you, was she? But now she does. And some part of her wonders why it feels like a beginning. You've lingered in the shadows long enough. The fire's waiting. Here's to the Black Serpents, blood, legacy, and love that bites back.

About the Author

Alana Dail is a dark romance author who crafts stories where love and obsession twist together in dangerous, unforgettable ways. Her debut novel, *Vows of Vengeance*, invites readers into a world of haunting beauty, unhinged passion, and secrets that refuse to stay buried.

Beyond the page, Alana treasures family life with her husband and children, often escaping into the wild for hiking, camping, and anything that keeps her close to the outdoors. An avid runner who thrives on competition, she finds strength and clarity on the open road. She also finds joy in coffee-fueled creativity and laughter-filled rants with her best friend, moments that balance the shadows in her writing.

She believes that the most powerful stories are those born from both darkness and light.

www.ingramcontent.com/pod-product-compliance
Lightning Source LLC
Chambersburg PA
CBHW020225010826

48973CB00006B/1376